WATCHING HIM DIE

The car bobbed halfway between both shores, about a hundred feet from safety. A hundred feet—it was less than the length of a swimming pool and an easy distance to swim. Except Josh had never learned how to swim.

He wanted to open the windows and cry for help, but he knew it would let the river in. He looked at the bridge for someone who might have seen him go off the road. The tailgater stood on the bridge in front of his SUV, leaning against the safety railing. The driver was watching him, watching his car sink, watching him drown. Josh screamed at him to help, to do something. The driver did nothing.

Josh couldn't see the man well enough to distinguish his features. Sunglasses and a baseball cap obscured the man's face, but he could make out the driver's movements. The driver removed a cell phone and started punching in a number.

"Thank God," Josh said aloud and let his head drop. Emergency services would be on their way. He hoped they would get to him before the car sank. It was going to be okay.

The driver put the phone away, then did something Josh didn't understand. He held out his right arm and put up his thumb as if he were thumbing a ride. Slowly, the driver twisted his arm around until his thumb pointed down, like a Roman emperor giving the thumbs-down to a vanquished gladiator.

*For Rod,
How Much Are
You Worth?*

ACCIDENTS WAITING TO HAPPEN

SIMON WOOD

Simon Wood 3/24/07

LEISURE BOOKS   NEW YORK CITY

A LEISURE BOOK®

March 2007

Published by

Dorchester Publishing Co., Inc.
200 Madison Avenue
New York, NY 10016

ISBN 0-8439-5830-8

The name "Leisure Books" and the stylized "L" with design are
trademarks of Dorchester Publishing Co., Inc.

Printed in the United States of America.

Visit us on the web at www.dorchesterpub.com.

ACCIDENTS
WAITING
TO HAPPEN

CHAPTER ONE

Josh Michaels took liberties with the speed limit on the quiet two-lane highway. And why shouldn't he? He was celebrating. His meeting with the supplier had proved worth the overnight stay in Bakersfield. He was looking forward to his performance bonus when the drinking water plant came online.

He rewarded himself by taking the winding highways instead of I–5 back to Sacramento. He enjoyed the challenge of the sharper bends and shorter straights that he couldn't experience outside of a racetrack. The lack of patrolling police cars on the back roads gave him the opportunity to bend the law as much as he wanted. And goddamn it, the reason he used the highways and not the freeways was because it was fun.

One hand on the wheel, Josh removed his cell phone from his shirt pocket. He selected a speed dial number and the phone chirped in his ear as it dialed.

"Hello, the Michaels's residence," a young girl's voice said.

"Hi, can I speak to the lady of the house, please?" Josh said pleasantly.

"Speaking."

"My darling wife, how are you? It's good to hear your voice. I've missed you so much. How is everything? Have you sent the adoption papers off so we will be free of our troublesome daughter?"

"Is that you, Daddy?"

"Oh no! You found me out," Josh said smiling.

"I knew it was you when you started speaking." His daughter sounded unimpressed with Josh's poor attempt at deception.

"I wouldn't make a very good superhero, would I?" Josh said, now grinning.

"No," she said disapprovingly.

Josh heard his wife speaking to his daughter in the background.

"Yes, it's Daddy and he's talking about giving me away again," she said to her mother before returning her attention to Josh. "Here's Mommy."

"I wish you wouldn't say that stuff to her," Kate said. "She'll believe you one day."

"Abby knows I'm playing."

"I hope she does, because if she doesn't, you can pay for her therapy. Anyway, where are you?"

"I'm about thirty minutes away."

"Are you going back to the office?"

"No, I'll give them a call in a minute, but I'll go in tomorrow."

"Okay then, see you later."

"See you at about four."

Josh hung up and punched in his office's number. He filled in the project manager on the site visit, the quality assessment and the new contract price. Josh promised to give him a full update in the morning. He hung up and put the phone on the seat next to him.

The calls out of the way, he settled into the final part of his drive. He slowed for another of the small towns that littered the seldom used highway. These once vibrant townships were now forgotten, squeezed out by all-powerful cities. These tiny places with forgettable names and a few hundred residents relied on passing trade for survival and barely received it. Storefronts displayed the names of the proprietors who ran them. No national chains here. There weren't enough consumers to warrant franchises. Leaving the town, he accelerated up to seventy-five. The road unraveled before him, snaking across the land like an asphalt carpet.

Cresting the hill, the road fell away toward the Sacramento River some two miles ahead. The Ford gathered speed on the descent. Josh glanced over at the rearview mirror and spotted a black SUV in the distance. The vehicle not only barreled along at the same speed as Josh, but exceeded it. It was reeling in Josh's Ford in short order. He checked his speedometer. The needle nudged seventy.

"Someone's in a bigger hurry than I am," he murmured to himself.

Over the next quarter mile, Josh watched in his mirror as the SUV closed in on his tail, until its large chrome radiator grill blotted out his view. Instead of passing, the black sports utility clung to the Contour's bumper.

"Pass me, damn it," Josh shouted at the tailgater.

As if answering Josh's request, the SUV darted out from behind him onto the left-hand side of the road. Side by side, both vehicles charged toward the steel truss bridge spanning the Sacramento River like it was a finish line. The SUV's chunky tires whined on the road and their sound droned in Josh's ears. The vehicle eased past Josh without effort, but Josh backed off the gas to help the tailgater on his way. The SUV's rear was just ahead of the Ford's hood when without warning it swerved back into his lane.

Josh stamped on the brakes and yanked on the steering wheel. The power steering exaggerated his intentions, jerking the car violently to the right. The vehicles missed each other by a distance that couldn't be measured in inches. Josh's car left the road for the dirt shoulder. The Ford slithered on the slippery surface, fishtailing and kicking up plumes of dust as the tires fought for traction. Cursing, Josh struggled to get the car under control, his actions as frantic as the vehicle's motions.

The bridge was ahead and the river loomed. Josh's Ford raced past the guardrail—there was no getting back on the road. There was no stopping the car in time.

"Jesus Christ!" he screamed. Did the tailgater know what he'd done?

He pushed the brake pedal even harder. Man and machine working in perfect harmony failed to stop the car in time.

The Ford leapt off the riverbank, trimming the tops of the scrub bushes as it went. Airborne, the car's nose pitched forward and it arced downward. The dark waters rushing up toward Josh filled his vision. Fear grabbed him when he saw his fate. His hands gripped tightly onto the wheel and his fingernails cut grooves into his palms. He continued to jam his foot on the brake pedal in the vain hope it would prevent the car from ever hitting water. The weightless feeling in his stomach made him nauseated. He wanted to slam his eyes shut, but morbid curiosity kept them open.

The purr of the car's engine died in time with the slowing wheel revolutions. The Contour sounded as if it were sighing, resigned to its impending fate.

The Ford struck the water like a sledgehammer. Inside the car a dull thud reverberated in conjunction with the roar of a thousand gallons of water being displaced around the vehicle. Water hissed on the hot exhaust and engine blocks.

The shock-resistant bumper, unable to resist the shock, was ripped off and dragged under the car as the hood buckled in sympathy. The side panels splayed and the trunk popped open, casting its contents into the river like a fisherman casting live bait. Clutter of the modern car owner—pens, CDs, gas receipts, cell phone and other diverse junk—clattered against the back of Josh's head and the windshield.

Josh didn't get to witness the impact. A billowing cloud mushroomed before him in an instant and his vision turned silver-white. He felt a jolt of pain across his chest and his right side tingled. For a moment, he thought he'd died and gone to heaven.

Josh wasn't in heaven. The seat belt had locked, pinning him in place and the driver's airbag had detonated, exploding into his face. The chilling water seeping into his shoes told him he wasn't dead and his ordeal wasn't over. The car was in the water and sinking.

He smashed his fists into the deflating air bag. He had to see how bad it was—and it was bad. The nose-heavy Ford tilted forward at an angle, the weight of the engine forcing the crumpled hood underwater. Small waves lapped the windshield, showing him glimpses of the depths of the river. Water leaked in from the door seals and from somewhere under the dashboard bulkhead.

The car bobbed halfway between both shores, about a hundred feet from safety. A hundred feet—it was less than the length of a swimming pool and an easy distance to swim. Except Josh had never learned how to swim.

He had taken lessons as a kid, but had scared the shit out of himself when he went down a waterslide and found himself at the bottom of the deep end. Since then, he had never been in water any deeper than his chest. The water slapped against the side windows.

It took a moment for him to realize his foot was still on the brake pedal. He wanted to open the windows and cry for help, but knew it would let the river in. He looked at the bridge for someone who might have seen him go off the road. The tailgater stood on the bridge in front of his SUV leaning against the safety railing. The driver was watching him, watching his car sink, watching him drown. Josh screamed at him to help, to do something. The driver did nothing.

Josh couldn't see the man well enough to distinguish his features. Sunglasses and a baseball cap obscured the man's face, but he could make out the driver's movements. The driver removed a cell phone and started punching in a number.

"Thank God," Josh said aloud and let his head drop. Emergency services would be on their way. He hoped they would get to him before the car sank. It was going to be okay.

The driver put the phone away, then did something Josh didn't understand. He held out his right arm perpendicular to his body and put his thumb up as if he were thumbing a ride. Slowly, the driver twisted his arm around until his thumb pointed down, like a Roman Emperor giving the thumbs-down to a vanquished gladiator.

Openmouthed, Josh stared at the man. He couldn't believe it. *What is he doing? Does this guy want me to die?* It had never occurred to him that malice had been intended. He'd assumed it was no more than an accident born from reckless stupidity. The gesture was bizarre. It didn't make sense. The only person who could help him didn't want to. Josh just couldn't wrap his mind around it. Hands against the window, he murmured, "Help."

The tailgater lowered his arm, got into his vehicle and accelerated off the bridge.

Shock galvanized Josh into action. He reassessed his position. Water circulated around his ankles. He had a submariner's view of the murky depths of the river. Even with most of the windshield submerged, the bottom was not revealed. Silt mingled with the water, obscuring the view. River debris slid past, dragged along by the current that also dragged Josh's sinking car along with it.

He needed his cell phone. Why hadn't he thought of that first? He unsnapped his seat belt and searched for it. He found it wedged between the windshield and the dashboard. The LCD display was cracked, but it looked operable. He powered it up, but couldn't get it to dial. The shock of the collision had broken it. Josh cursed and threw the phone into the rapidly filling foot well.

The car continued to sink. The windshield was totally underwater now and the driver's side door was three-quarters submerged. The water tugged at Josh's knees.

He could do only one thing. He could swim for it and hope for the best. He knew the techniques. He just lacked the confidence.

"I can do this, right?" he said to himself. He pulled on the door handle before he could disagree with himself, but the force of the water and the buckled panels kept the door closed. He tried the passenger door, but got the same result. He pressed the power window buttons, but the electrical system had crapped out.

His exit points were blocked in the front, but he had the rear passenger doors to try. He clambered into the car's rear; his every clumsy move made the car rock and roll in the water. Frantically, he tried the doors, kicking and banging them, but they were stuck just like the front ones. The windows were his last chance. Josh had not been able to afford power windows all around at the time of purchase and had cursed the inconvenience. He blessed his good fortune now.

He leaned on the handle. The mechanism strained against the damaged door. He looked into the dirty green water pressed up against the window. Flotsam nudged the glass. He didn't relish the prospect of the river and its crap gushing into the car with him, but he had no choice. He leaned harder on the handle and felt the mechanism shift under his weight.

Slowly, the window retracted into the body of the door and he smelled the air. He breathed in the pleasantly earthy freshness. He continued to wind the window down as the river broke over the level of the receding glass.

An arc of water flooded into the car with him. *Christ, it's cold,* he thought, as the water drenched his thighs and groin, taking his breath away. Struggling with the overwhelming chill of the river forced him to suck in sharp, hurried breaths. The invading water dragged the car down at an accelerated rate. It left Josh with a disorientating sense of falling.

He had opened the window, but not enough to get his athletic five foot ten body through. He forced the window open as the water climbed up his chest. Water swept through the Ford as swiftly as his fear. Knowing his head would be under the surface at any moment, he took deep breaths to fill his lungs.

For a moment, a long moment, he hesitated. His body seized and he held his head against the roof of the sinking vehicle, sucking at the diminishing pockets of air. *I can't do this. I don't wanna do this. Someone will save me, won't they?* Realizing doing nothing wouldn't help him and action would do everything, he gripped the window frame against the force of the incoming water.

Josh took a final breath and held it. He threw himself through the open window, but the river forced him back into the car. He tumbled back into the vehicle and swallowed water before he thrashed his way above the surface. He took refreshing gulps of the remaining air.

The car disappeared below the level of the river and Josh was subjected to a view he didn't want to see. The pressure equalized in the car as it dropped to the riverbed, allowing Josh to squeeze himself through the aperture and out of his watery would-be coffin. He made inefficient mauling motions with his arms and legs, but his natural buoyancy carried him upward. He lost most of his air on the way to the surface and gulped mouthfuls of the dirty river. He surfaced with a froth of effervescent bubbles spiraling up from the car.

Coughing and spluttering, Josh took lungs full of life-preserving air. Concentrating on breathing and not on swimming, he sank below the water. He reemerged, thrashing in some semblance of a crawl crossbred with a doggy paddle.

Josh looked toward the safety of the shore and nothing else. Fighting for breath, he took mouthful-sized bites out of the water and smashed at the river with his arms and legs as if he were beating off an attacker. His motions took him slowly toward the shore, but he had the added problem of the river current with which to contend. The Sacramento River was a powerful creature that had consumed many a good swimmer, but he would be damned if he would lose to the river. Not now that he'd come so far. He fought on.

His heart pounded against his rib cage, making his chest hurt. Water filled his ears and gurgled inside his head. His limbs were tired from kicking and punching at the water and he felt the energy drain from them. His head started sinking below the surface every few strokes and he still had fifty feet to swim.

Josh didn't know where the strength or the ability to swim came from but they were getting him to shore. He kept his eyes on the riverbank coming closer and closer. He wanted to make it. He *had* to make it. Invisible hands continued to tug at him, dragging him farther downriver, and robbing him of his landing point on solid ground. The shore wasn't far now. Or was it just an illusion?

Fearing he would be lost to the river, Josh lunged with his hands for the shore and a hand struck the ground. Silt compacted under his fingernails and he stopped swimming. His knees sank and touched down on the riverbed. To his relief, his head was still above water. He crawled like a babe on all fours and collapsed at the river's edge, his head barely clear of the water. He expelled air from his chest in sharp, short breaths. Stars twinkled in his blurred vision and remained there even when he closed his eyes. He wanted the sour taste in his mouth to go away. He was happy to be safe, but too tired to show it. Now that he had done what was necessary, his body relaxed and his bladder emptied its contents into the river.

"Yeah, piss on you," he murmured hoarsely to the river, smiling.

A buzzing rang in his head. The noise continued to get louder and he closed his eyes to put it out of his mind, but it increased in volume and voices joined it. He felt the water swell and shunt his body along the shore. He listened to the voices as he fell into the welcoming arms of unconsciousness. He was safe.

CHAPTER TWO

"Mr. Michaels . . . Mr. Michaels . . . Some people are here to see you," the soft voice said.

Josh opened his eyes. Kaleidoscopic images that made no sense came into view. His world twisted and turned, objects meshed into others to make new ones. Slowly, everything locked into place.

He was in a white bed in a white room. A man dressed in a white lab coat stood over him with a benevolent smile that exposed straight teeth. In the distance, a disembodied voice mumbled inaudibly. A scrubbed-clean freshness filled the air, but the sour taste remained in his mouth.

"Are you Saint Peter?" Josh said.

The man blurted out a laugh. "I've been called many things, but no, I'm not Saint Peter. I'm Dr. Robert Green—and you're not in heaven, you're in Sutter Memorial Hospital."

"How did I get here?"

"You were very lucky. Two guys in a boat found you on the riverbank," Dr. Green said, still smiling.

"I don't feel very lucky."

"I would say you are. You swallowed quite a bit of the Sacramento River, which is not exactly the cleanest water you can drink. That means your stomach is going to be upset for awhile. I've put you on a course of antibiotics to kill any organisms swimming inside you that should be swimming in the river. Other than that, you just have some superficial bruising."

"When will I be allowed to leave?"

Josh started to sit upright, but winced. His body told him where every bruise was hiding. The doctor helped his patient up and moved pillows for support.

"I want to keep you in tonight for observation, then you should be okay to go home. Anyway, like I said, some people are here to see you."

Dr. Green turned his head to indicate two people waiting expectantly by the door to the private room. Kate and Abby rushed to his bedside. Kate smiled weakly with a furrowed brow, but Abby smiled brightly at her father.

For Josh, it was easy to produce a big smile. Kate and Abby were the most important people in the world to him. Seeing them from the hospital bed, he saw them through new eyes.

Kate looked beautiful. She was the only woman he knew who could make jeans and a tank top look sexy. Her shoulder-length straw-colored hair hung loose around her face. Her beauty was at the crossroads of youth and maturity, creating a sensual fusion of what was and what was to come.

Abby was a reflection of her mother, possessing the same straw-colored hair, although hers was drawn back into a ponytail. She was his little girl, but Josh knew she would break his heart one day when she became someone else's.

"Hey, hon," Kate said from the side of the bed. She hugged and kissed her husband.

"Daddy, you're alive!"

The matter of fact statement made the adults in the room laugh.

"Abby!" Kate flicked a look at the doctor and Josh. "Don't say things like that."

"Well, she's not wrong," the doctor said in Abby's defense.

Abby looked at everyone, unaware of the impact of her remark. Quickly, she forgot about it and stood close to Josh's bedside.

Josh had never been so happy to see them and his smile extended into a broad grin. The pressure of the grin on his face squeezed out a couple of tears.

"I'll leave you all alone for awhile, but I'll be back in a few minutes to check up on you. Remember, you still need rest, so please, no excitement."

"Thank you, Doctor," Kate said.

Dr. Green smiled pleasantly and left the room.

"Oh, Josh, what happened?" Kate said.

"Somebody forced me off the fucking road and into the river." His anger spewed out at the recollection of the incident on the road.

"Josh . . . Abby." She indicated their daughter with her eyes. Kate disliked bad language spoken in front of her.

"Don't say bad words, Daddy," Abby said.

"I'm sorry. Daddy was mad, but I shouldn't say things like that. Forgive me?"

"Yes." Abby scrambled onto the hospital bed and hugged him.

He felt her small arms wrap around him as tightly as they could and he hugged her back. He ignored the ache from his bruises in favor of the affection. It felt like he'd been away from his family for a lifetime. He released Abby from his embrace.

"You're going to have to let Daddy go now, hon," he said.

"The police are waiting outside to talk to you," Kate said.

They were the last people he wanted to talk to right now, but if he wanted that son of a bitch caught, he'd have to talk to them.

"Wheel them in," he said with a frown.

Abby broke from the hug and snuggled herself next to Josh.

"Come on, Abby. Let's get the police officers. You're going to sit with Uncle Bobby while Daddy and I talk to the policemen."

"Is Bob here?" Josh said.

"Yeah, he brought us. He's waiting outside. They won't let him in since he's not family."

Bob Deuce had been Josh's friend since they were twelve. "Tell him thanks for coming."

Kate helped her daughter down from the bed after she had given Josh a kiss. He promised to tell Abby all about the accident when he returned home. They left and Kate returned with two uniformed officers.

The officers stood at the end of the bed. Kate sat on the bed next to her husband. The officers introduced themselves as Brady and Williams. Brady did the talking and Williams took notes. Brady was in his mid-forties and a good thirty pounds overweight for his six feet. He fixed Josh with a piercing look, like he was the guilty one. Josh thought he probably had too many people lie to him over the years. Williams was a young, well-groomed black man who looked as if he'd been out of the academy a couple of years and lacked the case-hardening that came with the position.

"Could you tell us what happened, Mr. Michaels?" Brady asked.

"I was driving back home on Highway One-sixty-two when a car overtook me approaching the river."

"What speed were you doing, sir?" Brady interrupted.

"Sixty-five."

Brady nodded to Williams, who made a note of the speed.

"And are you aware of the speed on that road, sir?" Brady inquired.

"Yes. It's not sixty-five. If you want to give me a ticket then do it, but do me the courtesy of letting me tell you what happened," Josh responded. His irritation blistered at the attempted slap on the wrist for speeding.

"Josh," Kate said softly. She put a hand on his arm.

"We're just trying to establish what happened," Brady said without apology. "Carry on, sir,"

"As we came to the bridge, the car behind me, I think it was an Explorer or Expedition—"

"Color, Mr. Michaels?" Williams asked.

"Black."

"New or old?" Williams said

"It was a current model. It looked as if it had come straight out of the box."

Williams's interruption of his account with simple, objective questions relieved Josh's tension, bringing his anger down to a simmer. Brady was a pain in the ass, but at least the other officer seemed genuinely interested in Josh's case.

"He overtook me as we reached the bridge, but when the SUV got just past me, it cut back across. I swerved to avoid it and went onto the shoulder. I tried to stop, but I was too close to the edge of the river. The car went over the embankment."

"So it was an accident," Brady said.

"No way, this guy meant for me to go over the side," Josh said, cutting the assumption down before it had a chance to become fact.

"What makes you say that?" Williams asked.

"When I was in the river I looked back and I saw him watching me, then the asshole gave me the thumbs-down. This bastard definitely wanted me dead," Josh said bitterly.

"He did what?" Williams asked.

"He gave me a thumbs-down." Josh demonstrated. He straightened his arm with his thumb up and twisted his arm until his thumb pointed down. It was an exact representation of the gesture the man on the bridge had performed.

Kate gripped his arm tighter. "Why did he do that?"

Josh shrugged.

"And why would this man, a stranger, want to kill you?" Brady added, seemingly unimpressed by Josh's account.

"I don't know. You're the ones I hope are going to find out," Josh said, incredulous at the lack of concern shown by the cop.

"Can you give us a description of this man, sir?" Williams asked.

"No, not really, the sun was in my face and I couldn't make out his features, but he was white. He wore sunglasses and a baseball cap. I couldn't tell you how tall he was."

"So, you're saying that a man you don't know and couldn't see ran you off the road without reason?"

"Yes, I am."

"I find that difficult to understand. Are you sure there isn't anything you aren't telling us, Mr. Michaels?"

"No, there fucking isn't."

"Mr. Michaels, there's no need for the profanity," Brady said sternly.

"Sorry," Josh snapped back.

"Nowadays, the department is getting more and more cases of road rage. Drivers are making it personal when they don't get their way. Everyone thinks they're a law-enforcing road vigilante. They're not. The police enforce the law, not citizens." Brady paused after his sermon. "Now are you sure nothing happened that would have provoked the SUV driver?"

"No. Nothing happened. We weren't racing each other. I hadn't cut him off and I hadn't been riding his tail. He just ran me off the road and waited around to see me drown."

"I think we have enough for now. We'll take another look at the area and we'll see if there's any physical evidence that will allow us to make any progress," Brady said, dismissing Josh's final statement like he'd already passed judgment.

"Is there anything else you can tell us about the man or his vehicle? Like a license plate number?" Williams asked.

"No, nothing."

"Your wife has given us your details and we'll be in contact in the next few days. And sir, can I recommend that you watch the speed? You never know, ten miles an hour slower and you might have stopped in time. Good night to you both," Brady said.

"Good night, sir . . . ma'am," Williams said.

"Good night officers," Kate said.

Williams pocketed his notebook and smiled. Brady put his hat back on and tipped it to both of them. The two policemen left the hospital room.

Josh waited for the policeman to get out of earshot before he exploded. "They didn't believe a word of it. They won't do a damn thing."

"Calm down," Kate said firmly. "You didn't give them much to work with. Give them a chance."

"Don't you side with them."

"I'm not, but I think you just came across some road crazy that thought he'd have some fun. He probably got off on terrorizing you. All we need to know is that it's over and you're okay." Kate hugged Josh tightly. She fought back tears, but they came anyway.

Kate's embrace felt tight enough to crack his ribs. It was hard to be angry when Kate was so upset. "You're probably right, but they didn't have to treat me like a criminal."

"Never mind that now, I'm just happy to see you alive." Gently, she rocked him while she spoke. "I have no idea how you swam to shore."

"Neither do I. God knows. Self-preservation, I suppose," Josh said, the anger subsiding. The rocking soothed his frustrations, but deep down, he wasn't satisfied. He was sure it was no accident. It didn't matter if the cops didn't believe him.

Dr. Green returned to his patient and called it a night for Josh's visitors. He told Josh to get some rest and ushered Kate out of the room.

CHAPTER THREE

When Dr. Green entered his room the next morning, Josh was feeling hungry, but not for hospital food. He'd left most of the breakfast they'd brought him. It had tasted like the contents of a bedpan. He would have killed for a turkey sandwich with a side of potato salad. He looked up from the magazine.

"Hi, Doctor."

"Hello, Mr. Michaels. I thought I'd check up on you to see how we're doing."

We? I don't remember you at the bottom of the river. I could have done with the help, he thought with good humor. "We're doing okay."

"Stand up for me, please. How'd you sleep?"

Josh put the magazine down and hopped out of bed. He let Green prod and poke him. "Not bad," he lied.

His sleep had been fitful. In his dreams, he had relived distorted versions of his attempted murder at the river. In one dream, the tailgater had been at the wheel of Josh's car and Josh had fought for control of the vehicle. Even at close quarters Josh was unable to see the man. In the dream, everything was distorted. The baseball cap's bill was three times its normal size. The man's mirrored aviator sunglasses covered half his face. After the fight of his life, Josh lost control to the tailgater and drove the car off the bridge with both of them in it. In another dream, the killer simply blew the bridge out from underneath Josh as he drove across. The bridge vaporized, engulfing him in flames as the car plunged into the river. More dreams had followed. Each time the events had varied but the outcome was the same. He hadn't survived. Waking at the moment of death had saved him.

Finishing his examination, the doctor asked, "How's your stomach acting?"

"I puked around three this morning."

"Sit down. How about now?"

"Okay, I suppose. I feel hungry."

"That's a good sign." Staring at Josh like he could see through to his internal organs, the doctor thought for a moment. "I think you're okay to go home. You seem all right, no serious physical injuries. I'll sign you off and you can go any time you want."

"Thanks."

"Go home, rest up, and take a few days for yourself. Take a holiday if you want. You've had a traumatic episode and it's time to put it behind you." With a smile, he pointed at Josh. "Doctor's orders, okay?"

"Okay, I'll try," Josh said begrudgingly.

Leaving the room, the doctor said. "Don't try. Do."

Easy for you to say, he thought. The doctor had not been there. He had not experienced what Josh had experienced. How many times had the doctor found himself trapped in a car at the bottom of the river? None, that's how many. He couldn't forget the experience just like that, nor could he forget the demented tailgater. He believed the driver had wanted to kill, not scare him.

As soon as Green left, Josh got out of his hospital johnny and into his own clothes from an overnight bag Kate had brought with her. He wanted out of the hospital. The facility was a reminder of the helplessness he'd felt in the sinking car. He was in an environment he had no control over, one where he couldn't dictate his next move. He picked up the phone and called Kate.

Kate and Abby picked him up from the hospital and took him home. It felt good to see the familiar surroundings of his home of the last six years. It was nothing special, just a two-story, three-bedroom Cape Cod on the southwest side of Sacramento. But it was comfortable and fit him like a favorite chair.

"Here we are, honey. Home," Kate said.

Looking from the passenger window, Josh said. "Yeah, I sure am."

Kate tugged at his arm and he turned to face her. She pulled him over to her and kissed him full on the mouth. Their kiss was interrupted by laughter. They stopped and looked at the person laughing in the backseat.

"What are you laughing at, Abby?" Josh said, fighting back a grin.

"You two," she replied.

"I wouldn't laugh too much if I were you. I haven't thrown away those adoption papers," he said, raising an eyebrow.

Lightly, Kate punched him in the arm. "Stop that."

Josh and his family clambered out of the minivan, and with a female on each arm he was led inside. They supported him as if he were a china doll that would break at any moment. He had the feeling this was going to be his treatment for the next few days. He imagined they would be attending to his every whim. He might as well enjoy it while he could. After Kate opened the door, Abby raced ahead.

"Wiener, we're home," she called and disappeared into the living room.

The three-year-old long-haired dachshund ran in from the kitchen with his tail wagging. The dog was black and tan with a smudge over each eye giving him a permanently surprised look. Josh had bought the dog after Kate had miscarried and they knew she would never have another child. The dog was to be Abby's substitute sibling. It was a stupid and insensitive gesture at a time when they were all looking for something to make up for the hurt, but that was forgotten now. Wiener was part of the family. The dog came up to Josh for a moment to be stroked before he bounded off to Abby.

Kate slid her arm around Josh's waist. "Is there anything you want?"

"I wouldn't mind a sandwich or something. The food in the hospital was what you'd expect." He frowned.

"Roast beef sound good?" Kate's eyes shone with love and affection.

Before Josh could answer, Abby interrupted. She raced up, clutching a picture in her hands, with Wiener close behind.

"I drew this for you." She held out the drawing for Josh to take.

Josh put his bag down and took it. He was at a loss for words.

Kate, who had already seen it, stifled a laugh and put a hand to her mouth to contain a giggle. "Tell him what it's called, sweetie."

"I call it *Daddy's Accident*," Abby said proudly.

Daddy's Accident was a crayon effort that depicted a bridge and Josh at the wheel of his car at the bottom of the river. The crudely drawn picture stunned him into silence. Only a child deciphering an adult's world could produce the picture's shocking honesty. After several moments, he smiled at the artwork.

"What do you think?"

"It's pretty much how it was," he said stiltedly.

"You like it then?" Abby said expectantly.

"Oh, I love it," he said, a little uncomfortable with the image in his hands. He bent down and kissed his daughter.

"Cool. It's just like Mommy told it to me."

"Is it now?" he said suspiciously.

"I'll get that sandwich for you." Kate left his side for the kitchen.

Josh heard a tinkle of laughter from the kitchen. His wife had left him to deal with the praise of the picture. He searched for a compliment.

The following morning, Josh had the house to himself. He packed off Kate and Abby to cruise the malls and fight it out with the other families with kids on spring break. The prospect of thrashing through the hordes of impatient people concentrated on the same outlet stores hadn't appealed to him. He wanted time to himself. Kate and Abby's affections had been suffocating. They didn't allow him a moment's peace without inquiring into his well-being. He told his employers he would be taking some time off and Kate had done the same with her job. He hoped his family would relax with time, otherwise his vacation would feel longer than two weeks.

He went into his home office down the hallway from the lounge. His office was his sanctuary from family life, an indulgence that focused entirely on Josh, the single man. Bookcases had the kind of books he liked and the shelves were filled with mementos of places visited and dearly held gifts. He only made one concession to family life—Abby's picture gallery.

He took Abby's picture off his desk and pinned it to the wall, which was a portfolio of significant events in her life. *Daddy's Accident* nestled neatly next to a portrait of Wiener and the killer whale from Marine World. He smiled at the latest addition. It was ridiculous but true and he loved the picture.

The phone rang and Josh reached across his desk to answer it.

"Josh Michaels," he said, still looking at his daughter's pictures.

"Hi, Josh," the female voice said.

Josh immediately recognized the voice, a voice he hadn't heard in nearly two years. His smile slid from his face. He looked away from the crayon gallery and sat down on his desk before his legs failed him. The river water he thought was gone lapped uncomfortably inside his stomach, its sour taste back in his mouth.

"Hello, Bell," he said. A stammer crept into his voice.

"How are you?" she said in a mocking tone.

Thank God Kate didn't answer. He counted his blessings that he'd answered the phone. "You shouldn't have called."

Ignoring him, she said, "I saw your adventure on TV the other night. Road rage is such a terrible reflection of society these days. You must have been very lucky. I thought you couldn't swim."

"I can't," he said sharply.

"So what saved you?"

"Fear," he said flatly.

"Very impressive. Just shows you what an incentive

fear is. I was surprised not to see you interviewed with that lovely wife and daughter of yours, but you never were a fan of publicity. How are they?"

"What do you want, Bell?" he said, changing the subject.

"Straight to business, eh, Josh? No, 'How you are, Bell?' 'Long time no hear, Bell?' 'What have you been up to, Bell?'" she snorted. "How you've changed, Josh. I remember you talking to me for hours. You loved to talk. Sometimes you'd talk too much and we know where that got you."

"I haven't got all day. What is it you want?" Josh chose anger to disguise his fear.

"It's not what I want, but what I can do for you."

"And what can you do for me?"

"I can protect that life you hold so dear. For five thousand dollars, I can guarantee that your dirty little secrets don't reach the ears of your family—or *Dateline* for that matter."

"I paid you."

"Yes, I know, but the cost of living is always increasing and money doesn't go as far as it once did."

"We had an arrangement."

"We did, but you thought it required a one-time payment and so did I. Alas, we were both wrong," she said with a sigh. "Now, all I need is another payment, which I might add is substantially smaller than the original sum. So you should consider you're getting a bargain."

Josh definitely didn't think Bell's sales pitch was a bargain. It was another shakedown and he hoped this wasn't the start of many such requests. "And will this be the last payment?"

"Honestly, Josh, I don't know."

"What if I don't pay?"

"Well, something unfortunate could happen. I'm

sure you can guess what that would be. But you don't have to decide now. I'll let you think about it and I'll call you in two days. It's so good to hear your voice again and it's been wonderful to speak to you. I would say give my regards to Kate, but I can't see you doing that. Ciao, Josh. It's been real," she said in an overly peppy, grating manner.

Josh said nothing and held the phone to his ear until he heard the dial tone. *Bitch!* He couldn't believe it was starting all over again. He thought he had paid for his stupid mistakes. He'd fucked up once, then again, only to prove that two wrongs didn't make a right. The sour taste in his mouth from the river became stronger and he thought he was drowning again.

Josh's crimes had been significant. He never thought it would come to prison, but it would if the truth ever came out. He thought he'd done everything necessary to cover his tracks, but it hadn't been enough. He stretched across his desk and brought the replica model of his Cessna C152 closer to examine its detail. *Will they let me keep this in my cell?* He dropped his head into his hands.

The phone rang again. Startled, Josh's head shot up. He stared at the phone like it was a hand grenade with the pin missing. On the fourth ring, cautiously, he picked it up.

"Hello," Josh said.

"Mr. Michaels?"

"Yes."

"Hello sir, it's Officer Dale Williams. My partner and I came to the hospital two days ago."

Relieved it wasn't Bell back on the phone, Josh's heart slowed to a near normal pace. He got up from his desk and settled into the swivel chair. "I remember you, Officer."

"I wanted to give you the latest on the investigation."

"Have you found him?"

"No, sir. We haven't come up with anything. There were no witnesses and there's no physical evidence at the scene other than your tire tracks. There isn't really anything for us to go on, unless you've remembered anything new or know of anyone who would have done this."

Josh hesitated. *Could Bell have masterminded the attack? Was this a warning to let me know what will happen if I don't play ball?* He fought the urge to blurt out everything—his mistakes, Bell's blackmail. He wanted to make amends for what he had done, but feared the consequences. He knew Kate would never understand. Somehow, he didn't see Officer Williams as the priestly type who would let him confess his sins and hand out contrition in return.

"Mr. Michaels?" the policeman prompted.

"No, Officer. I don't know of anyone who would want to harm me intentionally."

"Well sir . . . to be honest, I can't see us finding anyone. There's so little for us to go on," the young policeman confessed, a little embarrassed. "Personally, for what it's worth, I think you came across some psycho. You should count yourself lucky that things turned out so well. You wouldn't believe how many cases like this we get."

"Thank you for your honesty, Officer Williams."

"Sorry I couldn't do more, sir. If we find out anything, we'll contact you. Good-bye, sir."

"Thanks. Good-bye."

Josh put the phone down. *What are they thinking about me?* he wondered. Did Williams and Brady think it was an accident caused by two idiots fucking around on the roads or did they think he fell asleep at the wheel and dumped the car in the river himself? With his run of luck, he wouldn't be surprised if they charged him with reckless driving. A headache climbed in behind his eyes and settled in for the long haul. The morning hadn't gone well.

CHAPTER FOUR

The professional opened the door, took the DO NOT DISTURB sign off the hook on the back of the door and hung it on the knob outside. The motel room was clean, but lacked character or personality. It was a clone of the rooms on either side of it, furnished with two double beds, a television, a closet, a desk and assorted hotel toiletries. The room had been his home for the past week, but it looked as if he'd yet to check in. The maids rarely found any signs of disturbance to the room. The waste paper baskets were never used, the beds never looked slept in and the towels were always neatly folded after use. The only evidence of his existence was the locked aluminum briefcase and suitcase. He liked the kind of strong and resilient luggage that couldn't easily be tampered with. He didn't like people knowing what he did.

Removing the briefcase from the closet, he placed it on the bed. He dragged a chair over to the bed and sat down. Adjusting the combination locks, he snapped open the case and removed some files, spreading them across the bed. He scanned for something he'd missed, something he could use to his advantage to complete his task, to kill the targets. The files had arrived in the usual manner, delivered to his Boston post office box without his name on them and no return address, as instructed. This was more than the fiftieth such "care package" he had received over the last two years. However, this was the first time a package contained data on two targets in the same city for simultaneous termination. He didn't like the situation. Sacramento was a small city where murders were not that commonplace. It would be possible for someone to link the incidents if they dug deep enough, so it was important the deaths appeared totally unrelated.

Of the two targets, the older one, Margaret Macey, should be the easier to dispose of, and he had a novel idea for her elimination. Putting her file to one side, he picked up the other. Opening it, he leaned over in his chair, examined the photograph and frowned. This target had survived his first attempt. Josh Michaels hadn't drowned in the river. It was a screw-up that drew attention. He would have to be more accurate with his next attempt. He would dig a little deeper into Michaels's life before he exposed his position.

He had spent the first week watching his prey, seeing what they did, when they did it and whom they did it with. Michaels had offered him an opportunity when he left for a business trip. The professional had followed his target to Bakersfield. Seeing Michaels preferred driving on the deserted roads gave him the opening for which he was looking. He knew he would be chancing his luck on the open road when not all the conditions were under his control, but he liked his chances. An "innocent" road accident for Michaels on his return journey would be the order of the day. Except it was Michaels's lucky day, and that allowed him to survive. According to the television report, Michaels had swum to shore even though his file stated he couldn't swim. He hoped the rest of the information in the file was correct.

Thinking about his mistake, he cursed himself under his breath. He had to tighten up his act. Having drawn attention to himself, he was vulnerable and that was unforgivable. Mistakes were not his trademark and mistakes would get *him* killed. He closed Michaels's file, sat back and let his mind drift.

The hit man liked his work. He found it challenging and he had a talent for it. Killing people was something he was good at, but the challenge didn't come from the killing. It came from making the kill look like an accident. The concept was his employer's brainchild—he regularly needed people killed, but couldn't afford any suspicion falling upon him. He would think long and hard about what kind of accident suited each of his assigned targets to satisfy his employer. He kept news clippings of unusual accidents that he could reconstruct or improve on for his assignments. He took great care to make his kills look like accidents, although occasionally he did commit an obvious murder if the case warranted it. In his opinion, a seemingly motiveless murder was just as hard to solve as a well-planned accident.

However, it took time to set up the kills to make them look like accidents. Too much time in his employer's opinion—he wanted quicker and quicker turnarounds these days, and the caseload had significantly increased in the last twelve months. Obviously, a quicker kill meant less preparation, so the quality of the assassination couldn't be guaranteed. If his employer wanted quick kills he could do that, but it would look like murder and murder meant investigations.

He thought of himself as a craftsman rather than a ruthless killer; a member of a dying breed in a world of mass-produced lifestyles. The greatest compliment he could receive was to watch the nightly news and hear it, or read the newspaper and see it—the words "unfortunate accident" in conjunction with his target's name. Any monkey with a good aim and a cool nerve could take out a mark, but it took real intelligence, class and attention to detail to kill someone without anyone realizing it had been a contract hit.

Over time he began to need the applause after a superior performance. In the beginning, as soon as his mark was dead, he was out of there before the body was even cold. These days, he had little to fear cop-wise and hung around the kill zone awhile. The ultimate praise came from the mark's family and friends. On several occasions he had attended the funerals of his targets in person or viewed them from afar with listening devices. He loved hearing the target's loved ones discuss the circumstances of the death. An overwhelming pride filled him every time. Oh yes, he loved his work.

His work was his life, but it did come with its downsides. The hit man's life was a loner's life. His contact with the real world and the people in it was scant. Most of the time, the people he really saw were through the crosshairs of a gun sight. After years of practicing being unseen, practice became perfect and no one saw him. His career made his life very impersonal. Even after two years of dealing with the same employer and over half a million dollars of fees, he'd never met the man face-to-face. His home in Boston was like the motel room he sat in now. There were no photographs of him or his family, books, CDs or other material possessions. If someone walked into his house they couldn't tell if he had moved in, let alone lived there. He snapped out of his thoughts before he depressed himself. He had work to do.

He removed one of the three cellular phones from

the briefcase. This one, like the other two, was the pay-as-you-go type, unregistered and purchased with cash. This phone he used for his employer. He disposed of the phones regularly to prevent a regular record building up against any one person. He selected the preset number and listened to the phone dial. The call was picked up immediately.

"Yes?" his employer said.

"I have an update on the situation," the professional said.

"And?"

"The Michaels assignment was unsuccessful."

"What the hell do you mean? You told me it was completed yesterday."

"Your mark suddenly discovered he could swim. Your files were wrong." The professional emphasized that the blame wasn't his.

The employer put his temper on a leash, but it wouldn't take much to set it off again. "Is there any police involvement?"

"Yes, but they've got nothing to go on. I've been monitoring police dispatches on my scanner. I've caught a couple of transmissions and there are no further actions planned unless anything else comes to light. Which it won't."

"It better not. What's your next move?"

"I'm going to do some more research on Michaels, get involved in his life. The closer I am to him the easier it will be."

"I don't want you exposing us," the employer said. "What about the other project?"

"To be dealt with over the next few days. I see fewer problems with that one. She's less active than Michaels."

"Let's hope your next call reports success and not failure."

"Have I ever failed before?"

The professional heard the line disconnect and switched the phone off. He bore no resentment for his employer. The man was a greedy asshole who believed he was in control. That was fine with him. That thinking made his employer vulnerable, making it easy for the professional to eliminate him if the occasion arose.

He replaced the cell phone in the briefcase and removed another of the phones and an address book. The professional flicked through its pages. The names and addresses it contained didn't belong to friends, family or business contacts, but victims. Each name was the name of a person he'd killed on behalf of his current employer. He felt obliged to record their names for posterity. All craftsmen kept records of their work, so why shouldn't he? He knew carrying the book with him was highly risky, but he couldn't help himself.

He stopped at the Ms. It listed only one name. The names of Michaels and Macey were to be added very soon. He tapped the page and said, "Not long now."

He returned the book and the files to the briefcase and locked it. Taking the case with him, he left the motel room for his car. He got into a Ford Taurus, the Explorer's replacement. He knew the police didn't have a make on the license plate, but it wasn't worth taking risks. Opening the case again, he removed the 9mm semiautomatic pistol. He checked it and holstered it under his jacket.

"Let's see what Mr. Michaels is up to tonight," the professional said to himself.

CHAPTER FIVE

Josh walked into the sports bar and scanned the room for someone he knew. The bar was cool and the after work crowd was just arriving. The level of conversation was set on simmer, but Bob Deuce's voice could always be heard above the level of any conversation. There he was, two hundred and twenty-five pounds of happy man. His size was the product of beer, junk food and a voracious appetite for sports. Any sport would do; he had even developed a taste for soccer in recent years.

Sitting at the bar, Bob objected loudly to a baseball umpire's decision on the television. He expressed his dislike to a man sitting next to him that Josh didn't know. Knowing Bob, he didn't know the man either, but he had a way of picking up conversations with complete strangers. Bob's disgusted look turned into a broad grin when he saw Josh looking in his direction.

"Hey, glug, glug, Captain Nemo," Bob boomed across the room.

Everyone turned in Josh's direction and his face felt hot with embarrassment. He raised a hand at his friend and crossed the room, trying to avoid the unwanted gazes.

"Barkeep, a glass of your River City water for my good friend," Bob demanded.

"What can I get you, Nemo?" The barman failed to show the slightest interest in Bob's reference.

"A Sam Adams," Josh said.

The barman cracked open a bottle and put it in front of Josh.

"This is the man who climbed from his sinking car in the Sacramento River and swam to shore even though he can't swim," Bob expanded while paying for Josh's drink.

"You're the one," the barman responded flatly, then moved on to the next customer.

"I saw that on TV. You're a lucky man," the man sitting next to Bob said.

"Something like that," Josh said, before turning to Bob. "With your level of subtlety you should work with the terminally ill. You have a great bedside manner."

"Hey, man, you looked as though you needed a little tail pulling. Your face is longer than that jump you made into the river. But seriously, I'm glad you're okay, pal. You scared us for awhile," Bob said and slapped Josh on the back.

"I'm glad to be around and thanks for looking after Kate and Abby, I appreciate it," Josh said.

"You're not going to tell me you love me and get all metrosexual on me, are you?"

"Bite me," Josh said, smiling.

"That's my boy."

Josh swigged his beer and watched the game with Bob to allow a moment to compose himself before broaching the subject of his problems. Bob ruined his plan by speaking first.

"So why did you want to meet here?" Bob gestured

to the bar with the bottle. "We haven't been in a bar together for some time. What's up?"

"Come on, let's sit down where we won't be overheard."

Bob made his farewell to the man at the bar. As they
crossed the room, Josh felt the tension build between
them. They took up residence in a quiet booth by the
restrooms. Josh tried to prepare himself, putting all the
facts in order before speaking.

"I think I'm in big trouble."

"Why?"

"I don't believe my accident was an accident. I think
it was deliberate."

"Bullshit, buddy. I think you came across Roger
Ebert without his Prozac." Bob gave a limp-wristed
thumbs down. "No disrespect intended, but you aren't
that special."

"But I think I am. I did something that makes me
special."

"I don't think I'm going to want to hear this, so you'd
better tell me before I get the hell out of here," Bob said.

"You know that insurance policy I got you to cash in
for me about eighteen months ago?"

"Yeah."

"The money was for a payoff."

"Payoff who?"

"Belinda Wong. She was blackmailing me." Finally,
he'd said it. It was out. He'd admitted his predicament
to someone. He found relief in confession. It made the
problem less foreboding, although he imagined this relief would be short-lived.

"Your secretary? Jesus Christ. What was she blackmailing you over?"

"We had an affair for a year when things weren't too
good between Kate and me. When I broke it off she
said she would tell all."

"I got you over fifty thousand. You gave it all to her?"

"Yes, but it wasn't just for the affair. I gave her the money for what I told her during the affair. I took a kickback on a building project in Dixon after Abby was born."

"Shit." Bob sat back and struggled to comprehend what Josh was telling him.

"You know Abby had complications after her birth and I didn't have the insurance to cover the bills. I was inspecting this construction project in Dixon and the construction company knew it wouldn't pass because they'd cut corners. So when it came to the inspection, they offered me ten thousand to turn a blind eye. At the time it seemed like an answer to my prayers and I took it with both hands."

"Christ, what a train wreck," Bob said. "Where are the other bodies buried?"

"Thanks for making me feel better," Josh said bitterly.

"Christ, Josh, I can't believe you never told me. Jesus, I'm your best friend."

"It's not something you tell."

Bob shook his head. "Did Kate ever wonder where you got the money for Abby's treatment?"

"No. She never knew my medical plan didn't stretch that far. Unfortunately, the problem got worse when I moved on to the next project the company was building. They wanted to arrange a similar set-up. I had done it as a means to an end and not as a career enhancement. I couldn't squeal on them, so I got out of the building trade and became a buyer."

"And Bell knows all this?"

"The whole thing. My dick got the better of me. I wanted to show off." Josh went silent for a moment, reliving the events in his head. "Later, I realized I was an idiot for cheating on Kate and I told Bell it was all over. She wanted to get even. She wanted money to keep the details from Kate and the press."

Josh felt sick to his stomach. He'd hidden that part of his life so deep within him, he had forgotten all about his mistakes until now. Bell had brought them all back like drowned corpses rising to the surface. All his fears returned as if it had just happened. Josh emptied the remainder of the beer and brought the empty bottle down onto the table with a resounding crack.

"You bastard," Bob said and meant it. "Why did you have to tell me? I was in a good mood when I came in here."

"Because you're my friend and the only person I thought I could turn to."

"You're a bad advertisement for friendship."

"You won't tell anyone?"

"You know I won't because I'm your *friend*." Bob said the word "friend" like it was a dirty word.

"Thanks."

"I knew you were in the shit when you wanted that insurance policy cashed in. I thought you were over-stretched or something, but this." Bob shook his head. "If you hadn't told me, I wouldn't have believed it."

"Sometimes it's hard for me to believe."

"So, what's this got to do with your accident?"

"Bell called me today asking me for another five thousand and told me if I didn't pay, something bad would happen. I think she forced me off the bridge."

"But you said it was a male driver."

"It was, but maybe she paid someone."

"No, I don't buy that. It wouldn't be in her interests to kill you. She'd be killing the goose that lays the golden egg and all that crap."

"Maybe she wasn't trying to kill me—just scare me into paying."

"This is unreal," Bob said. "So what are you going to do?"

"I don't know."

"You've only got two choices. Pay her and refuel that gravy train or blow her off, tell Kate what you did and take your chances. What appeals to you most?"

"Neither."

"Can you afford to pay this time around?"

"Yeah, I have some savings that aren't in a joint account."

"Then buy yourself some time and pay her, but find out what the hell she's up to. I find it hard to believe she's going to all this trouble for the small sums of money involved. It's not as if she's tapping the Rockefeller fountain. Personally, I think she's using the accident as a lever to screw with you, and it's working."

"So you think the timing is coincidental?"

"Yes, I do. You've dug yourself in deep and you're panicking. You need to start thinking straight."

"Okay, I'll pay her. How do I diffuse the situation?"

"I don't know. We'll have to deal with that when we have more information."

"We?"

"Yes, we. As much as I dislike what you've done, I'm here to help you, man. You and Kate have too much going for you."

"Don't tell me what I already know."

"Well, why didn't you know it at the time?"

Josh didn't have an answer.

Bob Deuce sat in his office at Family Stop Insurance Services moving paperwork around. Josh's revelations in the bar the previous night preoccupied him. The impact had left him concussed. He'd never dreamt his closest friend could have got himself into so much shit. He'd stayed to watch the game but found his mind wandering back to Josh. He left twenty minutes after Josh did. His wife, Nancy, detected his mood, but he deflected her questions.

He slept little. Rather than sharing Josh's burden, he'd taken it all upon his shoulders. He realized the pressure Josh must be under keeping it a secret for all this time. It was bad enough experiencing the situation by proxy. He would find it difficult not to blurt it out the next time he saw Kate. Sharing was a bitch. But friendship was friendship and Josh needed his help now more than ever. Maria, Bob's receptionist, acted as a welcome distraction when she popped her head through the door.

"Bob, I have a James Mitchell from Pinnacle Investments outside. He says he's got an appointment with you, but I don't have a record of it. Is that right?"

"Yes, he does. He called after you'd gone. Sorry, I didn't write it down. Send him in." Bob managed a thin smile. He didn't really want to see this guy, but duty called.

Maria disappeared.

Bob looked at his desk. It was a sty. He thought about making a stab at clearing it up, but blew the idea off. He just didn't have the heart. *Let him see that I'm a slob.*

Maria returned with his ten o'clock appointment. "James Mitchell, Bob."

Maria saw herself out and the men introduced themselves and shook hands. The strength of the man's grip surprised Bob. He looked so ordinary. Everything about James Mitchell was average—medium build, average height, slightly receding hairline and an unremarkable face. If he had been the basis for "Where's Waldo," no one would have ever found him. He was about forty-five and dressed conservatively in a generic single-breasted suit.

"What can I do for you, Mr. Mitchell?" Bob said.

"James, please. I'm speaking to various insurance brokers in California to promote Pinnacle Investments and to remind them of our services, especially our unique ones. In the past you've been instrumental in providing us business, but things have dropped off and I would like to see what we can do for you and your clients," Mitchell said.

Bob saw no point in prolonging this meeting for nicety's sake. He wanted the salesman out of his office as soon as possible. "Okay, James. The main reason for the decline is most of your services are geared to investments and I'm an insurance agent. I've sold some of your life policies, but I do find that some of your competitors offer much better rates."

Mitchell asked Bob to outline where the differences were between Pinnacle Investments and their competitors. Mitchell wrote Bob's comments in a notebook on top of his briefcase, which he balanced on his knees.

Bob thought the exercise was a waste of his time, but it took his mind off his other worries.

"I see you've sold several of our viatical policies over the last few years—to a John S. Densmore, who is now deceased, a Margaret F. Macey and a Joshua K. Michaels."

Bob nodded in agreement.

"I wanted to update our records on Margaret Macey and Josh Michaels."

"Let me get their files." Bob left his desk for the archives in the rear of the building and returned with the files. Sitting down, he said, "What do you need to know?"

"Josh Michaels, does he still fly and rock climb?"

"Yes, he flies regularly, but I don't think he rock climbs much nowadays."

"And how's his health?"

"Good as far as I know."

"Good. And how about Margaret Macey's health?"

"Not so good. I saw her some months ago to renew her homeowner's insurance and she didn't look well. She's a very nervous woman. I think she's very drug dependent these days."

"So the treatment is not going well, eh?"

"No, I don't think the doctors have much chance of curing her heart problems."

"Is she terminal?"

"No, I think it's just that she's old and everything is worn out." Bob added, "She went for the viatical settlement because she needed cash, not because she was terminal."

"That's a shame." Mitchell looked suitably moved, but then suddenly brightened. "Thanks for the update, Bob. Do you have any other candidates for these unique insurance opportunities? It's a thriving division for us. I know it was originally intended to be a program for the terminally ill, but since then we've opened up the qualifications. It's fast becoming an alternative way to refinance."

"I don't have many terminal patients. It's something I have recommended to clients as and when the need has arisen. With regard to refinancing, that's something I don't really get involved in unless my clients ask me."

"I understand, as long as we're not losing out to our competitors on that one. We like to think that we offer the best viatical service on the market."

Bob didn't need to hear the pitch and wrapped up business with Mitchell. They bullshitted a while about the insurance industry, life, family and sports. He felt sorry for Mitchell. It wasn't much of a life flitting from motel to motel. He knew. He'd done it himself for six years. He'd given it up to start his own business and never looked back.

"How long are you in the area for, James?" Bob asked.

"Until the weekend, then I move to San Francisco, then LA."

"Well, if you feel up to it, I'm going to a barbecue on Saturday. Would you like to come? It's nothing fancy. Just a friend's birthday and he's one of your clients, Josh Michaels."

"One of our viatical clients," Mitchell said.

"Yeah, but please don't mention it. His wife doesn't know."

"Oh, I understand," Mitchell said, stumbling over himself. "Yeah, sounds good. I would love to come."

Mitchell thanked Bob for his time and hospitality. He gave Bob his motel address at the River City Inn, on the south side of the city, and they agreed on a time to meet on Saturday. The meeting had briefly perked Bob's spirits, but he fell back into his funk once the salesman was gone.

CHAPTER SIX

"Are you two going to play that game all day? It's beautiful outside and you should be out there," Kate complained.

"We're playing until I beat Daddy," Abby replied.

"Oh yeah?" Mock disbelief colored his words. "You're a long way from winning, my girl. I'll be victorious."

Josh and his daughter were playing the Sacramento version of Monopoly in the living room. The game had started after breakfast and was still in progress at three in the afternoon. Properties had been bought and skylines built. The pair fought for domination. Abby held her property cards fanned close to her face like a seasoned poker player, but her face told Josh she was pleased with herself. Occasionally she confided conspiratorially with her adviser, Wiener. He was meant to be representing the bank, but Josh was sure the dog knew something he didn't. He was losing to his daughter.

"Is that dog helping you, Abby?" he said, and raised an eyebrow.

"No, that would be cheating," she said, and hid her face behind her cards and giggled. "Your go."

Josh smiled at Abby. He picked up the dice and rolled them. A five and a two.

"Damn! Not again." This was the third time he'd been sent to the Traffic Jam square. He moved his riverboat piece to the square.

Abby erupted into laughter and Wiener barked in support.

"No two hundred dollars, no passing Go, Daddy," she squealed in delight and hugged the dachshund.

"Josh, I can't believe you're getting upset over losing to your daughter and the dog," Kate said, hoping to inject some sanity into the situation.

"That's the third time I've been on that damn Traffic Jam square in the last five circuits. That must be against the odds, and I bet that's gonna cost me another hundred bucks to get out," he said in dismay.

"Yeah, yeah, whatever. I'll be around for consolation hugs for the loser, okay?" Kate said to the industrialists at play.

Josh wasn't really upset. It was all for Abby's entertainment. He was actually enjoying himself. His talk with Bob had lightened his mood and so had his two weeks leave. He wasn't sure whether the combination of these events contributed to his high spirits, but he hoped so. He was getting back to a normal life, at last.

Abby rolled the dice. A double six. She giggled again.

"What games do you play at school?" Josh asked.

The doorbell rang.

"Can someone answer that please?" Kate called out.

"If you wouldn't mind, honey. I'm on the verge of scalping this little upstart," Josh called back.

"No, he's not, Mom," Abby shouted.

"Okay, I'll answer it, shall I?"

"Mommy's never understood business, not like us chickens," Josh said.

Wiener yawned and licked his nose.

Kate opened the door and spoke to the visitor on the porch. Her tone was one of confusion and alarm. "Are you sure you have the right address?"

Josh looked up from the game. Abby, oblivious to her mother's remarks, counted off her move around the perimeter of the board.

"Josh, would you come here a minute?" Kate called.

Getting up, he asked, "Is everything okay?"

"Don't go Daddy, it's your turn," Abby said.

"I'll be back in a minute, honey," he said over his shoulder.

Kate turned toward him. Her expression was one of shock. A delivery boy in his early twenties stood on the porch with a confused look on his face.

"What's up?" Josh slipped an arm around his wife's waist in a statement of solidarity.

"I have a delivery for the Michaels's household. I'm very sorry for your loss, please accept my condolences," the young man said in a solemn tone, but bewilderment furrowed his brow.

He proffered the delivery, a funeral wreath, for Josh to accept. Josh couldn't believe what the guy held in his hands and took an involuntary step backward.

"Is this a joke?" Josh demanded, his grip on his temper slipping.

"No, sir," the delivery boy said.

Josh looked at the boy dressed in a yellow and green windbreaker and peered over his shoulder at the van parked in the street. The van was from Forget-Me-Not Florists and displayed a free phone number and a local address. Appearances seemed to be honest enough; the delivery boy wasn't bogus. Josh looked back at the boy.

"It's for the recently departed Josh Michaels," the driver continued. He made another attempt to give the wreath to Josh.

"I'm Josh Michaels and I'm not fucking dead." Josh exploded at the expense of the messenger. The delivery boy took two steps back from the force of the blast.

"Josh, for Christ's sake, he didn't send it," Kate said.

"Who sent it?" Josh demanded.

The shaken Forget-Me-Not boy removed the card from the wreath to read it.

"Pinnacle Investments, sir," he said, offering the card to Josh.

Josh snatched the card from the delivery boy, almost removing a couple of fingers in the process. The boy snapped his arm back in reflex. Josh read the handwritten card:

> To the Michaels family,
> Please accept our heartfelt sympathies in your time of loss.
>
> *Pinnacle Investments*

"Why did they order this?" Josh shouted.

"I don't know, sir." The delivery boy took another step backward, the wreath still outstretched.

"Josh, leave him alone. He doesn't know anything." Kate snatched up her purse and moved between her husband and the scared driver.

"My husband has had a very traumatic time over the last few days. I'm very sorry."

She took the wreath and got a ten-dollar bill from her purse. She gave it to the boy and apologized to him again.

The driver took the money and thanked her, but his gaze was on Josh. He was wary just in case Josh launched into another attack. He marched back to his van, muttering obscenities as he went.

Kate closed the door.

"What's your problem?" she demanded. "What was all that about? That poor bastard didn't know anything."

"I wanted to know what was going on. What do Pinnacle Investments think they are playing at sending me a wreath? Why did they think I was dead?" Josh shouted.

"And bawling out some kid helps, does it?" Kate said, shouting almost as loud as Josh.

He hesitated and bit down his rage. "No, it doesn't."

"Who is Pinnacle Investments anyway?" she demanded.

Josh caught himself before he said something damaging. He couldn't afford to tell Kate the truth. In the moment he took to compose the lie, rationality took over and the rage subsided. "I have my life insurance with them," he said, his anger receding with every word.

"Well, I suggest you take it up with Bob, he's your insurance agent," she said.

The shouting died and another sound filled the air—crying. Abby stood in the living room doorway, sobbing. She buried her face into Wiener's body. The dog didn't move as her tears soaked into his coat.

Oh, shit, Josh thought.

"Well done, Josh," Kate said bitterly.

CHAPTER SEVEN

Dexter Tyrell sat at his desk in his executive office. It was five hundred square feet of office space luxuriously decorated with the best furniture, the best carpeting, the best of everything befitting a vice president of Pinnacle Investments.

The report lay on the desk in front of him, the result of weeks of number crunching and research. But it didn't matter how many times he juggled the numbers, he still failed to meet the return he'd promised the board. The growth in revenues would be ten percent, not fifteen, as he'd promised.

Seeing Greg Baxter's name on the cover filled him with bile. The little shit would be loving this. Ten years his junior, Baxter was the spitting image of himself— ruthless and hungry for success. *Did that bastard think I wouldn't find out?*

Baxter had been playing politics. He didn't want to be on the losing team and rather than fight for his successes, he wanted to jump ship. He'd been sucking up to the other divisions.

"I'll fix you, you little prick," Tyrell said to Baxter's name at the top of the report.

He'd see that Baxter's wings were clipped before he got to scale the corporate heights. He still possessed enough clout to arrange for a crap assignment. Baxter could never be like him. The man lacked the guts and the vision to be capable of what he had done for the division.

The telephone on his desk rang. "Yes?"

"Mr. Tyrell, Mr. Edgar has asked for all VPs to be in the board room in ten minutes for the quarterly review," Tyrell's personal assistant said.

"Thank you." He put the phone down.

He wasn't looking forward to this meeting. It was an opportunity for the big men to show their disappointment in him like parents reading their child's lackluster report card. At forty-one, Dexter Tyrell was the youngest vice president to make it to the board. Many in the organization resented his appointment, including three members of the board. They would love to watch him fail, even at their own personal expense. They were big men playing childish games. *Screw it,* he thought. *I make the rules.* He flicked through his copy of the report for the last time.

Tyrell had been appointed to the board eight years earlier, a rising star in the corporate heavens. However, he looked older than his years, the price for being the head of a failing business venture. His mop of hair had receded to a widow's peak with a balding spot on top. The golden blond had withered away to leave a tangle of gray growing out like weeds in a field.

His rapid rise to success came when he'd presented the board a guaranteed surefire winner. Dexter Tyrell had seen the future and it had been viatical settlements. A new and unique business opportunity was created and Tyrell was the man given the task of pulling it off.

Terminal illness in the early 1990s was creating a disaster area for its sufferers, especially AIDS victims. Medical insurance policies were not designed to cover the effects of long-term illness and this left the policy-holders out in the cold to fend for themselves. The patients found themselves footing the bills for expensive treatments to maintain their quality of life. Eventually, patients unable to pay were denied access to drugs because of the cost. But if the patient had a life insurance policy there was a way out for them, through a viatical settlement.

Dexter Tyrell saw the gap in the market. His division and several other competing companies jumped to the rescue. Pinnacle Investments's viatical division took over payment of the terminally ill's life insurance policies. In addition to paying the monthly dues, a generous cash payment was made to the patient. In return, Pinnacle Investments became the beneficiary of the policy. The cash payment could be a considerable percentage of the face value of the life policy. The percentage was based on the likelihood of the client's death—the closer the client was to dying, the greater the payment. And thus, an industry was born mainly thanks to the HIV virus providing so many potential customers. An industry where everyone got what they wanted. The investment companies returned a guaranteed profit. Patients had a relatively carefree life until their death. The medical insurance companies got a monkey off their back. Everybody won.

Dexter was the toast of Pinnacle Investments for four years. People died as projected, usually within a twelve to eighteen month period, and the company collected on the insurance policies. All was plain sailing, except for some problems with dependants. The surviving family members were often upset by the loss of their inheritance to the profit of corporate America. Dexter liked to think of it as sour grapes. It was their unsatisfied greed that was upset. He provided a public service, a good deed, and like all good deeds, someone received a reward. In this case, cash. Publicly he was the Good Samaritan, but honestly he believed he'd exploited a business opportunity to good effect.

The industry snowballed. Pinnacle Investments received the number of requests for viatical settlements in a week that it had received in a month two years before. At the rate at which their clients died, the company was able to take as many new clients as it wanted.

But disaster hit when the medical community discovered fantastic breakthroughs in the fields of treating terminal illnesses. The major advance had been in the treatment of HIV with reverse transcriptase inhibitors and protease inhibitor drugs. The new protease inhibitors seemed to purge the blood of virus. Drugs with names like Nofinivir, Thyrimmune, Thydex, and Xered cropped up from all quarters, with others following close behind. Dexter Tyrell's viatical clients had the cash to pay for the new treatments with the payouts from their settlements. As a result, clients stopped dying as scheduled.

The majority of Dexter Tyrell's clients were HIV positive patients. How he wished for the new drugs to fail. The new discoveries meant that life expectancy could be extended as much as ten to fifteen years with a quality of life previously unseen. Patients with an extended lifeline faced the prospect that in ten to fifteen years a cure could be found. The unwelcome possibility of financial ruin now greeted Pinnacle Investments and its competitors.

Pinnacle Investments's viatical division saw its income dry up and its costs increase over the next eighteen months. Many viatical policies' monthly dues needed paying. Dexter Tyrell was blamed for his shortsightedness. He was seen as the man who would sink the company.

To Tyrell's credit, he'd been inventive when his back was against the wall. He'd diversified, changed his investment mix, all but stopping the intake of HIV victims and replacing them with patients that were unlikely to survive from other illnesses such as cancer, heart disease, Alzheimer's, and multiple sclerosis. Also, individuals with dangerous jobs or hereditary conditions were welcome. Those actions and some other extreme measures he kept from the board had averted the collapse of the viatical division. He was a hero. The board should be thanking him. But they wouldn't.

The desk clock told Tyrell that his ten minutes were up. He picked up the copies of the quarterly report and his presentation materials and made his way to the boardroom.

CHAPTER EIGHT

Josh paced about the house on eggshells for hours. Bell had said she'd call at noon. It was twenty after. What made matters worse was Kate and Abby were still in the house. He'd hoped they would be out by now, but even after some prompting they'd decided to stay home.

Finally, the phone rang.

Dropping the newspaper he wasn't really reading, Josh leapt from the couch in the living room to grab the phone.

"Josh Michaels." He couldn't help but hear the overwrought tone to his voice.

"Josh, how are you?" Bell said smoothly.

He shifted to the open doorway between the living room and the foyer, giving him full view of all the downstairs rooms.

He'd have to put on a good show for his wife and daughter. He knew he had to make it sound natural, like he was talking to a good friend, not his blackmailer. He did a good job. "Fine, fine, and you?" he said pleasantly.

Coming downstairs with her arms full of laundry, Kate asked, "Who's that?"

"Hold on a second," Josh covered the mouthpiece with one hand. "Flying club."

Kate nodded and went into the kitchen with the dirty clothes.

Josh was forced to listen to Bell's laughter while he spoke to Kate. He wanted to bawl her out, but bit back the desire. He took his hand off the mouthpiece.

"Hello," he said.

"Oh, Josh. You make me laugh. You lie so well. You have a real flare for it."

Ignoring her derision, he kept a wary eye on Kate in the kitchen. "I think I know what I want to do."

"So you've made a decision?"

"Yes."

"What is it?"

"Yes."

"You'll pay?"

"Yes."

"Will you say 'yes' once more? Just for me."

Josh's grip on the phone tightened until his knuckles turned white. He ground out the word. "Yes."

"Good boy."

Josh hated Bell for getting a thrill out of making him squirm under these conditions, but he could do little else than pander to her.

Bell switched to a business-like tone. "I'll give you three hours to bring me the money."

"Where?"

"Sacramento Zoo."

The location surprised him. He almost repeated it, but caught himself. "Where?"

"In front of the white tiger and lion enclosures."

Smiling, Kate came toward him. Briefly, she held his

hand and mouthed, "I love you," before returning upstairs.

Josh smiled for appearances. "Okay, sounds good."

"Good. I'm glad you've come around to my way of
thinking. I'm quite enjoying this phone call. I feel I'm
in one of those cheesy spy movies. Quite the giggle,
don't you think?"

"Yeah," Josh said. "Quite the giggle."

"The clock's ticking, Josh." Bell hung up.

Josh called up stairs, "I'm going out for awhile. I'm
gonna borrow the car, okay?"

He didn't wait for a response.

Josh waited on a park bench in front of the white tiger
and lion enclosures as promised with the five thousand
dollars in a padded envelope he had bought from a
Rite-Aid on the way to the bank. There'd been no
problem removing the cash from the savings account.
The teller showed no surprise or interest. Kate wouldn't
notice the missing money. The residual cash came from
the remainder of the sale of his life insurance policy less
the initial blackmail money.

He sat in front of a bank of five habitats in the
middle of the zoo that contained the more impressive
animals—white tigers, lions, the polar bear, hyenas
and snow leopards. Josh ignored the people in front
of the caged animals, the burbling from the kids'
chatter and the sound of the animals themselves. Instead, he contemplated what he was going to say to
Bell, how he would finish it with her once and for all.
He wasn't doing very well; he hadn't come up with
anything good. Josh felt the balance of power was
with the blackmailer. He was the one who was willing
to pay to hide his secrets. He was holding the weaker
hand and a pair of threes never beat a full house. The

best he could do was bluff. Was he a good enough card player?

Josh checked his watch—ten after three. Bell was ten minutes late and he had arrived five minutes early. *She's doing this to get to me,* he thought and mumbled a curse under his breath.

He looked at the lion in its cage in front of him. It was a beautiful animal born to roam the plains of Africa, but this lion had never sampled that life. It had been born in captivity and transferred from the San Diego Zoo. It was just as unsatisfied with its situation as Josh was with his. The creature paced its inadequately sized habitat while its mate slept. Josh wasn't sure how lions lived in their natural surroundings, but he was sure they didn't live within twenty feet of where they shit. The lion dropped to the ground by its mate.

"There's no place like home, eh, Toto?" he murmured.

The crowd to Josh's right parted right on cue and Bell came through the gap they created for her. She caught Josh's eye, smiled seductively, walked over and stopped in front of him.

She was the same sexy Asian woman he'd had an affair with nearly two years before. She was a small woman, only a little more than five feet, with a delicate frame that looked as if she'd break if he held her too tightly. Her skin, the color of coffee with too much cream, was all too abundantly on show. Dressed for a warm spring day, she wore a khaki skirt that stopped three inches above the knee, more provocative than if she wore no skirt at all. The white tank top with spaghetti straps covered a minimal bra for her small breasts. She had the most provocative features he'd ever seen. Her almond shaped face had full lips, dark, knowing eyes and unusually curved eyebrows that always seemed to hint that she knew something he didn't. Although he detested her, he still couldn't help but drink her in.

"You look like a lost little boy, sitting there all on your own. Cheer up, things could be worse."

He stared up at her. "How?"

Bell sat down next to him on a bench donated by a local resident. She flicked her long hair with the back of her hand and the raven strands tumbled over her shoulder obediently. She stretched out an arm along the bench behind Josh.

Without looking at him, she said, "You could be at home explaining what you did all those years ago to your wife. Couldn't you, hmmm?"

Josh felt Bell's arm snake around his shoulders. Her touch repelled him, although it once would have made him instantly hard. He uncurled her arm, placing it on her lap.

"Don't you like that?"

Josh shot her a disapproving look. "I thought you were here to conduct some business."

"Oh, Josh. It doesn't have to be all business. I know you've got my money, but I thought we could socialize for awhile."

"I don't feel like socializing."

"But I haven't seen you in such a long time. You look good. I see you're still in shape. You're one of the few men I know who has the butt to pull off a pair of jeans," she said.

Josh steered the discussion back on track. "Bell, why have you come back?"

"I'm a Sacramento girl born and bred. I don't see why I should be away from my home, my friends . . . my lover." She flashed Josh a coy smile.

Did she honestly think they would pick up where they left off after what she had done? "We're not getting back together. Are you crazy?"

Bell seemed unaffected by the accusation. "You never can tell."

"Why did we have to come here? It's too public."

She looked away and briefly surveyed the zoo, its animals and its patrons. Without looking at Josh she spoke seriously, a side of her Josh rarely saw. "It's strange. I've been away less than two years and I have yearnings for the weirdest things. I don't know why, but it's the little things you miss. This is one of them. I haven't been to this zoo since I was a kid and a lot's changed since then. I'm not even a big zoo fan, but when I came back to Sac, the memories flooded back and I just had to come. Do you like zoos?"

Josh wasn't sure whether to believe what Bell was saying. She never seemed that sentimental before, but maybe San Diego hadn't been kind to her. "Not particularly."

Bell snapped out of her reverie and returned to her normal self. "Well, do you have my money?"

Josh removed the envelope from underneath his denim shirt. He placed the envelope on the bench between the two of them, letting his hand rest on it. As he went to ease his hand back, Bell placed her hand on the back of it and applied pressure to keep it in place for a moment. Josh yanked his hand out from under hers. The transaction looked more conspicuous than if Josh had just given her the five thousand straight from his wallet. Bell laughed and threw her head back. She picked up the envelope and slipped it into her purse.

People meandered past without noticing the transaction. Unable to comprehend their behavior, the lion watched with keen interest the activities of the two people on the bench.

"Josh, you're so easy."

Her sense of humor didn't impress him. "Does this money mean you'll keep out of my life here?"

"I don't know."

"Jesus, Bell, I can't have that. I can't live not knowing when you're going to pop up next." Josh felt his cool slip from his grasp.

"I'm sorry. That's the price you have to pay for being a criminal. If you'd been a good man, a faithful man, you wouldn't be in this situation." Bell's expression hardened into a sneer. "So you'd better get used to it."

"But every criminal eventually pays his debt to society," he said.

"Yeah, but some crimes warrant the death penalty."

Josh said nothing. She had him. He was cornered just like the animals. He couldn't live like this. His only way out was to confess and take his chances. He would only tie himself in frustrated knots waiting for Bell to issue another demand. He would tell Kate about the kickback and the affair and hope to God she would forgive him. It wasn't an enviable choice, but perhaps necessary.

"It won't be that easy to get rid of me, Josh."

"You wouldn't have much hold over me if I told Kate."

She looked at him with a crooked smile, amused by his attempt at trying to get the upper hand. "Do you think Kate would understand what you did? Besides, even if you did, I've still got you for the bribe. I'm sure that your employers, the police and the people living in that apartment complex would be most interested in your part in its dubious construction."

Josh looked around furtively, checking that someone hadn't overheard them.

"Don't worry, Josh. No one here cares about you and your sordid past," she reassured.

"So what will it take to get rid of you?"

She paused for a moment. "A lifetime of watching you squirm because of what you did to me."

He saw the hatred ablaze in her eyes. "What did I do to make you hate me that much?"

"You dumped me. You had your fun. You came to me when you had problems at home. You promised you'd leave her for me, but you chickened out when things got all lovey-dovey again. You shit on me, Josh."

A woman with her preschool age child walked past Josh and Bell. Offended by the foul language, she grabbed her daughter's hand and sped past. She muttered her disgust as she went.

Bell embarrassed him, but she ignored the woman.

"I don't regret breaking up with you. It was wrong to cheat on Kate. I regret the affair. I betrayed my family and I was wrong."

"What about me?" she demanded.

"What I did to you was wrong. I never should have gotten involved with you and I apologize to you, right now. I'm sorry."

"And you think that's enough?"

"I want it to be enough. I want to be left alone. I don't care about the money. I don't want to see you prosecuted for blackmail. I just want peace in my life."

"I'm not sure that I can grant you that." Bell stood up. "We all have wants, but we rarely get them."

Still seated, Josh grabbed her wrist. "This can't continue. You know that."

"I know." Her smile weakened and she looked away.

He let go of her wrist. Bell walked toward the exit. He watched the bustling crowd moving from one habitat to another swallow her up.

The professional was perfectly camouflaged amongst the tourists. His target hadn't spotted him in the crowd. He was good at just fitting in, disappearing amidst the masses. And he doubted anyone in the zoo would remember him by the time they got home. Not even that guy with his two brats in tow who walked right into him at the jaguar enclosure while he watched his target take a seat on the bench. The family man had looked stunned and apologized profusely, swearing blind he hadn't seen the professional. The hit man took the remark as a compliment.

He watched from no more than twenty feet away, but found it difficult to listen with all those damned kids whooping like monkeys.

The trip to the zoo had puzzled him. His target had left the house, visited a drugstore, gone to the bank, then come to the zoo. *Why hadn't he brought his daughter? What good father didn't bring his daughter to the zoo?* But a short fifteen-minute wait revealed all—a clandestine meeting with a woman. *What is Mr. Michaels up to? Is he a bad boy? A lady friend to keep perhaps?* This was something the professional would enjoy watching.

Sometimes in his investigations he came across some interesting alternative lifestyles his targets kept. One of his targets had a taste for peep shows and prostitutes when he was not with his happy family at home. Another had been a cross-dresser. It had been hard not to laugh when he saw an overweight middle-aged man prancing around like a little girl. Several had kept mistresses, and Michaels was turning out to be one of those. There'd been so many little oddities he had gazed upon in the course of his work. The human race never failed to amaze him.

This meeting was different, not quite what he had expected. His target didn't look too pleased to see the woman. The professional saw Michaels snap his arm away. *Rejecting her affections. Is that money I see being exchanged?* Michaels was turning out to be a very interesting assignment. The professional decided the woman wasn't a mistress. She might have been once, but not now. It looked like extortion was the name of the game these days.

The professional smiled. *There's an angle here I can exploit. Mr. Michaels, you're giving me a lot of material.* A germ of an idea began to grow. It would be messy, but it would be very dramatic if it worked. It would be one of his best efforts. He leaned his head against the rail of the polar bear habitat, one person among many, but his was the only head not turned toward the marine mammal.

He watched the woman get up and leave his target. It looked like a touching moment and he wished he could tell what was being said. He would look into lip reading classes after this contract. She headed in the direction of the exit and he followed. He could afford to leave Michaels alone, for now. He had what he needed on him for the moment. He wanted to find out more about this woman. She could be useful.

In the parking lot, the woman got into a black Chevy Cobalt coupe and the professional followed in his Taurus. He shadowed her progress north across town to the Radisson Hotel. She went in and he kept a reasonable distance behind. At the entrance, a doorman greeted her and he checked out her ass after she passed him. The professional was greeted similarly, but without having his ass checked. The woman walked up to the young female desk clerk.

The professional picked up a free local newspaper off a stand and made sure he got close enough to hear the conversation.

"Hello, how can I help you?" the desk clerk asked.

"Any messages for room three-oh-seven?" she asked.

The desk clerk checked and told her there weren't any. The woman headed over to the elevator.

The professional went up to the other clerk on duty, a bored looking man in his thirties. "Excuse me, could I use your restrooms?"

"Yes, sir. No problem, just turn left at the restaurant

and they're on your left." The desk clerk leaned over the counter and pointed to his right, in the opposite direction of the elevators.

"Thanks," the professional said and smiled.

"Not at all, sir."

The professional went off in search of the restrooms as directed. He locked himself into a stall and sat on the toilet for a respectable time before flushing and leaving the restroom.

He returned to the reception desk. The male desk clerk the professional had spoken to earlier was occupied with a customer. He approached the young female desk clerk who had dealt with Josh Michaels's secret woman.

She smiled at him.

"Excuse me, you have a lady in room three-oh-seven, an Asian woman, early thirties. Now I'm sure I know her from a company we used to work at and I wanted to check to see if it was her." The professional managed to look benign, hopeless and charming all at the same time.

She checked her computer records. "Room three-oh-seven is a Miss Belinda Wong."

"It *is* her," he beamed.

The desk clerk beamed back, happy for him and for her. It was probably the first interesting thing to happen all day.

"Do you have a card with a phone number I could call her back on?"

The desk clerk nodded. She gave him a matchbook and pointed to the number on the back. "Just change the last three numbers with her room number and you'll get straight through."

"Thanks very much," he fawned.

"But don't wait too long, she checks out tomorrow."

"Does she now?" A crooked smile trickled across his face. "Thank you very much indeed for your help."

The professional walked away from the reception back to the parking lot. He would be waiting here tomorrow to see where she went.

The professional didn't get far before the desk clerk called out to him. He stopped and turned around.

"Good luck sir," she said in a hoarse whisper and grinned.

The professional grinned back and gave her a thumbs-up.

The doorman showed the professional out of the hotel. *Hello, Miss Belinda Wong, who are you and what do you want?* The professional thought.

CHAPTER NINE

"Daddy, Daddy, I heard another car pull up," Abby said, bouncing on the spot excitedly.

"Well, isn't it your job to greet them?" Josh asked.

Abby agreed it was by nodding vigorously. She bounded off down the alley next to the Michaels's home to meet the visitors to the party. Wiener scampered behind her, acting as her second in command. As she got to the front of the house, she found people getting out of a Toyota Camry parked curbside.

"Uncle Bo-bo and Aunt Nancy!" Abby called. Her ribboned, pigtailed hair bounced as she ran, as did Wiener's, whose ears were tied with similar ribbons. She crashed into Bob Deuce and hugged him.

"Hi, Abby, you look pretty," Bob said, picking Abby up.

"Hello, Abby. Yes, you do look very grown-up," Nancy Deuce said, smiling.

"Thank you," Abby said, grinning.

Bob nodded at the dog. "What's up with Wiener's ears?"

"I wanted to put his ears in pigtails like mine," she replied.

"Oh, very nice," Nancy said.

"Who's this?" Abby asked.

"This is a colleague of mine, James Mitchell. I thought I'd bring him. Hope that's okay?"

"Yeah, that's okay," Abby said. "Hello, Mr. Mitchell."

"Call me James," Mitchell said.

Bob put Abby down at her request. She led the invited guests to her father in the backyard.

Josh was stocking an ice-filled bucket with beers on the lawn next to a trestle table. It was one of two tablecloth-covered tables smothered with snacks and drinks. At the rear of the yard Kate manned the barbecue and waved to her friends. Other early arrivals sat at a picnic table with drinks. The CD player, relocated to the rear porch, sent music across the backyard.

"Hey, buddy, happy birthday," Bob called across the yard.

"Happy thirty-eighth, Josh," Nancy added.

Josh looked up from the ice bucket and smiled at his approaching friends with a stranger in tow.

"I'm glad you made it." Josh checked his watch. "A fashionable thirty minutes late, I see."

The birthday invitations were for seven, but Josh didn't expect most people until eight. Bob's arrival swelled the numbers into double figures.

"Josh, I hope you don't mind me bringing someone. This is a colleague of mine, James Mitchell. He's in the area for a few days with nothing to do and you know what that's like, so I invited him."

"No, not a problem." Josh put out a hand to Mitchell. "Hi, James, I'm Josh. You're very welcome."

"Thanks very much. I hope you don't mind me gate

crashing. I'm not as desperate for a night out as Bob makes out."

"No, really, make yourself at home. There's plenty to drink and food soon," Josh said.

"Is Kate manning the barbecue?" Bob asked.

"Yeah, I'm on drinks and public relations tonight," Josh replied.

"Barbecuing, that's a man's job. You're losing your control, my man," Bob said, in mock indignation.

"Oh, shut up, Bob," Nancy said and punched her husband in the arm.

"You forget, Bob, when it's my birthday, my loving ladies do all the work for me and I get to enjoy my day. So, who is in control now?" Josh responded.

"I think I'll see if Kate needs any help now that the testosterone is flying," Nancy said. "I'll leave you to your fantasies."

"Thank you, my love," Bob called to her and blew her a kiss.

Nancy blew a kiss back.

"Can I get you guys a drink?" Josh asked. They nodded and Josh removed three bottles of beer from the freshly stocked ice bucket and popped the caps.

"Happy thirty-eighth," Bob said, producing an envelope from his back pocket.

Josh had a bemused look on his face when he opened the envelope. The present was a gift certificate for adult swimming lessons. "You bastard," he said, grinning.

"I thought you'd like it. I'm glad to see you smiling again," Bob said.

"Happy birthday, Josh!" a man holding Abby's hand called. He was in his early fifties, small, no more than five-five. He was slight and as thin as the silver hair that covered his balding scalp.

"Good to see you, Mark," Josh called back.

"I thought I'd show my face." Abby let go of his hand and bounded off.

"Bob, you know Mark Keegan," Josh said, and Bob nodded in agreement. "And this is a colleague of Bob's, James Mitchell."

The men shook hands.

"I brought you a couple bottles of wine. I thought I should, seeing as you owe me money. We still on for tomorrow?" Mark asked, giving the bottles to Josh.

"Yeah, and I'll bring a check with me." Josh put the bottles on the table with the rest of the alcohol.

"How is that plane of yours?" Bob asked.

"We just had it serviced, so it's as good as new. That's what the money's for," Mark said.

"So you've got a plane?" James said, breaking into the conversation.

"Yeah, a little Cessna C152 we bought four years ago. It needed some work, but we got it at a good price," Mark explained.

"Mark and I learned to fly at the same time, so we went partners on a plane," Josh added.

"Yeah, you can't miss it, either. Fancy paint job with their names on the doors like they're a pair of top gun aces," Bob joked.

"We had a bit of luck," Josh said. "We fly out of the Davis airstrip and a kid from the college there overheard us talking about repainting the plane. He offered to paint a design on it for a school project and we said yeah. All we had to pay for was the materials."

"That kid did a great job, it really stands out," Mark said.

"I've flown a couple of times, but I don't have a license," James said.

"Come out with us some time," Mark said.

"No, I'm only here until Monday," James explained.

"Oh, I thought you worked with Bob," Mark said.

"No, I'm an agent with Pinnacle Investments visiting some of the brokers in California."

"You work for Pinnacle Investments?" Josh asked. He wasn't about to let one of their employees get away. "I've got a big bone to pick with you."

"Well, if you people have business, I think I'll give my best to Kate. I'll see you about ten tomorrow," Mark said, excusing himself.

Josh nodded to him. "I'll catch you later."

"What's up, pal?" Bob asked.

"Thursday, Pinnacle Investments sent Kate a funeral wreath to the house with my name on it," Josh said angrily.

"Jesus, how did that happen?" Bob asked.

"That's what I wanted him to tell me."

"I haven't spoken to Pinnacle," Bob said in his defense. "Christ, I'm sorry, man. That's the last thing you needed."

"I don't know how it could have happened," James said. "Please let me apologize on behalf of the firm. Let me make a phone call now. There won't be anyone there, but I can leave a voice mail so they get it first thing Monday. Can I go into the house to make the call?"

"Yeah, no problem," Josh said sharply.

James Mitchell went into the house. Josh and Bob were alone together, the first time since the sports bar. They looked gravely at each other, their minds full of unspoken thoughts.

"How did it go with Bell?" Bob whispered.

"I paid her, but she's not going to stop." Josh sighed and his anger fizzled out.

"What does she want?"

"As far as I can see, just to screw me over."

"You know this'll never end unless you do something."

"Of course I know that."

"Then what are you going to do?"

"I don't know."

"I think it's time to tell the truth. It's the only way to stop this."

"Oh, shit," Josh muttered.

His response wasn't to Bob's comment, but as a reaction to who he saw over Bob's shoulder. Belinda Wong walked toward him, hand-in-hand with Abby. The color drained from Josh's face.

"She's here," Josh whispered.

"What?" Bob turned in the direction of Josh's gaze. "What's she doing here?"

"I think we're going to find out."

Josh left Bob by the beer bucket. He intercepted his blackmailer and daughter before they got too near the other partygoers.

"Daddy, this is Bell. It's short for Belinda," Abby said.

"I know, sweetie," Josh said with a plastic smile.

"Hi, Josh. Happy birthday," Bell said.

"Thanks, Bell." Josh hugged his ex-mistress and kissed her cheek. "What the fuck are you doing here?" he whispered into her ear.

"Having fun," she whispered back.

Josh broke the hug.

"It's so good to see you," Bell said.

"I think you've done enough meeting and greeting for awhile. You deserve a reward. Why don't you see Mommy?" Josh told his daughter.

Abby ran off toward her mother, weaving in and out of the crowd like a wide receiver making a run for the end zone.

"That's a lovely girl you've got there, Josh, so pretty,

so innocent, so trusting. I would hate to think what it would be like for her if her heart were broken. It would be hard to see that pretty face through those tears. I bet you'd do anything to prevent that."

"I would kill if necessary," Josh said.

"Would you now?" Bell smirked at Josh's poor show of strength. "Let's hope you're never put to the test."

"Yeah, let's hope so."

"Could I have a drink?"

Josh and Bell walked toward the drinks table and Bell slipped an arm into his. Josh shot her a look of rage.

"Now, now, Josh. Play it cool, we have an image to portray. You don't want these good people to suspect anything."

Josh poured her a white wine.

"It's Belinda Wong, isn't it?" Kate said, walking over to them from the barbecue.

"Yes it is, Kate. How are you?"

Josh stood stone still with the bottle of wine in his hands. *Don't say anything, please.* He sent telepathic messages to Bell, hoping she wouldn't blow the whistle on him. Fear prevented him from producing a smile.

"I thought you were in San Diego," Kate said.

"I was, but I've come back." Bell turned her head to Josh, smiled cruelly, then looked back at Kate. "I miss my old friends."

"Have you got a job?"

"No, but I was hoping that Josh could help me."

"Well, I'm sure he could put in a good word for you."

"Yeah, but like I was telling Bell, there aren't any open jobs at the moment, so she'll have to keep looking." He managed to make his words sound strong and convincing. Not a hint of his fear showed.

"Josh, I can't believe you didn't mention Bell was back. You always said she was your best secretary." Kate winked at Bell.

Bell grinned at the embarrassment Kate brought to her husband.

It was obscene, watching his wife playacting with his ex-mistress. Watching the macabre play was excruciating, but relief was soon to come. "I've only just found out myself."

"Kate, have you got a minute? Sorry to interrupt." A woman's voice called from a group of people nearby.

Kate excused herself and left, attending to the woman's needs.

"At least someone is happy to see me," Bell said, watching Kate go.

"Are you going now that you've had your fun?" Josh asked.

"No, of course not. The night is young. I think I'll mingle for awhile if you don't mind."

"I do mind."

She snorted. "Well, I don't care. Don't worry, I'm not going to tell on you. Your money bought my silence for now."

Bell refreshed her glass. Josh watched her turn on her heel and strike up a conversation with a group of his friends. *What does she have in store for me?* All he knew was that it wasn't going to be good.

It was a small room, poorly furnished with an eclectic combination of bargain basement purchases and long-held possessions now in a state of disrepair. The room smelled of musty neglect. The telephone rang on the small table next to the armchair in the living room.

The old woman shuffled in from the kitchen. Even this small exertion resulted in wheezing. She mumbled "Hold your horses," to the ringing phone before collapsing into the chair and picking up the receiver.

She hit the Mute button on the television remote. "Hello?"

"Is this Margaret Macey?"

"Yes, it is."

"Hi, I represent Mutual Life, Mrs. Macey. I was wondering if I could speak to you about life insurance for senior citizens."

Margaret got as far as, "I'm not really—"

"Good, I'll only take a few minutes of your time," he said, ignoring her.

"Mrs. Macey, our records show you are a senior citizen. You must think about having to make provisions for others when your time comes."

"No, not really."

"Do you have children, Mrs. Macey?"

"Yes, I have a daughter in New York."

"Do you know the average cost of a funeral nowadays?"

"No, I don't."

"It's over three thousand dollars." The telemarketer's voice rose two octaves to drive the point home. "Now, does that seem a fair price to burden your loved one with? Does it?" the terminally happy telemarketer asked.

"Well, no, but—"

"No buts, Mrs. Macey. Now this is where Mutual Life Insurance comes in. We will provide for you a low-cost life insurance that will serve as a lasting reminder to your family of your generosity."

The pitch was made and Margaret imagined the telemarketer's toothpaste advertisement smile shining into the telephone.

"I'm not really interested."

"Oh, come on, Margaret. Can I call you Margaret? It's only ten dollars a month. I'm sure it's not a lot to ask for peace of mind, is it now, eh, Margaret?"

"I don't really have ten dollars to spare."

"Oh, Margaret. I think you could afford ten bucks. I don't think anyone would miss ten bucks. What do you say, Margaret? Can I put you down? We can do the paperwork over the phone, right now. Come on, Margaret, what do you say? What do you say?"

The telemarketer offended her by trying to manipulate her just for the sake of his commission. *Surely these people are answerable to some government department,* she thought. She had a good mind to contact someone.

"No, I'm sorry, I'm not interested," Margaret said, her tone abrupt.

"Not interested? Not interested! You selfish bitch." Bile replaced the telemarketer's sickly sweet demeanor.

Her breath caught in her throat. It took a moment before she could speak again. "What?"

"No wonder your daughter lives in New York. She probably can't stand being near a twisted old bitch like you. Why don't you just die? You'd be doing the planet a favor. You're only taking up oxygen good people like me need to breathe."

The vile words burned the inside of Margaret's head. People didn't speak to people like this. She wanted to hang up, but her shock kept the phone pressed to her ear.

"How dare you talk to me like that. I'll report you to your superiors." Margaret's voice broke and tears built up behind her eyes.

"Oh, but I do dare, Margaret," he said, his voice controlled and level. "I've been watching you, Margaret. Oh, yes, I've been watching you for awhile now. You live in that shitty little house of yours. God knows what you find to do in there. You only ever go out to go to the store. I've seen you waiting for the bus, hunched up against the bus stop. Have you ever noticed how the people on the bus look at you? They see you and they think, Christ, I hope I never get to be like that. I hope someone will kill me first."

"That's not true." Margaret struggled to speak through the sobs that shook her body. She wanted to put the phone down, but she was too frightened of what the telemarketer would do if she hung up.

"How's that heart of yours? When's it going to give out? I do hope it's soon."

"Who are you?"

"Maybe you should be asking where am I?" He let that sink in before he broke into laughter.

Margaret leapt from the chair and tottered over to the window, receiver in hand. The telephone cord stretched to its full limit, sending the table with the phone on it crashing to the floor.

"Was that you, Margaret?"

She sniffed. "No, I'm still here."

"What a shame. I'll be coming to see you. I want to see the look on your face when you die."

"I'm going to call the police."

"I wouldn't do that if I were you. I'll know when they come and I'll take action if you do."

"What action?"

"Deadly."

Josh crossed the yard to where Bob stood. His overweight friend was the center of attention in a circle of five people. He'd tried to talk to Bob right after Bell left him, but two colleagues interrupted him to introduce their wives.

Josh arrived to find Bob at the tail end of one of his jokes. He was a good joke teller, although not all of them were in good taste. In his hands were the weapons of a good partygoer—a beer and a burger. Bob gesticulated with the booze and food to enhance his performance.

"When I go down, I go down in flames," Bob said in a bad French accent.

The group laughed loudly at the joke. Josh smiled. He'd heard that one before. He placed his hands on Bob's fleshy shoulders. "Can I relieve you of this very funny man?"

The people agreed on the condition that he brought him back. Before he could take Bob away, the group engaged him about his recent accident. Josh underplayed the magnitude of the event and the fear he had experienced. He didn't want to talk to them. He had bigger problems with which to deal.

As they walked away from the crowd, Bob asked, "What did Bell want?"

"She wants to mess with my head. A little reminder of what will happen if I don't play by her rules."

They stood against the fence and watched the people enjoying the party.

"Jesus, what a mess," Josh said.

Bob felt Josh's despair spread across his friend like an approaching storm front. He wanted to tell Josh everything was going to be okay. But he wasn't sure that was the case.

"Let me talk to her," Bob said.

"There's no point."

"There isn't if you talk to her. She's knows exactly how to yank your chain. It's not like that with me."

"I don't think you'll get anywhere."

"That's my problem. You go out there and talk to your friends. This is meant to be your party."

Josh looked at the crowd. It didn't feel like a birthday. Well, not a good one at least. He wasn't much in the mood for fun.

"Put on a good show for everyone. Let them know everything is cool and show that bitch she isn't getting to you."

"You're a good friend, Bob."

"That's nice. Now get out there, tell some jokes and for God's sake, cheer up." Bob shoved Josh in the back with both hands.

Bob watched Kate and her friends welcome Josh and draw him into their discussion. He scanned the party-goers for the blackmailer. Alone at the drinks table, she was pouring herself a glass of wine. Bob appeared at Belinda Wong's side and cracked open another beer.

"Hi there," Bob said.

"Hello," Bell replied.

"I'm Bob Deuce, a good friend of Josh Michaels, and of Kate and Abby, of course." Bob smiled and offered a hand.

"Of course. I'm Belinda Wong. A pleasure to meet you, Bob."

Bob saw the coldness in her eyes. "Yes, I'm sure."

"Josh has mentioned you before."

"Yeah, I think we met a long time ago. You used to work for Josh."

A middle-aged couple arrived at the drinks table to interrupt Bob's conversation. Bob and Bell moved out of their way.

"Shall we?" Bob indicated they should move on with a swing of his arm, bottle in hand. He needed to get Bell alone. "Are you enjoying yourself?"

"Yes, it's a nice party, and you?" Bell gave him a hint of a smile, but her eyes were filled with suspicion.

Bob took a swig from the bottle. "I wasn't talking about the party."

Bell narrowed her eyes. "I don't know what you mean."

"About you . . . coming here . . . uninvited. I know

about you and Josh, and the money you extorted." Bob gestured with the bottle.

The coldness in her eyes bled into her expression and her words. "And what the hell has it got to do with you?"

"Josh is my best friend and I stand by him. I don't condone what he did. Personally, I think he was an asshole to have an affair, no offense to you. I want you to leave Josh and his family alone."

Bell's features tightened into an angry knot. "Did that spineless bastard send you to speak to me?"

"No, he didn't. I came because I'm a friend. You have enough money from this. What more do you want?"

"I want to see him suffer."

"You hate him that much?"

"I love him that much." She paused for a moment. "You have no idea how hard it was to watch him leave me and go back to his wife and his daughter."

Bell's sincerity frightened Bob. She wouldn't leave Josh voluntarily. She'd go kicking and screaming. He couldn't see Josh surviving this one.

"He'll never be yours if you destroy what he has now."

"I know, but if I can't have him then no one will."

"Assholes!" Bell poured herself another drink. Anger prevented accuracy and she slopped most of it over the table and her hand.

"Who are?" James Mitchell said, joining the table.

"Men," she said.

Mitchell took the bottle from her hand and finished the job she'd started. He poured himself some wine.

"I'm afraid I fall into that category." He gave her a bemused smile. "Who particularly is an asshole?"

"Our lovely host."

"Josh Michaels?"

"Yes. Are you one of his cronies?"

"No, I only met him tonight. I'm an acquaintance of a friend of his."

"That makes you part asshole?" She took a big gulp from her glass.

Mitchell blurted a laugh. "Quite probably. Would you like to talk about it?"

It was a relief when Bob removed Josh from another discussion about his accident. It was the sixth time Josh had recounted the events of the incident. He kept his belief that someone was trying to kill him to himself. With every new telling the event seemed more and more like the incident happened to someone else.

"Josh, I spoke to her." Bob was grave.

"And what happened?"

"She is pretty fucked-up over you. She's not going to go away. This one's going down to the wire."

"Where is she now?"

"She's talking to Mitchell." Bob nodded to Bell and Mitchell over by the drink table.

Josh turned to see. "Do you think she's telling him?"

"No. She's angry, but she isn't ready to throw you to the wolves. Honestly, I don't think she knows what to do. She still loves you, did you know that?"

"No. No, I didn't." Josh's eyes were still fixed on Bell talking happily to James Mitchell.

The rest of the birthday party went without incident. It was the picture of respectability and mediocrity. No one got too drunk, the music wasn't too loud and the neighbors didn't complain too much. People left as the food and alcohol disappeared. The designated drivers were called to duty to perform their role.

Around eleven o'clock, Kate found Abby under a picnic table curled up in a ball with Wiener at her side. Kate put her to bed and discovered Wiener smelled of alcohol. She had no idea who had given the dog a drink. She mused that she'd never seen a dog with a hangover.

It was well after midnight when Josh decided to call it a night and send the party hyenas on their way. He climbed onto the picnic table and surveyed the stragglers. Bell was gone. He hadn't seen her go or whether she was with anyone when she had left. That worried him; she had drunk more than the legal limit and he hoped she hadn't spilled her guts to someone. Mark Keegan had left around ten-thirty. His flying partner wanted an early night since he and Josh were flying the next morning. Bob, of course, was still there with his colleague. Bob wouldn't leave until every plate was licked clean.

"Can I have everyone's attention," Josh called to the bleary-eyed congregation.

Dulled by alcohol and fatigue, they turned toward him.

"I would just like to say thanks to everyone who came, especially those who had the decency to have left already."

A titter of laughter came from the ensemble.

"But the party's over. There's no more alcohol left."

The surviving party revelers expressed a cry of sad comic despair.

Josh smiled. "So you'll have to go home now."

"I don't wanna go home," Bob said.

"I didn't want you to come. So that makes two of us disappointed tonight," he said and got another laugh.

Josh jumped down from the table and everybody took it as their cue to go. Josh, with Kate's help, ushered the party stragglers out. They watched their friends leave from the front yard.

Josh surveyed the battlefield of discarded bottles, plates, paper cups, glasses and other victims that fell during the festive clash in the backyard. "I think we'll leave everything tonight and clear up tomorrow."

"Yeah, I don't want to deal with it tonight," Kate said.

"Thanks for coming everyone." Hiding a smile, Josh ignored his wife and focused on his friends' departures. After a moment, he looked at Kate and winked.

"You bastard." She grinned. "You're flying tomorrow."

He put an arm around her and pulled her tight. "I probably won't go, anyway."

"Why?"

"I drank too much and I don't really feel like it." Although he had drunk too much, he hid his real feelings. Bell's arrival had taken the shine off his party and sapped his desire to enjoy himself.

"Now that everyone's gone, I thought we could play, maybe?" Kate said seductively. She made little circles with her finger on his chest.

"What—Scrabble, Twister, that sort of thing?"

"You know what I mean."

"Oh, you mean sex." He pretended to think for a moment. "I think I could manage that."

A car horn tooted as a vehicle went by. Josh waved. He spotted Bob and Mitchell talking animatedly, fueled by alcohol. The topic: basketball and who would make it to the playoffs. Nancy tried to ignore her husband and his colleague.

Then Josh's life changed dramatically, wiping the smile clean off his face as if it had been a smudge. In response to Bob's question, would the Sacramento Kings make it to the playoffs, Mitchell stuck his arm out straight with his thumb up. Slowly, the Pinnacle Investments representative twisted him arm until his thumb pointed down.

There was no mistaking the thumbs-down gesture. James Mitchell was the man from the bridge.

CHAPTER TEN

Shock paralyzed Josh's vocal chords. A cold wave washed over his body, as if a transfusion of ice were being pumped into his veins. He'd entertained the man who'd tried to kill him. Mitchell had drunk his alcohol, ate his food and probably pissed in his toilet. He had insufficient strength to stand unassisted. Josh slumped against Kate.

"Josh, are you okay? Do you feel sick?" Kate's expression was a mask of concern.

"That's him," Josh said, staring at the vehicles leaving. "He was here."

"Who?" Kate looked at her husband, then at their friends' disappearing cars.

"The man on the bridge." Josh became agitated and his voice rose in volume.

"Who? Where?"

"James Mitchell," he barked, his impotent frustration spilling over.

"The guy Bob brought?" Kate said, incredulous.

"He did that thumbs-down thing, the same as he did

on the bridge." Josh's frustration turned to rage. He jabbed a finger into the empty street. "James Mitchell tried to kill me."

"For Christ's sake, Josh. Calm down and come inside."

Kate dragged Josh, still babbling like a madman, into the house. She got him into the living room, sat him down in an armchair and knelt in front of him. With considerable effort, she held his flailing arms against his knees.

"Josh, you've got to get a hold of yourself. I'm not having you blow up at every little thing that reminds you of the accident. I know it must have been frightening, but I won't accept that behavior. You shouted at those cops in the hospital, you scared the shit out of that poor kid with the flowers and now you're accusing a man you've just met of being a killer. Listen to yourself. This is not the way Josh Michaels acts."

She scolded him like she did their daughter. But it worked. Josh felt his hysteria pass.

Before he could respond, Abby called from the top of the stairs. The arguing had upset her.

"I'm coming, honey," Kate said, and got to her feet. She looked down at Josh. "I'm going to settle Abby down. I suggest you do the same yourself. Gather your thoughts. When I get back, tell me calmly why you think James Mitchell tried to kill you." Her words were soft and comforting.

He watched her go. He sniffed and ran his hands through his hair. "Get a grip," he murmured. He started to think through all the events leading up to the car crashing into the river. The images were all too vivid. Josh unpacked the jumble of events and repacked them in a neat order. He heard Kate returning from upstairs.

She took a seat on the arm of the chair and slipped an arm around his shoulders. "Do you want to start?"

Josh took a deep breath and started. "I know I didn't see the guy's face at the river, but he did the thumbs-down thing like I was a vanquished Christian or something. Just like I told you in the hospital."

"Yeah, but I've seen lots of people do that. It's nothing special."

"I know, but not the way he did it. His way is different. And trust me, baby, when I say it was identical to what James Mitchell did. I was there, in that car thinking I was going to drown and I saw the guy standing on the bridge. He was my only hope for survival and he did *that*." Josh repeated Mitchell's action.

Tears spilled from Kate's eyes. She reached out and wrapped her delicate hand over his thumbs-down fist. She pulled his outstretched arm to her mouth and kissed the knuckles of his clenched hand. "Oh, Josh."

Josh's love intensified for her. For days after the incident, preoccupied with his own problems, he'd ignored his wife. Her support gave him the strength to get himself out of the briar patch he had fallen into. He drew her to him and hugged her tightly.

He spoke over her shoulder. "I'll never forget what he did."

"Nancy said Mitchell works for an insurance company. What sort of an insurance guy would do that?"

"I don't—" It struck Josh like an oncoming truck. "The sort of insurance agent that works for the same insurance company that sent the wreath."

Kate pulled away from him and stared at him incredulously. "He works for Pinnacle Investments?"

"That's what he said. I've only just realized."

"What are you saying, Josh?"

"Mitchell forced me off the road and had his company send me a wreath. Maybe he thought I was dead and has a sick sense of humor. It really doesn't make sense to me. It's like he's zeroing in on me, but why?"

"I don't know why and I don't care. It's not your job to find out. Talk to the cops. The ones from the hospital told you to contact them if anything develops, and it has."

"They don't believe me as it is. They think I was having a biggest dick competition with some idiot or I fell asleep at the wheel."

"It doesn't matter, Josh. You can give them something to go on. If this guy is a psycho, he might come back for more."

"I'll talk to Bob. He knows this guy."

"Josh, don't call tonight. Bob's already asleep by now. Don't wake him."

Josh frowned.

"For me, please. Sleep on it. Talk to him if you feel the same tomorrow, but call the *police*." Kate emphasized the word "police," reinforcing that it was their job to track down criminals, not Josh's.

Kate stood up and took Josh's hand. "Let's go to bed."

"Happy birthday to me," he said bitterly.

CHAPTER ELEVEN

Josh picked up the cordless telephone in the hall of his home and hit the speed dial.

"Hello?" Nancy said.

"Hi Nancy, is Bob there?"

"Hi Josh. No, he's still sleeping off last night. I can wake him if you like."

"No, it's okay. I've got to go off to the airport, but can you tell him that I called and that I'll drop by later?"

"Yeah, no problem, Josh." Nancy paused. "Is everything okay?"

"Yeah, just boys stuff," he said, injecting a smile into his response to allay her suspicions.

"See you later, Josh," she said, the concern gone from her voice.

Josh put the phone on the charger.

He went to pick it up again. He hesitated, his hand hovering over the handset. He wanted to scream through the phone to the cops that he'd found the bastard who ran him off the road, but the seeds of doubt had been sown. He couldn't be sure James Mitchell was his man. Kate had made him realize he'd been acting irrationally over the last week. He pulled his hand away from the phone.

He had to plan his actions instead of running head-on into the situation. He had to do the sensible thing—find out from Bob what he knew about Mitchell. If Mitchell's credibility was suspect, then he'd bring the cops in.

"I'm going now," Josh called to Kate.

She came to the doorway from the kitchen, where she was making Abby's breakfast. "How long will you be?"

"I'm only dropping the check off."

"I don't want to be clearing up on my own," she said and smiled.

"You've got Abby."

"You are just going to the airfield?" Kate insisted.

"Yes, I am. Trust me."

Taking a moment, Josh watched his wife from the doorway, going about her life. He loved her so much. He feared losing her. She caught sight of him staring at her and she smiled, but it didn't last. Her worried face was a reminder of last night. He smiled back and picked up the keys to Kate's '99 Dodge Caravan and closed the door.

Inside the minivan silence prevailed, but inside Josh's head his thoughts shouted. The car wreck, Belinda Wong clawing for more money, Pinnacle Investments's funeral wreath and James Mitchell consumed his mind. He wondered if all the events were connected and if they were, what it meant. He tried to make some semblance of order from it all, tried to make everything fit into little boxes, but he failed miserably. He switched on the radio to block his thoughts.

Josh stopped the car in the parking lot of the small

airport. The sound of a piston aero-engine spluttering into life greeted him as he got out of the vehicle. He headed toward the planning office where the club pilots mapped out routes, flight times and calculated fuel requirements. The unkempt outbuilding posing as an office consisted of charts of northern California and the type of plain-looking wooden design tables found in drawing offices forty years ago.

Mark Keegan wasn't in the planning office, but Nick Owen, an instructor with the flying school, was with a student. Nick was a young pilot with his eyes set on a commercial pilot's lifestyle with a major airline.

Josh leaned through the doorway with his arms outstretched, his hands supporting his weight against the doorframe. "Hi, Nick. Have you seen Mark Keegan today?"

Nick turned to Josh while his student busied himself with his route planning. "Yeah, I saw him talking to Jack Murphy earlier. If he's not with Jack, then he's probably checking out the Cessna."

"Thanks, Nick."

"You flying, Josh?"

"No, I have some business to deal with."

"Shame, it's a good day. You'll be missing out." Nick sounded like a car salesman with a "You'd be a fool to miss this bargain," pitch.

"It can't be helped," Josh said.

Nick returned his focus to his student and Josh went to the apron. He spotted Mark walking toward their Cessna from the workshop hangar, called out and jogged over to him.

Mark smiled and put his hands on his hips. "Hey, you're late—we said ten o'clock. What time do you call this? You turn up after I've done all the work. Too much celebrating last night?"

"Hey, sorry, man. You're going to have to go without me. Something's come up and I've got to deal with it," Josh said.

"Nothing serious I hope?" Mark's smile disappeared.

"No. Life crap. Nothing exciting." Josh dismissed his problem with a wave of the hand.

He and Mark were flying partners and their friendship was one of camaraderie rather than bonding. Neither man confided deep truths to the other, and Josh was not going to start now.

"What are you planning to do?" Josh asked.

"Oh, I'll still fly to Stockton, probably doing some exercises on the way. It never hurts to keep in practice." Mark offered an encouraging smile to show Josh there were no hard feelings.

"Sorry, Mark. Maybe next weekend." Josh removed the check from his back pocket and handed it to Mark. "Here's my half of the service bill."

Josh said good-bye and trotted back toward the parking lot, but Jack Murphy intercepted him by coming out from his workshop.

Damn. The aircraft mechanic was the last person to whom Josh wanted to speak. It wasn't that Josh didn't like the man; he did. Murphy was a conscientious mechanic and paid loving detail to the aircrafts he maintained. He nurtured the machines like prize blooms, and like all keen gardeners, the product of his labors was evident on his hands. Engine oil and grease were always caked under his fingernails and the same cocktail of fluids stained his meaty hands. Though not obvious at first glance, his hands had the delicate control of a surgeon's. Josh knew the mechanic would want to meticulously tell him every minute detail of the overhaul, but he didn't have the time or the desire to talk about his aircraft; he wanted to know what James Mitchell was after. "Hey, Jack," Josh said.

"Josh, I suppose you've spoken to Mark about the overhaul, but I wanted to let you know what I found," the mechanic began.

Josh feigned interest for about ten minutes before he managed to get a word in and made his excuses. Murphy seemed a little upset by Josh's brush-off, but he would have to live with it. Josh would make it up to him and let the mechanic bore him for an hour when he had his life back in order. Finally, he got back to the Caravan and set off to Bob's house to get some answers.

The professional cursed from the protection of the sun-bleached brush. *Where's he going? Goddamn it.* He saw his plans trashed, again. Michaels had survived the drowning in the Sacramento River and it looked like he was going to escape death again. He watched Michaels's minivan drive out of the parking lot.

His target wasn't doing what he was supposed to do. From his undercover work at the party, he'd discovered Michaels was meant to be flying this morning, but the view from his binoculars told a different tale, one that didn't follow the plot. How could something so good go so bad?

Getting invited to his target's barbecue had been the perfect example of serendipity. He'd only gone to Bob Deuce for background information, but finding out the insurance agent and Michaels were friends was fortuitous to say the least. He could have been knocked down with a feather when Deuce asked him to the party. And it got better when his target and his flying buddy blabbed about their plane—their pride and joy. The plan that came to him was so simple, so obvious.

He'd come out to the airfield after the party and gone to work. The plane was easy to spot with its ostentatious paint job. All it needed was a sign: "I'm Josh Michaels's plane. Cripple me." The lack of airport security made his deed simple. There were no gates or rent-a-cops. He had all the time in the world to do what he wanted.

The professional ran over to the aircraft with a few simple tools in his hands. He stared into the nose of the aircraft. It was child's play to tamper with a light aircraft. All its sensitive parts were exposed. It had pathetic door locks, no immobilizer, no alarm system, nothing. The professional got to work.

He disconnected the unions to the oil cooler in the aircraft's nose with a pair of wrenches. He snipped the split pins to the nuts on the elevator and rudder and loosened the nuts, just for luck. His work done, he slipped back into the night.

All had gone to according plan until he watched his target rendezvous with his partner, then walk away, get in his car and leave. The professional wasn't upset because the wrong person was about to fly the unsafe plane, but because it ruined his good work. Nothing could be done now. He couldn't remedy the situation.

He watched the multicolored airplane trundle onto the runway, wind up its engine, roar down the runway and lift off for the skies. He took the binoculars from around his neck, wrapped the leather neck strap around them and returned to his car. Michaels hadn't been aware he'd parked next to his predator. The closeness of their vehicles amused him. He got into his car and drove off to plan another accident.

As Mark Keegan roared down the runway, he failed to notice the oil dripping from the Cessna's cooler hoses. The plane climbed slowly. Mark leveled out at 2500 feet and saw the world below him. It was certainly a perfect day for flying—the crisp spring day brought with it an endless view of the San Joaquin Valley. He had to take advantage of days like these as often as he could. When the long California summer began, a yellow layer of smog smeared over the landscape would blight every flying day.

Josh will be kicking himself when I tell him what it's like up here. He enjoyed the solitude flying gave; the world and its problems stayed below while he rode above it all. Once he was in the air, his heart rate seemed to slow by five or more beats. This was therapy, not a hobby.

Thirty minutes into the flight, Mark didn't like the Cessna's performance. This was the third time he had to apply more throttle to maintain the engine revs and air speed. *The aircraft has just been serviced. Nothing better be wrong with it,* Mark thought. Even an aircraft as small and as simple as the C152 cost a lot of money to keep in the air. To Mark's and Josh's credit they took every precaution, but something was wrong with this airplane. Nervousness held him like the three-point harness that fixed him to his seat. He checked his coordinates and ETA to Stockton.

Mark's agitation made him cautious. He made a safety sweep of the instruments for some clue to his plane's poor performance. He closed his eyes for a moment, took a breath and let it out with a curse. He didn't want to believe what the oil pressure and temperature gauges told him. His nervousness changed to fear. The two indicators were in the red. The oil pressure had disappeared and the oil temperature was too high.

The dangerous levels meant this was an emergency. Mark had an agonizing decision to make. Did he shut the engine down and make an emergency landing or did he chance it and fly on to Stockton? He checked his position through the Plexiglas window. He had passed over Sacramento and was over empty fields, a good sign. Mark wiped a clammy hand over his dry mouth and tried to swallow.

"Murphy, what have you done to this plane?"

He wanted to blame someone for the fear he felt; to-day, it was his mechanic. He avoided the decision, hoping for a miracle. Mark stared at the pressure and temperature needles—they weren't returning to green. He knew they never would. He had to get with the program and follow his training. His training would save him. He murmured the steps for landing an aircraft without power.

Made keen by fear, Mark's oversensitive hearing heard every missed beat of the engine. He swore he heard the pistons binding up with every passing second. The plane jolted like a sledgehammer had struck it from beneath as it rode a thermal. Mark's heart skipped again. For a moment, he'd thought it was the end.

With a shaking hand he initiated the safety procedure. He pulled back the throttle to idle, the mixture to lean, switched off the fuel pump and turned the magnetos key to the Off position. The prop slowed and shuddered to a halt. The plane began to fall from the sky.

The silence was eerie. As a pilot, his ears had become accustomed to certain sounds in flight. Now, the whistle of the air flowing over the wings was the only sound to be heard. Mark's heart raced. His sweat chilled him and his clothes clung to his flesh.

Rapidly losing altitude, the plane fell at more than six hundred feet per minute. Mark saw the increasing rate of descent on his gauge. He focused on the crash landing simulations he'd practiced so many times, but this wasn't practice, it was for real. Josh had always ragged him about his compulsion to plan for the worst. Josh would be thanking him if he were here right now. Mark wished he was here to share the burden of this task, the most frightening of events. A crash landing.

Mark quickly established a glide descent that left him approximately four minutes of flight time. He looked out for a landing sight and focused on the field directly below. He would circle the damned thing until he ran out of altitude. He made his distress call to the Stockton Air Tower.

"Mayday . . . mayday . . . mayday. Stockton Tower, this is November, two, three, seven, two, niner." Dread filled Mark's voice, his words slow, hindered by an inflexible tongue that clung to the roof of his mouth. Relieved the words had come, the safety procedure started; he knew he could do it. The practice attempts never prepared him mentally to deal with the real thing, but he was coping. Silently, he thanked God that his mind hadn't seized. Everything was going to be okay.

A concerned air traffic controller at Stockton came back and allowed him to pass his message. Mark gave his details—the plane type, the nature of the emergency, location, plan of action, and who was on board. His monotone speech was textbook perfect—his instructor would be proud, although he probably would have complained about his slow delivery. But how many times had his instructor crash-landed? He gave cursory attention to Stockton Tower. He concentrated on landing the plane. They could do nothing for him. It was his bird to land. He just wanted them to know where to pick him up. Mark guided the plane on its downwind leg for landing.

The Cessna's rate of descent increased, increasing airspeed as a result. Mark eased back on the column to get the airspeed under control. Nothing happened. The plane continued to fall at a faster rate. He pulled back on the controls even more. The column moved without resistance. Something else was wrong. Mark stared back at the tail and pulled back on the column again. The elevator didn't move.

"No. This can't be happening."

He stamped on the rudder pedals. The rudder didn't

obey his inputs either. The tail-plane was dead. It was
still there, but it wasn't responding.

It can't all be going wrong. He'd kept his panic in
check, but he couldn't prevent it from overwhelming
him now. His aircraft was going down and he was just a
passenger at its controls. He glanced at the altimeter—
four hundred feet. It would all be over in less than a
minute.

Mark fought to control the Cessna. The plane de-
scended and the speed increased. Every knot in increased airspeed reduced his chances of survival. With
a paralyzed tail, he'd never be able to bring the plane
down for a soft landing.

The airspeed indicator read seventy knots . . . seventy five knots . . . eighty knots . . .

The altimeter read three hundred . . . two hundred
and fifty . . . two hundred . . .

Mark stared at the field rushing up at him with increasing velocity, pulling on controls that didn't comply while keeping his thumb on the radio transmit
button.

He screamed, "Mayday, mayday, mayday," over and
over again.

Josh peeled off the freeway to Bob Deuce's home. He
listened to an alternative rock station pump out track
after track from its latest playlist. He'd passed through
Sacramento and was in the residential district of Laguna when the newsflash interrupted the next scheduled track.

"Some tragic news. A small airplane has crashed between Sacramento and Stockton, not very far from Interstate Five. Rescue services have arrived and are at
the scene," the disc jockey said.

Josh stamped on the brakes, bringing the Dodge to a
shuddering halt. Vehicles behind did likewise, but with

angry hands on horns. Fortunately, nobody hit each other. Tires fighting for traction on the asphalt, Josh made a U-turn on the two-lane road. The minivan roared off in the direction of I–5.

Josh instinctively knew the downed aircraft was his and he had to see if Mark was okay. Not a believer in clairvoyance, premonitions or anything else found on the *X-Files*, he still knew the news report was linked to him. Without a care for himself and other road users, Josh tore along the interstate. He listened to the rest of the DJ's announcement for the approximate location site. He kept his eyes trained on the fields to either side of the four-lane highway. To his left he saw drivers rubbernecking out of their vehicles at something in the field.

Josh veered off I–5 onto the exit ramp at a steady seventy-five, ignoring the thirty-five miles per hour speed limit with impunity. He braked hard, the vehicle weaving under the stress. Without halting, Josh turned left onto the road, taking him over the highway and toward the spectacle in the field.

He closed in on the field and the concentration of people and vehicles came into clearer view. All the emergency services were represented—police, fire and paramedics. In the field, people were gathered around an object.

Josh's Caravan came to another shuddering halt, stopping with two wheels on the road and two wheels in the dirt. He saw it, recognizable from two hundred feet, the colorful tail of his Cessna C152 pointing skyward. It looked like a toy discarded by an angry child. The emergency services people and their vehicles obscured the rest of the plane from sight. He clambered out of the minivan and raced across the road without paying any attention to other vehicles.

The policemen keeping everyone back from the

scene closed upon him. "Where do you think you're going, sir?" one officer demanded.

Josh ignored him and ran on. He didn't have time for questions.

Two officers engaged him and swiftly halted his progress before he got to the three bar fence. They unceremoniously brought him to the ground. All three men crashed sprawling on the highway.

"I'm Josh Michaels and that's my plane!" he shouted, as one policeman started to handcuff him. He repeated himself twice more before they listened.

The cop uncuffed Josh and said without apology, "Next time have the presence of mind to approach an accident scene with more sense."

The officer led Josh to the scene, but Josh half-ran, half-walked and it looked like Josh led the cop. He ignored the whining pain from the cuts he'd taken to the hands, knees and chin when the policemen had brought him down.

"What makes you think this is your aircraft?" The cop's speech sounded choppy over the rough terrain.

"That tail section." Josh pointed at the colorful design. "Those are our colors. And I left my flying partner an hour ago before he took off for Stockton Metropolitan."

"How did you know the plane had crashed?"

Josh ignored the cop's question as he made it to the constellation of people circled around the crash site. Men tried to stop Josh from getting too close.

"Let him through. He may be the plane's owner," the out-of-breath policeman said.

The men parted to let him through. Josh came up on the rear of the plane, giving him his first sight of the Cessna. People were asking him questions. Josh didn't listen.

His plane was buried nose-down in the ground, resting on its starboard wing. The wing had buckled and split, dumping its fuel load onto the plowed earth. There'd been no fire, but fire extinguisher foam had been sprayed over the spilt fuel. Josh moved around to the side of the aircraft. Everything on the front end of the plane had been destroyed. The undercarriage was bent and twisted, the nose wheel invisible. The propeller had embedded itself into the ground. Struts had been torn from fixings. A spiderweb of cracks speckled the Plexiglas window. A trickle of blood ran along the dashboard. The plane's artwork looked vandalized on its wrecked canvas. Josh read his and Mark Keegan's names on the door.

"I'm Josh Michaels." He pointed at his name on the plane. "This is my plane."

Josh saw Mark Keegan's body flopped over the control column like an unwanted doll. Over twenty men from emergency services were just standing around. He went to open the copilot's door. A paramedic restrained him.

"Why aren't you helping him?" Josh demanded.

"There's nothing we can do for him. He's dead."

Mark was dead. Everyone could see that.

CHAPTER TWELVE

Again, Josh was talking to the police. He spent the next few hours at the aircraft crash site. For reasons of safety, the police had manhandled him away from the wreckage. The site had to be cleared, the crash area staked off and the downed plane screened from prying eyes.

Still in sight of the screened plane, he explained all he knew about Mark and the aircraft's history. He also identified Mark's corpse when it was finally removed from the Cessna. The questions asked seemed to be coming from a long way away, as if via an old transatlantic telephone line, and he answered in the same fashion.

Images of Mark flooded Josh's mind, alternating from the pilot's dead body to their last conversation before he took off. He thought about the check he'd given to Mark still in his back pocket. The concept of profiting from the unpaid debt because his friend was dead plagued him. Mark had no wife and Josh wondered whom he should contact. He felt obligated to inform someone and repay the money he owed. The only person he could think of was Mark's sister.

Eventually, the police told him to go home and expect an investigation from the Federal Aviation Authority and National Transport Safety Board. He didn't do as he was told.

Josh drove back to Laguna and got to Bob's house just after five in the evening. Bob welcomed Josh in typical Bob weekend-wear—baggy shorts, a big T-shirt and Teva sandals.

"Hey, Josh, I was expecting you earlier. C'mon in man." Bob ushered Josh into his house. "Nancy said you called this morning—what's up?"

"Mark Keegan's dead," Josh said.

"Dead?" Nancy asked, walking into the hall.

"Jesus. How?" Bob asked.

"He crashed our plane this morning, flying to Stockton. All I know is he radioed the tower with engine problems and he attempted an emergency landing. The last thing they heard was Mark screaming all the way into the ground."

Nancy put a hand to her mouth. She walked up to him and put a comforting hand on his arm. "Oh, Josh, that's awful."

"I heard about a plane going down on the radio and thought nothing of it," Bob said.

"What did Kate say?" Nancy said.

"I haven't told her. I was coming from the airport to here when I heard the radio report and I just knew it was Mark. Can I call her?"

"Of course you can, man. You don't need to ask." Bob retrieved the cordless telephone from the living room and handed it to Josh.

"Can I get you something to drink, Josh?" Nancy asked.

"Anything cold would be good," he replied, and dialed his home number.

"I'll give you a minute." Bob walked into the kitchen, where Nancy had gone moments earlier.

Kate picked up the telephone on the fourth ring and Josh told her what had happened to Mark Keegan. The accident shocked and upset her. She was also upset he had not come home first. He apologized and promised to be home soon. He hung up and went into the kitchen.

"How did she take it?" Nancy handed him the lemonade.

"About as well you'd expect. She's not too pleased I'm here when I should be at home." Josh took a sip from the lemonade. It was bitter, but good.

"She's not wrong, is she?" Nancy said.

"You make good lemonade, Nancy."

"What are you doing here, Josh?" Bob asked. "Weren't you meant to be flying with Mark?"

"Yeah, I was, but I wanted to see you about your colleague, James Mitchell."

"What about him?"

"Do you mind if we walk and talk? I just don't seem to be able to stay still." What Josh said was true, but he also didn't want Nancy hearing what he had to say.

"Yeah, sure," Bob said.

Josh took untidy gulps from his lemonade and placed the empty glass on the sink drainer. "Thanks for the lemonade, Nancy."

"Any time, Josh." Nancy smiled, but her concern for her husband's friend showed through.

They walked deeper into the housing development. To Josh, the street was eerily quiet. Sidewalks and front yards were deserted, but signs of recent life did exist.

Freshly washed and polished cars sat in driveways. Discarded baseball bats and soccer balls lay strewn across freshly mowed lawns. It was like a neutron bomb had gone off and he and Bob were the only ones left alive. His nuclear test theory was swiftly dispelled when a couple of kids came running out of a nearby house. A year or two older than Abby, they resumed kicking a soccer ball in the street.

Josh walked with his head down, staring at the oatmeal-colored concrete sidewalk. Bob walked alongside him looking forward with his hands behind his back. Neither of them had spoken for several minutes.

Bob stopped walking. "Josh, what did you want to know about James Mitchell?"

Josh took two more steps, stopped, turned and lifted his head to look at Bob. "What do you know about him?"

Bob shrugged. "Nothing, really. He's an insurance agent with Pinnacle and is in California scaring up business. He's on the road with nothing to do most of the time. I've been there and I felt sorry for him, so I invited him to your party. What's wrong, did he piss somebody off?"

"Yeah, me," Josh said.

"Shit, I'm sorry. Bad idea—"

Josh cut Bob off mid-sentence. "He drove me off the road. And you brought him to my home."

Bob's expression changed in increments as he absorbed Josh's words. It was as though layers of surprise were torn off his face one by one until the pure expression of shock came through. Bob walked forward and took hold of Josh's wrist like he was a disobedient child.

"What are you saying? That I knew this guy was the one on the bridge?" Bob demanded.

"I'm asking you what you know about him. That's all."

"That's all I know," Bob said.

"Let's keep walking. I don't want the neighbors listening," Josh said.

They walked again.

"What makes you think he's the one?" Bob asked.

"When you were leaving last night you and he were talking and he made the thumbs-down sign to you."

"That's it? That's what you've based this guy's guilt on? Oh, come on Josh, that's a little thin, don't you think?"

"He made exactly the same gesture. No two people would do it that way."

Bob frowned. "Josh, you're not convincing me, pal. It still seems you're reaching for something that isn't there."

"And it was Pinnacle Investments that sent the wreath," Josh said.

Bob shook his head in disbelief. "So you are saying James Mitchell ran you off the road, found out who you were, then sent you a wreath as some sort of sick joke. And by coincidence, you happen to be one of his firm's customers. Forgive me, Josh, but it doesn't sound plausible."

"Who says that he's an insurance agent? Don't you think it's funny that just as all this shit happens, Bell comes back on the scene wanting money? It occurred to me today they might be working together. I saw them talking last night."

"Jesus, Josh. You don't know that."

"Neither do you."

"No, I don't."

"Then help me find out. Prove me wrong," Josh said.

Bob looked down at his feet and kicked a small

chunk of gravel into the road. He thought for a minute. "How do we do that?"

"We'll pay him a visit. You picked him up from his hotel. You know where he's staying."

"Yeah, but I'm sure he was making off for San Francisco today or tomorrow."

"Well, we won't know if we don't try. Let's go now."

"No, Josh," Bob said. "Your friend has just been killed and your wife is worried sick. Go home."

"He'll get away."

Bob sighed. "I'll pick you up first thing in the morning and we'll go to the motel and check out James Mitchell, together. But you're going home right now. Okay?"

"Okay." Josh agreed reluctantly.

"Good. We'll settle this tomorrow."

Bob picked up Josh from his home before eight the following morning. They trudged across the city on commuter-clogged roads like blood struggling to flow through a diseased heart. Bob drove to the southeast side of the city, where he had picked up James Mitchell Saturday night.

Bob found it difficult to strike up a conversation. So far, Josh had given him a collection of one-word responses. This wasn't like him. He and Josh never ran out of things to say. He would make Josh talk to him.

"How are you and Kate?" he asked.

"Okay."

"No, really. And don't give another single word answer. Talk to me, damn it."

Josh sighed. "Not good. She feels I'm a different person. She thinks this accident has gotten to me more than I think. We argued again. Even Abby and Wiener are treating me differently," he said.

Bob guessed what it must be like living with Josh, if his friend's behavior was anything like his ramblings yesterday. Life must be hard for Kate, and it couldn't be doing the kid any good being exposed to Josh right now. Bob hoped their meeting with Mitchell would clear things up and Josh could move on. Of course, he still had the blackmail hanging over his head. Bell hadn't been worth it in his opinion. Jesus, Josh had screwed up and it was coming back at him tenfold. Bob pulled off the freeway and the motel came into view.

Bob slotted the Toyota into a parking space at the River City Inn. The motel was positioned on a development that was home to the social security office, a Shell service station, another motel chain and very little else. Bob had stayed in places like these when he was a salesman on the road. He was glad he'd established roots and built up his own insurance business. Bob didn't envy James Mitchell's life. He locked the car and he followed Josh to the motel reception.

"Let me do the talking," Bob said. "I don't want to freak anybody out if this turns out to be nothing, especially Mitchell. I still deal with Pinnacle Investments and I don't want to alienate them."

Josh nodded in agreement.

The motel receptionist, a pretty blond woman in her mid-twenties, all lipstick and cotton candy hair, looked up when Bob and Josh entered. Her name badge said TAMMY. She flashed a welcoming corporate smile. "Hi there, welcome to the River City Inn. Can I help you?"

Bob leaned on the reception desk and flashed the same plastic smile Tammy gave. "Yes, I hope so. I was looking for a colleague of mine, James Mitchell, but I can't remember what room he's in."

"Let me check that for you, sir." The receptionist looked up James Mitchell's name on the computer records. "I'm sorry, there's no James Mitchell here," Tammy said.

"Oh, he did say he was checking out either yesterday or today," Bob said. "Did he leave a forwarding address?"

"No, sir. I don't have a James Mitchell checked in or out," she said.

Bob looked at Josh in confusion. "I don't understand, I picked him up from . . ." Bob let his words trail off. "I must have the wrong motel. Thanks very much for your help. I'm really sorry to have put you to any trouble."

"No problem at all, sir," Tammy said, still smiling.

Josh shot Bob a baleful look that said everything.

"We may have his name wrong, he's only visiting us," Josh said.

"What did he look like?"

"He's about forty-five, average height, medium build, brown, graying hair, very ordinary looking," Josh said.

"We have a lot of men here who fit that description."

"C'mon, Josh, we've got the wrong place," Bob said, and started to move away from the reception desk.

Tammy's smile collapsed immediately when the two turned their back on her to leave. A non-corporate look of puzzlement replaced her smile.

In the parking lot, Josh couldn't contain his frustration. "What was that? You bailed on me, Bob."

"Hang on, Josh, wait a minute. I know this is the place I came to on Saturday and I don't know why they don't have a record of him, unless he gave them a false name. And I don't see a reason for an insurance agent to give a false name."

"So what are you saying?"

"I think you're right."

Josh calmed down. "Hey, I'm sorry. It's just that I feel no one's in my corner."

"Believe me man, I'm on your side. Something is beginning to smell here."

"How did you meet him on Saturday?"

"I met him in the reception area. He was ready and waiting."

Bob fished in his jacket pocket and pulled out a Pinnacle Investments business card. He always kept business cards. James Mitchell hadn't given him one, but Bob had one from another Pinnacle representative. He looked at the embossed card and brandished it like a winning lottery ticket.

Bob removed his cellular from his jacket pocket and dialed the telephone number on the card. "Moment of truth."

"Hello, Pinnacle Investments. Your life is in our hands. My name's Karen. How can I help you?" the receptionist said.

"Hi, Karen, could you give me a contact number for one of your insurance agents, James Mitchell, please?"

"Just checking for you, sir."

Silence greeted Bob for nearly a minute.

"I'm sorry, there's no one by that name working here. Are you sure you have the correct name?"

"I don't know. I'll check my paperwork and get back to you. Thank you so much for your help."

"Could I have your name, sir?" the telephone receptionist asked.

Bob hung up.

"What did they say?"

"They've never heard of James Mitchell."

"Why are we going to see a florist?" Bob asked.

"I want to know who sent that wreath," Josh said.

"Pinnacle Investments, right?" Bob answered.

"So the card said, but there's no proof. James Mitchell,

or whoever this guy is, said he was from Pinnacle Investments, but he wasn't. So who says they sent the wreath?"

The florist that sent the wreath was situated a few
blocks from Josh's home, a small business amongst
many on the strip mall put up to service the local community. Forget-Me-Nots was sandwiched between a
delivery pizza joint and a manicure parlor that sold
false nails for $7.95. Bob pulled into a parking space
directly in front of the store, just vacated by an old
woman in a Cadillac Seville.

They entered the store and the electronic buzzer
sounded. The staff consisted of one person—a tall
middle-aged woman who came out from the rear of the
shop. She was gaunt and a good fifteen pounds under-
weight. She looked as though someone had let the air
out of her. Her iron-gray hair was thick and loosely
curled to the middle of her back. Her jeans and big
wool sweater hung on her like clothes on a coat
hanger.

"Can I help you with anything?" she asked.

"We were after some information," Josh said. "You
sent a sympathy wreath to my house last week. It came
from Pinnacle Investments."

The woman pursed her thin lips as she narrowed her
eyes. "You're Josh Michaels?"

"Yes, I am."

"Oh, you're the one. Chris was none too pleased
with your . . . outburst."

Josh flushed a little, embarrassed by his misdemeanor
being brought to book. "Yeah, I'm sorry. I shouldn't
have tried to kill the messenger. And if Chris is here, I
would like to apologize to him in person."

Her face softened at Josh's apology. "Well, he's not
and I don't think he would be too interested in what
you had to say anyway."

Josh winced and looked at Bob. He smiled flatly.

"Is that all you wanted?" she asked.

"I hope you can understand that my friend was under a lot of stress and someone played a sick joke on him. His car was forced off the road into the river. And we are here to get to the bottom of it," Bob said.

"That was you? Wow. I saw the car dragged from the river on TV."

Josh nodded.

"Can you tell us who placed the order for the wreath?" Bob asked.

"Let me check." She disappeared into the rear of the store.

Bob placed his hands in his pockets and leaned back slightly, forcing his jacket open, displaying his ample belly. He looked approvingly around the store.

The florist returned through a string bead doorway.

"It was ordered by Pinnacle Investments from their head office, in Seattle."

"And it definitely came from Pinnacle Investments?" Bob asked.

"Yeah, I had to call them back to check some details."

Josh frowned.

"Is that the answer you were looking for?" the florist asked.

It wasn't.

Josh walked the five blocks from Forget-Me-Nots to his home with a bunch of roses in one hand. The flowers would be something nice for Kate. He hoped it would put a smile on her face. Also, the purchase was in some way Josh's apology to all those employed at the florist he'd offended. He hoped he would start making people happy.

But he was far from happy. He'd tracked James

Mitchell down to his motel, but that wasn't his name and there was no sign of his existence. He'd expected the man to have bought the wreath, but he hadn't. Pinnacle Investments had sent it. It didn't make sense. There was no connection, no conspiracy, no nothing. Maybe he was overwrought from the stressful events of the last week and his paranoia was unfounded. An irritated driver beeped her horn at him. Josh snapped back into the real world and found he had stepped onto the crosswalk when the light was against him.

Josh arrived at his home a few minutes later. He let himself in and called out to his family. He heard voices from the backyard and immediately put the flowers behind his back. He closed the door with his foot as Kate and Abby came in from the patio.

"Hi Dad," Abby said.

"Everything okay?" Kate said.

"Yeah." Josh produced the flowers from behind his back. "These are for you, babe."

At a loss for words, Kate took the flowers, put her arms around her husband and kissed him. "Thank you. I love you," she whispered in his ear.

"I've been such an idiot," he whispered back. "I'm sorry."

"Never mind that."

Their embrace was brought to a sharp conclusion by Abby. "What about me?" she said.

They looked down at their daughter.

"Oh yeah," Josh said.

He released Kate and removed a single rose from the bunch. Kneeling, he gave it to Abby. "Of course a rose for my other lady."

"I'll put it in my room," Abby said, and tore up the stairs.

"Don't forget to put it in water," Kate called after her.

"Am I a good husband?" he asked.

She smiled at him crookedly, bemused. "Yeah, I suppose."

Kate turned her back on him and went into the kitchen. She arranged the flowers in a vase and placed it on the kitchen table.

In the living room, Josh flopped onto the couch, exhaled and ran his hands through his hair. Kate came into the living room and sat on the coffee table in front of him.

"How did you get on?"

"Okay, I guess." He paused. "I don't know. We didn't find anything out really."

"Tell me," Kate said.

Abby bounded down the stairs and ran into the living room.

"I'll tell you later," he said.

Standing over Kate, looking as menacing as an eight-year-old could, Abby asked, "Can we go now?"

Kate smiled and slipped an arm around her daughter. "I suppose so."

"Go where?" Josh asked.

"The zoo," Kate said. "I was waiting until you got back. You coming?"

The zoo brought back a recent unpleasant memory. "No, I don't think so," he replied.

"Are you sure?"

"Yeah, I've got some paperwork to put together for the FAA."

"Okay. Your loss."

She got herself and Abby ready for their afternoon at the zoo. Josh saw them out. Before he closed the door, Kate said, "Miss you."

He busied himself with the task of producing the documentation for the destroyed Cessna. In his office, he removed his copies of the certificate of airworthiness, technical logs, insurance certificates and other mandatory documentation that would be requested for inspection.

He still had to inform the insurance company that the airplane had been destroyed. That was a nuisance he could do without. Insurance companies were the bane of his life at the moment. He picked up the phone and started to dial the claims line.

The doorbell chimed.

Josh put the phone down and answered the door, his thoughtful mood shattered upon opening it. Belinda Wong stood on the porch.

"You asshole!" Her beautiful oval shaped face was screwed up in hate. She pushed the door wide open and walked in without invitation.

Josh checked that none of his neighbors had seen Bell's arrival and quickly closed the door behind her. "What are you doing here?"

"You know why I'm here, Josh." She spat his name like she had venom in her mouth. "And don't worry. Your wife and kid didn't see me. I can see the look on your face."

She was right. Her invasion of his home in broad daylight terrified him. But she didn't have to rub his face in it. Throwing her out by the scruff of her neck seemed a very appealing option, but the undesirable scene it would bring prevented him.

"I've been waiting for your family to leave all morning," she continued.

"What do you want, Bell?" Josh demanded.

"You coward. Sending your fat friend, Bob, to tell me not to ruin your little family unit." She mocked him by speaking in baby talk. "Did you tell him to do that?"

"No, I didn't. And I don't have to explain myself to you."

Bell shook her head in disgust.

"Why did you crash the party, Bell? I paid you as you asked and I shouldn't have seen you again."

"Because I wanted to, because I want you to know that I can drop into your life any time I want and I don't need to ask." She scraped an index finger with a wicked looking manicured nail under Josh's chin. The nail rasped against his stubble when she curled her finger back sharply.

Anger, hate and frustration welled up inside him. He should have known that Bell's return hadn't been intended to be a brief encounter. She toyed with him like a cat with a mouse and he wondered when would she go in for the kill. He'd had enough.

"How much to make you disappear forever?" he asked.

"Josh, that's only half your problem. You think money will solve everything. If you hadn't been so fascinated with the stuff, you would never have gotten yourself into this shit pile you're in now."

"That's bullshit, Bell. I took that money because I needed it for Abby's medical treatment and you know it."

Suddenly, Bell softened. She became seductive, sexual. "Josh, you know it doesn't have to be like this. You know what you have to do to stop all this . . ."—she searched for the word—"unpleasantness. Don't you, Josh?"

Josh allowed her to come close to him. She slipped an arm around his neck and looked into his eyes. His body went rigid, unbending to her will. He resisted her.

"No, I don't, Bell."

"Leave that wife and brat of yours for me, of course. Silly boy." She oozed sex and temptation.

Raising a hand to his face, Bell caressed his cheek and kissed his mouth. The kiss was brief. He slapped her hand down, then gripped her wrist and twisted it behind her back. The kiss had been broken before she could make it openmouthed. Bell released a short laugh, taking pleasure from Josh's rough play.

"I don't think so," he whispered.

She laughed. "You seem in the mood to play. Are you sure?"

"Never in a million years would I ever want you back."

He released her arm and pushed her away with a sharp shove to the chest. He'd washed his hands of her. He didn't want her.

Bell stumbled back, nearly falling, but saved herself by steadying herself against a small table with the telephone on it. The impact rocked the table and the telephone fell, the receiver clattering to the hardwood floor.

Hatred consumed her face again. "You prick, Josh. You think you're so righteous, so perfect. Well, I'm not the one who took a bribe, cheated on my wife and screwed my secretary. Josh, you're going to be so sorry when I've finished with you."

"And are you going to do that alone, Bell? Or are you going to get your new friend involved?"

Bewilderment crossed Bell's face.

"You know, the guy who pushed me off the bridge. I saw you with him at the party."

After a long moment, recognition, then a malicious grin spread across her face. Still slumped against the table, Bell righted herself. "Wouldn't you like to know?"

"Well?" Josh wanted an answer. Was James Mitchell her partner?

"Fuck you, Josh. I think I have the answer I was looking for from you. And you will be hearing from me . . . in one way or another. Or your wife will."

"Get out!" he barked, shaking with rage.

"Suit yourself," she said, the evil grin still present on her face. She opened the door and let herself out.

"Dammit!" Josh said to himself, his hands balled up into fists.

CHAPTER THIRTEEN

The park was a full city block of grass in the downtown area, one of several plots scattered throughout downtown like green property squares on a Monopoly board. The children's playground occupied one corner of the park. Unsupervised and shrouded by trees, it was home to tire swing sets, slides, monkey bars, seesaws and a merry-go-round, all contained in a sandbox.

Abby had the playground to herself. It was late in the afternoon, and she had free run of the amusements and no petty arguments about whose turn was next. It was every child's dream and today, Abby's had come true.

Abby's good fortune wasn't because of good timing or knowing an out-of-the-way place. She had the playground to herself because most of the city parks were populated with bums spending their days lounging or panhandling, and parents feared their children coming in contact with an undesirable. They would rather take them to more secure places. However, this park playground was the exception. Not in a part of town heavily populated with city workers who had money to give, the park was virtually unmolested by bums who gravitated to places with better pickings.

Squealing, Abby came down the slide, her dress riding up and wedging under her bottom. Wagging his tail, Wiener waited at the bottom of the slide and barked in time to Abby's squeal. She ran back to the steps to climb up for another go.

Josh and Kate occupied two of the swings. The adults looked like giants on the swingset designed for children. Josh stretched out his long legs far in front of him, his heels digging into the sand. Kate rocked slowly back and forth. They watched their daughter at play. Neither said anything to the other.

Low in the sky, the sun cast shadows on the narrow streets. A gentle breeze ruffled the trees, producing a sound similar to waves lapping a sandy beach.

Kate shuddered. "I'm getting cold. What time is it?"

Josh looked at his watch. "Just after five."

"I think we'll go in a minute," Kate said to Josh; then called to Abby, "Another five minutes then we're going, sweets."

Both Abby and Wiener looked Kate's way at the bottom of the slide. "Oh, Mom! Can't we stay longer? I'm not tired or anything," Abby whined, as only kids can.

"We'll have five minutes to think about it and let you know. Okay?" Josh said.

Abby nodded happily and ran off toward the monkey bars, Wiener bouncing after her.

"Why the delay?" Kate asked.

Josh started to speak, but the words didn't come.

Kate turned in the swing, twisting the chains above her. "Come on, Josh, spit it out. You brought us here and you haven't had two words to say in the last hour. I've talked and you've stared into the distance."

Josh took a breath and released it as a sigh. After Bell's visit yesterday, he knew it was better he told her now rather than Bell telling her later. He turned to face Kate. "There's something I want to tell you. It's something I should have told you a long time ago. It's something I did. Something that I think is coming back to hurt me and indirectly can hurt us."

Fear passed across Kate's face like a shadow and the sparkle in her eyes dulled. He saw her mind working, trying to guess what he'd done. Would she be close? Could she imagine the things he'd done? If she couldn't, he would hurt her with his next statement. If she could, what did that say about them? Either way, it made this confession all the more difficult. Josh wrung his hands together and looked at them.

"Remember when Abby had that kidney and liver infection after she was born? She was in the hospital for such a long time and you didn't leave her side. You were with her virtually day and night."

Memories of that time bombarded him, cutting short his explanation. He relived those terrifying weeks seeing his first child fight to survive and him powerless to do anything to save her.

"Yes, of course I remember," she said softly.

"You've got to understand I did it for the right reasons and I didn't want to worry you."

Fear forced Kate to squirm. "Josh, tell me. Please."

"You were so scared for Abby. Worried whether she would pull through. I don't know what I would have done if she'd died."

Kate grabbed his wrist. "Jesus, Josh, don't say that. Don't even think things like that."

Josh stopped rocking on the swing and he stared into her eyes for recognition. "But I did and you can't say you didn't think the same, either."

She looked away from him. "Oh, Josh."

"It's okay to admit it. Look, she's okay, there's nothing wrong with her and she's great." He lifted

Kate's face so she looked at him, then turned his gaze to Abby.

Red-faced, Abby hung upside down from the climbing frame, her hair hanging down. Her arms outstretched, she stroked Wiener, who stood beneath her. She spotted her parents looking at her. "Are my five minutes up?"

"No, not yet," Josh said.

"Cool."

Josh couldn't help smiling.

"What did you do, Josh?"

His smile melted. "She wasn't getting better and the medical bills were piling up. The insurance was stretched to the max and Medi-Cal couldn't help us."

"Josh, you said the insurance would cover it."

"It didn't."

"What did you do?" she repeated, dread eating up her face.

"I remember the crying. I couldn't bear to listen to it. It was like listening to fingernails being drawn down a blackboard." He shuddered at memories of years past, the despair rising to the surface. "The insurance was saying they wouldn't pay out any further and the doctors said they needed to carry out more procedures. I didn't know what we were going to do."

Kate placed a comforting hand on Josh's knees. "Tell me."

"I was carrying out building inspections on an apartment development in Dixon. The construction company had cut corners to make a profit and they knew it would never make the grade." He stopped looking at Kate again and stared into the sand at his feet

"What did you do?" she whispered.

"They offered me ten thousand to sign the development off as safe."

"And you took it."

"Yes."

"Oh, Josh." Her hand slipped from his knee.

"I took it happily," he blurted. She needed to understand. "I saw it as our way to save Abby. You've got to understand I didn't do it for greed. I did it out of necessity."

Kate's face said it all. Disappointment scarred her expression, but Josh expected that. This kind of news didn't come with a round of applause and a ticker tape parade. He was just glad she wasn't angry.

"How dangerous is the development?"

"Not very. The owners are likely to have problems with subsidence or structural integrity over time. I don't know how well it would hold up in earthquake conditions, but it would have to be a very large quake to have an effect in Dixon and that's very unlikely."

"Josh, why didn't you tell me?" she asked.

"I couldn't. You were too preoccupied with Abby at the time and too happy when she was well. I didn't want to burst your bubble. But I promised myself I would tell you when the time was right." He paused. "I never found the right moment."

"Until now. Why?"

"Someone knows and they used it against me."

"What do you mean?"

"Blackmail."

"How much?"

"Fifty-five thousand, so far."

"Fifty-five thousand? Where did that money come from? You haven't been taking more bribes, have you?"

Josh recoiled. "Christ, no. I only did it the once. They did try me again, but I left rather than be in someone's pocket. That's why I got out of the construction business altogether. I didn't want to get involved again."

"So how did you pay the blackmailer?"

"With a life insurance policy. I sold it."

"You sold your life insurance? What if you'd been killed last week, what would have happened if you had no insurance?" Kate's temper began to slip.

"Don't worry, I've got insurance. I started a new policy after I sold the other one. It was a quick way to raise money."

Kate calmed down. "So why the big confession all of a sudden?"

"I think what's been happening to me recently has something to do with it—the car accident, the wreath, the guy at the party. I think the blackmailer is calling in the marker. I think someone is going to release my part to the press."

"Do you know who's doing this?"

"Yes."

"Was it the man with Bob?"

"No. I think he's a hired hand. We checked him out and he doesn't work for Pinnacle."

"Who is it?"

"I don't want to say."

"I think it's a bit late for what you want," Kate said sternly.

Josh had hoped to keep this detail from Kate. "It's Belinda Wong."

"Your secretary?" She was incredulous. "How did she find out?"

"She overheard a phone call," Josh lied. He couldn't bring himself to tell her about their affair. He would, but just not now. Neither of them could handle the enormity of it all. That was what he told himself.

"Go to the police."

"I can't."

"I don't care."

"I'll be ruined."

"You don't have a choice."

"Let me deal with it. I'll finish it."

"Abby, we're going," Kate fired across the playground.

"Oh," she whined.

"Now, Abby," Kate snapped. She stood up from the swing and walked away from her husband.

"Kate, tell me what you're thinking. Kate, Kate, please," Josh called after her.

She didn't answer.

CHAPTER FOURTEEN

Sitting at the front desk, two security guards occasionally glanced at the surveillance monitors. The main focus of their attention was on the fourteen-inch portable television perched on top of the bank of monitors. One guard got up from his seat and changed channels. The other guard checked his watch.

"Patrol time." He picked up his walkie-talkie and set off for the elevator. "Tell me if anything good happens, eh?"

"Sure," the other guard said, without taking his eyes off the screen.

At seven P.M., they were only two hours into their shift and a shitload of television would be watched before their time at Pinnacle Investments was over at seven the next morning.

The building was quiet in its slumber. The burble of activity of buying and selling investment interests was on hold. The only sounds came from the television and its bored viewers, the hum of the fluorescent lights and the bleeps of a phone being dialed from an office on the top floor in the east wing.

In his office, Dexter Tyrell tapped a number into a cellular phone. The phone was registered neither to him nor to Pinnacle Investments, per the professional's instructions. He was contacting his hired killer. He wanted a progress report, and more importantly, he wanted results. He needed results.

His meeting with the board had gone as he expected. The report hadn't been well received. Tyrell's viatical division was returning a profit, but it was again short of the fifteen-percent growth target required by the firm and promised by Tyrell. The results were better than the quarter before, and those were better than the quarter before that. He had it under control; all he needed was time and he would turn it around. He knew the board was turning against him. They wanted to be rid of him. He could see himself being replaced by someone who they thought could do the job more effectively.

The idiots, if they only knew. Would any of them have had the guts to do what he had done? He doubted it. His only way out was to increase the pace of his program. He knew he risked exposure and an investigation, but his back was against the wall and he would be damned if he would let them have his division. He had to risk it.

Tyrell listened to the *burr* of the telephone ringing. "Come on, come on, answer the phone. I want to know what you are doing," he muttered to himself.

After several rings, the professional picked up.

"Hello." His one word was impenetrable. It gave no indication to his feelings, his location, his well-being. It didn't even sound like a welcome.

"Where were you? Why didn't you answer the phone right away?" Tyrell demanded.

"What do you want?" the professional said dismissively.

"I want to know how far you have gotten with your assignments."

"They're proceeding."

"But when will they be completed?"

"Probably a week to ten days."

"I want them concluded as soon as possible, and that means less than a week," Tyrell snapped. "I have other assignments for you. I'm increasing the pace of the project."

"Do you consider that an acceptable risk?"

"Are you worried you'll be caught?" Tyrell liked his snide remark.

"I think *you* should be. If it ever came down to it, the police would never find me and neither would you."

"Are you sure? You seem to be losing your touch. You've missed this target once already. Have you managed to try again?"

"Yes, I have. This target is a fortunate man. I arranged for his aircraft to have some problems."

Tyrell interrupted. "Did you get him?" He already knew the answer.

"No, I followed him to the airport and he changed his mind."

"So? He'll probably use the plane again."

"No, his flying partner took it and was killed."

"Congratulations, you killed the wrong man," he scolded.

"Does that bother you?"

"No," Tyrell said bluntly. He was only bothered if the killing exposed him and his project. "Are you?"

The professional didn't answer.

"Is he suspicious with two accidents occurring so close together? If I were him, I'd be wondering about a third."

"Yes, I believe so."

"That makes your task harder. And does he have any suspicions regarding Pinnacle Investments?"

"Oh yes. The wreath that someone sent from your company did that. Was that you?"

The vice president was angrier with himself than his hit man. He'd indulged himself and it had backfired. Every time one of the viatical clients died he sent a wreath to the family. He got special enjoyment out of knowing the client was dead before the family did. He'd made the mistake after he'd received the phone call that Josh Michaels was dead. He'd sent a wreath, and why shouldn't he? His hired gun had never missed before. He wouldn't make that mistake again; no wreath until a kill was confirmed.

"If I hadn't been given the wrong fucking information about his apparent death, that mistake would have never been made," Tyrell said. "What have you got planned now?"

"The woman is proceeding according to plan, and I see a conclusion to that soon. My investigations have shown that Michaels has a dubious past. He is or was involved with a woman and I think there's a possibility for something spectacular that wouldn't raise suspicion. But it'll take a little arranging." The professional's pride shone through.

Tyrell's heart sank. Whatever it was the professional had planned, it didn't inspire confidence. "Just make sure that you don't miss this time. I don't want these failed attempts becoming habit. It's the wrong time for fuck-ups, for all of us."

"I've never failed you before, have I?" the professional asked.

"Good night," Tyrell said and hung up.

The vice president tossed the phone onto his desk. It bounced across the smooth surface and came to a halt at the edge of the table. His contract killer pissed him off. He was getting too flamboyant with his staged accidents, and his arrogance made him ineffective. For some time his hit man had worried him. The last three kills had gone according to plan, but the kills were so elaborate that the outcome could have easily gone the other way.

So, what were his options? Lay the hit man off? God knew he wanted to replace him with someone who had a more straightforward approach. Somehow, Tyrell didn't think hired killers were canned from jobs. It wasn't that sort of business. So what could he do with the professional? He was too much of a liability left to roam free, but he knew almost nothing about him. His thoughts were leading him to a conclusion his hit man wasn't going to like.

But for now Tyrell needed the hit man, and he really needed the kill rate increased. The life expectancy of his clients had to be shortened for the success of the company. He would love to show the board members who could make this company sparkle. Tyrell pocketed the discarded phone, picked up his briefcase and left his office. He hoped that tomorrow would be more promising.

An hour later the professional sat in a restaurant bar. The food and drink were expensive, like the clientele, which were a mix of state officials, businessmen and high-income white-collar workers. He wondered how many of these men had big life insurance policies in the hands of viatical companies like Pinnacle Investments. Would he be making a visit to any of them one day? He smiled at the thought. The human race's ability for creating complex problems amused him. His clean-living lifestyle, simple and without appendages, would never have him looking down the barrel of a gun.

He had a mineral water in one hand and his eyes

fixed on the television's baseball game. Disinterested, he watched the game, but his mind was elsewhere. He decided Dexter Tyrell was a prick. The businessman wanted everything to happen now, but this type of work needed planning. Tyrell's problem was greed, and greed meant sloppiness, which meant errors. He mused on the notion that he might blow off this gig, close the post office box and get rid of the cellular phones. And if he discovered Tyrell was becoming a liability, then he would take care of him. Permanently.

A hand lightly touched his shoulder and someone spoke, tearing him away from his thoughts.

"Hi, James." Belinda Wong was a vision in a scarlet dress that enhanced her to-die-for figure.

The professional had gotten her phone number at Josh Michaels's birthday party as part of a fallback plan. He'd called her after Mark Keegan had been killed in his aircraft. With that particular avenue closed for Michaels's demise, he turned to Josh's ex-mistress. He saw potential with this woman on his side. He thought Michaels was a fool to get involved with some one like this; she had trouble written all over her.

Belinda was pleased to hear from him. The professional took her interest in him as a positive sign and felt his luck change with the Michaels assignment. She'd suggested this place—expensive and exclusive.

"Belinda, you look breathtaking."

"Thank you. Call me Bell."

"Can I get you a drink, Bell?"

"Yes, I'll have a white wine." Bell slid onto the stool next to him.

He asked the barman to get the lady a white wine. The barman offered her a choice, and she selected a quality Chardonnay. The professional told her the table would be ready for them in a few minutes. She smiled, exposing teeth that could consume him in a single bite.

"Are you in a better mood than when we last met?" he asked.

"Yes, thank you." She smiled. "I wasn't having a good time at the party."

"What were all the bad feelings about?"

"Oh, a long story."

"I've got time."

"We'll see." Bell's perfectly manicured fingers with long bloodred fingernails gripped the wineglass as tightly as the scarlet dress hugged her delicate frame. She sipped her drink.

He looked at the woman. He studied her face, trying to see what was going on in that mind. *It is so obvious what kind of woman she is,* he thought. *As dangerous as she is beautiful.* The professional finished off his mineral water.

The maitre d' came over and told them their table was ready and showed them the way. The men noticed Bell, with her provocative dress and elegant good looks. Obvious stares meant to be stray glances were sent in her direction from all quarters of the restaurant. The men wanted her and she knew they did. They were seated at a window table for two. The table was an arm's width too narrow for the professional's comfort.

The server took their orders and left them. Their conversation was lost in a sea of voices. The appetizer course came and went, as did the exchange of words about everyday life, careers and other forgettable subjects. He'd noted boredom creeping into her demeanor. When the main course arrived, he decided it was time to make the meal more interesting.

"Do you want to play something? Just for fun."

Suspicion flashed in her eyes. "Like what?"

"I used to work with a guy many years ago and he

had the perfect way of breaking the ice with new people. He always swore that this one question gave him more insight into people than weeks of working with them," the professional lied.

"Was he a salesman?" She dabbed her mouth with the napkin and sipped her wine.

"Yeah, he used to spring this question on his clients at social functions. You know, business dinners and lunches—stuff like that," the professional said, embellishing the lie.

"So what was the question?"

"So you're interested?"

"Yes." Bell's dark eyes bored into him.

She was interested. He had her.

"What is the worst thing you've ever done?"

"That's the question?"

Smiling, the professional nodded. He took another mouthful of food from his fork.

"Why not the nicest thing you've ever done?"

He put down his fork, swallowed his food, placed his elbows on the table, and interlaced his fingers. "Because the nice things aren't that interesting. But people are very keen to tell you the worst they have done, because in some twisted way we're all turned on by the evil that men or women do. People would rather hear that I hung out with Al Capone than Mother Teresa. There's something inherently sexy about being bad, as twisted as it may sound."

Bell paused on the thought. She picked up her knife and fork.

He smirked. "Well?"

"Well what?" She glanced at him and cut into the fish on her plate.

"What's the worst thing you've ever done?" he repeated.

"You really want to know?"

"Yes. I think I do."

"Okay then."

The professional grinned.

"I blackmailed someone."

Although she tried to pass off the comment as no big thing, it was impossible for her to hide her pride. The professional smiled. His question never failed.

"Wow. That is bad."

"It is, isn't it? I thought you might be impressed."

Picking up his knife and fork, the professional started to eat again. Just the confession for which he was looking. He had the reason why Michaels had sold his life policy. Michaels had to have money for the blackmail. "So, what was the blackmail about?"

"That isn't enough for you?" she asked, her tone provocative.

"No. I want details. You've given me the answer. I've seen the menu, but you haven't let me sample the food. Without the details there's no way for me to judge what kind of person you are."

"I blackmailed a man I was having an affair with."

"Good. Tell me more."

The server interrupted them to check on drinks. The professional asked for another bottle of wine.

"So you blackmailed him over the affair?"

"Partly."

"What was the other part?"

"He once told me he took kickbacks when he was a building inspector. I suppose he was playing true to form. As your friend was saying, he told me his worst to impress me."

The server returned with the wine and topped off their glasses, then moved on to another table.

"Did you blackmail him after he told you?"

"No, I did that when he tried to break up with me."

"Did you know about his wife?"

"Oh, yes."

"So you were under no illusions that he was unattached."

"Oh, no. I knew about his marriage and I had even met his wife a few times."

The professional laughed. "You are a dangerous woman."

Smiling, she said, "I'll take that as a compliment."

The professional nodded.

"I found it quite stimulating, having a conversation with his wife while she was completely unaware that I was fucking her husband. It used to make sex very intense after seeing her. I liked to have my tête-à-tête with his wife and then screw him afterwards."

"So why the blackmail?"

"He got an attack of the guilts and wanted to break things off. That wasn't acceptable to me. He'd made a decision to start a relationship with me, but hadn't had the courtesy to break it off with his wife. So when he decided that his relationship with me had been a mistake and that it was over, I decided I would make him pay a price for his betrayal."

"To his wife?"

Bell laughed. "No, to me. He betrayed me as well as his wife. I wasn't concerned with her feelings. It was up to her to do whatever she wanted to take revenge for her husband's infidelity."

The professional noticed the more she talked about Josh, the colder she became. Bell's deep-rooted hatred for Josh Michaels became very apparent. This was the kind of woman with whom the professional could do business. He stopped eating and gave his full and undivided attention to Bell.

"So, when did you stop blackmailing him?" he asked.

"Who says I have?" Bell hid her smirk behind her wineglass.

The professional grinned again. He was getting all the information he wanted.

"What's his name? This unfortunate betrayer of trust and breaker of hearts."

"I'm not sure I should say," she said, the smirk still on her face.

"Oh, come on, Bell, you can't leave me hanging. It's not like I would know him or anything."

Bell moved her food around her plate while contemplating the question, deciding whether she should answer. "But you do know him."

"Do I?" he replied, trying not to show he knew the answer already.

"It's Josh Michaels."

The professional had surmised correctly. He knew the hold she had over Michaels; now it was time to exploit it, and her.

"So is that why you were upset at his party?"

"Yes. He's starting to refuse to play along with my demands and he used one of his friends to try to talk me out of hurting his happy home."

"It sounds like he's trying to call your bluff."

"Maybe. But what can I do about it?"

"Show him that you're not bluffing."

"How would I do that?"

"I could show you."

Surprised, Bell raised an eyebrow. "Could you now."

"Is the money your main concern?"

"No. It's a punishment."

"Well that gives us options."

"Us?"

"Yes. Us."

"I think we should discuss this somewhere else. The dinner table is not the right place," Bell said.

"That's fine with me."

"So, what's the worst thing you've ever done?" Bell asked.

CHAPTER FIFTEEN

While sitting at the kitchen table eating breakfast, Josh leafed through the initial findings of the joint FAA and National Transport Safety Board investigation that had come through the letter slot that morning. In brief, the report stated that the Cessna had run dry of oil and the elevator and rudder bolts had detached themselves. The reason the engine sump had been devoid of oil was because the oil cooler hoses were not sufficiently tightened. It was assumed that the missing bolts had come loose and fallen from the plane during flight, which meant it was probable that the split pins weren't secured through the nuts and bolts. In the opinion of the NTSB, these simple mechanical failures should have been detected during the overhaul prior to the fatal flight, and the pilot should have taken better care during the pre-takeoff checks. The NTSB planned to put the majority of the blame on the mechanic and the remainder on pilot negligence. The findings were preliminary and were in no way to be taken as final. He read through the brief report again.

Josh refused to accept the findings, and he refused to believe Jack Murphy had failed to carry out a thorough inspection of his airplane. Jack was too much of a perfectionist and too much of a craftsman not to have tightened any bolt to the torque setting laid out in the Cessna maintenance manual. Unsatisfied with the report, he drove to Davis Airfield.

Josh parked the car in the same spot he had the day of Mark's death. He walked over to Jack Murphy's hangar. The orange windsock at the end of the runway hung limply against its pole. The sock looked like it was at half-mast in tribute. Josh thought it was fitting, seeing as the airfield had lost one of its own. Davis Airfield had never lost a pilot in its fifty-two-year history.

Josh entered Murphy's workshop. The hangar had the appearance of an elephant's graveyard. A Cessna 172 in flying school colors lay slumped at the mouth of the building. The engine and its cowling had been removed along with the nose wheel assembly. Tubular steel stuck out from the fireproof bulkhead like polished bones, and a tangle of colored wires hung down like veins. The aircraft unceremoniously rested on its tail, no longer able to stand upright without its engine in place. A Piper Archer PA-32 stood propellerless on its wheels looking sadly at the gutted Cessna in front of it. A misshapen object lay hidden under a tarp like a corpse under a mortician's sheet, but it was probably another of Jack's unfinished projects.

The workshop was silent. This wasn't right; it was guaranteed that Jack's workshop rang with the sounds of him and his employees putting their best efforts into keeping these and other aircraft aloft. Josh called out. The odor of used engine oil and grease filled his nose. A rustle of movement came from the small, shabby office at the rear of the hangar. Jack Murphy appeared at the doorway.

Josh crossed the hangar. His footsteps echoed on the concrete floor.

"Hello, Josh. I thought I might be seeing you." Murphy sounded defeated. "I suppose this is to do with Mark."

Josh raised his hands in surrender. "Don't worry, I haven't come to accuse you of anything. I've just come to talk."

"So you got the news from the FAA?"

"Yeah. Shall we go into the office?"

Murphy didn't look good. It was obvious the loss of a plane and pilot from his workshop had hit him hard. Murphy looked like dried fruit with all the goodness sucked out of it. To Josh, he had aged ten years in the days since Sunday.

The two men entered the cluttered office. Murphy squeezed past the bulging filing cabinets and sat behind his wooden desk. Josh removed a stack of magazines from one of the two shabby office chairs before sitting. He remembered seeing these types of chairs in dentist's waiting rooms twenty years ago. Aircraft component manufacturers' calendars, wall planners covered in a graffiti of hastily written notes and magazine articles of aircrafts of interest covered the wall behind the mechanic. The flying club and the private aircraft owners excused Murphy's clutter because of his first-class abilities as an engineer.

"Do you want a coffee, Josh?" Murphy asked.

"No, I'm good, Jack."

"What did you want to talk about?"

"Why aren't you working?" Josh asked. "Where is everyone?"

"I'm not sure there's much point. The FAA is blaming me for the crash and they're likely to take action against me. They'll probably close me down." Murphy doodled on his desk blotter with a pencil, unaware of what he drew.

"But people rely on you."

"Well, that's not a very wise thing to do. Letting me touch their birds is likely to get them killed," the mechanic said pointedly.

"Jack."

"Jack, nothing. One of my planes went and killed someone."

Josh let the subject die. Murphy wasn't going to see sense right now.

"What do you say to their report that you left the oil cooler hoses loose and tail section bolts without split pins?" Josh noticed Murphy was unaware he now doodled on an invoice on his desk and not the blotter.

"I don't believe it." Murphy threw the pencil down. It went skittering across the desk and onto the floor. "I always do a wrench check after servicing. I even do an engine run to make sure everything is sealing. The oil cooler hoses shouldn't have been loose in the first place, because I had no reason to take them off. What they found are fundamental errors that no mechanic would make. If I were that bad I wouldn't have been surprised if the prop fell off."

"So did you undo, then tighten the hose connections?"

"No. I didn't need to. The same goes for the elevator and rudder controls. I had no need to touch the split pins. The pins were in good shape. I only tighten them when there is movement."

"How do you know whether there's movement?" Josh asked.

"I paint a white line across the nut and bolt. If the white lines aren't matched up then the bolt has moved, but they were all lined up. I swear to you that aircraft left me in better condition than it did the day it left the factory."

Murphy's explanation disturbed Josh. Murphy was an honest man and a good mechanic. Josh believed his story. He was sure he'd done everything correctly and hadn't touched the parts of the aircraft that had caused the crash. Josh's paranoia antenna twitched. Why was he getting the feeling that Mark Keegan's death wasn't an accident?

"The thing is, in the twenty-five years I've been involved with aircraft, I've never known the bolts or the hose connection to come undone before." Murphy spoke as if he were in the witness box. With the way things were going, he would have to be before long.

An uncomfortable silence wedged itself between the two men.

Josh knew no more could be learned. He stood up and offered his hand to the distraught mechanic. "Thanks for talking to me, Jack. I really appreciate it. For what it's worth, I don't blame you for what happened to Mark."

Murphy shrugged.

Josh left Murphy's office and headed out of the shade of the hangar for the harsh brightness of day. He was only halfway to the hangar doors when Murphy called to his back. He stopped and turned to face him.

"If I didn't know better . . ." He paused. "I would say that someone wanted that plane to go down." Ominously, Murphy's words echoed throughout the hangar, ricocheting off the walls like bullets, each one burying itself in Josh.

Josh opened the front door to let Abby and Wiener into the house. He unclasped the dog's leash from his collar and hung it on a coat hook. The dachshund shook himself and trotted over to his water bowl. The dog was tired after his walk to the park and thirty minutes of chasing a ball around.

Abby rolled a squeaky ball after the dog. "We're home," she called.

Kate came halfway down the stairs. "You're just in time. I'm running a bath for my little girl."

"Oh. Do I have to?" Abby whined.

"Yes. If you don't, I don't think we can let you stay up this late on vacation." Kate kept her tone firm, but not unkind. She was just negotiating her position with her daughter. It was a regular occurrence for Abby to take Wiener for an evening walk with one of them, but because Abby was on spring break Josh had taken them late, after nine o'clock.

"Dad." Abby turned to Josh for support.

"I think your mother's right. A bath before bed." He paused. "Or you could go to bed now. Your choice?"

The child thought for a moment. "I'll have a bath."

"Good girl," Josh said.

Turning on her heel, Abby ran up the stairs, following her mother.

Josh sat in the living room reading a book and could hear the noise of splashing and giggling coming from the upstairs bathroom. Wiener sat on the floor in front of Josh washing his tufted feet. The phone rang and Josh picked up the cordless handset from the coffee table.

"Hello," he said.

"Josh, it's Bob. Have you got the television on?" Bob's tone was urgent.

"No, I was reading. Is everything okay? You sound—"

Bob cut him off. "Turn on Channel Three. Look at the news. It's on the TV."

Whatever it was, it was bound to be bad news. Josh looked at the remote control on the coffee table and hesitated. If he didn't turn the television on he would be ignorant. Ignorance sounded nice.

"Hold on, Bob. Let me turn the TV on."

Channel Three was in the middle of a commercial break.

"Bob, what am I meant to be watching?"

"It was on the headlines. It's the next story up."

"Can't you just tell me?"

"Here it comes."

The commercials ended and the cameras went to the news anchor, a sharp-looking black man in his thirties with a pencil moustache and glasses.

"We have a breaking story of corruption in the building industry. An anonymous source contacted the station this evening and made the allegation that the Mountain Vista Apartments in Dixon were built to unsafe construction standards. We don't have exact details, as yet, but Channel Three will be investigating all angles of this claim when we receive more information. We now go live to Howard Decker outside Mountain Vista Apartments in Dixon," the anchor said.

The television image switched from inside the studio to the reporter, illuminated by television and security lights. He stood outside the apartments, kept out by security gates. The reporter looked serious and concerned at the same time. He was conservatively dressed in a blue suit and white shirt.

"Thanks, Doug. Howard Decker reporting live from the Mountain Vista Apartments in Dixon. The apartments behind me were built eight years ago. The development consists of over three hundred apartments and condos. The anonymous informant alleges the apartments were built to inferior standards to save money.

"Our informant, who wishes to remain nameless, says they have information detailing the major players involved and the shortcuts made.

"We've spoken to some concerned occupants who didn't want to be filmed tonight but expressed their concern at the revelation. We, of course, will be pressing for an investigation by the apartment management company to establish the validity of the claim made exclusively to Channel Three. This is Howard Decker reporting live from Dixon. Back to you, Doug." Howard Decker's serious face immediately brightened as he switched on a broad smile at the end of his report.

The screen returned to the grave-looking anchor. "A disturbing story—let's hope we can get to the bottom of it. Debbie?"

The camera went to the female coanchor and she began a story about a farming policy going through the state capitol. Josh turned off the television before she could finish.

"Josh, is that the apartment complex you were telling me about?"

Josh didn't answer.

"Josh, are you there?"

Josh had known as soon as they mentioned the name of the apartments that it was the construction project he had taken the bribe on. He couldn't believe Bell had gone and done it. A chill ran through him, as if a chunk of ice circulated through his bloodstream. Gooseflesh broke out along his arms and down his back. Josh fell back onto the couch, relieved to be sitting down.

Bob was still asking if he was there. Josh interrupted him. "Yeah, that's the project I worked on."

"Do you think it was Bell?"

"It wouldn't be anyone else. She came around after I came back from Forget-Me-Nots. She said if I refused to play along with her, she would do something to hurt me."

"At least she didn't mention any names."

"This is a warning. She will if I don't comply with her demands."

"Which are what?"

"I have no idea, but I'm sure I'll find out."

"Hey, man, are you okay?" Bob said. "You don't sound good."

"Everything just seems to be going to hell. I think I'm losing this one."

"Well, if you feel that way, you might as well give up and concede defeat. Tell Kate about the blackmail and the affair, walk into the cops and tell them about the kickback and tell Bell to go fuck herself," Bob said sharply.

Josh didn't understand Bob's hostility, and the change in character shocked him. "What's crawled up your ass?" he asked.

"You. You've surrendered."

"I haven't given up."

"Then don't act like it. And if you need my help, call me. I'm here for you. But don't give up on me, and more importantly don't give up on you. You've got to bring this mess to a close."

Bob was right. It was time to drop the self-pity. He had too much to lose by giving up.

"Thanks, Bob. I'll be talking to you." Josh hung up.

"Josh, is everything okay down there?" Kate called from the upstairs landing.

"It's nothing. Everything's going to be okay," he said, but didn't know if he believed it.

CHAPTER SIXTEEN

The professional sat in his rental car, parked several houses down the street from Margaret Macey's ranch home. He tutted his disapproval.

"Margaret, Margaret, Margaret, what have you done?" he asked.

A police cruiser was parked outside the old woman's house.

The cops won't save you, Margaret. No one can save you. I told you that. The professional had warned her not to call the police; told her it wouldn't do her any good. He'd discovered the police involvement on his scanner three days ago when he heard a request for a patrol to visit Margaret Macey. And here they were again, and he was certainly surprised to find them when he had something new planned for his target. But he could wait for the police to go. He had underestimated Margaret. She had more strength of character than he gave her credit for. Her file had stated she was weak in all respects, but no matter, she could do little to hurt him and the police wouldn't be able to track him. The police were more of a nuisance than a problem. She would still die and it would look like natural causes. He waited.

He cast a quizzical eye over Margaret's house. The siding had seen better days and looked as if it had been run through the washer one too many times. The moss-covered wood shake was curled and hung at curious angles like the teeth of a none-too-proficient boxer. The small, unkempt yard was ugly, filled with dead plants and overgrown weeds. Margaret's house was no different than the neighboring homes. *A shitty little house on a shitty side of town,* he thought. He mused this was no way for someone to live out their twilight years. In the same position for over twenty minutes, his butt was going to sleep, so he shifted in his seat.

Like a cat watching its prey, he waited for the right time to pounce while he thought of the woman inside the house. *A hundred and fifty grand—who'd've of thought it?* An outsider would have never guessed Margaret Macey was worth a considerable six-figure sum, dead. But how many times had he read about some old bird who lived like a bum with millions in the bank? Sometimes he failed to comprehend what made people tick. He could get into the lives of those he killed, establishing what they did and when they did things, but the why always eluded him. A horn blared from behind and the professional checked his mirror. One car had cut off another turning onto his street and the cars had narrowly missed each other.

He returned his gaze and his thoughts to Margaret Macey. What a sad and pointless life she led. Life to her was a malignant disease prolonging her suffering. He wondered if anyone besides Pinnacle Investments wanted to see her dead. He considered that he would be doing her a favor, ending her life, like a considerate owner knowing when to have his beloved pet put out of its misery. The near-miss cars sped past. The force made his car shudder on its wheels.

Josh Michaels's life was in stark contrast to Margaret's. He had so much to live for. And if the professional was brutally honest, Michaels was a more challenging target and he couldn't wait to get back into the thick of that assignment. But to deal with Michaels effectively he had to be totally focused on the younger man and not have the distraction of Margaret Macey on his plate. Anyway, it wouldn't take much for the professional to rid himself of Mrs. Macey. A couple more phone calls and a personal visit should do it. He would be glad when he had disposed of her.

He remembered his nocturnal visit to Margaret's house two days after his first phone call from Josh Michaels's party. His investigation revealed no security systems and poor quality door locks, making it easy to get in and out when the time came. The operation had all the hallmarks of a slick assignment. It would be like taking candy from a baby—or life from an old lady. The professional smiled smugly.

His smile hardened. A swift disposal of one of his targets would get that prick, Dexter Tyrell, off his back. Tyrell's attitude annoyed him. The executive knew nothing of the work the professional did for him and the inventiveness needed to meet Tyrell's criteria.

"I want the people in the files killed in a way that does not raise suspicion. It has to look like an accident or a random act of violence. You know, accidents with machine tools, heart attacks, muggings, car accidents, hit and runs. I'm sure you don't need me to tell you what to do," Dexter Tyrell had said to him during their initial phone conversation two years ago.

It had been easy for him to say, but not as easy for the professional to carry out. With the hassle he was getting from Tyrell these days, it hardly seemed worth the ten grand per head. It might be time to move on to higher-paying assignments.

The professional was distracted from his thoughts by two police officers coming out of Margaret's house and saying something the hit man couldn't hear before closing the door. They climbed into the squad car and pulled away, the purr of the thudding V8 heavy in the air.

Time for some food, the professional thought. He unfolded a sheet of paper he removed from the car door pocket. He dialed a number listed at the top of the pizza delivery flyer. He gave his order, a name, and an address.

"When will it be ready?" he asked.

"Thirty minutes, sir," the disinterested pizza chain employee replied, and said, "Thank you for choosing Supreme Pizza."

"Perfect," he said and hung up.

He waited for his food to arrive.

"Like I said, we have a name to go with the number that called here Saturday night, thanks to Pacific Bell," the police officer summarized. "It was lucky you only had the one call Saturday. It certainly made our job easier."

"Can you tell me his name?" Margaret asked.

"Not until we've had the chance to speak to him ourselves."

"Are you sure he hasn't called since?" the other officer asked.

Margaret hesitated. There'd been the first call—the one where the caller changed from an insurance agent into a monster hell-bent on her destruction. Since then it had been a series of calls at all hours of the day and night, but he'd hung up before she could answer. She didn't know if it was him, her monster, but she thought it was. She'd learned to live in fear without ever seeing her intruder. But it hadn't stopped with just the calls—there'd also been noises. She was sure he'd been outside her home—footsteps on the deck, fingertips drawn down windows and the laughter, that evil laughter. No one without evil on their mind could laugh like that. She wanted to tell the officers, but she couldn't. She'd made two allegations to the police last year about trespassers at night and they hadn't believed her then and she didn't think they believed her now. They didn't need to know more; they had a name. It didn't matter whether it had been one call or a hundred, as long as they ended his reign of terror.

"Mrs. Macey," the officer prompted.

"No," she said, "there haven't been any other calls."

The officer looked unconvinced and frowned. "Anyway, we'll let you know what happens in due course. But it looks like we've got our man. I'm just glad you called. But you shouldn't have left it so long."

Three days had gone by before she called them. Three days of peering through the drapes at the slightest disturbance. Three days of receiving telephone hang ups and the visit to her door. Three days was a long time to live in fear.

How could she venture outside when he could be there waiting for her, just waiting to pounce? But confined to her home, her supplies ran out, supplies she needed. Toilet paper ran out on the third day. Lacking the courage to buy more, she forced herself to use torn strips of newspaper. Had it really come down to this, wiping her ass on scraps of paper like a common tramp? It had been a humiliating experience. Afterward, she'd cried for a long time. That demeaning act had made her mind up for her. Margaret called the police.

She was fully aware of the punishment if she was caught calling the police. He'd said he would know if she went to the cops. She had little choice. She was dead if she did and dead if she didn't. Deciding it was better to die trying, Margaret called them.

With no more to be said, the police officers saw themselves out. Margaret had done it. She'd made a stand against her assailant. And now the police had a name to go with the threatening caller's voice. It was over. She sighed with relief.

Although she was relieved, explaining herself to the police had overexcited her heart. She felt it pounding like a rock on a piece of elastic forever crashing inside her chest. Her breathing became strained, as if she were breathing through a sock jammed down her throat. Although her exertions were brief, she was sweating and her wet clothes clung to her old flesh. She staggered into the bathroom to take her medication.

Snatching her pills from the medicine chest, she swallowed down another two capsules with the help of some water. In an effort to calm her excited heart over the last few days, she no longer adhered to the prescribed dosages of her medication, instead taking the pills as and when she needed them. She surmised it couldn't be any worse than not taking them. Wiping her mouth on a towel, Margaret returned to the living room.

Instead of her symptoms abating after taking her drugs, they got worse. Her heart worked harder, her throat constricted and perspiration broke out at every pore like she had been running for a bus. But she wasn't running. She wasn't exerting herself. She stood rock solid still. The telephone was ringing.

The phone rang for the third time. Subconsciously, she knew it was *him,* her evil caller calling again. She could always tell when it was him. Somehow the tone of the phone changed when he called.

Margaret answered the phone.

"Ah, Margaret, you're there."

It was him. He sounded so congenial, but he always

started out that way. She clutched the phone with both hands—one hand held the handset normally and the other cradled the base of the receiver like it was a baby.

"It's been such a long time since we spoke."

"I've called the police, you know. They were here a minute ago. They're on to you. It won't be long before they pick you up," Margaret said triumphantly. He wouldn't be frightening her for very much longer.

"Oh, I know that, but I don't think they'll find me. And what did I say?" He paused. "I said don't call the police, didn't I, Margaret?"

"I'm going to put the phone down. I don't have to listen to you." She tried to sound strong, but her voice cracked.

"I don't hear that phone being put down," the oily voice said, a cruel smile hidden inside it.

"I will."

"Go on then, but I wouldn't recommend it."

Margaret had been standing, but the warning sapped the last of her energy and she fell into the chair next to the phone. What did he have in store this time? What torture would the caller inflict if she didn't comply with his demands? Terror became a serpent encircled around her chest and it squeezed. "Why?"

"Well, if I can't talk to you on the phone . . ."—he paused for dramatic effect—"then I'll have to make a personal visit. I know where you live."

That sent a chill through Margaret's body that made her shiver, and the sweat cooled on her skin. It felt like his hands touched her throat, not warm like a lover's, but cold like a killer's. Margaret mouthed a reply, but the words didn't come. She didn't know what to say.

"I could get into your home at any time. It's poorly maintained with shitty little locks that could be broken with a snap of my fingers." He snapped his fingers and a sharp crack resounded down the telephone line. "It would be child's play for a man like me. Christ! It would be child's play for a child."

"You're not a man," Margaret blurted.

Laughter echoed down the receiver and into Margaret's ear. She flinched at his mockery.

Someone banged on the door.

Involuntarily, Margaret jumped in her seat and released a short, startled scream lacking volume and power. Her hands tightened around the receiver until her knuckles glowed white under papery, translucent skin. Margaret stared at the door. Unlike Superman, she couldn't see through walls, but she knew it was him outside.

"Who's at the door, Margaret?" he whispered.

If Margaret had possessed the strength she would have shattered the phone in her grasp. She wanted the man to be on the other end of the phone. She wanted him there, not outside her door. Gripping the handset tighter was her way of keeping the monster in the phone and out of her living world.

Margaret froze. She saw him. The nondescript body behind the door moved and appeared at the window, his silhouette outlined against the drapes. He peered through the window, but the drapes prevented him from seeing anything. He wore a baseball cap turned backward on his head and what appeared to be a windbreaker fluttered in the breeze. He carried something bulky in his hands. Fear of what the object could be drove Margaret's mind into a frenzy. The figure moved back in front of the door.

"Have you guessed who it is?" he whispered once more.

Margaret jumped in her seat when he banged on the door again.

"Hello," he said from behind the door and paused. "Is anybody there?"

"Go away, go away," Margaret shouted back.

"Hey, it's pizza delivery," the man at the door said.

"I didn't order a pizza."

"I've got a delivery for this address for a medium thin crust pepperoni pizza that was ordered in the name of Macey."

"I didn't order anything."

"Well, somebody did, and I need to be paid for it," he said.

Margaret started to get out of her chair.

The man at the door mumbled something inaudibly and the voice whispered on the phone.

"How do you know who is at the door, hmmm? I could be lying my head off waiting for you to answer. Think about it, Margaret."

Margaret fell back into her seat, afraid of the warning the voice had given her. She had no idea who was at the door. It could be him ready and waiting for her to open the door, to blast her with a shotgun or stab her with a knife. Kill her right on her doorstep and laugh as he watched her die. Driven by fear, her heart accelerated another ten beats per minute. The serpent tightened its grip around her chest.

"Go away," she said.

"Hey, lady. I want to be paid for this pizza. I get stiffed with the bill if you don't pay."

"Go away," she said and burst into tears.

"Okay, okay. Thanks a lot."

Margaret heard him walking away, cursing her as he went. Relieved, she dropped the phone and wept uncontrollably. For a moment, she didn't notice the laughter coming from the phone. The voice called her from the receiver. She raised it to her ear.

"Gotcha," he said.

"What?" Tears choked Margaret's voice.

He waited for the crying to stop. "Margaret, go to

your door, you pissed off some poor pizza boy trying to make an honest buck."

Margaret hesitated, afraid that this was another of his falsehoods to make her come to the door.

"C'mon Margaret. Hurry before he goes. I wouldn't lie to you. I only did it to you make you realize the error of your ways—letting the cops know about our little chat. Chop, chop. Take a peek."

Margaret went to the window and pushed the drapes to one side. She saw the figure at the door had indeed been a pizza delivery boy, wearing a Supreme Pizza baseball cap and windbreaker. He was getting into a crappy, battered Honda sedan that was all dents and faded paintwork. A small flag on a small plastic pole was stuck on the roof with Supreme Pizza's name and logo emblazoned on it. He looked back at Margaret's house before racing away in a cloud of black smoke and squealing tires.

Relieved that her tormentor wasn't behind the door threatening to break her into pieces, Margaret's knees buckled and she collapsed, striking the wooden door. Slumped, she held herself up against the door and slowly, she slid to the floor in a crumpled heap. It was all a joke. A sick joke to scare, to torture, to put the fear of God inside her and he'd been successful.

Relaxing, she let her bodily systems slow and stabilize themselves. In the distance *his* voice babbled endlessly. Margaret ignored him. In the pit of her stomach a sensation relayed its rebellion. She felt unwell. She was going to be sick. Margaret tottered to her feet and made for the bathroom, where she puked. It was physical release from her mental torture. Dryly, she retched several times before finally vomiting.

"So, can I interest you in that life insurance policy Margaret?" he said to no one. The phone rested on its side on the armchair. He laughed, knowing that he was talking to an absent Margaret Macey.

The professional slipped the phone into his pocket. He was pleased with his efforts. He felt he had made real progress this time. He would have to follow up this incident with another very soon to ensure his target didn't get a respite. Margaret Macey was being reeled in like a prize marlin. She was tired and beginning to lose her strength. It wouldn't be long before she was another trophy to go above his fireplace.

But now he had a date to keep.

CHAPTER SEVENTEEN

Dressed in his sweats, Josh bounded down the stairs with his running shoes in one hand. He ran on the weekends and sometimes a couple of times during the week. A normal run was three to five miles, depending on how much time he had available. Since coming out of the hospital, he hadn't been running. It was time to get back into the swing of things. He sat down on the bottom stair and pulled on his shoes.

Kate came out from the living room. "Are you going for a run?"

"Yeah. I thought I would."

"Do you want breakfast now or when you get back?"

"I'll eat when I get back."

"How far do you think you'll go?"

"I might try a longer one, six miles or so, to make up for slacking, but I'll see how I go." Josh looked up as he tied his shoes.

"It'll do you good to get out and do something."

He saw Kate was pleased to see him settling back

into old routines. She probably hoped it was a sign their lives were returning to normal.

"I'll see you later." Josh gave his wife a kiss and slipped out the front door.

It was after nine and the daily commuters from Josh's neighborhood had already left for their jobs. He ran in the relative comfort of being free of thoughtless motorists. It was a good time to run.

Sweat displayed itself on his clothes and face. The morning was cool, but there was warmth from the sun unhindered by sparse clouds. Dark rings stained his gray sweatshirt under the arms and around the neck. His matching pants showed an unflattering dark line between the buttocks. Perspiration glistened on Josh's flushed face and hung in beads from his black hair like melting icicles. He hadn't intended to push himself that hard. His mind had been elsewhere. It had been fixed on Bell. She hadn't called since she'd turned informer to Channel Three. If she wouldn't come to him, then he'd go to her.

Instead of running his usual route, a circuit of the horseshoe shaped Pocket neighborhood, he jogged the roads that took him northward toward downtown. His Adidas-shod feet beat a path to Belinda Wong's new Sacramento home. The bitch had the audacity to give her address and telephone number to Kate at the barbecue. His anger drove him to run even harder.

He came to a gradual halt outside the small ranch style house. It was a corner plot and still had the FOR SALE sign outside that hung from a post buried in the lawn close to the sidewalk. Bent over with his hands on his knees, he panted heavily. Sweat fell from his forehead and hair, the droplets splashing on the sidewalk.

He crossed the short path to the front door and pressed the doorbell. No one answered. He pressed the doorbell again. This time he kept his finger on the button, which made the chimes drone tunelessly. He heard movement and took his finger off the bell. He disliked its sound as much as the person who moved unhappily inside the house did.

The door opened and Josh didn't wait to be invited inside. He barged in, knocking the door from the occupant's hand. If she could barge her way into his home uninvited, then he could do the same to her.

"Good morning, Josh. You found me. Thanks for the wake-up call." Bell showed no sign of annoyance at the abrupt entry. In fact, she smiled.

Josh looked about him, staring at the starkly furnished living room. "I suppose my money went to buy this place," he said.

Bell looked at him approvingly. She closed the door and leaned against it with her arms crossed over her electric blue silk robe. "Don't flatter yourself—you didn't give me that much money. No, I have a friend who's a realtor and I'm staying here while they sell it. It's a repo from a family that couldn't keep up with the payments. They just couldn't keep up with the changing pace of life."

"Is that last remark supposed to mean anything?"

"Read into it whatever you want."

Not waiting for a response, she walked into the kitchen, retying the belt to her robe as she went. Her feet made sticking noises on the vinyl floor. She filled the coffeemaker with water and grounds before switching it on. "Do you want coffee?"

Josh followed her into the kitchen and stood against the sink behind her. "No, I'm not here for a social visit."

"Shame," she said.

She stood on tiptoe to retrieve a mug from the cupboard in front of her. The robe climbed up the backs of her thighs to expose more of her slender legs. The material clung to Bell's stretching body. It accentuated her waist and buttocks hidden beneath the rich blue silk, becoming nothing more than a second skin. Josh's gaze crawled over her body—its structure, proportions and form. Her body moved gracefully, almost in a dance, all so very enticing. Once. She removed the mug and placed it on the counter next to the coffeemaker.

"Still attracted to me, Josh? Still want to fuck me, Josh? You can if you want." Her back still faced him.

The remarks took him by surprise. She knew him so well. He cursed himself for still being caught by her stupid games. Nothing about Bell was innocent. Everything she did was carefully calculated. She was tempting him. She knew he'd look, and look lustfully. She knew exactly how to pull his strings. But that was then and this was now. He was no longer her plaything. He was cutting the strings. "No thanks. Like I said, I'm not here to socialize."

Bell turned around to face him and met him with a grin. She pulled the sides of the robe apart, exposing her small firm breasts and erect nipples. Leaning against the work surface, she slid her right leg up her left and the flimsy cloth fell from her smooth legs, exposing her completely. "Are you sure? Are you sure I can't offer you something from the dessert cart?"

The coffeemaker coughed and spluttered as boiling water dropped onto the grounds. Steam rose through the vents and a rising cloud appeared from behind Bell's head.

Josh ignored Bell's offer, but not her exposed body. He cast a glance over what his senses had already experienced, then looked Bell in the eye. "I'm here about the latest television scoop on Channel Three."

She blurted out a laugh. She lowered her leg to the floor and her naked body disappeared behind the curtains of swaying silk. She wrapped the robe around her and retied it. "Is there more sweat on your brow than I remember seeing earlier, Josh?"

"Channel Three, last night. Was that you?"

"What do you mean? Is your past coming back to bite you in the ass?"

"You know exactly what I mean."

"Well, I cannot tell a lie. Yes, it was me."

"Why? I paid you."

Bell dropped the smile in favor of a sneer. "Yeah, but you thought you could push me around. So I thought I would apply a little pressure to ensure you don't do something stupid again."

"So, what's the next step, leak them my name?"

"No, you keep your end up and I'll make sure that they don't find out any more."

Josh knew that one day the money would dry up. It wasn't far off. "But what happens when I can't?"

She leered. "What do you think will happen?"

"So be it. If you're going to skewer me, it might as well be sooner than later. Go to hell. I'm not paying you anymore."

Bell looked as if he'd slapped her. "How dare you speak to me like that."

Josh was in no mood to listen to a tirade, and headed back to the front door. He ignored the expletives that followed him.

He opened the front door, but stopped in the doorway. "Here's the deal, Bell. I'm willing to give you a one-off payment that will buy your silence for good. After that, I never want to hear from you again. Let me know your answer in your own time."

She followed Josh out into the front yard. Her response mostly never graduated higher than four-letter words. "You'll be sorry, Josh."

Josh didn't know if he would, but he felt good. He

liked pushing people who pushed him. He broke into a jog.

Bell shouted after him from the lawn. Her threats soon lagged behind his pace somewhere in the distance.

Josh's run back home invigorated him. He felt stronger and more positive than he had in some time. Finally, he'd taken some control of the situation with Bell. She would no longer screw him up. He'd tipped the balance of power in his favor. Not even the notion that Bell could go straight to the media with his part in the Mountain Vista Apartments scandal could dampen his spirits. His inner strength came from the ability to bring closure to the subject. He no longer had to hide behind a wall of cash to keep the truth from coming out. He would take his chances and deal with whatever consequences arose.

Josh sprinted the last hundred yards to his home and shaved five minutes off the two and a half miles from Bell's. Although sweat ran down his body and he breathed like an asthmatic wood saw, he felt good. Josh took the key from his zipped pants pocket and opened the door.

"I'm back," he called out to anyone who would listen.

Not waiting for anyone to answer, he started pulling off his sweatshirt and made his way to the bathroom to shower. He had the sweatshirt over his head and one foot on the first stair when he was called back.

"Josh," Kate said.

He had completely pulled the aptly named sweatshirt over his head but still had his arms through the sleeves as he turned to face his wife. She sat on the couch in the living room with Abby and Wiener. The image reminded him of Russian dolls. Each doll removed from inside the others and stacked in descending order of size—Kate, Abby and Wiener. Like the dolls, the three of them possessed the same blank looks. The policemen from the hospital, Officers Brady and Williams, stood adjacent to his family in front of the fireplace. Josh had been blind to the patrol car parked curbside outside his house.

"Oh, hi, I didn't see you there," Josh said.

The policemen nodded in acknowledgment.

"Please excuse my condition. I'll just have a quick shower and I'll be with you." Josh smiled.

Nobody returned the smile.

"If you could be quick, sir. We have some details to go over with you and we do have other calls to make," Officer Brady said.

"Of course. I'll only be a minute." Josh shot up the stairs. He hoped they had good news about finding evidence on Mitchell, but judging by the look on everyone's faces, it didn't look like good news. He had no idea what else could have gone wrong.

Josh showered and dried himself swiftly, but not thoroughly. The T-shirt soaked up the damp patches from his body and a dark ring of wetness showed on his neck from where his hair had dripped. The jersey shorts did a similar drying job to his lower half. Barefoot, he returned to the living room. The two police officers were sitting on the couch opposite his wife. The room was in silence.

"Sorry to keep you waiting," Josh said.

"Not a problem, sir," Officer Williams said.

Josh sat on the arm of the couch next to Kate. "So you got my phone call?"

"Josh," Kate said, and placed a hand on his arm.

"Could we go somewhere a little more private? I prefer not to discuss this in front of your family," Officer Brady said.

Kate squeezed his arm. Josh looked at her and saw fear in her eyes. She nodded at him.

"We could go into my office," Josh suggested.

"Sounds fine," Officer Williams said.

Josh led the policemen to the small office toward the rear of the house. The policemen's boots squeaked on the hardwood floor. The way they walked on either side of him made him feel like the proverbial dead man walking, being led to execution.

Josh sat at his desk. The two officers bulged from the amply filled loveseat on the opposite wall. He asked the policemen if they wanted a beverage. They declined his offer.

"So you received my phone call at the beginning of the week about the man who ran me into the river? Well, like I said, I met—"

"Mr. Michaels, we aren't here about the traffic accident," Brady interrupted.

Josh was confused. "Then why are you here?"

"We're here regarding the threatening phone calls you made from this house," Brady said, and started to read Josh his Miranda rights.

CHAPTER EIGHTEEN

"What?" Josh's feel-good high drained out of him and a tingle of fear ran down his spine. He shifted in his seat. It no longer seemed to fit the contours of his body. He struggled for words to respond. Panic and guilt swam through his mind, bumping into things. Had Bell made some trumped-up accusation against him about their phone call? Could she have recorded their phone call? He couldn't remember if he'd said anything that could be construed as threatening. "I don't know what you're talking about."

"Margaret Macey alleged she received a threatening phone call. One in which a man claiming to be from an insurance company became abusive and made threats on her life," Williams said, reading from his notes.

Hearing the name, Josh relaxed. The name meant nothing. Whoever made the call, it had nothing to do with his problems.

"What can you tell us, Mr. Michaels?" Brady asked.

"Nothing. I have no idea what you're talking about."

The policemen didn't look as if they were going to accept Josh's denial as a defense. Brady eyeballed Josh with a stare hard enough to crack concrete. Josh felt the man didn't believe a word he'd said from the moment they'd met.

Brady sighed, "Mr. Michaels, you are the only male in the house."

"Yes."

"Then I find it difficult to accept you couldn't have made the call," Brady said.

"Why? I've never heard of this woman."

Josh showed signs of guilt. More than just water from his shower moistened his clothes—sweat appeared under his arms. He didn't know the woman, so why did he feel so damn guilty? His palms were sweating and he wiped them on his shorts under the cover of the desk, but fresh sweat immediately sprang from his dryed palms.

"Telephone records tell us the call was made from this house."

Brady leaned forward, placing more weight on his accusation. It was a cheap intimidation tactic and it worked. Josh felt a noose tightening around his neck.

"So how do you explain who made the phone call from here?"

"I don't know what to tell you. Honestly, I don't know anything. Maybe I misdialed her number and she's confusing it with her threatening caller."

"A fifteen minute wrong number conversation?" Brady said. "I don't think so, Mr. Michaels. Your call was the only one she received on Saturday night."

"Saturday night?" Josh's panic dissipated.

"Yes, Saturday night. Can you tell us what you were doing from seven forty-two P.M. until seven fifty-seven P.M.?" Williams asked.

"I was having a birthday party," Josh said.

"Where?" Brady asked.

"Here."

"And you have witnesses that will verify you weren't on the telephone at the times stated?" Williams asked.

"To the minute, I don't know," Josh snorted. "All I can tell you is that I was at my party and there are plenty of people who can confirm it."

"I'm afraid that isn't enough."

"Then what is?"

"There's nothing to say that you weren't on the phone to Mrs. Macey. You could have easily slipped out from your party to call her and returned with no one being the wiser," Brady said.

"That's a bit of a stretch, Officer," Josh said.

"Then what's your explanation, sir?" Brady asked. Flecks of spittle appeared on his bottom lip.

Brady worried Josh. The cop was convinced he was lying about something and he didn't see how he could shift the guilt. If he weren't careful, he'd end up getting arrested for something he didn't do.

"There were lots of people here—any one of them could have done it."

"That's not particularly nice, Mr. Michaels, placing the blame on your friends," Brady said. "Who needs enemies?"

Josh ignored the slur.

"It's convenient you were having a party when this phone call was made," Brady said

The cop just wasn't going to let this one go, Josh decided. "I didn't know I needed an airtight alibi."

"I think we have enough for now," Williams said, rising to his feet. "We may request you make a sample recording of your voice for analysis and for Mrs. Macey to identify. We'll let you know in due course."

Brady followed suit and stood next to his partner. "We'll see ourselves out, Mr. Michaels."

"Hey, hold on." Josh came around his desk to stop the policemen from leaving. "I want to tell you about the man I saw on the bridge who ran me off the road. I saw him again."

"Mr. Michaels, I would worry about yourself right now. You could be facing serious charges. I think sighting the man who cut you off on the road, while disturbing, is the least of your worries. And as I remember it, you didn't get a very good look at him," Brady said. He motioned to his partner to leave. Williams already had the door open. The officers left Josh's office and he watched them walk out the door. The door slammed shut with a sound reminiscent of a cell door.

The professional arrived at Bell's ranch house at six in the evening. The sun was descending on another perfect California spring day. He parked on a neighboring street to avoid any connection between him and the rental car.

That morning, he had been drinking coffee in Arden Fair's food court, reading the newspaper and observing a very bizarre physic reading between two black women when she called. She was pissed at the ultimatum Michaels had issued her. Her anger more than boiled over. It threatened to scald the professional as he listened on his cellular phone. She'd called minutes after Michaels left her and decided she wanted to vent her rage at someone. The professional was glad he wasn't with Bell. He didn't fancy being that close to the epicenter of her eruption and said he couldn't make it over for at least an hour. In that time she should have cooled off.

He decided that Michaels's blowup with Bell could only be to his advantage. Bell made the perfect puppet now. She wouldn't need much coercing to get her to do what he wanted. It was time to make Josh and Bell's relationship more volatile and bring it to a head. Mix the appropriate two elements to produce the explosive effect. It was basic chemistry.

He knocked at the door and Bell greeted him. She looked ready to kill. The more he got to know Bell, the more he knew not to get on the wrong side of her. He did plan to cross her, but by the time she realized it, it would be too late for her to do anything about it.

"Can I get you a beer?" she asked.

"Yeah, a beer would be good."

The professional took a seat in the sparsely furnished living room while Bell went to the kitchen. He recalled their initial date at the downtown restaurant after which Bell had brought him here. They'd discussed Josh, the affair and the subsequent money she'd blackmailed out of him. She expanded on her reasons for returning to Sacramento. She wanted be in her hometown instead of living in exile in San Diego.

Although bored by her personal outpourings, he absorbed every piece of information on a professional level. He'd offered ideas to get back at her adulterous lover, and she'd reveled in those ideas. It was after that she'd bedded him. It wasn't lovemaking, but lustful sex. The professional's revenge-filled suggestions had been an aphrodisiac. After an hour of adventurous sex, which the professional hadn't had in a long time, he suggested that she drop hints to the media about her ex-lover's crimes.

Bell returned from the kitchen, handed him an opened bottle of beer and sat down on the couch next to him. He positioned himself so he could face her when he spoke.

"Have you had time to calm down since you called me?" the professional asked.

"Does it look like it?" Bell demanded.

The professional smiled. "No, it doesn't, but that's

fine. The question is how are you going to use that anger to your advantage?"

"What do you mean?"

"You can be angry all week, but what good does it do you?"

He watched the gears turn in her skull. She was trying to think. That was fine. She could believe that she needed to, but he was doing the thinking for her.

The tension went out of her body. "It doesn't do me any good."

"That's right. So what are you going to do instead?"

"I'll do whatever I want," she said emphatically.

He smiled a snake's smile. "That's right. So what did Josh say?"

"He told me he wants me out of his life for good and he's willing to pay once more, then that's it. He doesn't care what I do after that."

"So he is willing to take his chances with the truth." The professional mused on that point. "That takes a strong man who believes he can survive the bullets you have to fire at him."

"He's not strong," Bell barked. "He's weak."

"So what do you want to do? Do you want more money?"

"I have enough of his money."

"Do you want him to go to prison?"

"I want him to appreciate me. To know the damage he's done to *me*." She jabbed a finger into her chest. "I want him to know I loved him and he trashed what we had."

Bell poured out a list of Michaels's wrongdoings and ranted about how he should be made to regret them. It was music to the professional's ears. Between him and Michaels, they'd created a monster hell-bent on destruction. "So revenge it is?"

She mulled that over, then smiled. "I suppose so.

What do you suggest—another call to Channel Three with more revelations?"

"Something like that. Something to grab his attention," the professional said. "A test of his convictions, if you will."

"Sounds good to me."

Bell took the professional's hand and placed it between her thighs. He felt the heat of her sex on his fingertips through the material of her shorts.

"James, let's discuss it further in the bedroom," she said.

The professional didn't object.

CHAPTER NINETEEN

"Jeez, I feel perfectly angelic. I've never been this high up before," Bob complained.

Josh found Bob's third crack about their bad seats annoying.

Bob nodded in the direction of the vendor trawling the aisles. "I wonder if the beer man has cotton balls for nose bleeds."

"I couldn't help it. You knew the Lakers game was going to be popular, and I've apologized for forgetting to book tickets earlier." Josh had bought the tickets on game day after Brady and Williams had interrogated him. After explaining himself to Kate he'd slipped out to the box office, but seating choices were limited.

ARCO Arena was busy, bubbling with excitement leading up to the tipoff for the Kings home game against the LA Lakers. Hopes were high for a good result. This year's team showed promise for a good playoff position. Even the basketball commentators had been kind to the Kings in their reviews of the team's chances. The lower levels of the arena were filled and very few plastic seats didn't have someone's ass filling them.

Josh and Bob sat way up in the northeast wedge of the arena, three rows from the wall. Even these less popular, cheaper seats were occupied. Josh didn't mind being this far away from the action. He'd offered the tickets to Bob more as an excuse to talk than to watch the game.

"Do you want a cold one from the vendor?" Bob asked.

"No, I'm okay." Josh felt cold. The temperature of the stadium seemed a degree or two too chilly for his liking.

Bob called to the overweight vendor. The middle-aged man, whose gut seemed genetically engineered to perfectly hold the tray of beverages, came over to Bob. Bob relieved him of a cup of Coors Light and the vendor relieved Bob of an excessive amount of cash. The vendor moved on to the next guy requesting his wares.

Bob looked at what his money had bought him. "Shit, I'm sure they're jacking the prices around here to pay players and coaches."

"You know you're going to be scalped in places like this," Josh remarked.

"They should have a beer cap as well as a salary cap," Bob muttered.

The respective coaching staffs called the players to the benches. After several minutes, the starting line-ups were announced and the players were met with a rapturous chorus of cheers, whistles, applause and abuse—the abuse, of course, aimed in the direction of the Lakers players. Like the fans, Bob was on his feet, the overpriced beer spilling from the plastic cup. On his feet too, Josh clapped appreciatively, though not really party to the frenzy going on below him; not to-night.

The crowd retook their seats in anticipation of the tipoff and Josh and Bob took theirs. As they watched the action on the court as the game neared its start, Bob spoke endlessly about the players' form, playoff chances, the NBA, who was hot and who was a waste of space. Josh listened, but said little.

The game began and Bob focused on the play.

"The cops came around this morning." Josh sat with his legs apart, bent forward with his forearms resting on his knees and his head down staring at the litter-strewn ground.

"Oh, yeah?" Bob said, not really listening. He was as alert as a prairie dog, twitching and shadow boxing with the flow of the game. "So they finally got around to talking to you about Mitchell?"

"No."

"So what were they doing?" Bob cursed when the Kings lost the ball and the Lakers gathered it up for an easy two points.

"They're looking to prosecute me for threatening some woman on the phone," Josh said.

The crowd moaned in disappointment as the Lakers made another basket. But to Josh it sounded like they were upset at his revelation.

Bob turned to Josh. "What woman did you threaten?"

"No one," Josh said. "I have no idea who this woman is who's making the allegations."

"You wanna find out her name?"

"I know her name, but I've never heard of her."

"So what are the cops saying?"

"They said that someone made a call from my home phone to this woman threatening to kill her. They have telephone records proving it was my phone."

"Shit."

"And because I'm the only man in the house, I'm their prime suspect."

"So what's her name?"

"Margaret Macey."

"That rings a bell," Bob said.

"You know her?" Josh said in surprise.

"I don't know. It's just that the name sounds familiar for some reason." Bob shook his head in failure. "Anyway, when did this threatening behavior take place?"

"That's the thing. It happened around eight last Saturday night."

"But you were having your birthday party."

"I know. I think that's the only reason that I'm not trying to post bail right now. They may want to make a recording of my voice for identification. That cop from the hospital has got it in for me. He didn't believe me about Mitchell bouncing me into the river and he doesn't believe that I had nothing to do with this threatening phone call."

Recounting the events from earlier that day brought Josh's fears back to the forefront of his mind. He felt he was going down for something, whether it was for his crimes or somebody else's. Nervous excitement consumed him like a plague, the disease breaking down his immunity to stress until it destroyed him. He stared blankly at the players on the court.

Bob looked around him to check if people were listening to Josh's excitable ramblings. The Kings fans were concentrating on their team's performance too avidly to notice their conversation.

"What cop?"

"Brady. Didn't you meet him at the hospital?"

"No. I knew they were around, but I didn't see them."

"Anyway, he's got it in for me," Josh said.

"Personally, you don't have anything to worry about. They can't prove it was you who made that phone call. Any one of us could have done it. And I think you'd have to be a special kind of stupid to threaten someone from your own phone. It's all circumstantial. They've got nothing."

"Yeah, but the cops think that's what I did to cover my ass. They think I arranged the party just to have lots of suspects present."

"Bullshit! They're screwing with you because they've nothing better to run with. So they're hoping you'll do something stupid to give them a lead. From their point of view they know they've got a no-hoper."

Bob made sense. If the cops had any evidence, they would have charged him. He could breathe easily, for now.

"Do they have a recording of the phone call?"

"Not as far as I know."

"If they take a voiceprint from you, they can't compare it. All they can do is play it to this . . ." Bob snapped his fingers as he searched for the name.

"Margaret Macey," Josh finished for him.

"I think a lawyer would have a fine time if the cops didn't interview all the other possible suspects at the party. How have they left things?"

"Just that they would get in contact."

"What about this voice recording?"

"They'll let me know."

"Yeah. They don't have a thing. What about James Mitchell?"

"What about him? They didn't want to listen. They didn't want to talk about anything except this phone call."

"So you never got to speak to them about the party?"

"No, they weren't interested."

"Bastards. We've got to get them to listen to us."

"What do we do?"

"Never mind that now, sit back and enjoy the game.

Let the Kings entertain you." Bob patted Josh's shoulder. "We'll worry about it after the game."

Josh sat back and joined in with the thousands of fans enjoying the game.

Bob sped along the interstate with the other drivers leaving the game. He was quiet, lost in thought, and Josh was no different. Bob's silence had little to do with the King's collapse during overtime. Something in his brain itched and he couldn't quite reach to scratch it. When Josh had told him about the police visit, something had clicked in his head, but the connection eluded him. It was the woman who had called the police, Margaret Macey. Her name meant something to him.

Suddenly, a car horn blared in annoyance. In a world of his own, Bob had let his car wander to straddle the line separating the second and third lanes. The noise snapped him out of his deep contemplation and back to the matter of car control. He jerked the car back into his lane. The disgruntled driver accelerated past Bob's Toyota.

"Shit, Bob. I can do without two traffic accidents in the same calendar month," Josh said just for Bob's benefit—he rarely got the chance to inflict the same brand of humor on his friend that his friend did on him.

"Hey, sorry, man. I wasn't concentrating," Bob said. He stared straight out into the darkness that lay at the end of the headlight beams.

"I'm waiting."

"For what?" Confused, Bob glanced over at Josh.

"For the caustic 'fuck you' remark," Josh said. "Are you okay?"

"Yeah, sorry. I was miles away, thinking."

"I'm sorry, did it hurt?" Josh said and laughed.

A pained expression appeared on Bob's face. "I'm

serious, Josh. I was thinking about that woman the cops told you about."

That brought Josh's humor to an abrupt end. "Margaret Macey, you mean?"

"Yeah, I remember hearing her name recently. And I think I know why. She's a client."

The remark silenced both men for a moment. The *thump-thump* of the tires striking the all too regular breaks in the worn concrete road punctuated the quiet.

"Shit," Josh said. "I don't know if that's something to feel good or bad about."

"Neither do I," Bob said.

"I don't think it adds much to my case that the woman I allegedly threatened is a client of a close friend of mine. I'm sure if Brady knew that he would have both of us in front of a judge in the morning."

"I'm not sure it means anything. It's probably a coincidence that you are both my clients. Now forget about it. I'll take you home and I'll look into it. If I find anything, I'll let you know."

"That's easier said than done," Josh said.

"All right, I shouldn't have told you. I can do without you going postal on me."

Josh conceded to Bob's request with little resistance. They lapsed into silence once more, their minds filled with more questions and fears. The car's interior reverberated with the drone of engine noise and the Doppler effect of passing vehicles.

Bob dropped off Josh outside his house, told him not to worry and promised he would get back to him. He waited until Josh let himself into his house and closed the door before driving away.

In his office, Bob returned the handset to the receiver. He'd just informed his wife that he'd be home late from the Kings game. He had to check out something at the office. Nancy had slammed the phone down with a sharp crack. *That's gonna cost me,* Bob thought.

He switched on the computer on his desk. While it booted up, Bob left his office and went to the filing cabinets in the archive. His computer database would have details regarding all his clients, including Margaret Macey, if she was a client of his firm. But his filing cabinets contained the personal correspondence he received from his clients and copies of original documentation.

He searched the deep drawer cabinet for Macey. The double cabinet contained two rows of files side by side, but didn't contain a record for Margaret Macey; only a Harrison F. Macey, who had a car insurance policy with Bob.

"Shit. That woman is a client. I know it," he muttered to himself.

He went back to his office. The computer's screen bathed the room in a spectral glow. He hit the light switch on the wall by the door. The fluorescent strips flickered into life with a *bink-bink* sound.

Bob shifted the heaps of paperwork strewn across his desk to the floor to make a clear spot.

"A messy desk is a sign of a sharp mind," he'd told his wife.

She'd responded with, "No, that's the sign of a lazy bastard."

In his opinion, both sayings had merit.

He sat at his desk and logged onto the network. He selected a file that provided client information. Typing Margaret Macey's name in the appropriate data fields, he started a search. The computer blinked a dialog box: *Searching . . . Please wait.*

"Thanks for the advice," he said.

The screen flashed up the information. There she

was—Margaret F. Macey, her address, age, social security number, and past business transactions.

"She *is* a customer," he exclaimed to his empty office.

With the mouse, Bob clicked the Print icon at the top of the screen. A whirring came from the printer in the main office and sheets of paper emerged from the machine like a white tongue.

Hungrily, he read through the information and the grin dropped from his face like a rock. Margaret Macey had made a viatical settlement with Pinnacle Investments less than two years ago and he'd acted as the agent. Bob's brief notes detailed that the medical treatment she had undergone for a weak heart was beyond what her medical insurance would cover. He'd helped her to pay for medical bills and provide cash for further treatment with the viatical settlement of her hundred and fifty thousand dollar life insurance policy that her dead husband had made her take out years before.

It wasn't the revelation that he'd acted as agent to Pinnacle Investments to both Josh and Margaret Macey that left him slack-jawed. He had hundreds of clients he'd dealt with for years, but he rarely remembered their names a few days after dealing with their accounts. But in this case, he remembered the senior citizen's name because James Mitchell had asked about her and Josh at their meeting.

Bob moved his chair back from his desk in shock and it came to an abrupt halt against something on the floor. He looked down. One of the castors on the swivel chair was wedged under some of the files he had placed on the floor. He leaned down and picked up the offending items. He looked at the names on the file covers—they read *Joshua Michaels* and *Margaret Macey*. He had removed the files to show them to James Mitchell.

*   *   *

Josh groaned when the telephone on the bedside table rang. Cursing, he reached across for it. The digital clock radio displayed the time—12:01 A.M.; he had been asleep less than half an hour. Kate stirred in the bed next to him.

"Hello," he said sleepily.

"Josh, it's me," the excited voice said.

"Bob?"

"I've found something. Margaret Macey is a client and you two are connected."

"What?" Josh sat bolt upright, taking the comforter with him. The sleep that had fogged his mind burned away like a morning mist.

"Josh, what's going on?" Kate asked, disturbed by the phone, then by her husband stealing the covers.

Josh stuffed the phone into the bedclothes for privacy. "Honey, go back to sleep. It's Bob and he has got something on that woman the cops say I threatened."

"Oh, Jesus, Josh. Leave it alone. This household has been in enough turmoil over the last two weeks without you looking for more."

"I'll tell you what he knows. Go back to sleep." Josh put the phone to his ear. "Bob, I'm going to change phones, hold on."

Josh got out of bed and slipped into a pair of shorts. He wondered if Bob had something that made sense of the situation he was being drawn into. Was there finally a beacon in the night leading him to safe waters? "Honey, will you put the phone down when I pick it up downstairs?"

Kate nodded, taking the phone from him, and started interrogating Bob on what he was doing.

Josh rushed downstairs in the darkness and switched on the lights. He took the cordless in the living room. Kate put the receiver down.

"What did you find out?" Josh asked.

"Margaret Macey is a seventy-seven-year-old woman living over in the rough part of downtown. And she had a life insurance policy with me," Bob said.

"She had?" Josh paced. He went from the living room to the dining room to the kitchen to the hall and back to the living room, switching lights on as he went. Disapprovingly, Wiener looked up from his bed in the kitchen. Josh couldn't be still when he was excited.

"Yeah. Like you, she made a viatical settlement and I was the agent."

"She sold her life insurance. When?"

"About this time two years ago."

He wasn't getting information quick enough; it was maddening—he wanted to scream. *Who did she sell the insurance policy to?* The fear grew within him that he already knew the answer. Josh paced even faster, as if to outrun his anxiety, and threatened to cut a groove in the carpets and floorboards. "Who to, Bob?"

"Our good friends at Pinnacle Investments."

He was right and hated it. Patterns were emerging. The truth was presenting itself. But it wasn't making any of this go away.

"I should have known," Josh said. "You've got a good memory to remember that, pal."

"But that's not the reason I remembered her."

Invisible spider's feet crawled up Josh's spine. "What do you mean?"

"The reason why her name meant something was because I had her file out. When James Mitchell saw me, he remarked on my past clients with Pinnacle Investments and he raised your name, Margaret Macey's and some other guy who died a couple of years ago. We discussed your files."

Josh stopped pacing. James Mitchell was his would-be killer, and apparently Josh wasn't the only one Mitchell had his sights on. But why? What was the point? The invisible spider crawled across his face.

Mitchell claimed he was an employee of Pinnacle Investments, but he wasn't. Josh could hear the penny dropping, but he didn't know what he was getting for his money. "I'm not insane. That bastard wants to kill me and this woman, but for what possible gain?" Josh asked.

"You've got me, pal," Bob said.

Josh started pacing again, this time faster. His mind worked through events as he lapped the first floor of his home at a brisk pace. Wiener, fascinated by his master's actions, joined him on his walk. "He must have used the phone here to call Margaret Macey. I gave him the chance when I told him about Pinnacle Investments sending the wreath."

"He's got some balls on him—big brass ones. You've got to admit that," Bob said.

Josh agreed. He couldn't deny it, but he didn't have to like it. The man had been in his home and committed a crime for which Josh was now the primary suspect.

"But why use your phone?" Bob said.

"God knows. Maybe he didn't expect Margaret Macey or me to be in any state to get the cops involved."

"Maybe. It all sounds risky."

"Only if it doesn't work."

"And it hasn't so far," Bob said. "Where do we go from here?"

Josh thought. The answer was to the cops. The more menacing this situation became, the more he knew he was out of his depth. Also, it was an opportunity to stick it to that disbelieving bastard Brady. That would be especially sweet. He now had a reason for his telephone number to be on Margaret Macey's telephone records. It was his chance to get the police off his back and prompt an investigation into James Mitchell.

"I'll talk to the two officers who were here and at the hospital. I'll tell them that not only did James Mitchell run me off the road, but that he had been checking up on Margaret Maccy and me, then came to my party and made the phone call to Margaret while he was here," Josh said.

"You're forgetting he doesn't exist. We couldn't find him. If these two cops think you're their man, they won't really give a shit about this invisible man. They'll think it's a bullshit story to get you off the hook," Bob said.

"But they have nothing better on me. Suddenly I decide to call a woman I have never met and threaten to kill her? What sort of case is that to convict on?" Josh asked. He knew Bob had his best interests at heart. Bob was right—the police could dismiss him for putting up a smokescreen. Nevertheless, he knew he needed to apprise the authorities of the latest developments.

"I don't know," Bob said.

"I'll see the cops in the morning," Josh restated.

"No, don't."

"Then what do you suggest?"

"I'll go to the cops. I'll tell them I had James Mitchell at my office. I have a record of his appointment and Maria saw him. And I'll tell them he made a call from your house and that you believe that he was the man on the bridge," Bob said.

Josh paced in silence, considering Bob's offer. "Okay. You're probably right. It'll sound better if someone independent can verify the story." He gave Bob the police officers' names.

Josh felt tired and excited at the same time. Tired because he'd walked at least a mile around the first floor of his home and excited because he felt he was finally getting somewhere.

"I'll tell you something I *do* know," Bob said.

"What?"

"Mitchell may have missed you so far, but I guarantee he'll try again."

CHAPTER TWENTY

The noise of the landing twin prop drowned out the minivan's radio. Josh knew the FAA building was close to Sacramento Executive Airport, but did not know its exact location. He spotted it on the opposite side of the road from the airport and made a U-turn at the light.

Pulling up in the parking lot, the jitters took hold of Josh. He had a plan, but now he wasn't sure how to play it. How could he convince the FAA the plane crash had been intentional? When he received the initial findings from them, he was just unsatisfied with the report; after seeing Jack Murphy, he was convinced it was not an accident.

According to Jack, the mechanical failures were possible, but unlikely. If the attempts on his life hadn't occurred, Josh would have brushed Murphy's comments off as ludicrous. However, recent events told him it wasn't that insane to believe his aircraft had been tampered with on purpose. And deep down he really knew Mark's death hadn't been an accident—the same way he had known it was his plane that had crashed with

his friend aboard as soon as he heard the newsflash on
the radio.

With the knowledge that his aircraft had been intentionally disabled to kill him came guilt. Mark wasn't
the intended victim. Christ, did he feel like the scum of
the earth. He'd been leaving Jack Murphy's hangar
when it hit him and the sour river taste returned to his
mouth. His mistakes had killed an innocent person.
Josh didn't know how he would live with himself, but
one way was to get the FAA and the NTSB to look for
signs of foul play and nail the bastard who'd done this.

Josh knew James Mitchell was Mark's killer. Mitchell
had forced him off the road into the river and he was
at his birthday party. He knew Josh and Mark were
flying partners and he knew when and where they
would be flying next. Josh had remembered the details
and put it all together once Jack Murphy had made it
click for him. All he needed was a look at his airplane
to be sure.

The FAA district office in Sacramento looked unas-
suming for its significance and was nestled uncomfortably amidst a number of drab commercial enterprises,
from mini-storage centers to breakdown recovery services to a smog check center. The office's jurisdiction
stretched out from Sacramento to the Sierras and up to
the Oregon State line. Responsible for enforcing FAA
rules and regulations from aircraft safety to pilot certification, the officials had the unenviable task of crash
investigations as part of their duties.

The district office was the headquarters for the investigation into the crash of his Cessna. The fatal nature of the crash caused it to be classified as an
accident and not an incident. The Safety Board called
the shots, and they'd assigned an investigator and sent
him to Sacramento.

Josh entered the building. The sign at the entrance

said, WARNING—ALL ACTIVITIES ARE RECORDED ON
VIDEOTAPE TO AID IN THE PROSECUTION OF ANY
CRIME COMMITTED AGAINST THIS FACILITY. That message didn't offer a warm welcome. In the reception for
pilot certification, a small middle-aged woman met
Josh with a broad smile. Her shoulders barely cleared
the L-shaped service counter.

"Hi there. How can I help you?" she asked.

"Yeah. I wanted to speak to Terrance Reid of NTSB,"
Josh said.

"Sure thing. Can I tell him who is calling?" She picked
up a phone on her desk and punched in a number.

"Josh Michaels. I'm the owner of the Cessna he's
investigating."

She relayed Josh's request and put the phone down.
"I'll take you up to him."

She led Josh along a corridor and up the back stairs
of the building to a small office in the corner of the second floor. She knocked on the door and entered without waiting for a reply.

"Josh Michaels," she said, ushering him into the office before closing the door.

The twelve-by-twelve office had several cardboard
storage boxes on the floor and a desk strewn with papers on either side of a laptop computer. Terrance Reid
was in his mid-fifties and efficient looking with a bald
head edged with a rim of iron gray at the sides and
back. A small portly man, the investigator stood up
from behind the desk and shook hands with Josh. His
welcome was businesslike. He was neither happy nor
annoyed to see Josh. Reid offered Josh a chair and he
sat down.

"Apologies for the room—I've got this while its
owner is on vacation. What can I do for you, Mr.
Michaels?" Reid asked.

"I wanted to speak about the investigation," Josh said.

"There is little I can tell you at the moment. An initial report is not due for another few days, and the final report will not be due for another month. And that won't be the end of the matter."

"I know you've spoken to the mechanic."

Reid nodded.

"You suspect the mechanic was negligent?"

Reid raised a finger and interrupted. "The mechanic may have been negligent, but no accusation has been made. However, initial findings have shown that several components were found unfastened, and the mechanic should have detected these at the time of inspection. Especially as this was the aircraft's maiden flight after a major overhaul. But Mr. Michaels, we are a long way off from a decision. Please don't jump to conclusions."

"Jack Murphy is convinced you're going to have him convicted for negligence," Josh said.

"I assure you that negligence hasn't been proven, but we do have concerns regarding Mr. Murphy's conduct."

"What about foul play?"

Reid looked puzzled. "I'm not sure there is any grounds for it. What makes you think that?"

"Jack Murphy is a good mechanic and Mark Keegan is . . . ," Josh corrected himself, "*was* a good pilot."

"However, things can go wrong and obviously did. There's nothing to give us grounds to suspect foul play."

Reid's response gave Josh an answer and a problem. The NTSB didn't think foul play was a factor, so how was he going to get them to consider it since Reid had dismissed the notion? He saw no point in explaining himself, as it was likely Reid would react to his claims the same way as the police had. "Can I see the aircraft?" Josh asked.

"No, I'm sorry."

"But, it's my plane," Josh protested.

"I have to inform you that it's not."

"Excuse me?"

"The aircraft became the property of the insurance company once you made the claim. The plane is in the ownership of the NTSB and the FAA until our investigation is over, then we hand it back to them."

"But I might be able to show you something you haven't seen."

"Mr. Michaels, my FAA counterparts and I are very experienced in this type of work. If we need you, we'll contact you. Anyway, the aircraft is still potentially a biohazard."

"A biohazard?"

"Yes. In a fatality, blood is spilled. Toxins, poisons and all manner of potentially dangerous hazardous materials may have been released as a result of the accident and may still be harmful to the investigation team." Reid sighed. "Look, Mr. Michaels, we investigate everything—toxicology, metallurgy, pilot performance, as well as mechanical failures. Rest assured we look into every aspect of an aircraft accident."

"How long before I'll be told what is happening?"

"I couldn't say for sure. I believe this case to be a straight forward one and a final result should be published in six months."

Josh frowned. He wondered if he'd still be alive in six months.

"Some cases can take years," Reid concluded.

"What about Jack Murphy?"

"If we find that he was at fault, then the NTSB will take action. We only have the power to fine or suspend. Only the federal justice system and you or Mr. Keegan's family may take things to another level—criminally, that is."

Josh gave it one more shot. "With all your years of experience, have you ever known of an accident of this type—loose bolts and unions?"

"Personally, I haven't. It is unusual, but not impossible. Don't let the uniqueness of the accident make you think there was foul play."

Josh opened his mouth to speak, but closed it. He wanted to ask more questions, but he knew it was pointless. Reid wasn't interested in Josh's beliefs. Josh read between the lines. The investigator saw him as a hindrance. His manner said Josh was a man too close to the disaster to be objective. Josh created an uncomfortable silence between the two men.

"Well, Mr. Michaels. I do have a case to investigate, so if you will excuse me." Terrance Reid went to the door and opened it. He offered his hand to Josh.

Josh stood up and shook the investigator's hand.

"Thanks for coming in, Mr. Michaels. I'll be in touch."

Josh knew he stood no chance of seeing his aircraft again. Nothing short of breaking into the hangar would gain him access to his plane. He couldn't afford to add a federal crime to his list of mistakes.

Josh was still preoccupied with his visit with Reid when he let himself into his home. He decided to leave the NTSB to do their job. There was little point in pushing them. Mitchell had done his job too well. They would never believe someone had planned the crash. There was too much room for doubt.

He walked into the house as Abby bounded down the stairs with an unstable looking Wiener sliding down with her. "Daddy, you're back!"

At least someone was pleased to see him.

"Abby, Abby, please be quiet for a moment, I'm talking," Kate said in a firm tone.

Abby stopped in her tracks and bit her bottom lip. "Sorry, Mom."

"That's okay, hon," Kate said.

Josh bent down to pet the excited dachshund at his ankles.

Kate put the phone back to her ear. "Sorry about that. Josh just came in. Well, like I was saying, I'll be coming back to work tomorrow." She paused while the other person responded. "Okay then, I'll see you Tuesday," she said and hung up.

Kate's decision surprised him. She hadn't mentioned returning to work early. He'd assumed she'd return to work when he did. He'd already informed his company he'd be back late Thursday morning after Mark's funeral. He felt betrayed. Abby held out her arms and Josh picked her up. "I thought you were going back to work after Mark's funeral on Thursday."

"I've decided to go back tomorrow. Abby's school started today and you're okay now. I've used most of my leave for this year and I want to keep some."

He frowned. Somehow he didn't quite believe Kate. It felt like she wanted to distance herself from him and his problems. She was pushing him away; rejecting him. He didn't think her decision was part of a healthy answer.

It wasn't going as well as Bob Deuce thought it would. He'd expected the police to be pleased that he had some evidence and logic to support Josh's wild account of the man on the bridge who now seemingly stalked his every move. Bob detailed Mitchell's visit to his office under the guise of an investment representative and his inquiry into Josh's and Margaret Macey's personal lives. Bob thought that Mitchell's presence at Josh's birthday party gave him the means and opportunity to make the threatening phone call. He hoped that his account would be the inspiration the officers needed to go after Mitchell and take the heat off Josh.

It didn't. The cops weren't biting. The bait wasn't juicy enough for them.

Bob had called the Sacramento Police Department from his office and made an appointment to see them. Luckily, he'd gotten a hold of Officer Williams, the more open of the two policemen—or so Josh had said. Williams promised Bob five minutes around lunchtime and he'd made the trip downtown to the city police station and parked opposite the library.

They led Bob to a drab looking interview room with gray walls, plastic chairs and a Formica-topped table. He sat in one of the uncomfortable chairs and Williams did likewise on the opposite side of the table, while Brady parked his rear on the corner of the table next to his colleague. Brady looked stony-faced and as impenetrable as a rock. Williams, as Josh described, was amicable and willing to offer his time. Bob could see that the police officers wanted to dump him and get on with their jobs.

"Do you know where we can find James Mitchell?" Officer Williams asked.

"I have no idea. That's the problem. I tried to get a hold of this guy after Josh told me about him, but he doesn't exist. The company he said he worked for has never heard of him."

"That's not a lot of help to us, is it, sir?" Officer Brady picked at a fingernail.

Bob felt his irritation grow. "I don't know. You're the cops, not me. What does your training tell you to do—eat doughnuts?"

Brady leapt up from the table. "You think that's funny, huh?"

Williams jumped to his feet, sending the chair sliding back behind him and snapped a hand to Brady's arm. "Cool it. Everyone, please."

The two men did as Williams demanded and retook their places.

"Mr. Deuce . . . can I call you Bob?"

Bob nodded.

"Bob, I appreciate what you are trying to do for Mr. Michaels and for us, too. But you aren't giving us very much to work with," William's said.

Brady's eyes smoldered. He looked like a restrained Rottweiler that needed feeding.

Bob took a breath, held it for a moment and released it. "I know it sounds weak, but it's all I have. I want you to know there's something to Josh's claims. I don't promise to understand it, but there's something odd happening."

Seeing the cops' response was less than enthusiastic, Bob decided to keep Mark Keegan's death and the funeral wreath incident to himself. Information based on Josh's gut feeling could be best described as weak even if it was bizarre. If they weren't going with the best he had to give them, they weren't about to be bowled over with the rest. He was reminded of something his fifth grade teacher used to say to him when she caught him daydreaming. *There's no point chasing after rainbows, Robert. You'll never catch up to one.*

Bob knew Josh's problems weren't illusions. They were problems worth chasing, but this wasn't the place to start.

Williams asked, "Can you give us a description of the man?"

Bob detailed a description of the ordinary-looking man. He was amazed how hard it was to describe Mitchell. He recalled the comment the cotton candy-headed receptionist had made at the River City Inn. "We have a lot of men here who fit that description."

"Thank you, Bob." The young, black officer wrote

down the description, but his enthusiastic smile couldn't hide the fact he thought the information was useless.

"What happens now?" Bob asked.

"We will follow up on your claims and we'll let you know in due course," Williams said.

The answer straight out of the police training manual, Bob thought.

"But with what we have gotten from you and Mr. Michaels, I'm not sure what we will turn up," Williams added.

Bob frowned. "Thanks for your time."

"No problem at all, sir." Officer Williams offered a hand.

Bob shook it and then Brady's, who said nothing, but glared intensely at him. Bob dismissed Brady's attitude as sour grapes and let himself be shown out of the station.

Unlocking his car door, he noticed the fifteen minutes left on the thirty-minute parking meter. *Someone else's lucky day*, he thought as he got into his car and drove back to his office.

Back in his office, Bob stared out the window. *Screw the cops*, he thought. *They won't take this seriously until they had Josh's corpse lying on the ground and Mitchell standing over him with a smoking gun.* If the police weren't going to do anything, then he would. Someone had to get to the bottom of the matter. Besides, he didn't fancy telling Josh the police intended to do nothing. He wanted to give his friend something positive, but what? Then it came to him—what about Margaret Macey?

Bob called up Margaret Macey's file on the computer. He picked up the phone and dialed her number off of the screen.

A trembling voice said, "Hello."

"Is this Margaret Macey?" Bob asked.

"Yes."

She was on the verge of tears. Her distress unnerved him. She sounded petrified. He spoke in a level tone, without emotion. "Hi, I'm Bob Deuce. Do you remember me at all?"

"No," came the short response.

"I'm from Family Stop Insurance Services."

"Oh, no. Not you again. You just want me dead. You want to kill me."

The old woman transmitted her fear through the telephone line and into Bob. The hair on the back of his neck prickled and sweat broke out across his forehead. Stammering, he tried to explain himself, but he couldn't get her to understand him. She fired off outrageous accusation after outrageous accusation at him.

"I know it's you and don't tell me you're the pizza boy this time. I'm not that stupid," she raved.

Bob struggled to get a word in between her rants. "No . . . no . . . Mrs. Macey, you don't understand. You're not listening."

"I knew it was you calling. I can always tell, and I know you've been inside my house."

"But Mrs. Macey—"

"You won't hurt me, you bastard!"

Before he could say anything further the phone line went dead. Margaret Macey had hung up.

The encounter left him breathless. He sat there for several minutes trying to let his heart rate settle. The sound of his blood pumping around his body sloshed in his ears. He felt very old for his age. He wiped the sweat from his brow. What the hell had happened to this woman?

"Well, that wasn't the positive news I was hoping to give you, Josh," Bob muttered to himself.

* * *

Josh and Kate didn't speak. They sat at either end of
the couch with a distance between them measurable in
more than just feet. Abby was in bed asleep. Prime-
time television had come to an end, making way for the
nightly news. The station went to commercial. A pre-
view for the Channel 3 News flashed up and the anchor ran through the main stories for the upcoming
program. The lead story was something Josh had been
expecting.

"More on that exclusive to Channel Three—
corruption in the construction of the Mountain Vista
Apartments in Dixon. Our source has named names involved," the anchor said.

Flatly, Kate spoke over the television. "Is that you?"

"I imagine so," Josh said in the same tone.

Sitting in renewed silence, Josh braced himself for
the news program to start.

The news began with a summary of the headlines before the concerned-looking anchor went into the lead
story.

"Last week, we brought you an exclusive story about
the alleged scandal over the building of the Mountain
Vista apartments in Dixon. Our source, who still
wishes to remain nameless at this point, has provided
further details of the corrupt activities conducted during the building of the apartments.

"Allegedly, Johnston Construction, Inc. intentionally built the apartments below standard to ensure
they made a substantial profit. Knowing full well the
construction wouldn't pass the inspection, Johnston
Construction's owner, Mike Johnston, bribed the
building inspector, Joshua Michaels. Our source alleges Mr. Michaels accepted ten thousand dollars
from Mr. Johnston.

"I must express we as yet have not sought comment
from either Mike Johnston or Joshua Michaels."

The anchor introduced the field reporter and the camera switched to the reporter outside the Dixon apartments. The reporter relayed information similar to what the anchor had expressed.

Josh had his answer. Bell had made her decision. He supposed she'd decided to decline the money offer and go with revenge. The bonds of the blackmail that held him so tightly were broken. Josh was free. But he was now in the hands of others over whom he had no control. He'd gone from the mercy of Bell, his blackmailer, to the mercy of the media, police and anybody else investigating the claim. He was now fair game to anyone who wanted a piece of him. He'd seen enough and reached for the remote control on the coffee table.

"I'm still watching that," Kate said icily.

Josh turned to her. She stared intently at the screen, her face devoid of any facial expression. He left the remote and leaned back into the couch.

The Channel 3 Nightly News team moved onto another story.

"Do you think Belinda is their source?"

"Yes. I gave her the opportunity to make her final demands because I refused to be blackmailed anymore," he said.

"What was her final amount?"

"Nothing. She hadn't given me an answer, until now." Josh nodded at the television. "I think she would prefer to see me pay in other ways." His mind drifted away to his affair with Bell. She had cut some of the puppet strings, but the ones that made Josh dance were still attached.

He continued. "I want you to understand things are probably going to get worse before they get better."

"Life with you over the past two weeks has prepared me for every eventuality. Shock after shock—the impact is reduced with every new occurrence. Josh, I don't think anything would totally surprise me," she said.

It was difficult for Josh to respond to her coldness. He composed himself before speaking.

"If someone inspects those apartments, they will find faults and they have a record of my report giving the construction the green light. They'll have enough evidence to convict," Josh said.

"What will they do to you?" Kate asked.

"I don't know what they do in these cases." Josh was silent for a moment. "What will you do?"

"What will *I* do?"

Josh moved across the couch to be close to her and took her hand in his.

For a moment, Kate stiffened at his contact, but then she relaxed.

"Will you stay with me regardless of the outcome?" he said.

Kate looked away.

Josh placed a gentle hand on her jaw and turned her head toward him. "Look at me, please. Will you?"

"I don't know, Josh." Tears welled in Kate's eyes. "I really don't know."

CHAPTER TWENTY-ONE

For Dexter Tyrell, this was a rare excursion from his two usual haunts—his home and Pinnacle Investments. He'd booked the hotel room for the day although he only intended using it for a few hours. It may have seemed extravagant at five hundred dollars, but in the long run it was a drop in the ocean. The room was for work-related business, but not the sort of business his colleagues would understand. It was better for everyone if his colleagues didn't observe him.

His subversive program, killing the firm's viatical clients, was faltering. Two case files worth over six hundred thousand dollars in company revenues were being held up because of the incompetence of the hit man, and that impacted dearly on the disposal of other clients. Tyrell's decision might be risky, but it would certainly get his project moving.

Slumped in the comfortable padded armchair of the well-appointed hotel room, Tyrell sat cross-legged, his left over his right. The left leg rocked back and forth while he listened to the ringing of the cell phone in his hand. *Last chance, my friend.* His hit man had one more opportunity to put things right. Tyrell straightened in his chair and uncrossed his legs when the phone was answered.

"Yes?" the professional said.

"I haven't heard from you in the past couple of days. I assume from that you haven't succeeded in your tasks," Tyrell said.

"Like I've told you before, these things take time. You just have to be patient. Rest assured, I have laid the foundations."

Tyrell's snide remarks failed to raise the hit man's ire. That pissed Tyrell off. He wanted something out of this son of a bitch.

"My patience in running thin. You've had more than enough time to take care of these people and you haven't."

"How would you know how much time it takes?"

Prima donnas, they all think they're God's gift, he thought. "Based on your previous assignments. And don't get pissy with me. I know I haven't got any experience in your profession, but I do have realistic expectations and you're not living up to them. How long do you think it will take until you have completed your assignment?"

"Another week."

"No," Tyrell said matter-of-factly. "I have another three targets lined up for you worth over one point five million dollars. I want them all cleared up in the next two weeks."

"I don't think I can do that. The plans are laid and they'll have to run their course. I may be able to advance them a little, but I can't make any guarantees."

"I don't care about your plans. Do something different." Tyrell was losing his temper with the professional. "The time has come for an alternative approach. I don't care how you do it, but I want them killed. No more fancy plans for accidents—just straightforward assassinations."

"Are you suggesting I just shoot them from the nearest clock tower?"

Tyrell ignored the crack. "How many times have we seen tragic house fires? We live in a world of muggings, hit and runs, rapes, murders, et cetera. Pick one. Impress me. You have two days." He hung up without letting the professional comment further.

The conversation had gone the way Tyrell had expected. The professional wasn't the man he'd hired two years ago. He was incapable of the quick turnaround Tyrell needed. It was time to bring in someone else. A new broom always swept better than an old one and maybe that new broom could dispose of the old broom as well.

"The job's yours if you want it," Tyrell said to the other man in the room.

The other man stood in front of the window looking out over the pleasant grounds from the fifth floor room. The trees and well-manicured lawns were illuminated in the early evening darkness by the security lights positioned all around the premises. He turned his back on the view and faced Tyrell.

He was a big man, tall and muscular, and his suit did little to disguise it. His crew cut hinted that he might be a military man or some outcast from a government agency. Tyrell didn't really care or want to know. He never wanted to get that close to his outsourced talent. His colleagues were bean counters and analysts, not killers. These people made him uncomfortable, but they were a necessary evil to ensure success. They were resources to be used for specific functions—like a computer or a subordinate, a means to an end. Because of the extreme course of action Tyrell had undertaken, these people were essential if he was to get back in favor with the Pinnacle Investments board.

"Don't you believe your man will succeed?" he asked.

"To be honest, I don't. I think he'll prefer to stick to his own plans," Tyrell said.

"Wouldn't you prefer I take care of your next targets while he finished his current assignments?"

"No, I wouldn't."

"Personally, I prefer not to take over another operative's assignment."

Jesus Christ, these guys are paid killers. They murder for financial gain, but they have all these fucking ethics. Honor amongst thieves . . . what a load of bullshit. Tyrell had no time for the politics of the industry. He just wanted results. "Do you want this job?"

"Yes," his new killer answered.

"So we understand each other?"

"Yes."

"Good." Tyrell picked up his briefcase and placed it on his lap. He removed two files from it and dropped them on the bed.

The newly hired killer picked up the files. He sat in another of the comfortable chairs by the window. He opened the first file and flicked through the documents, then did the same with the second file.

"Like I told your brother in firearms, you have two days to make Joshua Michaels and Margaret Macey into obituary articles. No fancy stuff, okay?"

The killer looked up from the files and nodded. "What about my . . . colleague? What do you want done with him?"

"He's a liability. I would like to have him removed from my employ, as it were. If you can find him, you can kill him. I'll make it worth your while."

"How do I find him?"

Tyrell removed another file from his briefcase and dropped it on the bed. "I thought you might be interested. The file contains all the information I have on him."

The killer picked up the scant file, much thinner than the previous two. He sat down again, scanned the file and nodded in agreement.

"I don't know his name or his address. All I have is a post office box that all monies and files are directed to. I've included the cell phone number I've contacted him on. Be warned, he regularly changes his number. I thought a man of your profession could trace his location by the number," Tyrell said.

The killer placed the files in his briefcase, stood up and went over to Tyrell with an outstretched hand. Locking his briefcase, Tyrell got up and shook the hand offered.

"I don't think there's anything else I need to know. If you'll excuse me, I'll see if I can't get a flight out tonight. I'll contact you as soon as I have news."

"What do I call you? Our intermediary didn't say."

The killer paused for a moment, then smiled. "Mr. Smith."

Tyrell smiled back. "I'm sure there are a lot of men in your business with that name."

"A few." At that, Smith released Tyrell's hand and departed.

Tyrell checked to make sure he had everything he'd brought with him. He was pleased with himself. Things would be changing for the better, and fast. *I can see the checks rolling in,* he thought.

"Bang, bang, who's dead?" he joked to himself.

CHAPTER TWENTY-TWO

Mark Keegan's service was at St. Thomas's Anglican Church. Josh's flying partner hadn't been a religious man, but his sister was and she wanted a religious ceremony. The church was half filled with relatives, co-workers, flying club members, airport officials, and friends. Josh sat with his wife and daughter in a row of pews waiting for the ceremony to begin.

Organ music and echoing conversations drowned out the silence within Josh's family. He looked at them. Kate stared into an infinite distance beyond the walls of the church. Abby sat between Kate and him, studying the floor and absently clacking her shoe heels together. They weren't a happy family. It was a blessing that Kate had returned to work, Abby had school and he had the house to himself. Everybody had their space.

Josh let his gaze wander and it fell upon the coffin. The simple pine casket with brass fixings rested at the head of the church, garnished with funeral wreaths. Josh struggled to believe Mark was dead. It didn't seem real. He couldn't imagine Mark's body was inside the box. It couldn't be true. Mark was his friend and his living image preoccupied Josh's mind, but it kept being replaced with the one of him slumped over the Cessna's control column. It seemed the funeral was a hoax, a big joke played on Josh by his friends as a belated birthday prank. The urge to go up to the coffin and tear off the coffin lid was becoming impossible to resist. But deep down, Josh knew the truth. Mark was dead, killed by the man trying to kill him. An innocent man lay dead because of him. He didn't want to be there. He shouldn't be there. His presence seemed sacrilegious.

Josh felt a hand on his shoulder.

"Hey, Josh," Bob said.

Josh turned to the row behind him, where Bob was taking his seat. "Hey, Bob."

Kate and Abby turned to Bob and they said "Hi" to each other. Abby managed a smile for the first time that day.

"Thanks for coming, man. You didn't have to," Josh said.

Bob leaned forward. "Yeah, I know, but I was talking to the guy the day before the crash." He leaned farther forward and whispered, "Can I talk to you afterwards?"

"Yeah, no problem."

Bob sat back. The wooden pew creaked under his weight. He nodded to a group of four people and moved over to let them sit down.

The minister took his place at the lectern and the organ music died. A hush came over the congregation. The minister introduced a hymn and everyone stood and sang. The service echoed throughout the bowels of the church and sniffs and gentle sobs punctuated the proceedings. Mark's sister, Mary, gave a tearful eulogy about Mark's love for life. The service ended with a final hymn.

Those gathered slowly filed out of the church and into the courtyard. The mourners clumped into groups and made awkward conversation. Josh excused himself from his family and made a beeline for Jack Murphy, who was heading toward the parking lot.

"Jack." Josh placed a hand on the mechanic's shoulder. "I'm glad you came."

"I wasn't going to, but Mary asked me," he said.

"Why weren't you going to come?"

"Why do you think?"

"Don't be stupid, nobody blames you. Mary doesn't and I don't."

"Well, I do."

"I spoke to the NTSB investigator a few days ago. They aren't blaming you. They have their suspicions, but no reason to take any action against you." Josh exaggerated the truth, hoping to alleviate the mechanic's depression.

"For now," Murphy said.

Josh frowned.

"I've gotta go," Murphy said. Quickly, he moved away from Josh.

"Jack, it's going to be okay. Trust me." Josh spoke to the mechanic's back. He watched Murphy get into his car before returning to his family.

He spotted Kate and Abby speaking to Mary and her husband. Bob intercepted Josh before he got to them.

"Hey, pal," Bob said.

"You talk to the cops?" asked Josh.

"Yeah," Bob replied.

"I assume it didn't go well, judging by that answer."

Josh and Bob were interrupted before any more could be said.

"Josh."

Mary stood behind him. He turned to her. She was

the female embodiment of her brother Mark—small, only five feet, slight of frame with the minimum of curves. Only two years Mark's junior, she possessed the same salt and pepper gray hair.

"Thanks for coming." Smiling, she took Josh's hand in hers and clasped another on top of his.

"Oh, it's the least I could do," Josh said.

"He thought of you as a good friend."

"Thank you."

"The will has been read. You got the letter from the attorney?"

"Yes, I did. I know about the plane."

"I just want you to know I'm glad he left you his share of the aircraft. God knows what I would have done with it." Momentarily, the smile slipped. "Although I'm not sure what good it is to you now."

"I don't know. It's in the hands of the insurance company."

The smile came back, bigger and brighter. "I hope you will do some good with the settlement."

"Of course."

"Are you following on to the cemetery?"

"Yes."

"Good." Mary turned her head to Bob. "And you?"

"Oh, Mary, this is a friend of mine, Bob Deuce."

Mary shook hands with Bob.

Bob hemmed and hawed, but Josh answered for him. "Yes, he'll be coming along."

"Good. We'll be leaving in five minutes." Mary moved onto the other well-wishers.

"We'll talk on the way to the cemetery, okay?" Josh said.

Bob agreed.

They joined Kate and Abby. "Are you going on or leaving?" Josh asked.

"I'm going to take Abby back to school, then I'll go back to work. I can see you and Bob have something to discuss."

Josh frowned. He dropped to one knee and kissed Abby. "I'll see you after school, kiddo."

"Okay, Dad," Abby said.

Getting up, Josh said to Kate, "I'll see you later."

"Yeah," Kate conceded. Taking Abby's hand, she turned on her heel and strode off for the Dodge Caravan.

Bob waited until Kate and Abby were out of earshot. "It got a bit chilly all of a sudden, don't you think?"

"Yeah. Things aren't going too well, as you can imagine. She's none too pleased with me these days ever since Channel Three turned up on the doorstep."

The morning after Josh's name had been given out on Channel 3, the news crew landed demanding a comment. Kate had answered the door to them. Pictures of a flustered Kate before Josh had intervened with a stern, "No comment," made the evening news. Other local news stations repeated the process, as did the rest of the press. Josh had been screening calls ever since.

"You can't blame her," Bob said.

"Yeah, you're right," Josh agreed.

Bob looked at him. "Are they still trying to get an interview?"

"I've told them 'No comment' about a dozen times. I think they've got the message." Josh stared at his wife and child. "Come on, let's talk in the car. I'll drive."

"You got a new car?"

"The loaner from the insurance came through yesterday."

A hush came over the crowd. Josh turned. Mark Keegan's coffin was brought out and loaded into the hearse. This heralded the end of the service and the mourners filed into the parking lot. In respectful fashion, the hearse, limos and cars poured out of the church onto the roads.

Josh merged with the flow of traffic, taking his own route to the graveyard. The cemetery was a twenty-minute drive from the church, which gave him the perfect opportunity to talk privately with Bob. Murder and attempted murder weren't appropriate conversation for the graveside.

"What happened with Starsky and Hutch?" Josh asked.

"Wipeout. You're right about them, though. Brady certainly has a stick up his ass. But I couldn't make out whether it's about you or if he's just made that way. Williams listened, though."

Josh nodded, agreeing with the character assessments.

Bob continued, "I don't think they're going to do anything. To be honest, we don't have anything to give them."

"What do you mean?" Josh snapped.

"We have a man with a fake name, a fake job and no permanent address. In their opinion, we ain't doing them any favors."

Josh cursed. "So we got nothing out of it."

"I dunno, Josh. I think I put the seed of doubt in their minds about the phone call to Margaret Macey."

"How did you end it with them?"

"They said they'd call me if they needed me further."

With his mind on the conversation, Josh's focus wasn't on the road. He failed to see the woman with the stroller stepping into the crosswalk until the last moment. He slammed on his brakes and the front wheels skidded over the first of the two white lines. The force threw both men forward, but the seatbelts kept them restrained. The woman jerked the stroller and child back from the brink.

People on either side of the road stared and frowned

disapprovingly. The woman with the stroller attempted the crossing for the second time. She chewed Josh a new asshole as she crossed. The windshield muted her abuse and protected him from the evil she would do if given the chance. Blissfully unaware, the child slept through the drama.

Josh released the breath he had held since violently applying the brakes. Openmouthed, he fixed his eyes on the woman insulting him as she walked.

"Nice one, Centurion. I nearly had a cardiac arrest. If we're lucky, we can ask the minister if he'll do a group booking at the graveyard," Bob said.

Josh wiped his hands over his face. "Shit, sorry, man. I was miles away."

"Unfortunately, I was right here in the thick of it."

A car horn tooted from behind and Josh glanced in the rearview mirror.

"C'mon pal. Focus now and let's see if we can't get to where we're going in one piece," Bob said.

Josh removed his foot from the brake and inched down on the gas. Slowly, the car accelerated away from the intersection.

Again, Josh's focus wasn't on driving or his problems. His mind was a blank. Occasionally, his mind flicked back to what could have happened if he had hit the stroller. He shuddered at the thought.

"I did something you may not thank me for," Bob confessed.

"What do you mean?"

"After the cops, I wasn't happy with their lack of interest in the case. I wanted to do something more . . ."—Bob searched for a suitable word—"more proactive."

"And?" Josh prompted.

"I called Margaret Macey." Bob was already wincing as the old woman's name came out.

Josh felt the air around him squeeze. Anything anybody did to improve things only made them worse. He swore if he did nothing, it would make matters worse. He switched lanes to make a left turn.

"I thought I could get some information from her that could help us," Bob said in his defense. He clutched the overhead door strap for support as the car made the turn.

"Well?"

"She went into wild hysterics."

"Shit, don't do me any favors."

"Yeah, I know, but listen!"

Josh fell silent.

"She went loopy as soon as she heard I was from an insurance company." He paused. "She really does think someone's trying to kill her."

"What do you mean?"

"Margaret Macey thinks someone at her insurance company is trying to kill her." Bob allowed the information to sink in for a moment. "What have you and she got in common?"

"We've both cashed in a life insurance policy?"

"Yeah, not only that, but you cashed them in with the same insurance company—Pinnacle Investments."

"What are you getting at?"

"James Mitchell said he was from Pinnacle Investments and when he came to me, he asked about you two. I know we've considered Mitchell may be working with Bell, but we haven't considered that he's working with Pinnacle. I think Pinnacle Investments may be at the root of all this."

"Where did you get that idea from?" Josh asked.

"It came to me last night, while I was in the tub."

"The tub?" Josh scoffed.

Bob sighed. "I know it sounds wild, but to me it seems worth further investigation."

"No, I'm sorry, Bob."

"It's no wilder than the shit you've come up with in the last few weeks."

The remark struck Josh hard, a kidney punch when he wasn't looking. He knew he'd driven family and close friends mad with his rants, complaints, revelations and general paranoia. In days of old, they would have probably bored holes in his head to let the demons out.

"Okay," Josh conceded. "What do you want to do about it?"

"I don't really know. I thought I would check out Pinnacle Investments's operations," Bob offered.

"Before you poke your nose into things too far, I think I'll pay Margaret Macey a visit."

"Are you crazy?"

"No, not if we have something in common like some psycho trying to kill us. Maybe she knows something we don't."

"What about the cops?"

"At the moment, I'm damned if I do and damned if I don't. I haven't got anything to lose."

Bob frowned. "I don't know about that."

Josh glanced at his friend. Bob looked like he was trying to pass a football-sized kidney stone. Josh smiled at him.

"I don't see what you have to fucking smile about," Bob said, nonplussed.

"Bob, I don't say it often. You're a good man and a good friend. And I do appreciate it."

The big man's cheeks reddened with embarrassment. "Just drive."

Josh's good mood didn't last as the cemetery came into view. He swung the car into the garden of bad memories with the other arriving vehicles.

* * *

Josh felt strange pulling into the parking lot of Red Circle Engineering. It felt like the first day of school all over again. He'd only been away from the company less than three weeks, but in that time, his world had been turned on its head. The place felt unfamiliar, as if he'd been away for a hundred years.

Once he was in the building, he didn't want to be there. Work was pointless. The decisions he made here paled in significance to the life and death decisions he needed to make outside. He stayed, though. He had a façade to portray. He had to let those people know he was doing okay and all was well with the world.

He flashed a car salesman's smile to Tanya on reception duty, an attractive blonde in her late twenties. Her smile looked stapled in place. She looked at him as if he carried a collection of severed heads by the hair in one hand instead of his briefcase.

"Hi, Tanya. I'm back," Josh said, like he was on happy pills.

"Hello, Josh. It's nice to see you." Tanya spoke like she was trying out the words for the first time.

Josh left Tanya and her constipated smile to their own devices. Between the reception area and his office, he encountered a number of colleagues who seemed to lack the time to chat beyond the merest of pleasantries. Others at desks ensured they didn't make eye contact with him. He found it increasingly difficult to smile. By the time he reached his office, he'd worn the happy façade to the bone.

"Hi, Jenny," he said despondently.

Deep in concentration, Jennifer Costas, the procurement department's administrative assistant, looked up from her computer. A plain-looking woman in her forties, tall with narrow shoulders and big hips, she was Josh's invaluable sidekick. Surprise replaced her look of concentration.

"Josh, it's good to see you," she said.

"Hopefully, you can fill me in on recent events," he said and went into his office.

Jenny followed Josh into his office.

He put his briefcase on the floor by his desk and dropped into his chair. Surprisingly, his desk was relatively bare. Usually, after a week on vacation, paperwork would be spilling off the sides.

"What's going on? Fill me in," Josh said.

"Josh, Mike Behan wants to see you right away." Jenny wrung her hands in front of her, guilt-ridden anxiety etched into her face.

"What now?"

"As soon as you arrived, he said."

Mike Behan, the commercial vice president of the firm, had his office on the opposite side of the building. Josh had to make an uneasy return journey in front of his equally uneasy coworkers. Again, heads buried themselves into paperwork that didn't deserve the attention.

Why doesn't this feel like it's going to be a pep talk from the boss? he thought as he approached Mike Behan's secretary. Lisa saw him immediately.

"Hello, Josh. Mike will see you right away," she said.

Josh went in and found Behan speaking on the phone. He leaned back in the leather executive chair with one hand on the desk. Seeing Josh, he beckoned him in with a wave of his arm and a smile. Behan finished up his conversation and put the phone down. He straightened in his chair and sat with his forearms on the desk and his fingers interlaced.

Josh sat down on one of the seats at the board table abutting Behan's desk. Lisa closed Behan's office door. A closed-door meeting meant something was wrong. It put him on his guard.

"Good to see you, Josh," he said.

"Thank you."

"Are you recovered from your accident?"

"Sure, no problem. Dry as a bone."

Behan laughed. "Tell me what happened."

Josh recounted the events on the bridge, but slightly distorted the facts. He didn't mention the thumbs-down incident; instead he replaced it with the assailant giving him the finger once the car was in the river. Behan nodded and looked shocked at the appropriate times.

"And the cops can't do a thing?" Behan asked, incredulous.

"No. They've got nothing to go on. They suggest I should put it behind me. Reading between the lines—shit happens, live with it," Josh said.

"Kate and Abby, how are they holding up? Good?"

Josh nodded. "They're good."

"And sorry about your flying buddy. Tragic, tragic. You must be waiting for the next bad thing to happen." Behan reddened as soon as he completed his sentence.

Seeing Behan flush, Josh guessed what was coming. "But, I'm back. Ready to pick up where I left off," he said.

"That's what I wanted to speak to you about, Josh." Behan shifted awkwardly in his seat. The chair swiveled when he moved. "I saw something on the news while you were on leave. I think you know what I mean."

A block of concrete sank in Josh's gut and rested uncomfortably on his bladder. He didn't acknowledge Behan.

"The television report is very damaging, regardless of its validity. And I hope the situation is quickly resolved for everyone's sake, especially yours. We, as a company, cannot afford to be at risk—we have investors, customers and employees to consider. I think you understand that it would be unfair to them to put their livelihoods in considerable peril over one man."

Son of a bitch. No wonder everyone is so jumpy. Josh couldn't believe what he was hearing. Were they going to can him over an allegation? He knew the allegations were true, but he had yet to be charged. He cut Behan's soft soap short.

He slammed his fist on the table and ignored the flame of pain up his arm. "Get to the point," he barked.

Behan jumped in his chair. He spoke again, this time with the corporate voice torn away. "Shit, Josh. You've been accused of taking a payoff on a previous job. People's safety could be at risk and you overlooked that in favor of a chunk of money."

"You have no fucking idea of the situation," Josh spat.

"Okay. You're right. I don't. I have no idea of the circumstances of your guilt or innocence. But I do know I have a responsibility, and it's hard to carry it off when I have my procurement manager's name splashed over the news. The press has been calling here."

Josh stared hard into the table's polished wood surface and gazed at his reflection. The surface twisted his features and his baleful gaze threatened to burn holes in the table. Behan spoke again and Josh met his eyes.

"Josh, you'll have to deal with vendors who'll be wondering whether they've lost contracts to a payoff or will gain new ones if they offer you a bribe."

"You don't know that. You don't know that our suppliers will think any differently."

"I do," Behan said softly, but with the impact of a sledgehammer. "I thought it and human nature tells me others will too. I can't have that . . . neither can the CEO of this company. This comes all the way from the top with no disagreements. I'm sorry, Josh. I truly am."

Josh struggled for something to say, but the words

failed to come. The next bad thing had been duly received. He understood the company position, but their distance mortally wounded him. He was against the ropes and another of his seconds had disappeared into the crowd, leaving him to his disgrace. Finally, the words came.

He said, "So I'm fired."

"No, I'm not doing that. I'm suspending you."

"But what image does that portray? It assures people of my guilt."

"I'm sorry, Josh, it's the best I can do. I've agreed to a suspension with pay, but if you are formally charged, I will have to terminate your employment here."

He wanted to say it felt like a sentence had already been passed. "That could be a long time, Mike. I have a family."

"I know that, but there's little I can do."

"Or want to," Josh interrupted.

"Hey, that's unfair," Behan said. "You brought this on yourself."

"Okay, okay, but it depends on what side of the table you're sitting at, doesn't it?"

"I suggest you go home and work on getting these allegations cleared up and come back to me when they are."

Silently, Josh fumed.

"I'll get Jenny to escort you off the premises." Behan reached for the phone.

"Christ, Mike. Escort me off the premises? I'm not going to do anything. Give me some credit. I'll go, but don't make me look like a criminal doing it." Anguish filled his throat and Josh spoke in a hoarse whisper.

Phone in hand, Behan hesitated, but returned the phone to its receiver. "Okay, Josh. Call me when this is cleared up. I'm here for you."

Josh got up and tottered to the door on legs that dissolved with every step. The sentiment seemed hollow to him. The son of a bitch was just doing his job and nothing more. He twisted the door handle to leave.

"Josh—is there anything you can tell me?"

Josh looked over his shoulder. Behan seemed small in his big leather chair and looked like a disobedient child waiting for punishment outside the principal's office. He imagined Behan swinging his legs to and fro, anxiously waiting for his name to be called. He almost laughed.

"No, Mike. I can't say anything. Anything I say may be used against me in a court of law."

CHAPTER TWENTY-THREE

His ex-coworkers were ready for him the moment he left Behan's office. The corporate grapevine must have glowed red with news of his demise. They watched him trudge back through the halls, never once engaging him. Being gawked at by all the knowing faces was more than he could bear. It was a relief to be back in his office where he could hide. Josh pulled open his desk drawers and removed his personal possessions.

Jenny entered his office and immediately burst into tears. "I'm so sorry, Josh."

Josh went over to her and put a comforting arm around the tall woman. "It's okay."

"But I knew what they were going to do. I should have told you," she said through the tears.

"It's not important." Strangely, it wasn't. A month ago the suspension would have been the supreme downfall in his life but now it was an inconvenience, just another nail in the coffin of normality in Josh Michaels's life. It wasn't great, but it wasn't the end of the world.

Certain elements in his life had the ability to bring about a personal apocalypse, but losing his job wasn't one.

Jenny regained her composure and left his office. She returned with a cardboard storage box and helped Josh pack his things. He doubted he would return.

On the drive home, he considered his downfall. He felt himself cowering under the volley of stones thrown at him. It was time he started lobbing a few rocks himself. Who would be first?

He pulled up in front of his garage and got out of the car. At this time in the afternoon, a quiet had fallen over his street. It was a place between events, the time of day when kids were at school and parents were either at work or on their way to collect their children. Screams, shouts and laughter from a neighborhood school less than a mile away carried easily on the afternoon breeze.

Josh went to the passenger side of the car and clumsily removed the cardboard storage box. The box contained the possessions from his office he wanted to keep—framed photographs, a mug from Abby with a picture of his plane on it, an expensive Parker pen from Kate and other personal belongings.

After locking the car, he carried the file box to the front door. Awkwardly, he tried to open the door with the box in his arms. He managed it with some effort and dexterity. The door clicked open and he knocked the door ajar with his knee. Just as he stepped inside, someone called him back.

"Mr. Michaels . . . Mr. Joshua Michaels?" the man asked.

Josh didn't recognize the man walking up the path toward him. He was a big man with an army-style haircut wearing a cheap sport jacket and non-matching pants.

You're either a cop or another reporter. Please be neither. "Yeah, I'm Josh Michaels. What can I do for you?"

"I wonder if I could have a moment of your time, sir." The stranger dug inside his jacket for something and produced a wallet, flashed a shield and returned it to his jacket pocket before he reached Josh. "Lieutenant Tom Jenks, Sacramento Police Department."

Bingo, my day keeps getting better and better. He had guessed right—his visitor was a cop. Maybe he wouldn't get his chance to fight back today. It was another banana peel he hadn't seen until it was too late. He nodded to the policeman.

Jenks stopped about one pace too close for Josh's liking. The encroachment into his personal space made him take one step back, and he backed into the door. It shuddered open. Imperceptibly, Josh stumbled, but regained his poise.

"You'd better come in," Josh said.

"Thank you, sir." The detective followed Josh into his house.

Josh placed the box on the floor next to the living room doorway, then gave the lieutenant his full attention. "What can I help you with today?"

"I would like you to accompany me, sir."

"Where to?"

"I would prefer to show you at this point."

"What's it in connection with?"

Jenks sighed. "All will become clear later. If we could make a move, I would appreciate it, sir."

Josh narrowed his eyes. *Why doesn't he just drop the cloak and dagger stuff and spit it out?* It had taken this cop sixty seconds to piss him off. "Is this to do with Margaret Macey?"

"Sir, can we go? I don't have all day." Jenks extended an arm and showed Josh the way out from his own home.

"I'll write my wife a note first."

"That won't be necessary." He saw Josh's frown. "We won't be long."

Josh didn't like being bullied, but he wasn't in the police's good books as it stood, so he didn't see the point in antagonizing them any further. He followed Jenks out the open front door to his car, a new Chevy Malibu. They got in the Malibu and pulled away from the curb.

"Am I under arrest?" Josh asked.

"No, sir. All will become apparent very soon."

Some of these guys really get off on their jobs. This is probably some technique for sweating the suspect. He was convinced this had something to do with either Margaret Macey or the Dixon development. The cops were just dying for him to incriminate himself. He wouldn't give them the satisfaction. He settled back to enjoy the ride.

After several moments of quiet, Josh noticed the car didn't have a police radio or any other police equipment, for that matter. He hadn't been in enough cop cars to be sure, but that didn't seem right. He shifted in his seat. "Where's your police radio?"

Jenks shot Josh a look, then glanced at the space where Josh was staring, the place where the police radio should be. "It's a new car—I only picked it up today. It hasn't been fitted yet. Anyway, we all use cell phones and beepers these days."

Josh glanced over to the odometer. "The clock reads over three thousand miles. You've been busy for one day."

Jenks hesitated. "It's only new to the department. The city can't always afford new cars these days. Federal cuts to the city's budget. Not enough tax dollars."

"Oh, yeah," Josh said suspiciously. "Those buttheads on Capitol Hill don't know their ass from their elbow."

Jenks blurted out a laugh. "Yeah, I like that."

Where's this guy taking me? Josh decided it was advisable to be aware of what was happening outside the car as well as what was happening inside. They were still on I-5 northbound heading toward downtown.

Josh shot a glance at Jenks's waist. His sport jacket was splayed open and exposed his trim gut. He wore no shoulder holster and no gun was to be seen. Something cold and clammy crept up Josh's spine with small hard fingers. He had no idea who he was sitting next to, but he wasn't law enforcement. Perspiration formed on Josh's brow.

The Chevy peeled off I-5 and traveled east on J Street. Jenks threaded the car through the grid of streets that constructed the downtown district. The familiar and comfortingly populated blocks became increasingly desolate as they entered the partly derelict and unused commercial areas scarred by the light rail lines.

They were a long way from police headquarters and this part of town had nothing to do with Margaret Macey or the Dixon job. Fear charged through Josh's system.

"Could I call my wife on your phone?" Josh asked. "I think she'll be wondering where I am."

"No. In a few moments our business will be complete."

Josh smelled it. The smell was the stink of his own sweat in the air-conditioned chill of the car's cabin. Was Jenks aware of the manifestation of his fear? It didn't matter how much he put up a strong defense, his body ratted him out. To Josh the odor was gathering momentum, so he squeezed his arms tight against his body. Disgustingly, the dampness spread further over his armpits and down his sides, soaking into dry shirt material.

Josh glanced at Jenks. If he wasn't a cop, who was he? James Mitchell's partner? In retrospect, nothing made Jenks an officer of the law. He had the suspicion he was being taken to meet James Mitchell. He didn't care to be around to find out whether he was right or not.

The Malibu slowed and came to a gentle stop at the intersection. Jenks surveyed the road, waiting for the sporadic traffic to clear. Josh took his chance. Simultaneously, he punched the safety belt release and yanked on the door handle. The belt recoiled, making a whizzing sound like a bottle rocket. The door lock clunked and the door opened. Josh made for the street.

A ratcheting click came from behind. Jenks produced a gun from God knows where and roughly stuck it in Josh's face. Josh felt the coldness of hard metal against his cheek. The smell of oil and burnt firecrackers filled his nose. He flicked his eyes to the black pistol jammed hard against his flesh. The weapon rubbed uncomfortably against his cheekbone and the gun felt as heavy as it looked.

"Now, Mr. Michaels. Close the door and buckle up. Our journey isn't over—yet," Jenks said without irritation, but there was a hardness to the word "yet" that could crack diamonds.

Josh's escape had amounted to a half-opened door and one foot on the doorsill. He sat back in his seat and closed the door with Jenks' gun muzzle pressed against his cheek. He fastened the seatbelt and Jenks drove across the intersection.

"No more thrills, Josh. I hope you don't mind me calling you Josh?"

Josh said nothing and stared straight ahead.

"Just so we understand each other." Jenks shoved the gun into Josh's groin.

Josh winced at the intrusion.

"Move it and lose it," Jenks snarled.

The car bounced over the light rail crossing onto cracked asphalt. A layer of rubble from a nearby demolition site coated the road. The pieces crackled against the underside of the car as they bounced over another poorly covered, unused rail line. The gun muzzle bounced between Josh's thighs. He gasped in fear of the weapon going off by accident.

Jenks heard the gasp, looked at Josh and laughed. "I suppose I should be careful with your valu-balls," he said and laughed again.

Jenks made a left and drove the car down an alley between two vacant, whitewashed factories. The signs were long since gone, giving anonymity to the last occupants.

The car came to a halt behind a Dumpster. "Time for business," Jenks said. He pressed both of the seatbelt releases and the belts whizzed back against the door pillars. "Get out."

Jenks removed the semiautomatic from Josh's crotch and both men climbed from the car. He motioned with the pistol for Josh to move. Josh moved ahead of the car with his head cocked over his shoulder at Jenks several feet behind.

A smile cracked across Jenks's angular face. "I bet you have no idea what this is about, do you?"

Josh thought for a moment. "You're right. To be honest I haven't a clue."

"Well, I'm not going to explain it all, but you're worth a lot of money to some people."

What was this guy talking about? He wasn't worth anything to anyone. All he had was his life insurance and Kate and Abby were the beneficiaries. "Who?"

"That's not important, but what is . . . is that you have to be dead for them to get it. Get it?"

Jenks came closer to Josh. Josh made tentative steps backward. Seeing Josh squirm, the killer smiled and holstered the gun in the back of his pants.

"But first you'll have to be roughed up a little," he said.

Josh stopped and stared beyond Jenks and the Malibu. Slowly, a car rounded the corner into the alley.

Oh, my God, a witness, Josh thought. He was saved. Jenks couldn't try anything now. Not with someone else around. The tension drained from him.

The white Ford's driver stamped on the gas and the car's engine roared. The sedan accelerated under full power, tires spitting debris and kicking up plumes of dust in its wake.

The car wasn't coming to save him. It was coming straight for them.

Josh bolted. Without thought or plan he pounded down the alley away from Jenks and the charging Ford.

Forgetting Josh, Jenks whipped around to face the speeding car and in one fluid motion, he jacked out the semiautomatic from the back of his pants. Snapping into a shooter's stance, he readied the gun to fire.

Jenks never had a chance. As he aimed to fire, the car was upon him. Before releasing a shot, the Ford struck him head-on.

The car took his legs from under him, breaking them below the knees. His head thudded into the hood as he collapsed forward on broken legs. The velocity of the car and the angled windshield flipped Jenks over the top. He somersaulted one and a half times before crashing to the ground on his back. The car came to a skidding halt, the rear snapping around to overtake the front. The driver got out of the Ford, a gun in his hand, readied for use.

Josh ducked into an empty factory for cover and stared through the broken windows. He saw the driver get out of the car after mowing down Jenks.

"You've got to be kidding." He couldn't believe who stood over Jenks. It was James Mitchell. The indestructible cockroach had appeared out of the woodwork again. Josh had to be content with seeing the play unfold, since he couldn't hear what was being said. Something nailed his feet to the floor. He had to see what Mitchell would do next. He'd thought Jenks and Mitchell were partners, but Mitchell had just run him down. Now, he didn't know what think. Everything was thrown into the mix and he had yet to make something else from the ingredients.

Mitchell finished speaking to Jenks. He fired the gun twice into Jenks's face. At the sight of the spearheads of flame leaving the gun, Josh jerked twice in shock. He'd seen enough and ran. He burst out the other side of the building into another alley and turned left, away from the killers. At the end of the alley, he came to a scrabbling halt. He had a choice—left or right. He chose right and ran to where the alley narrowed to less than the width of a car.

The alley ended and Josh found himself in the quiet of a residential street with a café and other businesses occupying the corners. The street had old factories on one side and seedy-looking, poorly kept townhouses on the other. Cars beyond their prime littered the roadsides. People were absent from the thoroughfare.

He stopped running. The only noises to be heard were the sound of his heart pounding against his ribcage and the sharp wracking breaths tearing in and out of his lungs. New sweat intermingled with old, coating his entire body. He wanted to stop, catch his breath, but there was no time. He looked as if he'd run a marathon in his work clothes. Josh disappeared into the alleys and side streets to safety.

The professional had chosen to keep an eye on Josh Michaels today, although it wasn't necessary. He'd done all he needed to eliminate Michaels. The wheels were in motion and it was inevitable that the train would roll over his hapless victim. Interest, more than anything else, made him keep up his surveillance on

Michaels. Today was funeral day, or so it seemed. The
Michaels family, dressed in black, set off in their cars.
He followed them at a distance.

It had been unfortunate that Michaels's friend Keegan had been killed instead of his target. It was the first
time he'd killed an innocent party in the pursuit of an
assignment. He would have had no regrets if Keegan
had gone down with Michaels, but killing Keegan
without the target aboard was embarrassing.

Michaels dribbled out of the church with the rest of
the congregation. The professional watched him speak
to various mourners through binoculars. After separating from his wife and child, he got into a car with Bob
Deuce.

The professional continued to follow his target to
the cemetery and back to the church to drop Bob
Deuce at his car. His target's next stop was at his job.
He'd expected to settle in for the afternoon, but after
an hour Michaels was out the front door with a box in
his arms.

"Looks like someone got canned. I suppose that's the
power of television," he murmured to himself.

He followed Michaels home, parked five houses down
and watched his target get out. A car, a red Chevy Malibu, passed him and pulled up outside the Michaels
home. The guy in the Malibu intercepted Michaels. He
produced something out of his pocket and accompa-
nied his target into the house.

"Damn, I don't like this," he said to himself. "This
isn't good at all." The professional hadn't picked up
anything on the scanner, so it was unlikely to be a cop,
but his presentation gave the impression he was. Something about the man was familiar, though. He was sure
he'd seen him before.

Moments later, the man led Michaels out of his
home. The professional started his car when Michaels

got into the Chevy. He shadowed the Malibu into the matrix of downtown streets. The Malibu avoided the police department and was leaving the familiar landmarks for the dead side of town. *Something's going down, Josh, can't you see it?*

The professional lagged one block behind his target and waited longer than necessary at the intersections. "Shit!" he exclaimed. He saw Michaels's failed attempt to make a run for it at the intersection ahead and saw the gun at his head. The Malibu drove on and he followed suit.

The professional seethed. The moment he saw the gun, he realized what was going down. *That fuck has hired someone else to finish up my work. He couldn't wait. Son of a bitch!* He had it all under control. Tyrell just had to give him time. The executive had cheated him. Moreover, he had insulted him by hiring another hitter. It was like finding your wife in bed with your brother. Tyrell would be sorry for the betrayal.

Angry, the professional screeched to a halt at the next intersection, where the failed escape had taken place. He was stuck there longer than he liked. Traffic poured past in what seemed a never ending stream. He watched the car cross the rail lines and disappear down one of the alleys by the abandoned factories.

The traffic parted and he raced the white car across the junction. Once past the light rail crossing, he slowed and turned into the alley where the red Chevy had stopped.

They were out of the car. Michaels was walking backward away from the killer as he bore down on him. Michaels spotted him and the professional reacted to it.

The professional floored the accelerator into the carpet. The car lurched forward, slithering on the loose surface. Michaels made off like a rat up a drainpipe. His competition went for his weapon.

"Too late, my friend, far too late," the professional murmured.

He drove straight at his would-be replacement. His eyes filled with the man with the gun. Upon impact, the man blocked out the world, but he swiftly disappeared as he bumped over the roof. Josh Michaels had gone. The professional slammed on the brakes and the Ford came to a sliding stop.

Grabbing his Colt and its suppressor from the glove compartment, the professional clambered from the Taurus. Screwing the silencer onto the pistol, he walked over to the battered body of the other killer.

He lay on his back, blood oozing from contusions to his face and head. His legs were unnaturally positioned, as if he possessed a pair of additional joints between the knees and ankles. His hands no longer gripped a gun nor would they; most of his fingers were shattered and skin was missing at the tips. A trickle of blood ran from the corner of his mouth and down the side of his dust-frosted face. He looked like a rejected china doll.

The professional pointed the gun at the competition. "I know you. It's Joseph Henderson, isn't it?"

The man struggled to stay conscious. "Yeah," he croaked. "You must be the opposition."

The professional nodded. "You know about me, then? We have a mutual friend, don't we?"

"Dexter Tyrell." The shattered man coughed and winced.

"That's right, Dexter Tyrell," he said, and smiled.

Henderson made pathetic attempts to move his broken body.

"Don't move. There isn't much point."

Henderson ignored him and continued to drag his body across the dirt. The professional wasn't sure if Henderson's movements were voluntary or not.

"I can't believe the bastard brought another player into the game. You must have known there would be unhealthy competition. And now that you've lost there will be repercussions." The professional paused for a moment and surveyed the dying man. "All I can say is your résumé read better than it should have."

"Fuck you," Henderson spat.

"No, fuck *you*," he said and unleashed two rounds from the semiautomatic. The dulled hiss from the silenced pistol echoed gently off the walls.

The shots were precise. The first struck the bridge of his nose, causing his face to implode; the second shot tore his mouth open to produce an inhuman smile.

"That should make the coroner work hard for his money. Not even a loving mother would recognize that face," he said to the corpse.

The professional bent over his competitor and removed all identification from his pockets. He found the detective's shield for a New York City cop called Jenks. "Josh, you should look more carefully when you talk to strangers. Didn't your mother teach you anything?" He pocketed the items and the 9mm Henderson had been holding.

The professional looked over at the Malibu. Michaels's prints would be all over it. It would do him no good if his target were picked up in connection with this mess. Even if Dexter Tyrell had tried to shaft him, he still had a job to do and he would do it. Josh Michaels and Margaret Macey would die, as would Tyrell himself. It was a matter of principle.

His opposition had done one good thing. The location was perfect. It was secluded. No one was watching and no one had heard. He went to the Taurus, removed a can of gasoline and splashed it over and inside the car. With a handkerchief he removed the gas cap, then soaked the handkerchief in gas and shoved it in the car's filler nozzle. He ran a trail of gas from the car to the dead man's body and dumped the remaining gasoline over the corpse. He packed up the Ford, started it, turned it around and stopped a suitable distance from the Chevy. Leaving the car running, he got out and produced a matchbook from his pocket. He lit a match and set the matchbook alight. It flared, then he dropped it onto the dead hit man's body.

Henderson's corpse erupted into flames and immediately ignited the trail of fuel. The flame leapt up the side of the car and spread out across its surface like spilt milk. Within seconds, the fire took hold of the car and smoke lifted from all quarters of the vehicle.

The professional ran back to his car. He checked the progress of the fire and once suitably satisfied he drove off. He was more than a block away when he heard the muffled explosion.

Josh Michaels had gone, but that didn't matter. His fate was sealed. This inconvenience would only hasten his demise.

CHAPTER TWENTY-FOUR

Eventually, Josh encountered civilization. He traversed a straight line from the derelict buildings and ended up on Broadway. Lively businesses, traffic and living, breathing people populated Broadway. Relief flooded over him and his heart slowed to a normal pace. He was safe. He was amongst witnesses, lots of them, too many of them for one killer to eradicate. He was out of no man's land and on the right side of enemy lines. He needed more safety; he needed home. He knew the killer could be heading there right now, but where else could he go?

He spotted the bus stop opposite the Tower Theater. The bus was a good, safe means of transport that would get him home in one piece. Mitchell couldn't do anything to him on a bus. He knew his assassin couldn't afford to make such a brazen attempt. A bus was as good as a tank, impregnable. Josh jogged over to the bus stop.

After several moments of sitting on the bench, vulnerability struck him across the face with an open hand. He realized sitting at the bus stop wasn't such a good idea. What if his killer spotted him on the bench? He might take a chance with a drive-by shooting. Josh had no idea when the bus was coming. It could be in ten minutes, thirty, an hour. He never used them regularly. He was a sitting duck waiting to be picked off. Nervously, he crossed the road and ducked inside the bookshop.

He flicked through paperbacks, magazines and newspapers, never once looking at the printed pages, but instead out of the window at the vacant bus stop. Staff and customers viewed Josh with interest, but never once challenged him. A giggle from behind jolted him from his surveillance. Realizing he was a spectacle, he placed the book back on the shelf and left.

The theater foyer offered some protection from spying eyes. After some negotiation to get inside the cinema without a ticket, he bought a soda from the snack counter. Leaning against a poster for coming attractions, he sucked on the soda's straw.

A pneumatic hiss drew Josh's attention, and he looked out the window to see the mobile billboard slowing to take the corner. Emerging from the foyer's darkened mouth, he jogged over to the bus stop, ditching the half-drunk soda in the trash as he went. The bus stopped for him. It felt good climbing the three steps into the welcoming arms of Regional Transit.

Josh paid three dollars for the ride home, seventy-five cents over the top. CORRECT CHANGE ONLY the black-and-white notice pointed out. Josh didn't care. He paid the money gladly. He took a seat next to a teenage girl just out of high school with a ring through her nose. She had a Virgin employee's nametag pinned to her chest. He sat, relaxed and exhaled loudly. She looked at him, as did several other rush hour passengers on the three-quarter full bus.

"Hard day at work," Josh explained to the girl.

"Every day." The girl from Virgin dismissed Josh and stared out the window.

The doors rattled shut. The air brakes wheezed and the bus eased into traffic.

From the end of the road, Josh took the opportunity to scope out his street. The vapor lights shone down on his car and Kate's minivan. The lights were on in the house and there was no sign of the white Ford he'd seen tossing Jenks's body like a rag doll. He recognized the cars parked in the street and driveways, so he started to walk. Someone could have staked out his neighborhood, but if they had, he'd missed the signs. Although it seemed obvious his street and home were safe, he'd learned not to believe his instincts. With shaking hands, he opened the front door to his home.

He found the hall was neither packed with cops waiting to gun him down nor with James Mitchell holding a knife to Kate and Abby's throats. Reassured, he ventured farther inside his house. His wife and child sat in front of the television.

"Josh, where have you been?" Concern and annoyance were evident in Kate's voice. "Your car was parked outside."

"I want to check something," he said, interrupting her.

He snatched up the remote control from Abby's hand and started channel-hopping.

"Dad," Abby whined.

"Josh, I asked you a question." The irritation dissolved as Kate noticed his disheveled state. "What happened to you? You look like you've been dragged through a hedge backwards."

Josh ignored her and continued channel-hopping. He found what he was looking for, the news. Slowly, Josh backed up and sat on the arm of the chair next to Abby.

Kate started to complain, but Josh shushed her. "Give me a minute and I'll explain."

The television screen showed a cordoned police scene with police and fire services present. Spotlights illuminated the area. In the background, the burnt carcass of a car lay slumped on melted tires. A screen shielded the television cameras from what Josh knew to be the dead body of Tom Jenks. The field reporter with suitably furrowed brow spoke.

"To recap, the police have found the body of a dead man next to this charred Chevy Malibu." The reporter motioned with a hand in the direction of the wreck. "The man has no identification, was shot twice in the face and burned. Police, as yet, have no witnesses to the grizzly murder and appeal to witnesses to come forward. Initial indications lead the authorities to believe this killing may be a drug deal gone bad. . . ."

"Kate, come with me," Josh said.

"Okay." She saw the fear in Josh's eyes; fear that was contagious.

"There you go, sweetie." Josh gave Abby the remote control. "We'll be back in a minute."

Josh led Kate by the hand toward the stairs, but their daughter halted their progress.

"Daddy, why don't you tell me what is happening?"

Josh returned to his daughter's side and knelt by her so that he was eye to eye. "Daddy is having some big problems he's trying to get through. You know sometimes you struggle with math problems and you scratch your head for a while before you get it?"

Abby nodded.

"Well, Daddy has a whole big bunch of them"—he gestured with his hands out wide like a fisherman telling a tale—"and it's going to take me a long time before I can work them all out. But I promise, when

I've got it all sorted out, I'll tell you all about it." Josh put a finger to her nose. "Is that okay? Can you wait for a little while?"

Abby nodded vigorously and gave him a hug.

"Thank you, honey. You can watch your cartoons now."

Josh returned to Kate and took her up to their bedroom. He sat her on the bed and knelt in front of her, holding her hands in his.

"Are you going to tell me what's going on?" Kate asked.

He took a deep breath. "If I knew I would tell you, but I don't understand it all myself."

"But what *do* you know?"

"I went to the office and Mike Behan wanted to see me." Josh hesitated. "They've suspended me, indefinitely."

"Why?"

"Because of the Dixon apartments bribe. They can't have an employee suspected of bribery in such a sensitive position." Josh frowned in apology.

"The bastards. Is this suspension paid?"

"Until an arrest is made. Then they cut me loose. But I think it'll be all over by then."

"How can you say that?"

"Trust me, it will."

"But that doesn't explain your condition."

At that moment, Josh realized how badly he smelled. Briefly, he thought of the girl on the bus and what she must have endured sitting next to him. He caught a glimpse of himself in the closet mirror. It wasn't a pretty sight. Jenks and his foiled assassination attempt quickly obliterated the images of the nose ring girl.

"I think someone wants me dead." Kate started to challenge his wild accusation, but he knocked her protest aside. "Listen, I came home from work and I was picked up by some guy called Tom Jenks, who said he was a cop."

Kate looked puzzled. "Who *said* he was a cop?"

"Yeah, he said he needed me to go with him and I did. After a few minutes, I realized he wasn't—the car, his manner, lots of things didn't ring true. When I tried to get away, he pulled a gun and told me I was worth money to someone, but only if I was dead. He took me to the old factories over by the rail lines."

Kate slapped a hand over her mouth. "That was him, wasn't it? The murdered man on the news. You killed him?"

Josh shook his head. "No, I didn't. He was going to kill me and someone else killed him."

"Who?"

"James Mitchell. He ran him down, then shot him and must have burnt him and the car. I was out of there once the killing started."

"But I thought Mitchell was trying to kill you, not rescue you."

"That's what I thought, but I really don't have a clue now."

Kate wrapped her arms around him. "Oh, Josh, what have you got us into?"

The word *us* stung. His actions, his deceits, his mistakes, had dragged his family and friends into a sinkhole with no bottom. It was his fault and his alone, but he'd affected everyone close to him. His only comfort was she still thought of them as an *us,* not as individuals. He hoped he could keep it that way.

"I don't know." He pulled her back. "But I think it's connected to Margaret Macey, the woman who got the threatening phone call. Someone wants both of us dead. I'm going to see her."

"No, Josh."

"But I've got to. I might be able to save her and she might be able to explain to me what's going on."

"No, Josh. That's what the police are for."

"But they won't be interested until I wind up face-down in an alley with a bullet in my head."

Kate flinched.

"I'm sorry, but it's true."

"Josh, I'm scared. I don't want you leaving this house tonight. The more involved you get, the more things go wrong. People are dying. I don't want you to be next."

"I can't just do nothing. I have to go."

"If you go, I won't be here when you come back. I mean it."

The professional lounged on the bed in his motel room with pillows propped behind his back, the remote control in one hand and a cellular phone in the other. He watched his handiwork, the cremated car and the mutilated body, on the television. *Not bad for a spur of the moment effort,* he thought to himself. It was him they were talking about. He dialed the number and the phone was answered immediately.

"Dexter Tyrell."

He hit the mute button on the TV, but continued to watch the newscast.

"You dumb fuck, Tyrell." The professional was cool, showing no hint of the anger boiling up inside.

Feebly, Tyrell muttered something in the way of ignorance.

The professional chopped him off short. "Don't play the innocent. You know why I'm calling. You sent a second man in to finish my work. Didn't you?"

Silence filled the telephone line except for a roaring hiss that made Tyrell sound like he was in a wind tunnel.

"Yes, I did," Tyrell admitted.

"I'm glad you admitted it. It shows strength of character when a man can admit his mistakes. Don't you think?"

The television report went back to the studio and the program moved on to other news. Disinterested in the mute talking head, the professional switched the TV off.

"How is he?"

"Funny you should ask. I've just been watching the evening news. Your man is one of the top stories tonight."

"Is he dead?"

"Yes, he is. Don't worry, it'll be some time before they can make a positive ID."

The professional grinned. He thought he heard an audible wince through the phone line.

"It was lucky I was there or he would have robbed me of my fee."

"What do you mean?"

"He was about to kill Josh Michaels, but luckily, I interceded."

"You stopped him?"

"Of course, Mr. Tyrell. It was my assignment. Mine to carry out. Mine to finish."

"But Michaels will go to the police," Tyrell said, his voice rising in pitch.

"No, I shouldn't think so. It wouldn't be in his best interests."

Tyrell paused before answering. "What's your plan?"

"My plan? I'll do as I was assigned. Within the next forty-eight hours, your request will be fulfilled. I'll confirm my plans tomorrow. And then . . . we should discuss terms. A new arrangement after your breach of trust."

"Of course."

"I think we should meet face-to-face." The professional made the simple request sound ominous.

"Let . . . let me know when you . . . you're ready," Tyrell stammered.

"Good night, Mr. Tyrell." The professional hung up.

The professional switched the television back on and flicked through the stations for something to watch other than news.

He knew Tyrell would be panicking over whether the man he hired would kill him after the assignment was complete. He could almost smell the businessman's fear. He stopped the channel surfing when he came to PBS. A cheetah had just brought down a gazelle and was reveling in its new kill.

Gently, Dexter Tyrell put the cell phone on the passenger seat next to him. His focus drifted from the other cars and the road ahead to the phone call he'd received from the professional. In the years he'd dealt with the killer, he'd never believed their relationship would take a turn for the worse. But it had now. He found it difficult to think straight. For the first time, he hoped it would take some time before Josh Michaels and Margaret Macey were dead. He tightened his grip on the steering wheel.

Involuntarily, his foot eased down on the gas pedal. In hindsight, which was always twenty-twenty, he'd made a mistake bringing in another contractor. Hiring Smith seemed like a good idea at the time and he'd come highly recommended, but never for one minute did Tyrell think he'd be killed two days after meeting him. He shot out of the righthand lane and blew by a Greyhound bus at eighty-five.

Tyrell's Mercedes continued to increase in speed. He considered the situation. If the professional could take out a man like Smith, how difficult would it be for the

hit man to take care of him? The answer: it wouldn't
be hard. Different thoughts, scenarios and questions
flashed inside his head like icons on a slot machine.
Maybe he was jumping to conclusions assuming the
professional would want to kill him. He was a businessman as well. It didn't make good business sense to
bite the hand that fed him or to tear it off in spite.
Tyrell was deluding himself and he knew it. He just
wished he knew what the professional was thinking. In
the financial world, people were as easy to read as a
book, but the professional was written in a different
language. He pressed the accelerator pedal into the
carpet.

The siren wail made Tyrell jump, waking him from
his living nightmare. The police cruiser's blue and red
lights flashed excitedly in his rearview mirror. He
looked down at the speedometer. It read 105.

CHAPTER TWENTY-FIVE

Kate's threat was a kick in the guts. Josh had never thought for one moment that Kate would consider leaving him. But there it was—if he went to see Margaret Macey, Kate would leave him. So he did as he was told and stayed home, threw his clothes in the hamper, had a bath and put the eventful day behind him.

But that was yesterday. Today was a whole new day. Kate was at work, Abby was at school, and he was at home, alone. Kate would never know if he slipped out of the house and visited the old woman. Something twisted the blade of guilt between his ribs. He'd been deceitful to Kate before and the deceit had come back to take its revenge. But he had to find out what Margaret Macey knew about this conspiracy and do it without being caught. He knew the price and consequences of failure. If he screwed up, he lost Kate and Abby—he lost everything. He was gambling with higher and higher stakes. He raised the bet one more time.

Josh guided his car down the street and brought it to a halt outside Margaret Macey's house. He remembered the address Bob had told him, though he knew his friend wouldn't approve of what he was doing. From the appearance of the street, he couldn't imagine this woman was worth murdering. He crossed over to the other side of the street and went up to the front door.

He rang the doorbell. It didn't work. Josh wasn't surprised. He knocked on the door. No one answered. "Shit," he murmured. He hoped she was in. He didn't want to hang around all day waiting. Out of the corner of his eye, he saw movement, a blur darting back from the window. He knocked again.

"Hello," he said.

No one responded.

"Mrs. Macey? Margaret Macey? I know you're in there. I saw you moving." Josh had his head close to the door and spoke loudly.

Realizing how sinister he must sound, Josh glanced behind him into the street. He hoped the neighbors hadn't heard, put two and two together and come up with five. The last thing he wanted was to give the cops another nail for his coffin. He saw no one.

Whoever was in the house didn't move or make a sound.

"Margaret—can I call you Margaret? I'm here as a friend. I need to speak to you. It's about the insurance company, Pinnacle Investments."

"Go away," she shrieked.

Shocked by the sudden outburst, Josh's head snapped back from the door and he took one step back. He peered through the grubby window to the right of the door and only made out shapes in the gloom.

"Mrs. Macey, I'm here to help." A tinge of resignation clouded his resolve. *This isn't going to be easy,* he thought.

*   *   *

Ever since the pizza boy incident, Margaret Macey had made herself a recluse. The evil man on the phone had called twice since then. Now, she feared the phone, the outside and people. She'd never seen her tormentor and he could be anyone. He could be the man standing next to her at the bus stop, the man who packed her groceries at Albertson's or the man at the front door right now.

The police had told her they'd spoken to a suspect. By going to the cops had she aggravated the wound, only making the situation worse for herself? Maybe if she told the cops to drop the investigation he would leave her alone. She would do anything for peace. The man at the door interrupted her train of thought.

"Margaret, can't we talk? I think the same man who is trying to hurt you is trying to hurt me," he said, his words muffled by the windowpane.

He sounded convincing to Margaret, but he'd sounded convincing when he called the first time. He'd sounded just like a salesman, all bright persona and fake interest in her welfare, but he'd turned into a monster. He could be doing the same now, offering her something sweet before the bad medicine came.

"Please, leave me alone. I know you're him. You're the one on the phone calling at all hours," she said.

He started talking to her again, but she didn't hear him. Sweat broke out across her body. For a moment, objects became shapes, losing their integrity as solid forms. As Margaret's heart beat faster and faster, a tingle crept along her arm, numbing it. She needed her medication.

"Please, let me in, Margaret," he pleaded. "I know I can help you and you can help me."

"Please, don't kill me," Margaret said.

"I'm not trying to. Please, don't think that."

Margaret picked herself up from behind the armchair. She'd ducked behind it after she glanced at the visitor at the door. Getting up was easier said than done. The strength needed to do so was an effort at the best of times; currently, it was a near impossibility. Using supreme effort and her one good arm she pushed herself to her feet and tottered like a babe for a moment before gaining her balance.

"Margaret, I can see you. Please let me in. I only need a few minutes of your time." He sounded excited by the sighting and charged with new vigor.

She ignored him in favor of her medication. The stuff was here somewhere. The bathroom cabinet was full of nothing, filled with medication for coughs and colds, Band-Aids and toothpaste, although it was hard to see anything as her vision faded to primary colors, then back to Technicolor. She grappled with the cabinet's contents, which went tumbling into the sink below. The pills weren't there. She couldn't remember where she'd last seen her drugs. *Why can't I think straight?*

In her bedroom, the nightstand proved as fruitful as the bathroom. She stumbled back to the lounge with the ever-present visitor still whining at the window. He was telling her something, but she didn't care what he had to say.

Margaret moaned the feeble utterance of a creature without a tongue. She didn't feel good. Something bad was happening. It felt as if her heart had been folded into a shape it was never meant to be in. The pain in her chest was excruciating and the tingle in her arm was ablaze; millions of hot needles pressed into her flesh at once. She fought to take a breath, but the air stopped in her mouth. Breathing, something she'd done all her life, was now an alien concept.

Standing became too much. Her legs buckled and she

crashed to the floor. She struck the telephone table, sending it and the phone smashing to the floor in sympathy. She hardly registered the impact on her body. It no longer fed the information back to her brain.

Margaret lay on her back. The visitor rattled the door and tried to force it. A recorded female voice from the telephone told her to hang up and try again or dial the operator. Margaret wasn't compliant to the request.

"I'm coming round the back," he called.

She could hear it—the rustling of his movements, the creak of the screen door, the attempts on the door before the tinkle of shattering glass cascading onto the vinyl flooring. She saw the figure come for her, the Michelin man, crudely shaped without definition. Even now, she still couldn't identify the man coming to kill her.

Margaret Macey was in bad shape. Josh dropped to his knees at her side. He propped her up on his lap. Her eyes looked at him, but didn't focus.

"Is there anything I can do? What can I do? Tell me, Margaret."

"You got what you wanted. I'm dying," she said.

"No. That's not what I wanted. I wanted to talk to you about the man who's been calling you. He's been pursuing me as well."

The old woman stared back blankly. She wasn't going to tell him anything now. She was the color of the dead and breathing erratically. She needed a hospital. But that was a problem. Suspected of frightening this woman, he'd now broken into her home and given her a heart attack. It wouldn't look good for him with the cops. He cursed.

"Margaret, do you take any medicine for your condition?" The woman didn't seem to hear him. "Do you have any pills or shots? Is there anyone I can contact?"

The woman in Josh's arms stiffened. Her face contorted in pain. Tightly, her boney hands balled up. White knots at every joint threatened to break through the paper-thin skin. He cradled the old woman like she was a bomb with the seconds disappearing off the clock. Flecks of spittle sprayed over her chin.

Josh didn't know what to do for her.

Her last word came out as an accusation. "Killer," she said.

She gurgled like a blocked drain before her body relaxed and became still. Josh knew he was holding a dead woman.

CHAPTER TWENTY-SIX

"Oh, Christ. Oh, no. Please, don't be dead." He clutched the frail old woman to his chest and rocked back and forth. He thought fast. What could he do? What should he do? Gently, he placed her body on the floor and started CPR. He had his CPR certificate, but he couldn't remember a damn thing now. He hoped to God he was doing it right. He tilted the woman's neck back, pinched her nose and breathed into her mouth. Disgusted, Josh dismissed the unpleasantness of her spittle on his mouth. After several attempts, he stopped. She was dead and Josh gave up.

He wiped a shaking hand across his mouth and tried to swallow, but his throat was dry and his tongue stuck to the roof his mouth. He couldn't bear to look at the blank, staring eyes of the dead woman and brushed a hand over the lids, closing them. On hands and knees, he moved away from the corpse and slumped against the threadbare couch.

Josh noticed the monotonous tone of the recorded voice coming from the discarded telephone. He went over to the handset to call 911. With his hand about to touch the receiver, he hesitated and retracted it. He realized what he'd done.

Guilty. Josh was guilty of the crime the police had accused him of, whether it was intentional or not. He'd scared Margaret Macey into a heart attack and she was dead. The cops didn't need a smoking gun to convict on this one. Josh had given them all they needed. He should have done what Kate had told him and not gone. Here was another mistake to add to the growing pile.

Josh stared blankly at the dead woman in front of him. He'd come to help this woman and himself, but instead of helping her, he'd killed her. How long would she be on his conscience? As long as Mark Keegan would? Another innocent person had died because of him.

After several minutes, Josh got up and retraced his steps, making sure to wipe clean anything that he may have touched. He knew it was wrong to leave Margaret Macey's body without calling an ambulance, but he didn't want to be the one they found with the body. Someone would notice the broken door before long.

Josh crept along the side of the house and checked the street for witnesses before returning to his car. The street was clear. Josh ran to his car, got in and accelerated away.

The professional recognized the figure getting into the car as he pulled away. *What is Michaels doing at Margaret's?* His targets had no reason to be talking to each other; had someone made a connection? Michaels probably had, but it was too late for them.

As he watched Josh's car disappear onto another street, the professional dialed the old woman's number. He got the busy signal.

Curiouser and curiouser, he thought. What were his

little people up to? No good to be sure, he decided. The professional hung up and pocketed the cellular. He approached Margaret Macey's house and knocked gently on the door, but received no answer. His visit to the rear of the house gave rise to further curiosity. The back door was broken. Glass was scattered over the kitchen floor. Removing a handkerchief from his pocket, the professional entered the house, ensuring he didn't leave any prints behind.

Moments after entering the house, he spotted feet sticking out from behind the armchair in the sitting room, one shoe hanging off the left foot. The professional closed in on the unmoving body. He knew who he'd find. His target lay on her back—still, quiet, and very obviously dead. He knelt down by her side and placed two fingers over the vein in her neck. He felt no pulse.

The professional laughed out loud. He just got the joke. One of his targets had accidentally taken out the other. Days like these were very rare in his profession. He wished he could share this moment with someone.

"Josh, I would split the money with you if I didn't have to kill you," he said to the room.

The killer wandered into the bathroom and shook his head at the mess of items scattered over the sink and floor. He removed a baggie from his shirt pocket with a bottle of pills inside; without touching the contents, he dropped the bottle into the sink with the rest of the junk.

"You can have those back, Margaret. I bet you've been looking for them," he said.

He left the way he came. And like Josh Michaels, he swiftly drove off, unseen by the neighbors.

The professional stopped at a strip mall with a pay phone and called 911.

"What is the nature of your emergency?" the female dispatcher asked.

"I want to report a break-in, possibly violent," the professional said, sounding suitably distressed.

"What can you tell me, sir?" The dispatcher's level tone had a mannish quality to it.

"I heard breaking glass and shouting, then I saw a man leave and get into a blue sedan. And I know an old lady lives alone in that house." *An Oscar winning performance in a telephone role*, he thought.

"Do you have an address, sir?"

The professional reeled off Margaret Macey's address.

"Can I have your name, sir?"

The professional dropped two fingers on the hook and broke the connection. Smiling, he got into the Taurus. He had final preparations to make for Josh Michaels's demise.

Bob Deuce's desk, as messy as ever, was awash with paper, but the paperwork wasn't related to his clients. The debris was his research on Pinnacle Investments. Since returning to the office after the funeral the day before, he'd immersed himself in the company's history. After calling friends in the industry, reading reports and financial data, he felt he had it all. What he'd discovered was amazing; no, not amazing, fantastic. It may have seemed wild, but what he believed to be the truth wasn't impossible. If it hadn't been for the tragic events that occurred in the last few weeks, he wouldn't have believed it.

His phone rang from under a wad of papers and he waded through the mess to find it. "Yes, Maria?"

"Call on line one for you, Bob," she said.

He pressed the glowing key on the keypad. "Bob Deuce, how can—"

"Bob, it's me."

"Josh, what's up?" The nervous edge to Josh's voice frightened Bob. Every time his friend called him, something bad had happened. He dreaded the new turn of events.

"Have you got time to see me?"

"Yes, I suppose. Where are you?" Bob leaned over his desk on his elbows, his body stiff with fear.

"I'm outside on one of the pay phones."

"Here? Josh, what's this about?"

"I'll be waiting by the phones."

Bob sighed. "Okay."

The line went dead.

"Damn it," he said to himself, with the phone still to his ear.

He replaced the receiver. This was more bad news and he knew it. He went into the office reception area.

Maria looked up from her computer and smiled.

"I'm just going to get myself a coffee and something to eat. I've got the munchies." He beamed a big smile and placed a hand on the door.

"Bob, you'll be going home in a couple of hours, can't you wait?" Maria was still smiling, but she deplored his overeating.

"Gotta keep the wheels of the food industry turning. Can I get you something?"

"No, thank you," she said and shook her head in dismay.

Once Bob passed out of view of Maria, he dropped the act. The grin slipped into a frown. He trotted across the shopping center parking lot to where Josh stood by the pay phones.

"Bob, two people are dead," Josh said.

Bob swallowed the shock instantly. *It isn't healthy being Josh Michaels's friend,* he thought. "Not here."

He guided Josh to a coffee shop on the corner of the mini mall next to the fitness center. He sat Josh down on the plastic garden furniture in the farthest corner of the terrace, away from prying ears. Only a middle-aged woman in sunglasses reading a newspaper sat outside, but she was on the other corner of the terrace. Bob went into the coffee shop and returned with two coffees.

Bob hunched over his coffee and the small table. "Who's dead? What's happened?"

"I went to see Margaret Macey and I killed her," Josh said.

The news slammed into Bob, leaving him bewildered. He couldn't quite comprehend what he was hearing.

Josh brought a hand to his forehead and rubbed it. He stared wide-eyed through the table as he rambled. "She wouldn't answer her damned door so I called to her through the window and she had a heart attack or something. I broke into the house to give her CPR, but it didn't work. She died."

"Josh, listen to me. You didn't kill her. She had a heart attack. You're being stupid."

"She was so scared someone was going to kill her. Those phone calls must have been a nightmare."

"Look at me, Josh."

He looked up.

"You didn't kill her. She had a heart attack." Josh attempted to interrupt him, but Bob raised a hand. "She had a heart attack. She would have had it with or without you."

"Yeah, but it was me who caused it."

"Yeah, it could have been the mailman, telephone repairman or the Jehovah's witnesses. You were the unlucky SOB who triggered it." Bob placed a supportive hand on Josh's shoulder. "Okay?"

Slowly, Josh nodded.

"Did you call for an ambulance?"

"No."

"Christ, Josh, you can't leave her there."

"But I can't be seen at her home."

Bob hated to admit it, but Josh was right. The cops would be suspicious if he was found at the scene of her death. He understood Josh's logic. "All right, I'll drop by. If she's still there then I'll make a nine-one-one call."

"Thanks."

"You said two people were dead."

Bob surprised himself. A month ago he wouldn't have been so causal about dead people with whom he was personally involved. Now, it was almost a way of life and he treated it as such. He didn't like that.

"I came home yesterday afternoon and I was picked up by this cop. But he wasn't a cop. He was about to kill me when James Mitchell ran him down and shot him."

From Josh's brief description, Bob found it hard to take in the information. He got Josh to expand on his account.

"James Mitchell. I don't get it." After a moment it dawned on him. "Are you talking about this guy they found with his face shot off?"

Josh nodded.

"Jesus, I really don't get it. Why did Mitchell save you after trying to kill you?" This mystified Bob. It didn't make sense.

"I don't understand it myself, but I think if I hadn't got my ass out of there, there would have been two bodies found."

"Go home, Josh, and stay there. I need time to think." Bob paused. "I'll pick you up and take you to breakfast. I've found some things out about Pinnacle Investments. I think I can make some sense of this mess and you might be able to fill in some of the blanks."

"Kate said she'd leave me if I went to Margaret Macey's."

"Go home," Bob said sternly. "Put on a good show

and don't tell Kate. You're not going to lose that woman. She's the best thing to ever happen to you. I won't let you screw it up."

"He'll be coming for me next and there's nothing to stop him."

"I know."

CHAPTER TWENTY-SEVEN

The diner was busy for a Saturday morning, but not so busy that Josh and Bob couldn't select their table. Bob picked the corner booth and a hostess showed them to it. They slid into the booth and she gave them each a large laminated menu. Bob put down the manila envelope he'd brought with him.

"Your server will be with you in a minute," the hostess said and left.

Josh waited until she was out of earshot. "Did you go to her house?"

"Yeah, when I got there they were loading her into the ambulance," Bob said.

Josh sighed with relief.

"Don't relax too much. That means someone either found her or saw something that made them call it in."

Josh frowned; Bob was right. Who had called the ambulance? He hoped no one could identify him or his car. He started to speak, but saw the approaching waitress.

She was a plain-looking woman in her late forties,

tall, but her dyed brown hair scooped up into a pineapple sprout made her look even taller. She seemed like a seasoned waitress—sharp and straight talking with asbestos hands for easy handling of hot plates and jugs of coffee without the aid of mitts.

"My name's Laura and I'll be your server today. What can I get you gents this morning?" A Southern twang scrubbed thin by years of living in California's melting pot tinged her speech. "Coffee to start, maybe?"

Bob and Josh agreed and she filled the mugs already present on the table. Both men quickly scanned their menus. Bob went for a sausage skillet with home fries and eggs sunny side up. Josh ordered the scrambled eggs, hash browns and toast. The waitress thanked them with a smile and relieved them of the cumbersome menus.

They sat in silence drinking coffee and pondering Josh's problems. Neither knew what to say or where to start. Laura returned with their breakfasts. After several moments of eating, Bob spoke.

"How's Kate? Does she suspect anything?" Bob asked.

"No," Josh replied.

The waitress returned with a steaming pot of coffee and overheard a snippet of the two men's conversation. "Refill?" she asked sternly.

"Yes, please." Bob saw the hate smoldering in her eyes. "Wedding anniversaries. We men can never plan surprises. It's a very fine line we walk, as husbands."

The extinguished hateful look became a warm smile. "How many is it, darlin'?" she asked Josh.

Momentarily confused, he picked up the thread. "Tenth," he said.

She tapped Josh on the shoulder and wrinkled her nose at Bob. "Still a kid. He's still got lots to learn."

Bob laughed. "That he has."

The waitress topped off their mugs and moved to another table in need of service.

Bob explained what he'd found out about Pinnacle Investments. His discovery was punctuated with mouthfuls of food snatched from the plate in front of him.

"The first thing you need to understand is you didn't cash in your life insurance policy." Bob swallowed the mouthful of food and waved a fork at Josh.

"But that's what you did for me, isn't it?"

"No. I made a viatical settlement. That basically means Pinnacle Investments gave you a cash settlement that was a percentage of the face value of your policy. They continue paying your monthly contributions until you die."

"Why do that? Why continue paying my contributions?"

"Because when you're dead, they collect on the policy. That's how viatical settlements work. In effect, you made them the beneficiary of your life insurance."

Josh picked up his coffee. "So why did you do that and not cash in the policy?"

"Because you wanted a lot of money quick. If I surrendered your policy, I would have gotten next to nothing, a few thousand at best. But by making a viatical settlement, I got you a serious slice of your policy back."

"The fifty-seven thousand."

"Right, which is about ten percent of the face value. And that's still a poor payout. If you were terminally ill or very old, you would have received a cut of up to seventy-five percent of the face value."

"Jeez, that would have been well into six figures." Wide-eyed, Josh was astonished by the money that could be raked in.

"Yeah, that's what got viatical companies into trouble—the large up front payoffs. Viatical settlements became big business at the beginning of the nineties when people saw easy money could be made."

"How?"

"AIDS. Many medical insurance polices wouldn't cover AIDS patients, so a lot of people would have become destitute if a number of companies hadn't popped up giving them a large cut of their life policy while they were still alive. Bingo—a lot of very sick people lived out their last days worry and debt free. And viatical companies got what they wanted, a quick, surefire return on an investment. The estimated life expectancy of an AIDS patient was a year, maybe two. The investment firms paid the monthly dues and passed over some cash. Everybody was happy."

Josh sneered. "Sounds a bit ghoulish, living off the dead and profiteering off someone's misery. They must be willing their clients to die."

"Yeah, but they did you a good turn when you needed it."

No denying it, he had benefited from the system—at the time. "So what went wrong? We wouldn't be here unless something had happened."

"Smart boy. Medical breakthroughs. There have been several successful AIDS drugs put on the market over the last few years that have changed the world for their patients. The life expectancy of AIDS patients has increased by ten years, and in ten years, who knows, there might even be a cure. So the viatical companies were screwed. Suddenly the big short-term profits dried up. Their clients had the cash to buy the drugs and got the better end of the deal. The companies started going to the wall, paying out too much too soon with no likely return in sight, plus they still had all those monthly dues to cover. The ones that diversified survived. They moved onto other terminal illnesses like cancer, heart disease—all the biggies medical science doesn't have an answer for."

Bob stopped to drink his coffee and Josh let the information sink in.

Bob continued. "The other way some viatical companies survived was to act as an agent. They acted as intermediaries for private investors or investment clubs who made large cash payments for some poor sap's life insurance. Little did they know they might have to wait a decade to get anything when they thought a check would be in the mail in twelve months. I remember seeing the late night infomercials ages ago."

"So what's Pinnacle Investments's story?"

"They were one of the founding companies in the industry, setting up a division to specifically get a steal on the rest. They bought big and were paid out bigger. Most of their clients were AIDS patients, but they'd already moved into all kinds of terminal diseases. The annual report was a shareholder's dream, with major growth in the early nineties. But, the ninety-eight report was the complete opposite. The viatical division was sinking the rest of the firm. But in ninety-nine they almost broke even, two thousand they showed a profit again. Tiny in comparison, but a profit." Bob illustrated his information with printouts of financial data taken from Pinnacle Investments's Web pages. He removed a sheaf of papers from the envelope he brought with him and passed it to Josh.

Briefly, Josh scanned the papers. "So they got over the hump," he said, offering a logical conclusion he didn't believe.

"Yeah, but for their success their clients had to die when the trend was for them to live. The rest of their competitors either went bust or were bought out."

"How do they account for their success?" Josh pushed his plate away. The discussion had sapped his hunger.

"Are you finished with that?" Bob asked, nodding at Josh's plate.

"Yeah, knock yourself out."

Bob hijacked the remainder of the hash brown between his knife and fork, and put it onto his plate. "You should never let food go to waste. It should be a crime," he said, and made a piece of Josh's breakfast disappear. "To answer your question, the official statement for their renewed fortunes is shrewd management. They say their investment spread is much wider and not as vulnerable as their competition. The laws have relaxed on who can make a viatical settlement. It used to be the terminally ill, but now it's anyone over seventy-five."

"But I was neither of those."

"That's right, but I got you in on your lifestyle as a pilot and recreational rock climber."

"Yeah, I used to rock climb, but I stopped after Abby was born." Once an avid climber in the Sierras, he had given it up at Kate's request. Although he'd never had a serious fall—only a minor mishap that landed him two days in the hospital—she didn't relish the thought of bringing up a baby with no father.

"Yeah, but you might take it up again and I told them there's hereditary cancer on the male side."

Josh studied the black coffee in his mug. His reflection stared back, dark and distorted in the shimmering liquid. Cancer was one of his greatest fears, and he tried to hide it deep within himself and do his best to forget. His father had died of prostate cancer at forty-nine when Josh was twenty-one, and his paternal uncle had died of the same thing three years younger. His grandfather had died at a similar age of lung cancer, but he'd been a lifelong smoker. He didn't know what had happened to his great-grandfather. He didn't dare to find out.

"They took you because you were a high-risk candidate and worth a flutter in their opinion," Bob added.

Their Southern waitress took the plates away. Both men rejected the offer to see the menu again, but accepted coffee. She refilled their mugs and promised to return with the bill later.

"Okay. They say good management made them survive, but what do you say?" Josh said.

"Considering what has been happening to you, I think they're killing their clients, and the figures bear it out. The average Pinnacle Investments viatical client lives two point four years, but their closest competitor's rate is five years and getting longer. They don't care who their clients are, because they'll decide when it is time to collect." Bob paused. "And you, my friend, are on their endangered list."

"Bob, if it hadn't been for that guy Jenks, I would tell you that you are talking out of your ass, but he said I was worth money when I was dead. I'm only of value to three people—Kate, Abby and Pinnacle Investments. And I don't believe Kate and Abby are trying to kill me."

Bob took a swig from his coffee. "I contacted my buddies in the insurance trade to see if they'd done any business with Pinnacle Investments. They had, and several of them had clients die in unusual, but explicable accidents. One of them crashed into a river and drowned."

In the parking lot of the diner, Josh leaned against Bob's Toyota and placed his folded arms on the roof of the car. Bob was about to get into the car and asked, "What's up?"

"We may know who's doing this, but how do we stop it? How do we call them off? We've got nothing concrete to give the cops."

"What do you suggest?" Bob asked.

"You buy my policy back."

Bob frowned and shook his head. "I don't think they'd go for it. It wouldn't be in their interests."

"We'll compensate them. I have insurance coming on the Cessna that would cover their losses."

"I don't know, Josh."

"You're going to have to try. It's my only option."

It seemed everyone in Sacramento had converged on the mall this Saturday morning. The parking lot were a roadblock. Parking had been a bitch, but Kate had found a space for the minivan after fifteen minutes. Once out of the car, the sidewalks were a wave of people and she always seemed to be swimming against the tide. She clutched Abby's hand and at the first opportunity darted inside the mall.

In a lot of ways, Kate wanted the hustle and bustle of the mall. The crowds and piped classical music were a welcome distraction from her unwanted thoughts. Abby aided this desire. The girl's demands and blindness to the problems at home diverted Kate's attention. Without a distraction, Josh preoccupied her mind 24/7. It had become increasingly difficult to live with him. She loved him, but she couldn't cope with the curveballs his life kept throwing at them. The two murder attempts, Mark Keegan's death, police, mystery men, a television exposé and the lies were too much—the lies more than anything. Josh had betrayed her, he'd said what he'd done was for the better good, but it didn't make it easier to swallow. If he'd lied about the bribe, then what else was he keeping to himself? The prospect of living on a knife edge didn't appeal—there were always lacerations.

Abby bounced up and down threatening to take off, restrained only by the hold of her mother's hand. "Where can we go?"

Kate looked down at her daughter's beaming face and painfully smiled back. "Anywhere you want, honey."

Abby led Kate through a merry dance of stores. Kate indulged Abby's every whim, letting her play with toys and try on clothes. Her daughter's energy warmed her. She found it easier to smile, to laugh, and be happy with every passing minute.

In the food court, they sat surrounded by their purchases, the result of the day's indulgences. Although most of the bags were for Abby, she egged Kate on to splurge on herself. Armed with a hotdog and milkshake, Abby munched and slurped happily. Kate, with only a muffin and a latte, looked on in disbelief at her blissful daughter. She wouldn't normally let her daughter eat junk food, but today she let it slide.

"Don't think you can live like this every day," Kate said. "Today is a special day, okay?"

"Special? How?" Abby asked through hotdog-packed chipmunk cheeks.

"Don't speak with your mouth full. And I hope you're not going to tell Wiener what you're eating."

Abby shook her head and made an especially large swallow.

Kate smiled. "It's a special day because we haven't had one in a while, so I thought we should have one. So, are you enjoying it?"

Abby beamed. "You bet, Mom."

"I thought we could catch a movie, but you can go to one more store before we go. So, where's it to be?" Kate cocked her head to one side.

"The Disney Store," she said without a moment's hesitation.

Kate nodded at the food. "Are you finished with that?"

Abby made an extraordinarily large suck on the milkshake straw. "I am now."

Kate couldn't help herself and laughed out loud and
Abby joined in. "Let's go then," Kate said.

Kate dumped Abby's half-eaten food and milkshake
in the trash, but kept hold of her latte. Abby set off
ahead at a half-running, half-walking pace toward the
escalators for the Disney Store on the upper level. Kate
told her daughter to slow down, which Abby did reluctantly. Mother and daughter hopped onto the empty
moving staircase.

Halfway up the escalator, Kate's good mood evaporated at the sight of a head emerging on the upper
level. Resting on the top stair of the escalator, looking
disembodied, the head smiled. The higher the escalator climbed the more Kate could see of the person
waiting for them. Belinda Wong appeared to grow out
of the ground. Kate twisted around to move against
the moving staircase, but people had climbed on behind her. The last thing she wanted was to speak to
this woman, but invisible hands pushed her forward
against her will. Inexorably, the escalator drew Kate
closer to the woman who was blackmailing her husband.

Belinda leered as Kate stepped off the escalator with
her daughter. The coldness in her dark eyes held a de-
structive element. Kate was sure the deadly force was
intended for them. She was no match for Belinda
armed with a multitude of store bags and a daughter.
Kate's stomach made a complete revolution. Her grip
around the cardboard coffee cup weakened and it almost slipped from her grasp.

"Kate. Abby. I saw you down there and I thought I'd
say hi," Bell said, as smooth as silk.

"Hi, Bell," Abby said.

"Hello, Belinda," Kate echoed.

Kate didn't stop and proceeded toward the Disney

Store, but Abby stopped her by choosing to stick by the blackmailer.

"Come on, Abby. I thought you wanted the Disney Store. We don't have much time if we want to catch that movie." Kate tried not to sound too harsh, but failed to a large extent.

"I was just going to talk for a minute, Mommy," Abby pleaded.

"I'll tell you what, I'll come along with you. I wanted to talk to you, Kate," Bell said.

The suggestion sounded as palatable as cyanide, but Kate conceded at Abby's support of the request. The three walked in unison into the store. It was sickening for Kate to be this close to the woman, but she had to keep up appearances for the world and her daughter.

"Hi, Mickey," Abby said and waved at the oversized mouse with its human occupant inside.

The mouse waved back and stared longingly at the Asian woman's figure when she passed by.

Dropping the bags to the floor, Abby ran over to the stuffed toy section.

Bell took advantage of the moment alone with her ex-lover's wife. "Kate, I thought we'd chat about things—life, you know."

"Belinda, we—"

Bell interrupted with a raised hand. "Bell, please. We're all friends here, Kate."

"Bell, we've got nothing to talk about."

"Oh, I disagree, Kate. We have a lot in common."

"Nothing you've got to say will be of interest to me," Kate said.

"But I think it will."

"I don't care what you think. Josh has told me all about you and your blackmailing scheme for the bribe.

I know it all. I suppose it's you who's been feeding Channel Three all the dirt."

Bell raised an eyebrow in surprise. "You *are* well informed."

"We have no secrets," Kate said.

"I'm not so sure I would be that forgiving if I were you. You must be a very understanding woman. Far too good for a man like Josh."

Containing her frustrations no longer, Kate stormed away toward her daughter. "Come on, Abby, it's time to go," she snapped.

"Oh, Mom," Abby whined.

"No, Abby. I said we're going. So let's go," Kate snapped.

Abby relented with low-pitched mumbles. She picked up her bags and stormily strode out of the shop with her mother.

"Stay away from us, Bell. We don't need you around," Kate said, passing Bell on the way out. Kate sneered contemptuously at the Asian woman. Bell's pretense that they were friends and had something in common disgusted her.

"You're a good woman, Kate. I don't know many women who would forgive their husband's infidelity," Bell called loudly to Kate's back.

Kate stopped and spun around in the entrance of the store, jerking Abby around with her, while the seven-foot cartoon mouse looked on behind them. Bewildered, Kate didn't know what Bell was talking about, but she was beginning to understand. Bell recognized the look of bewilderment on Kate's face and squeaked a laugh, clamping her hands over her mouth and bending forward in amusement. After a moment, she straightened and let her hands drop, the laughter knocked aside by spiteful rage.

"So, you don't know I was fucking him for over a year?" she spat loudly and triumphantly.

Slack-jawed, Kate dropped the half-drunk latte. The coffee exploded on impact and sent the hot liquid splashing over Kate's bare legs and feet, but she was too numb to feel it.

"Oh, shit," Mickey Mouse said.

CHAPTER TWENTY-EIGHT

Family Stop Insurance Services was closed on Saturdays, but Bob Deuce opened up his office, not for business, but for his friend. Buying back Josh's viatical settlement from Pinnacle Investments was worth a try. Bob had little else to suggest.

He sat at his desk and removed the papers from the envelope he'd taken to the diner. Leafing through the pages, he pulled out a printout from Pinnacle Investments's Web site. The page detailed the names of the important people for each of the company's divisions. He tapped his finger on the vice president in charge of the Viatical Settlement Division, Dexter Tyrell.

"I'll start with you."

Pinnacle Investments was open for business six days a week, so someone would be there. Bob hoped to speak to Dexter Tyrell, but he doubted he would be there on a Saturday. Mentally, he crossed his fingers for luck, picked up the phone and dialed the number listed.

"Pinnacle Investments Viatical Settlements Division,

your life is in our hands. My name is Julie," the receptionist said. "How can I assist you?"

"Hi, I'd like to speak to Dexter Tyrell, please."

"Can I tell him who is calling?"

"It's Bob Deuce, from Family Stop Insurance Services. I'm an agent for Pinnacle Investments."

"I'll just see if he's available."

Bob was put on hold and something from Easy Listening's Greatest Hits, Volume Umpteen, dripped down
the phone line. The music ended.

"Hello, Mr. Deuce. I'll just connect you," Julie said.

Bob was in luck; Tyrell worked Saturdays.

"Dexter Tyrell," the executive said, in a time-is-
money tone.

"I'm Bob Deuce from Family Stop Insurance Services. I've acted as an agent for Pinnacle Investments in
the past."

"It's nice to speak to someone who creates business
for us," Tyrell said condescendingly.

"Well, Mr. Tyrell, I have a request from one of our
clients."

"Okay, Bob, fire away."

Bob raised an eyebrow at Tyrell's use of his first
name. Bob supposed Tyrell thought of him as one of
the boys, being in the insurance game and all. The in-
formality amused him. Tyrell seemed insincere, so Bob
thought he'd be playful.

"You see, it's like this, Dexter." Bob placed a lot of
topspin on Tyrell's name. He smirked and paused.

"Yes," Tyrell said, stretching the word out.

"I have a client who made a viatical settlement eighteen months or so ago. And I'm inquiring whether it
would be possible for him to reverse the settlement."

Tyrell didn't answer. The question hung in the air,
turning stale.

"I'm not sure that's possible, Bob." Tyrell seemed embarrassed by his unfortunate answer.

"Any reason?"

"Obviously, you understand the process of a viatical settlement."

"Obviously."

"Then, you understand the costs incurred by Pinnacle Investments with the cash settlement and the existing monthly dues, et cetera."

"Yes."

"It isn't in our interests to reverse the settlement."

"My client would be prepared to return the cash remuneration and any other costs involved," Bob offered.

"Why is our client doing this?"

Bob shifted uncomfortably in his chair. His mind raced for an answer. "His financial circumstances have changed and he's interested in getting his life insurance policy back because of its sizeable face value."

"How much?"

"Five hundred thousand dollars." A nervous tone crept into Bob's voice. The source of his anxiety was clear. He had the distinct feeling he was conversing with a spider while he was the fly that trembled on the web.

"Who is our client?"

"His name is Joshua Michaels."

A pregnant pause intervened, a pause in dire need of inducing.

Does he know? Is he the one? In the silence of the telephone line Bob wondered if Tyrell was the man sanctioning the murder of his clients. Contact with this man frightened him. It made sense for the order to come from up high. It was unlikely a minion of Pinnacle Investments would have the corporate clout to order people's deaths. Also, it would be possible for a top executive to hide the excessive expenses needed to hire a professional killer. Chipped ice ran down Bob's collar; Tyrell knew his name.

"I don't remember his file,"—Tyrell paused again—"but I don't think I can accommodate your friend this time around."

Bob's mouth went dry. *Friend? Who said Josh was my friend?* The insinuation Tyrell knew Bob and Josh were friends only reinforced his fear that Pinnacle Investments's vice president was killing his viatical clients. Bob couldn't be sure whether Tyrell was aware of his slip or not. Either way, he was scared.

Tyrell continued. "Even if he did reimburse Pinnacle Investments for monies paid, it wouldn't provide the company a return on its investment. We do have investors to think about. As you can understand, we are a profit-making organization, not a charity."

"Thank you for your time, Dexter."

"Thank you for your call. And I hope we can do business again. On behalf of Pinnacle Investments, we do appreciate the business we receive from our agents. Good-bye Bob, it's been a pleasure."

Bob had only seconds to decide. He knew a killer pursued Josh. He knew it was more than likely someone at Pinnacle Investments was at the heart of it. He had the feeling Dexter Tyrell was the man giving that order. But he couldn't be sure—it was all supposition. In a moment, the connection would be broken and contact lost and it was unlikely Tyrell would take further calls. Should he bluff Tyrell and risk his own life? He couldn't hesitate any longer.

"I know what you're up to, Mr. Tyrell." Bob's voice trembled. He had just stepped into the ring and sized up the opposition. He feared his decision and hoped it was the right one.

"What do you know, Bob?"

Tyrell's coldness trickled down the line and Bob shivered.

"I know what you're doing to your clients."

"Providing them with first-class service at reasonable prices?" Tyrell mocked.

Bob composed himself before asking the five hundred thousand dollar question. "You're killing your viatical clients, aren't you?"

Tyrell roared with laughter. "Bob, Bob, Bob, where did you come up with that cock-and-bull story? *The X-Files*? Or *Days of Our Lives* maybe?"

Instead of being embarrassed by Tyrell's mockery, Bob took strength from it. The evidence to support his belief was in front of him and what he and Josh knew made a compelling story, even if it was all circumstantial. He took a deep breath and let the executive have it, both barrels.

"Pinnacle Investments is the most successful viatical company in the industry." Tyrell tried to interrupt, but Bob spoke over the vice president. "You are the only successful viatical company in the industry, especially with an AIDS client base as big as yours. AIDS patients are living longer. Yours are dying quicker. So are your other clients. A number of my colleagues have had their viatical clients with Pinnacle Investments die from unusual accidents, just as their health improved."

"This sounds like a crank call to me. I'm putting the phone down," Tyrell said.

"I think your next two targets are Josh Michaels and Margaret Macey. Both of them are my clients, Mr. Tyrell." Bob said Tyrell's name like he chewed sour lemons. "And Margaret Macey is dead."

Bob had nothing left to say. He waited for Tyrell to respond. He didn't.

"Dexter, I don't hear you putting that phone down," Bob said.

Dexter Tyrell said nothing.

Bob felt he was on a roll. He'd rattled Tyrell. The executive would be weighing his options. Bob decided to push until he left Tyrell no option. "There is a man passing himself off as an employee of Pinnacle Investments called James Mitchell. I think he's your hired gun."

"What do you want?" Tyrell asked.

"I want you to stop."

"What if I don't?"

"I'll go to the cops."

"With what you've got?" Tyrell snorted. "They'll laugh you out of the precinct or lock you up."

"Maybe, but I'll give them enough to make someone look into Pinnacle Investments's operations, and that wouldn't be good for business, would it now?" Bob smiled.

Tyrell was silent for a very long time. Bob was happy to wait. He could almost hear Tyrell squirm.

"I have an offer to make to you, Bob."

Bob listened.

Josh returned home after his breakfast with Bob and found no one home. He kept playing over Bob's theories in his head. Would Pinnacle go for the buyback option? He hoped so. He waited for Bob's call, but it didn't come. He tried calling, but Bob didn't pick up.

He couldn't just sit there. He had to do something with himself. He decided to indulge in something he had not done in ages—climbing. Bob's mention of his old hobby had a nice ring to it. Josh dug his gear out from his home office. The kit, ten years old or more, was very much out of date compared to the modern lightweight rigs people now used. He drove down to the indoor climbing center and knocked the rust off his old skills. He found he was better off using the equipment provided at the center.

After ten minutes, Josh was back in the fold; no hint of staleness showed after his eight-year absence. As the hours shot by, Josh went from their basic climbs to the most difficult, conquering each level with great aplomb. Amazed, he couldn't understand why he had not gone to an indoor center before. The risk was so minimal he was sure Kate wouldn't have minded. But even with this brief taste, he knew if he came here regularly he would end up wanting to hit the mountains for the real climbs. Yosemite was too much of a temptation to be ignored.

He came home in a good mood. It had been a good day. He parked next to Kate's minivan. Kit bag over his shoulder, Josh unlocked the door to the house and pushed it open. The door opened only a few inches before bouncing off the security chain. The door's recoil knocked the keys out of his hand and he jumped back before the charging door took a finger or a toe as a trophy.

"Kate, it's me. The chain's on, can you take it off?" Josh called through the crack of the door and picked up his keys.

No one answered.

Fear rushed through him. Had Mitchell tried something?

"Kate, are you there? Is everything okay?"

"Josh, you aren't coming in."

Fear turned into confusion. "What?"

"You're not welcome here anymore." Kate's voice cracked under her tears.

Josh peered through the gap the door allowed. He couldn't see Kate.

"What's wrong? Let me in."

Kate broke into sobs, which were echoed by someone Josh presumed was Abby. Kate spoke to Abby, but he couldn't hear what she said.

"Just go. Please, Josh, go away."

His stomach clenched. A vivid recollection of the events at Margaret Macey's house struck him between the eyes. But this was his house, his family. He wouldn't be kept out of his own home.

"Don't panic, I'm coming round the back," he paused. "Okay?"

For a moment, Josh waited for a response and heard only stifled weeping. He raced over to the gate to get to the backyard, but it was locked. He dropped his kit bag and clambered over the top. He glimpsed a neighbor across the road watching the real-life soap opera unfold; but he didn't give his neighbor a second thought. He darted over to the patio doors and found them locked, but he had the keys to the lock and rushed inside.

Drowning in worry, he called, "Kate, Kate, it's me. It's okay."

Josh found his wife and child huddled together in the living room. Kate stood with her back against the fireplace and Abby's face buried in her stomach. Seemingly, they were okay. He detected no visible wounds or injuries other than their tears. His panic subsided.

"Thank God, you're okay. I was really worried," he said. "Why the security chain?"

"Josh, get the hell out." Kate's tone was as hard as steel.

The demand was hard enough to stop him in his tracks. Kate's hostility made no sense. He was at a loss for words.

Kate unpeeled Abby from her. "Abby, go up to your room. It's going to be okay, but I need you to do this for me. Can you do this for Mommy? Can you?"

Sobbing, Abby didn't want to leave, but she relented at Kate's insistence. Kate pulled Abby to her and hugged her.

"You'd better go. Wiener's waiting for you in your room. He needs you." Kate said.

The sight of his wife and daughter in such turmoil tore Josh up inside. *What's happened to cause so much misery?* He had no idea for the reason of the heartbreak.

Abby raced past him for the stairs and her room. She took an exaggerated path around him and stared at him like he was a monster. Josh murmured her name and put an arm out to her, but she dodged his touch.

Husband and wife said nothing until they heard the bang of the bedroom door upstairs. The muffled sobs through the ceiling made an unbearable soundtrack for their encounter.

"You bastard, Josh. How could you? How could you do it to us?" Kate said through bitter tears.

Josh didn't have an answer. He didn't know what she was referring to. He'd done so much to them.

"With the pain and misery you've brought to this family, you aren't entitled to any of the love you've been given." Kate's nose had run. She sniffed and wiped the back of her hand across her nose. "You deserve all you get."

Shaking his head, Josh was still at a loss to understand. "What have I done, Kate?"

"You didn't tell me everything. In the park, you gave me the edited version. Keep the family on a need-to-know basis—was that the plan? Keep the really bad stuff to yourself and make sure you don't get into some real trouble? You coward," Kate spat. Each word was a shard of glass meant to cut deep. "Any of this ringing any bells, Josh?"

It was. He didn't understand how she could have

found out. Who would have told her? Josh swallowed the knot in his throat.

"We met Bell in the mall today. She told me all about you two. No, she broadcast it across the store. What a fool I've been to believe in you. Moments before, I was defending you to her, when all along she knew the real you and I only knew the fucking fairy tale." Kate paused to get a grip. Her emotions were taking over. "Your secretary! Couldn't you have been more original and fucked a Nobel scientist or something?"

Bell. How she must have enjoyed the moment. He should have known she'd do this once she'd lost her hold over him. Destroying his reputation wouldn't have been enough. She needed to crush him under her heel. Well, she'd done that.

She could destroy everything else, but he'd be damned if he'd let her destroy his marriage. He rushed toward his wife with arms outstretched.

Kate stiffened. Backed up against the fireplace, she clutched for something to protect herself with, and picked up the poker from the rack. Brandishing the weapon with deadly intent, she jabbed it at Josh. She looked like a cornered animal. "Keep away from me. God help you, I'll use it on you."

Josh stopped abruptly, only inches from the end of the poker. "Oh, Kate. You don't understand," Josh pleaded.

"Educate me, Josh. Tell me why. Why did you do it? Come on now, the spotlight's on you." Kate positioned her arms like a magician's assistant highlighting a master illusionist's achievement.

Fighting with himself to give a delicate, more softened version, Josh struggled to speak. But knowing lies and deceit were useless currency, he paid with the truth. "I started the affair three months after you lost the baby. We were strangers to each other. We were both unsure what we wanted or even if we wanted each other."

"That's it? Because we had a rough patch you ran off to find the first bitch you could fuck?"

"No," he recoiled. "You didn't want to know me, you pushed me away like it was my fault."

"I'm so sorry. It must be my fault you put your dick in your secretary." Sarcasm laced the tirade.

"No, I'm not saying that. I'm telling you the truth—something I should have done a long time ago. I had an affair for my own selfish reasons, but I realized it was wrong. I came back for you and I made this family work, did my best to make us happy. I love you, Kate, and I want you." Josh maintained his distance; Kate still had the poker and he feared what she would do with it in this distraught state.

"How do I know you won't run off with the next pair of pretty tits that jiggles by?"

"Because I'm here now and I'm not going anywhere. I'm one hundred percent behind this family, for this family."

Kate glared. Her face, screwed tight with the fury and pain, suddenly relaxed. She dropped the poker to the floor. It twanged against the fireplace tiles.

The Kate Josh knew came into focus. It was going to be okay. He managed a weak smile.

The house was silent; not even a noise from Abby's bedroom.

"I want you to go, Josh," Kate said.

He couldn't believe it. He had lost. He tried to challenge, but she knocked his pleas down with a raised hand.

All the emotion had drained from Kate. "I don't know what I want, but I do know I don't want you."

Kate's fury, present moments earlier, now possessed

Josh. He knew he could do nothing here. He'd lost his family and stormed out of the living room.

He yanked on the door, but the security chain was still attached. The door ripped itself from his grasp and slammed shut. He jerked on the door even harder. With a crack of splintering wood, the fixings tore from the door frame. The chain attached to the door recoiled and swung out, narrowly missing Josh's face. The door's momentum sent him sprawling.

Josh tore over to his car and flung himself behind the wheel. He gunned the engine, yanked the gearshift into reverse and the car roared backward into the street. He jammed the car into drive and floored the gas pedal, trails of black smoke pouring off the screaming tires.

"Fucking bitch," Josh growled. He would be damned if Bell would be allowed to get away with this. She would pay dearly for what she had done.

CHAPTER TWENTY-NINE

The journey to Bell's house took mere minutes. The rules of the road didn't apply to Josh. He bullied his way past every vehicle in his path. The engine screaming in pain, Josh tore along the roads, taking each bend too fast and stopping too late.

The car screeched to a halt outside Belinda Wong's borrowed house. The car rode up over the rolled curb and positioned itself untidily on the sidewalk, trailing a pair of black, wavy lines on the pale road surface. Josh leapt from the driver's seat. A Pontiac Grand Am missed him by inches as it passed him. He ignored the driver's violent overcorrection and the subsequent insult. Blinded by rage, he charged up to the house.

Josh yanked on the door. It was unlocked and opened easily. It wouldn't have mattered if the door was locked—nothing would have prevented him from getting in.

Bell appeared from the bedroom dressed only in a white silk teddy and skimpy panties. The silk was opaque, but it clung to her delicate frame. The peaks of her nipples were easily highlighted under the seamless material. When she moved, the material momentarily stuck to her like wet cotton, giving glimpses of the contours beneath.

"You bitch. You *fucking bitch*." His rage was so intense he thought he would puke.

She smiled sweetly, not showing a hint of surprise at his uninvited intrusion. "Josh, so good to see you. You must have gotten the news."

"You had to tell her. You couldn't have taken the money. You had to destroy my family."

Bell cocked her head to one side and flashed a tight-lipped smile of regret. "Things not too good at home then?"

"You knew what Kate's reaction would be." Violently, Josh grabbed her by the shoulders, his fingers digging into her supple flesh. He shook her in some vain hope of making her understand the significance of what she'd done. Bell's raven hair scattered over her face and shoulders.

Still in Josh's grasp, she shook her head, revealing blazing eyes and an open mouth excited by Josh's energy. "God, you have no idea how horny you're making me."

There was no talking to her and he found it hard to speak. Different emotional states fast-forwarded through his mind—anger, rage, desperation, loss and defeat. He didn't know whether to laugh or cry. A knotted ball of frustration in his brain prevented him from doing either. Releasing a primal growl of frustration, Josh shoved Bell away from him. Stumbling, she fell backward, striking the floor unceremoniously. Legs in the air, panties showing, Bell lost all the seductive allure she'd ever inspired. Frustrated, Josh collapsed onto the couch behind him.

Bell got to her feet. She dropped her mocking tone

and in all seriousness said, "What did you expect me to do, Josh?"

"Accept what happened. I don't know."

Bell glanced out the window. "Nice parking job, by the way."

She came over to him. She looked at him with a pitying expression.

"Why did you do it?" Without the rage, he sounded tired.

Crouching on her haunches, she placed her hands on his knees. "You gave me no choice. You refused to give me what I wanted. I wasn't just going to disappear to make it convenient for you."

"But this way, you've destroyed everything you wanted. You don't get any more money. You've destroyed my family, so you don't get me. You've lost as much as I have."

"You still don't get it, do you? This has never been about money. It was about making you pay for what you did to me." Pain was evident in Bell's rising voice.

She pushed herself away from him and stood up. She went into the kitchen, got herself a beer from the refrigerator and popped the top with the bottle opener on the fridge door.

Josh followed Bell into the kitchen after a moment. His face was long, stretched by a more powerful gravity than that experienced by anyone else on the planet.

Bell saw the sad expression and moved toward him. She wrapped her arms around him. The condensation from the bottle soaked Josh's shirt where it touched it. Its coldness burned against his flesh. She raised herself on tiptoe, bringing her head close to his. The instability made her teeter on her toes and Josh steadied her, putting his hands around her waist. Taking that as her signal, she kissed Josh, her tongue seeking entry to his mouth.

Sickened by the intrusion, Josh's face contorted in disgust. He twisted his head to break the kiss. He tasted the sharp bite of alcohol from her in his mouth and its odor filled his nostrils. She'd been drinking, and more than one beer. It wasn't a good sign.

Bell leaned into him, applying more pressure. Her heat marked an outline against Josh's body. Although slight, her weight seemed heavy on him and resistance was difficult. Finally, he broke the cloying embrace with a powerful shove that almost made him topple.

The force propelled Bell backward. She lost her hold on Josh and her balance. In an attempt to save herself, she let go of the bottle of beer. The bottle slammed into one of the overhead cabinets before striking the vinyl flooring without breaking. The spilt contents fizzed on the floor. Bell crashed into the cupboards and grabbed onto them to save herself from falling.

Josh dragged the back of his hand across his mouth and looked at it, half expecting to see blood.

"What do you think you're doing?" he demanded.

"You still don't get it, do you?"

"You're right. I don't."

"I love you. I want you back. Why do you think I've been doing this?" Bell answered her own question. "Because I want you free from all things so you have only me left."

Bell's motives shocked and abhorred him. She was crazy. She had to be to think destroying him would drive them together. It was a madness he never thought possible in Bell. Did she expect him to thank her, flattered by the lengths she had gone to? Josh shook his head.

"Do you honestly think I would come back to you? I broke up with you because I made a choice. I chose my family. And even though you've taken that away from me, I still wouldn't come back to you."

Josh stopped. He had expected a tirade of verbal

abuse fueled by disappointment and rejection, but there was silence. There was nothing further to be said. Bell had stopped looking at him. Her gaze was aimed over his shoulder. A blank look took over her face, as if she didn't understand what she saw. Josh turned his head to the point of interest.

A flash of colors was all he saw. At the speed it was moving, Josh didn't get enough time to focus on the object, only its blur, before it hit him. He felt it, though. It smashed across his head, numbing him with its force. Josh fell forward, out cold before he hit the ground.

Josh came to. He had no idea how long he'd been unconscious. An intense ache emanated from the back of his head. It rippled outward from its epicenter like waves in a millpond. He raised a hand to the ache, but the briefest movement drove knives through his skull. He found a lump the size of an egg on the back of his head and the pain forced his eyes closed. He left the bump alone, but became aware of his sore cheek, which must have broken his fall.

Bell looked very concerned with her head cocked to one side, her face so sad, so disappointed. For the first time since her return, she looked human, possessing a weak as well as a strong side. She looked like a nervous child waiting her turn to go into the doctor's office for her shots. She spoke, but the words came out as an inaudible murmur.

He saw the knife. Not the whole knife, just the handle, its blade embedded in her chest below her left breast. He noticed the blood. Too much blood. It stained the white teddy; the harsh crimson made more vivid by the pale silk. The material clung tightly to her punctured body. The blood, still oozing from the wound, ran down her onto the floor and formed a pool around her legs. His slow-witted brain hadn't registered that she was sitting. Before the blow she had been standing, but now she was slumped untidily against the cupboards. He tried not to entertain thoughts of who had done this to Bell, but failed. He had to get out, but he couldn't stop staring at the blood.

Slowly, the pool expanded across the floor in Josh's direction. He recoiled on hands and knees from the creeping mass like it was scalding lava. Josh had seen deep cuts before and there'd been blood, but he had never seen a cut so deep or with as much blood as this. Doctors dealt with these sights every day, but he couldn't cope. Josh slunk further away from the injured woman.

Bell raised her right arm with her hand outstretched and beckoned to him. Blood trickled between her pale lips. "Josh."

Josh stopped moving. He stared at the pool, the light reflected on its smooth surface. He got to his feet. His head swam. He wasn't sure if the blow or the bloody sight caused it. He came as close as he could without stepping in the mess. Still, it wasn't close enough for Bell. She called to him. He had no choice. He walked in her blood and crouched at her side.

Bell looked at him with sad eyes. The color of her rich Asian skin had drained to a jaundiced yellow. "I love you, Josh," she whispered.

"I know you do." Josh honestly believed she did and though he didn't return that love, this wasn't the time to be brutally honest with her. She was dying and he wasn't going to give her cause to curse his name with her dying breath, even after all she'd done to him. He had possessed feelings for her once.

Josh's eyes flicked between her face and the wooden knife handle poking out from her chest, disconcerted by its movement. The handle shifted back and forth with the weak breaths she took. He found it hard to concentrate on Bell with the knife moving in time with her breathing, as if the blade were part of her body. Should he remove the knife or leave it? Josh didn't know what was best, but watching Bell die wasn't the answer.

"I'll get help," he said.

He went to get up, but Bell snapped a grip on his arm with a strength that terrified him. He looked at her bloody hand on his wrist. He sneered as the fluid squeezed out either side of her palm and between her fingers. Her bloodstained handprint on his forearm was his first physical contact with the stabbing. Up until then, he'd been a witness to the wound, but the blood on his arm made him part of it, tainted him by its contact.

"No. I want you to stay. I want you to be near me," Bell said.

Josh hesitated. He nodded to her and shifted from a crouch to kneel beside her, so he was better positioned to comfort her. As his knees dipped into the blood, he felt its lukewarm heat soaking through the fabric of his jeans. He clasped a hand over hers and squeezed out a thin smile.

He wanted to tell her everything was going to be okay, the doctors would sort her out, but the lies didn't come. Instead, he watched Bell die, the blood slipping from her punctured body taking her life with its flow.

"Josh," she called. She didn't look at him, but directly ahead into the dark of the living room.

"Yes, Bell?" Josh couldn't take his eyes off her, not out of lust, which he once held for her, but out of a bizarre compulsion to see this woman die.

"I'm so sorry, Josh."

"It's a bit late to be sorry. We've done what we have done and there's nothing we can do to change that."

"I'm sorry about what I did."

"I know you are." He slipped an arm around her, and being careful not to push the knife any further into her, he half-hugged her.

Bell coughed and flecks of blood speckled her mouth and chin and landed on Josh's face. "I'm sorry I didn't tell you."

"It doesn't matter."

"I need to tell you."

"Only if you have to, but it doesn't matter now."

"I'm HIV positive."

A blow, as powerful as the one to the back of his head, slammed him. His arm trembled around Bell's shoulders in shock. He stared at the pool at his feet, teeming with the killer virus. It was invisible to the human eye, but it was there. He was kneeling in poison. This woman's blood had the most devastating disease of the last thirty years. He'd had unprotected sex with this woman.

Am I infected? Is Kate infected? Abby? His thoughts scared him. The ramifications of his possible contraction of HIV were horrific. His death sentence would be the death sentence of the people he loved.

"I was diagnosed in San Diego. I was never going to tell you, but . . ." Her final words trailed off before she finished them.

He held another dead woman in his arms. He withdrew his arm from around her and got to his feet. His shoes made sticking noises on the vinyl. He turned to leave.

"I'd prefer if you stayed for a while, Josh."

CHAPTER THIRTY

James Mitchell stepped out from the shadows, a gun in his hand. "A murdered woman and that blood all over you. That wasn't very smart, was it now?"

"I suppose you killed her," Josh said.

Josh wasn't only angry with Mitchell for killing Bell, but with himself. It had never occurred to him that Mitchell was at the core of this carnage, but it should have.

"Why did you kill her?"

"Because I need her for this." Mitchell waved the gun in the direction of the slaughter. "To make your murder more convincing. It would be totally understandable if your blackmailing ex-mistress confessed your sins to the TV news and your wife, driving you to kill her in a fit of rage. Makes total sense. Don't you think?"

"How did you know her?"

"Oh, Bell and I have become, or I should say had become, good friends. We had a lot in common—you, for instance." Mitchell jabbed the gun at Josh. "She was pissed at you for dumping her. A lot of unresolved issues there."

"And you call that resolved?" Josh pointed at Bell's corpse.

"You could say that. You two certainly had a touching farewell." Mitchell cut Josh off before he asked another question. "What I need before we go any further is for your fingerprints to be on that knife handle. Then I can get all this wrapped up."

"What if I don't?" Josh asked. It was a feeble attempt at resistance, nothing more than a schoolyard boast lacking any power or muscle to support it.

"I'll shoot you, drag you over there and stick your hand on the knife."

Josh studied the floor. It wasn't much of a choice. The killer would shoot him anyway. It was just a matter of when. He could either make the hit man's job easy or difficult.

"Why did you kill Jenks?"

Mitchell laughed and shook his head like he'd heard an old joke for the hundredth time. "That wasn't his real name. He was a competitor of mine employed to do my job. Career infighting—you know how it is."

Josh didn't. He had no concept of what internal conflicts were encountered in the professional killing industry. Nor did he want to.

Mitchell's tone turned cold. "And I'll be damned if one of my contracts will be taken away from me. That's why I killed Jenks. You were lucky you got away, otherwise both of you would have made it on the six o'clock news."

Josh had guessed right about Mitchell's intent to kill him along with Jenks, and it still made his gut churn. Another realization did little to help settle his troubled stomach. If he hadn't fled the derelict factories, Bell wouldn't be dead. There would have been no reason to kill her. She'd been a bitch, but she hadn't deserved to die so violently. Was his life more valuable than Bell's? Was it better he lived and she died? Only if he lived through this night and stopped Mitchell from killing anyone else. It was also the only way he could ever forgive himself for Mark Keegan and Margaret Macey's deaths. Josh couldn't let himself be the victim tonight.

"I don't see your fingerprints on that knife yet," Mitchell said.

"So, who's your employer—Pinnacle Investments?"

"Yes."

Bob was right. Josh smiled.

"Happy that you know?" Mitchell asked.

"Yeah. It makes sense of all this," Josh said.

Mitchell indicated Bell with the gun. "So can we get on?"

"Sure," Josh said, "I just needed to know."

He turned his back on the killer and faced Bell. He hoped that Mitchell didn't shoot him in the back of the head before he had the chance to do anything. He took a deep breath before he stepped into the bloody mess to grab the knife in Bell's chest. He gripped the blade with his right hand. The wooden handle felt comfortable in his grasp. It was the sight of the knife buried up to the hilt in his ex-mistress that was uncomfortable.

"That's it, Josh, get some nice thick prints on that handle. Come on, do it like you mean it," his killer said, peering over Josh on tiptoe from the kitchen doorway.

"Are you sure you can make this look like a convincing lover's disagreement turned murder, story at eleven?"

"Oh, you wouldn't believe how I'll make this look. You'd be impressed. It's a shame you won't see it."

"So how did you make Margaret Macey's death look?"

"Margaret Macey, Jesus." Mitchell blurted out a laugh. "I didn't do a thing. You did it all for me. I wasn't expecting that, I can tell you. It was a dream come true. I saw you running out and I was worried. I thought you had screwed everything up, but instead you finished my job just as I wanted. It was beautiful."

Josh glanced over his shoulder at Mitchell. Mitchell's focus was on the recollection rather than him. His guard was down. He hoped Mitchell thought he was a willing victim who was going to roll over and die for him. Josh pulled on the knife embedded in Bell's chest.

"What did you do to scare her?" Mitchell asked.

"She thought I was you."

Mitchell laughed again.

The knife was stuck tight and required more effort than Josh expected. He'd forgotten the blade was in a person until he looked at Bell. Her eyes didn't register Josh's desecration. He felt nauseated.

He glanced back at Mitchell. He hoped the killer wouldn't see him tug on the handle. If Mitchell saw him, the hit man would put a bullet in his head without a second thought. Josh's brains would be splattered all over the wall, game over. The resistance broke, the blade slid from its human scabbard.

"That's enough. You don't have to hold the thing all night," Mitchell said.

Josh snapped around in a heartbeat with the knife in his hand and threw it at Mitchell. Slipping in Bell's blood at the moment of release, Josh fell backward onto the blood-soaked floor. He crashed into the cabinet behind him, knocking his head on its door.

Mitchell reacted in an instant. He aimed and fired the gun.

The knife hit Mitchell in the chest as he squeezed the trigger on the semiautomatic. Josh's slip caused the thrown knife to skew its trajectory and the blade batted flatly against the killer before it clattered to the floor. The knife did knock Mitchell's aim off and his shot went wild into the ceiling.

Josh clambered to his feet and rushed the hit man. Before Mitchell could aim again, Josh smashed into the smaller man, driving him into the kitchen door frame. Mitchell yelped, but brought his knee up into Josh's gut. Josh lost his grip on the would-be killer. The hit man brought his knee up again, this time into Josh's face.

The force of the blow jerked Josh's head back and he released the hit man and clutched his nose, surprised to find it intact. The pain was nauseating. He stumbled backward, trod on Bell's discarded beer bottle and fell again.

Mitchell steadied his aim at the falling man and fired the weapon.

Josh fell and struck the floor, the bottle slithering across the vinyl. He saw the flash of flame and a two-inch hole appeared in the particleboard door to the left of his head. The odor of burnt wood and hot glue from the door's wound smelled like a sawmill.

The bottle banged against the skirting board and ricocheted back across the floor toward Josh's outstretched hand. Acting on reflex, he grabbed the bottle by the neck and threw it at Mitchell.

This time Josh's aim was true. The bottle hit Mitchell in the head, thudding into his left eyebrow. Smashing on impact, fragments of glass sprayed over the man's face. He yelled through gritted teeth, his free hand to his eyes. His gun hand pointed in the general direction of Josh. The killer tottered backward into the living room.

Josh got to his feet and charged the hit man. He knew he had to disarm the killer before he had the chance to recover. Throwing household items was no defense against a gun. Charging at the blinded Mitchell, Josh grabbed the wooden chopping block from the counter-top. Raising the board above his head, Josh brought the block down, edge on, onto Mitchell's gun arm.

The resulting sharp crack told both men Mitchell's arm was broken. The hit man screamed in agony and the pistol went flying from his grasp.

Driven on by his initial success, Josh swung the wooden board like a major league batter. This time the board smashed into Mitchell's face just as he removed his hand from in front of it. The resounding thud echoed like the crack of a baseball going out of the park.

Mitchell careened back, clipping an armchair, and fell to the floor. Blood spread between the hit man's fingers covering his nose and eyes, spilling down his face. He grimaced and exposed teeth rimmed with red in a split and rapidly swelling mouth.

Shocked by the carnage inflicted on the man's face, Josh turned the chopping block over and saw a blood-spattered bloom the size of an open hand smeared over its surface. Disgusted, he sneered, dropped the wooden board and looked for the gun.

Mitchell moaned.

Searching the carpeted floor, Josh found the gun. The weapon had landed in the corner of the room. He snatched the weapon up. It was heavier than he expected. Having never owned or fired a gun, he never imagined the pistol would be such an effort to hold, let alone shoot.

Josh turned the gun on the killer. He would hold the hit man at bay with it while he called the cops. *They can sort the whole fucking thing out now*. Josh had done his part. He'd found the killer who knew every-thing the police needed to know. They could take it from here. The gunshot surprised Josh and he fell backward against the wall. He immediately checked himself for a wound and found none.

Mitchell was sitting up with another gun in his left hand, this weapon smaller than the one Josh held. He was grinning through an open wound of a mouth and squinting through lacerated and bloody eyes. His right arm hung limply at his side. The hit man fired again. The second shot also missed its target.

"It always pays to bring two guns," Mitchell said through his broken face.

Without hesitation, Josh jerked his arm out at the killer and fired once, twice, three times in rapid succession. The first bullet went wild, the second hit Mitchell's right shoulder and the third hit him in the chest.

Mitchell jerked with each impact from the bullets, but didn't go down. He did not fire his weapon. Josh, not taking it as a sign of surrender, took another step forward and fired for the fourth time. Another burst of light flared from the gun muzzle, another simultaneous explosion deafened, another spent cartridge ejected onto the carpet, more burnt cordite filled the room and Mitchell took a second hit to the chest. This time, he went down.

Please be dead. Please be fucking dead, Josh's mind chanted as he rushed over to the killer. Mitchell might have been on his back, but that gun was still in his hand. And as much as he hated having to go near the man, it wasn't over until he saw a corpse. He stood over Mitchell and saw rasping breaths leaving the hit man's body. Josh prepared to fire for the last time.

The professional winced in pain. His body sent messages to his brain, none of them good. How could three small chunks of metal feel like cannonballs thrown at his chest? Talking was a bitch—it felt as if his teeth were dice shaken in a cup and scattered across a table. He knew several of them were loose. He breathed through his mouth. Breathing through his nose made his face ache. He thanked God there was no glass in his eyes. Pain was relative. His broken arm stung when stationary, but it screamed when he moved it. It all hurt, but it hurt less if he kept still.

Michaels stood over him. His own 9mm pistol was in Michaels's hand. He found the situation funny. The hunted had turned hunter. Michaels aimed the pistol at his face.

"Don't do it." The professional's teeth shifted when he spoke. He sucked a gasp of air into his mouth to cool his aching gums.

"Why shouldn't I? I doubt you'd do the same for me if I was lying there."

Michaels shook. The professional didn't know if it was from fear or anger.

"You're probably right, but I want you to know something."

Michaels showed little interest in anything the professional had to say. However, he let the gun drop to his side.

A man joined Josh Michaels. He stood behind him and peered over his shoulder. The professional didn't recognize the man, who was dressed in running clothes, and Michaels seemed unaware of the man at his back. Even though the professional saw the man, he wasn't sure if he was really there. Unlike Michaels, the ceiling or walls, the jogger lacked substance. The running man was like a reflection off a lake.

"Know what?" Josh said.

It clicked. The professional now knew the running man. The runner was Stuart Shore, an AIDS patient. He had been the first. The first one Dexter Tyrell had hired him to kill. He'd mowed down the jogger on a deserted Seattle highway one rainy fall morning almost two and a half years ago. But Stuart was unharmed, exhibiting none of the lacerations or broken bones from the last time he had seen him. He was as he had been the moment before his murder. The last time the hit man had seen Stuart, he'd crushed his neck under the wheels of a car to make his death look like a hit-and-run.

Stuart looked down at the professional like Josh Michaels did. He wanted to know what his murderer had to say, too. Others joined Michaels and Stuart. The room was filling with them, all a transparent reflection of who they once were. People stood behind Michaels and the dead jogger. The murdered poured in from the kitchen and the bedroom. Much to his discomfort, he turned his head over his shoulder and saw them filing in through the front door. They were all there. All the innocent people he had killed for Pinnacle Investments.

They swarmed around him jostling for position, hoping to get a better look. There must have been over fifty people crammed into that house. All the people he had killed. He didn't remember all their names, but he did remember how and where he'd killed them. The farmer he'd pushed into his threshing machine poked his head between two others. His family and friends never knew if it had been an accident or suicide. Jesse Torino—he'd beaten and shot her before stealing her purse to make it look like a smash 'n grab gone wrong. The professional recognized a guy who worked with computers. He'd tampered with his car to make it look like a bad overhaul and the car had crashed into a truck, killing the computer analyst and seriously injuring the truck driver. Two people were allowed front-row access. Mark Keegan led Margaret Macey to the head of the throng. Keegan glanced at Josh and flashed him a smile Josh didn't see. Keegan turned his gaze back to his killer, his features hardening.

All of them wanted to know. They wanted to know his name, his real name. Not the names he'd used to get close to them to gain their trust before killing them. It was time to tell.

More than that, the professional *wanted* to tell them his real name. For years he'd lived a life where the people he came in contact with never knew who he truly was. He couldn't remember the last time someone said his real name, and it made his heart sink. He wanted someone to say his name. Just once.

The professional smiled. In a bizarre twist, the killer was touched that so many would turn out for this occasion. He had always thought he would die alone, without a friend or foe present.

"I want you to know my name," the professional said. The blood in his throat made speech difficult.

"I didn't think it was James Mitchell. But tell it to someone who gives a shit," Josh said.

Michaels's lack of interest hurt the hit man. Seeing the gun being raised, he feared Michaels would shoot him before he got the chance to say him name. He didn't wait for an invitation.

"John Kelso. My name is John Kelso." He blurted out his own name like a stool pigeon under the bright lights of a cop's interview room.

The murdered victims of John Kelso murmured his name amongst themselves.

"Jesus, is that important to you?" Josh asked.

Kelso swallowed and tasted his blood running back down his nose. "Yes."

Michaels snapped his head away from Kelso and out the window. Police sirens filled the air with their wail.

Their sound was muted by distance, but it wouldn't be long before their arrival. Neighbors must have called them during the gunplay.

Michaels, panicked by the sound of approaching police cars, lost his hardness. He recognized time was running out.

"Tell me, did you tamper with my plane?" he demanded.

Kelso glanced at Keegan at the front of the crowd. "Yes, I did."

Michaels drew in a deep breath and exhaled, closing his eyes momentarily. "I wish I could kill you all over again."

Slowly, Kelso's victims became more solid and Josh Michaels and the house took on a hazy quality. Kelso knew his time was running out.

The sirens grew louder. Michaels made for the front door. Kelso grabbed his leg. Josh stopped and looked down at him.

"Say my name," Kelso commanded.

"Fuck you," Michaels spat.

"Say my name and I'll tell you something you should really know."

"Like what?"

"Say my name," Kelso insisted.

Michaels hesitated. The sirens were close now, too close for comfort. "Okay. John Kelso. Your name is John Kelso. Now tell me."

"You can't save them. You're too late."

"Save who?" The puzzled look returned to Michaels's face.

"Your family. You can't save them."

CHAPTER THIRTY-ONE

Josh's blood froze. His body became brittle—he would shatter at the slightest touch. He refused to accept it. Regardless of what Kelso said, it wasn't too late. He could still do something about it. He kicked off Kelso's grip on his leg.

"What have you done to Kate and Abby?"

The hit man laughed. His eyes darted in all directions, focusing on nothing. "You're too late," he said again.

"Don't say that."

Josh's head swam in the confusion of the screaming sirens and Kelso's boast. The man was laughing at him. His anger made him want to inflict a lifetime of pain on Kelso. He wanted to make him sorry for the misery he'd caused him, his family, his friend and Bell. The sirens sounded like they were outside the door. There was no more time.

"Are they still alive?"

"They won't be when you get to them."

"What does that mean?"

Kelso shook his head and laughed. Josh knew he wasn't going to get any more from the hit man.

"Time for a taste of your own medicine," Josh said.

Josh put out his arm with his thumb up and gradually turned his arm. When his thumb pointed down, Josh shot Kelso in the face.

John Kelso's laughing stopped.

Josh tore out of the house, the gun still in his hand. Faces at the windows of the neighboring houses peered through curtained windows. He leapt into the car, throwing the gun into the passenger side foot well. Police cars approached from both ends of the street, still several hundred yards off in the distance. He roared off in his car, not bothering to turn on his lights. He turned left into a small residential street without stopping at the four-way stop. It was a minor diversion that would slow his journey by moments, but he would avoid the cops.

He checked his mirrors and was relieved to find no police cars in pursuit. Josh made a turn onto another street and he saw a speeding squad car tear across the next intersection heading for Bell's house. He was clear of them. The cops wouldn't be knocking at his door; well, for a while, anyway. Neighbors probably had his license plate number and his fingerprints were all over the house. It wouldn't take them too long to track him down.

His journey home was more frantic than the road race to Bell's. Josh drove more recklessly and more dangerously. With what was at stake, he had no choice. His family's safety was paramount.

What has Kelso done? How has he gotten to Kate and Abby? They were questions he could only guess at with a deep-rooted fear that scared him. He would never forgive himself if they were killed as a result of his mistakes. His fear and loathing tasted sour in his mouth.

Although Josh reached speeds of eighty miles an hour in some places on the residential roads, it was still too slow. The speed of light would have been too slow for him. He didn't know how much time his family had before it was too late, so every second counted.

He turned onto his street. The car slewed across the road, the back end threatening to overtake the front. Rubber shredded off the tread as the tires squealed in pain. He raced up to his house and stamped on the brakes. The car ground to a halt in his neighbor's front yard after plowing two wild furrows with its wheels.

Kate's minivan was parked outside. It meant they were inside, or so he hoped. If they weren't, he didn't have a clue where they could be or have a hope in hell of finding them. Josh had put a bullet through the face of the only man who knew where his wife and child were. He should have brought the hit man with him.

Josh reached for the gun in the foot well. His reckless driving had tossed it around inside. Blindly, his hand leapt from place to place in the car's darkened interior. The vapor lights provided poor illumination for the vehicle's cabin. His hand found the bulky steel lump under the front passenger seat and his fingers wrapped around the weapon. He burst out of the car.

"Please be okay. Please be okay," he quietly chanted.

Josh tried opening the door, but it was locked. He fumbled in his pockets for his key and cursed when he realized his keys were still in the car. He tore back to the car and yanked them out of the ignition, almost snapping the ignition key off.

"Kate, Abby," he bellowed. "Are you okay? Answer me, it's important."

Running back to the door, he searched for the door key, finger dexterity impaired by the cumbersome pis-

tol in one hand. Finding the key, Josh jammed it into
the lock, twisted it and threw himself against the door.

The explosion tore the house apart. The blast blew
windows outward, scattering glass far and wide. Flam-
ing wood shake was projected high into the air, im-
printing the sky with comet-like heavenly bodies.
Lengths of siding snaked across the neighborhood like
balloons inflated, then released. The concussion spat
the house contents into the street. The garage door
shoved Kate's minivan aside and embedded itself in an
SUV three houses down the street.

The sound, although deafening, was impressive—
orchestral in nature. The blast's thunderclap was interlaced with shattering glass. Glass fragments tinkled on
the road surface like waves crashing on shingle. Burning shakes thudded into lawns like the hooves of Derby
runners approaching the first furlong. Crackling house
materials rounded out the symphony.

Neighbors already awakened by Josh Michaels's dramatic arrival had time to witness his house be torn
asunder in a spectacle of color and sound. The price of
admission was expensive. Neighboring homes had their
windows blown in and debris burned on their lawns.

Josh was flung into the air, protected from projectiles,
the blast, and the heat by the door ripped off by the explosion. He landed in the front yard with the door on top
of him. He kicked off the door and got to his feet. He ignored the ringing in his head and the aching in his bones.

Hearing and feeling the blast was no preparation for
what he saw. His home was a burning skeleton—every
single part was aflame. Nothing and no one could have
survived that. It struck him. His family was dead. He
dropped to his knees, his hands to his head, the gun in
his right hand pressed up against his ear.

"They're dead. I've killed them," he screamed above
the roar of the fire.

* * *

For several moments, Josh was alone in the street. None of his neighbors ventured from the confines of their homes. The event was too astounding. Exploding houses didn't happen here. Eventually people appeared and gathered into groups discussing the occurrence. No one approached Josh. Everyone kept a healthy distance from the blaze and the homeowner with the gun. Even from the other side of the street the flames dried the skin on their shocked faces. God alone knew what perils lay ahead for any person who went near the catastrophe.

Josh knelt on his scorched lawn unable to come to terms with the meaning of the disaster. The people he cared most about, Kate and Abby, were dead because of him. It didn't matter what he did to improve his plight. He had now suffered the worst kind of punishment. If he had let it happen, let Kelso kill him, maybe his family would be alive—maybe a lot of people would be alive. But there wasn't much point to *if*; there wasn't much point to anything anymore. Everything he held most dear was gone. Josh raised the pistol to his temple.

The blaze-watching crowd gasped as their neighbor put the gun to his head. What were things coming to— was their neighborhood going to hell?

A car screeched to a halt behind Josh.

"Josh! Put the gun down." Bob Deuce flew out of the car.

Josh ignored the shouts and closed his eyes. The flames were so strong that even through his eyelids, red and yellow images danced before him. He took a deep breath and held it. He tightened his finger around the trigger.

Bob threw himself on top of Josh and slapped the gun away from his head. The gun roared and the slug kicked up a chunk of lawn. Sprawling, both men fell closer to the burning house, the heat intense on their bodies. Their clothes, heated by the flames, felt hot enough to combust. Bob wrenched the gun from Josh's grasp, then yanked his friend to his feet. He shoved Josh toward his neighbors.

The crowd parted at the sight of the weapon.

"I've got to get you out of here."

Grabbing on to anything he could grasp—an arm, a shirt collar—Bob dragged Josh forward. The man had no will and was as malleable as a puppet, but he was a living dead weight. Using his bulk, Bob managed to move his friend away from the blaze.

"What the hell were you thinking?"

Josh stared into the burning wreckage of his home.

Bob looked at the gun, then at Josh. He jammed the gun in the waistband of his pants against the small of his back and said, "You don't need this, you don't need this at all."

"They're dead, Bob," Josh said.

Bob grabbed Josh, digging his fingers into Josh's T-shirt, handfuls of material in his fists. "Yes, but you're alive and that's what matters now. Pinnacle Investments will sell you your life back."

"None of that matters anymore. It's not important." Josh was dead inside; his words lacked emotion.

"God damn you, Josh. This isn't going to be for nothing. Kate and Abby aren't going to die in vain."

Taking the lead, Bob took Josh sternly, one hand on his arm and the other on his back, and ushered him into his Toyota. Bob ran around to the other side of the car, removed the pistol from his waistband and climbed in.

The onlookers' flickering faces watched the sedan roar off into the night.

* * *

Bob raced through the suburban streets just as Josh had twice that night. Jumping red lights and running stop signals, he only heeded the rules of the road when three fire engines raced across a four-way stop bound for Josh's burning house.

Inside the car the mood was tense. Except for the whine of the thrashing engine and Bob's mumbled curses to other road users, silence filled the car. Josh's silence disturbed Bob. He snatched glances at his friend's catatonic state.

Bob snapped his fingers in front of Josh's face. "Come on, Josh. I need you with me."

Josh acknowledged Bob's presence and looked at his anxious friend.

"Where have you been? I've been looking all over for you," Bob said.

"I got home and Kate wouldn't let me in. She'd found out about Bell."

"How?"

"Bell told her in the mall."

"What a bitch," Bob said.

"I had it out with Bell and someone slugged me. When I came around, she had a knife in her chest. This is her blood." Josh held out his hands for Bob to see.

"Is she dead?"

"Yes. John Kelso killed her."

"Who?"

"James Mitchell—it's his real name. He was going to kill me and make it look like a revenge killing."

"Jesus Christ." Bob struggled to comprehend the facts. These weren't the happenings of the average Joe living his life. Everyday life, if they ever got back to it, would never be the same. "So all the shit that's been stirred up with Bell was an act to get you two linked up for a murder-suicide?"

"Not at the beginning. She came back for me, but Kelso saw an opportunity and twisted her to his will. She was just his puppet."

"Where's Kelso?"

"He's dead. I shot him. You've got his gun."

The more Josh spoke of recent traumatic events, the more he became himself. His despair evaporated and life returned to his voice. It couldn't be said that he was back to normal. Normal was a lifetime ago.

Josh was silent again. Lost in his thoughts, he relived his escapes from death and the losses that night. He'd survived again, but those close to him hadn't. It was hard to accept his survival. A tear ran down his cheek.

"Bell had AIDS," Josh said matter-of-factly.

Bob teetered on the brink of saying something, but didn't. Josh's life was too much for him to comment on.

Untidily, Bob swung the Toyota into a parking space. The parking lot was relatively empty, with only a few cars in the spaces. There would be no one to complain about Bob's bad parking for a while.

Josh stared at the illuminated sign belonging to Sacramento Executive Airport. "What are we doing here?"

"There's a plane waiting for us, my friend. It's about time we straightened this out."

The men crossed the parking lot and entered the lobby. The small airport was busy. Josh always heard light and small commercial aircraft flying over his home at all hours of the day. He knew the airport's layout well, having landed there on several occasions.

After a short flight of stairs, a bored looking man in a pilot's uniform sitting in the airport's lounge greeted Josh and Bob. He was younger than Josh, no more than thirty, a young pilot earning his hours in order to be picked up by one of the big commercial airlines. He got up and approached them.

"Josh Michaels and Bob Deuce?" the man asked.

"Yeah," Bob said.

The pilot's gaze fell on Josh. The younger man stared in amazement at Josh's condition. His appearance could be best described as disturbing. Blood stained the knees of his jeans and continued down his shins. Cuts and bruises paraded themselves across his face and arms. The smell of smoke permeated the air like Josh had spent a weekend next to a campfire.

"Are you from Pinnacle Investments?" Bob asked to distract the pilot.

"Er, sorry. Yes. I'm here to fly you to Seattle. My name is Martin Trent and I am your copilot. We're all ready for you. So if you're ready, we can take off immediately."

Josh nodded in agreement.

Trent led the way out of the foyer and onto the apron, where a number of aircraft were parked. Aircraft noise replaced the echoing hollowness of the airport lounge. A Navajo touched down on the asphalt.

"I was expecting you earlier," Trent said over the din of a turboprop carrying out its checks at the holding point.

"I know, but my friend had an accident," Bob said.

Josh became conscious of his physical condition and apparel. He looked distinctly conspicuous in his soiled clothes, and his muscles reported their discomfort. "I was wondering, do you have any spare clothes on board that I could borrow?"

Relief at the plausible explanation was obvious on Trent's face. "I've probably got something in an overnight bag you could use."

"Thanks."

Trent led Josh and Bob to a waiting Lear jet. The three climbed into the cramped confinement of the executive plane. All three hunched instinctively upon embarking. The young copilot closed and secured the door.

"Okay, gentlemen, if you can buckle yourselves in, we'll be taking off very soon. And Mr. Michaels, once we're at cruising altitude I'll get you those clothes. Oh, and there is a bathroom if you want to clean up." Trent flashed an airline smile and disappeared into the cockpit.

Josh and Bob took seats toward the rear of the aircraft in one of the twelve first-class seats. Normally this level of luxury would have excited Josh, but the knowledge he was onboard a jet taking him to Pinnacle Investments filled him with disgust.

"Why are we going to Pinnacle Investments, Bob?"

"That's why I've been looking for you. I've gotten them to sell you your policy back. It's over, Josh." Bob placed a heavy hand on Josh's shoulder.

Slowly building in speed, the engines whined.

"Fuck you, Bob. My family is dead. Four other people are dead because of this insurance policy. It's not going to put things right. It's not going to bring Kate and Abby back." Josh seethed. It had gone far beyond just getting the hit man off his back. He wasn't about to let Pinnacle Investments off the hook. He needed someone to pay for killing his family.

"Trust me, Josh. We have nothing on these people. We go to the cops once more and we're screwed. They've probably got enough on you to put you away for life. You have the blood of a murdered woman on your clothes and your fingerprints on the gun that killed a man. No, I can't bring your wife and child back, but I can stop the killing. It's the best I can do."

Trent's professional voice broke in through the intercom. Josh and Bob both stared at the closed door of the cockpit.

"Gentlemen, we've started engines and should be departing in approximately ten minutes. Flight time should be one hour and forty-five minutes. As I said, I'll return to you once we are airborne. Thank you for listening," he said.

"What am I meant to do afterward, Bob? Once I've bought my life back."

Bob frowned. "Start again. Disappear somewhere. Get away from all this shit."

Josh looked away, out of the aircraft window into the darkness.

The engines rose in pitch and the aircraft trundled forward. The Lear jet rolled to the holding point, paused and finally taxied onto the runway. The plane roared down the runway and lifted into the night.

Once the plane reached cruising altitude, Martin Trent came back to the passenger area as promised. He grabbed a duffle from a storage locker and removed a pair of jeans and a shirt for Josh. He showed both men where refreshments were kept.

Josh excused himself and squeezed into the bathroom. He removed his T-shirt and washed himself in the small stainless steel sink. He stared at himself in the mirror. He looked at the puffy bruising on his face and his singed hair. Lipstick colored bruises covered his chest and soot streaked his face. He looked like he'd been engaged in combat. Had it all been worth it? Was his survival worth the lives of his friends and family? It would be, if he lived their lives as well.

He finished washing by dunking his head into the soapy, clouded water, soaking it for a moment, trying to wash the bad images from his mind. Water slopped out of the sink, splashing his jeans and feet. A watery, bloody pool formed on the rubber matted floor. He dried his hair with a towel and combed it into position with his fingers. He wasn't pretty, but presentable.

Josh came out of the bathroom with his T-shirt in his

hand. His bloody footprints were lost in the dark blue carpeting. Bob spoke on the onboard telephone. Trent was gone. Josh stripped out of his jeans and slipped into the young man's clothes. The shirt fit fine, but the jeans were too tight in the waist and an inch too short in the leg. He would make do.

"Okay, Mr. Tyrell," Bob said and hung up the phone.

"Who's that?"

"Dexter Tyrell. He's the VP in charge of viatical settlements."

"Are we meeting him?" Josh asked.

Bob nodded. "Do you want a drink?"

"Not if it's paid for by Pinnacle Investments."

Crashing into another of the ample seats, Josh tilted it back and swiftly fell into a deep sleep. Although deep, the sleep wasn't peaceful. Images of Kate and Abby haunted him—their bodies ravaged by flames in the wreckage of their house, their clothes seared away, calling out to him while he watched them burn. Josh tried to help, but he was frozen to the spot. The conflagration took hold of their bodies and they melted into the flames, although their dying screams didn't. A fist struck him and he found himself pinned to the ground by a bullet-ridden John Kelso as Bell fired a gun into Josh's limbs. As Bell fired a final round into his head, Josh found himself at the controls of the crippled Cessna with Mark Keegan. Keegan screamed obscenities and accused Josh of betraying him as Josh uselessly fought with the disobedient controls.

The jet touched down onto the runway, jerking Josh awake. He inhaled and rubbed his face. A thin veneer of sweat coated his body. He tilted the seat upright and stared out the window. An unknown landscape rushed past. The Lear jet shuddered to a stop before it taxied over to the apron.

"I thought I'd let you sleep," Bob said.

"What time is it?"

"It's eleven-fifteen." Bob paused. "Are you ready for this?"

"As ready as I'll ever be."

Josh thanked Trent for the clothes as they disembarked. He promised to give them back on the return flight.

The airport was small. Not a soul wandered the terminal. As they stepped out of the airport, the Pacific Northwest chill bit into Josh. A taxi fired its engine and the lights came on. The sedan pulled up in front of Josh and Bob. The front passenger window retracted and the driver leaned over to address them.

"Bob Deuce?" the cabby asked.

"Yeah," Bob said and got in.

"Pinnacle Investments, right?" the cabby asked.

The cabby was a white-haired man in his sixties. He looked like he'd been driving a taxi since he was a kid. He hunched over the wheel with what seemed to be a permanent stoop. It looked doubtful he could stand upright. He glanced back at his two passengers in the rearview mirror.

"Yeah, as quick as you can," Bob said.

"No hotel then?"

"No," Bob said.

"Business is it?"

"Yeah," Bob said.

"You must be pretty important people to be flown in at this hour for a business meeting. What's the emergency?"

"That's our business," Josh said.

The cabby held Josh's stare in the mirror, his old face wrinkled into a sneer. He mumbled a curse under his breath. He didn't speak for the rest of the journey. There was silence except for the occasional crackle from the CB radio transmissions.

The taxi pulled off the highway into a wooded area that swiftly opened up into a secluded business park. A portion of the woodland had been harvested to house three clinical-looking tinted glass and brick blocks. Each three-story building was a clone of the other two, but each had different corporate logos glued to the outside. Pinnacle Investments occupied the center building. Floodlit parking lots capable of holding several hundred cars surrounded each building. A few minutes before the witching hour on a Saturday night, the parking lots were bare.

The cab stopped in front of Pinnacle Investments's reception with a squeak from the brakes. Bob reached for his wallet, but the disgruntled cabby shut him down with a raised hand.

"The tab's been picked up by this place," he said sharply as he flicked his head in the direction of Pinnacle Investments's building. "They paid more than enough."

Bob stuck his wallet back into his pocket and he and Josh opened the rear passenger doors. They started to get out of the car, but the cabby interrupted them.

"Do you want me to wait?"

"No, you can go," Bob said.

The cabby nodded curtly. He barely waited for Josh and Bob to close the doors before he tore off into the night.

The two men walked up the concrete steps past the manicured landscaping. The lights in the reception illuminated the area from behind the darkened glass. Two security men manning the reception desk watched them approach the front doors.

One security guard, a streetwise looking black man in his mid-thirties, got up from his seat and met Josh and Bob at the doors. He looked as if he had experienced a few unorthodox events in his life. They waited for a moment while the guard opened the door and poked his head through, his face a question mark.

"Dexter Tyrell is expecting us," Bob said.

"Your names, please?"

"Bob Deuce and Josh Michaels," Bob said.

The guard opened one of the glass doors wide and Josh and Bob entered. He locked the doors after them.

The guard went back to the reception desk. "I'll tell him you're here."

The other guard, an overweight white man a good ten years older than his coworker, looked up from his magazine and nodded an acknowledgment to the visitors.

Josh and Bob nodded back.

The black guard picked up a phone from the switchboard and dialed a number. After a moment his call was answered.

"Mr. Tyrell, I have those gentlemen you were expecting." The guard paused and listened to the response. "I'll send them up, sir. Thank you."

The guard put the phone down and pointed in the direction of the elevators. "If you would like to take the elevator to the third floor, Mr. Tyrell will be waiting for you."

Josh and Bob did as they were told. Josh pressed the button for the elevator and they got in.

"Right, Josh, we're here. Play it cool. We may know what he has done, but we have no proof. I want to get out of here in the shortest period of time possible and still be alive. Remember what this guy is capable of, okay?"

Josh pursed his lips and nodded.

Bob grabbed Josh's arm. "You're with me on this, right?"

Josh shook Bob's arm off. "I know exactly where we stand," he said, sharply.

The imitation bronze elevator doors, polished to reflect a distorted image of the occupants, opened. Dexter Tyrell stood on the other side to meet them. He looked as if he'd just stepped off the nineteenth hole. He flashed a shark's smile and welcomed them into his lair.

Tyrell ushered the two men off the elevator car. "Welcome, gentlemen, do come this way."

Tyrell led them along the thick pile-carpeted corridor and directed them into his office.

Josh's hatred for Dexter Tyrell boiled inside. Up until then, he'd sunk into a pit of self-pity and self-reproach for his own actions. But now, he was face-to-face with the devil himself, the man who had ordered his death. This monster would be sorry for what he'd done. Josh didn't care what Bob said. Tyrell wouldn't be allowed to escape scot-free. His family was dead because of this man's command.

"I hope the arrangements were satisfactory to you both." Tyrell followed them into his office.

Bob turned to Tyrell. "Yeah, great. A nice way to travel. Private jet, I mean."

Josh nodded his agreement.

"Yes, it's a charter firm we use now and then. A reliable outfit." Tyrell took a seat at his desk. He gestured to the leather club chairs in front of him. "Please, take a seat."

"I prefer to stand," Josh said, remaining in front of Tyrell's desk.

Bob had moved toward the chairs, but stopped when Josh made his decision to stand. He took a step to one side and stood by the bookcases. "So will I," Bob said.

"As you prefer." The courtesies over, Dexter Tyrell got down to business. He leaned back in his high-backed leather chair. "So, Mr. Deuce tells me you want to reverse your viatical settlement."

"Yes, I do." Josh fought the desire to launch himself over the desk and throttle Tyrell's smug smile from his face.

"Well, I have given the subject great consideration since speaking to Bob and I have decided that it won't be possible, Mr. Michaels."

"What?"

"You see, we have made a substantial payment to you and we have been paying your monthly dues over the last eighteen months. We've placed a significant investment in you and I personally would prefer to see a return on that investment."

"I can pay you your money back."

Tyrell interlaced his fingers, brought them up to his lips and feigned contemplation. "No, Mr. Michaels. I think I'd prefer to collect. There's no profit for Pinnacle Investments if we give your life policy back. We aren't a charity."

The vice president's sickly sweet manner was cloying. It made Josh sick. He couldn't stick to the plan any longer. He grabbed the chair back in front of him and sunk his fingers into the soft fabric. He wished it was Tyrell's throat.

"Look here, you son of a bitch. Let's cut the bullshit. I know what you did. Your company was going to the wall because of this viatical shit." Josh waved a dismissive hand in disgust for the viatical principle. "People stopped dying when you wanted them to, so you started killing them. You sent a man to kill an old woman and me, and God knows how many others. How many are there? How many have you killed?"

"Hold on, Josh," Bob said. "This isn't what we agreed."

"Not enough." Tyrell replaced his business smile with a hateful leer.

Tyrell's candor amazed Josh. He'd just called Tyrell's

bluff and the man didn't give a shit. Dexter Tyrell gave the impression he was bulletproof. What did the executive know that he didn't?

"You bastard. What gives you the right to kill people for profit?"

Tyrell unlocked his fingers and pointed at Josh. "You do. You and all the others like you, who coming rushing to this company, to me, and ask to be saved. Those with AIDS who fucked one too many times with the wrong john. The sick that are hoping for the miracle cure that will never come. And people like you, who rustle up a shit storm so big, only money can buy them out.

"But I solve all that for them. They just sign a piece of paper and all the bad stuff goes away. I grant them a second chance. The opportunity to live out their days in fine style until I decide they die."

"Until *you* decide they die," Josh said.

"Yes, me. And you wouldn't believe how many are willing to sign up."

"You disgust me," Josh said.

"Why? You're all going to die anyway. It's inevitable. Once you've made a settlement, your life is no longer your own. It belongs to me and it's my decision when it should end."

"Oh, bullshit. People weren't dying as quickly as you liked so you started wiping them out to balance the books."

"Admit it, Josh, you don't care about the other people, only about you. You're pissed that your life has caught up with you."

"My wife and child are dead because of you."

"No, your wife and child are dead because of *you*, Mr. Michaels. Your problems killed them."

Josh went for Tyrell, throwing the chair aside and sending it crashing into the one next to it.

Suddenly, a bullet turned the corner of the desk blotter into confetti and a chunk of wood exploded from the table, taking a pen with it.

Josh froze in his position.

Tyrell smiled.

"Josh, you should have played along," Bob said.

CHAPTER THIRTY-TWO

Dexter Tyrell's grin broadened by the second. It was a winner's smile. His cold eyes sparkled with delight. Josh could see it, anybody could see it—he had lost to Tyrell. Josh shook his head in defeat and turned to his friend. Bob pointed John Kelso's semiautomatic pistol at Josh. His fear evident, the gun trembled in Bob's hand.

Not Bob, it can't be Bob. How long has he been involved? He couldn't believe his best friend had sold him out. When had Bob's part started? When John Kelso turned up in California? Or had Bob known Josh had signed his own death warrant when he made the viatical settlement? No wonder Tyrell hadn't looked concerned at Josh's accusations; he already knew the game was rigged in his favor. A week ago, he would have hated Bob for his betrayal, but now, he had no more hate left. He was prepared for the executioner's bullet.

"Bob," Josh said.

Bob swallowed hard. "Shut up, Josh. I'm not too

good with guns and I don't want to shoot the wrong person."

Josh braced himself for the next shot to rip through his brain. He didn't fear his life ending; he welcomed it. He couldn't wait for that bullet to pierce his skull and end his misery. Josh had lost everything he held dear—his wife and child burnt alive in their home, one friend murdered and the other a betrayer. All he had left was his life. Now the betrayer had him in his sights. It would be a fitting end for Josh—he'd done everything for the right reasons, even the bribe had been for the benefit of his daughter, but every decision he made had only wreaked more havoc.

Tyrell laughed. "Oh, dear, Mr. Michaels, you're not a good judge of character. I bet you didn't see this one coming. You're always putting your trust in the wrong person."

Josh ignored him. "Just do it, Bob, if you're going to."

"Josh, you don't understand," Bob pleaded.

"I don't care why you did it. I just hope you were well paid," Josh said, defeated.

"Don't worry, Josh, Bob will be well looked after. He knows when there's a good offer on the table. I think that's part of your problem. You don't know a good opportunity when you see it. If you'd done the right thing and drowned in your car, just think of all the destruction that you would have saved your family and friends. A lot of people wouldn't be dead, if you'd thought this through."

"Just order it done, Tyrell. I don't need to listen to your crap."

"Oh, good God, no. You don't think we're going to kill you here, in my office? What do you take me for, an idiot? We'll take you somewhere," he said.

"*I* think you're an idiot, Mr. Tyrell," Bob said, the

gun still aimed in the direction of the other two men in the office.

Bob's remark knocked the smile off Tyrell's face. "Excuse me?"

"I'm sorry, Josh. I had to do it this way. He offered me a deal and I took it. It was the only way to get this close to the man. I was meant to come here to make a deal after you were killed, but I couldn't let him do it. Once I found you and you told me Kelso was dead, I made a change of plans. I told him I was bringing you here to get rid of you."

Josh felt as confused as Tyrell. Bob's rambling was going straight over his head.

"Kate and Abby aren't dead," Bob added.

They're alive? Josh heard the revelation, but it was too much for him. He buckled at the knees and slumped against Tyrell's desk to catch his fall.

"What are you doing, Bob?" Fear and caution were evident in Tyrell's question.

Bob produced a small tape recorder from his pocket. The spools were revolving and the record button was depressed. "It was the only way I could see us trapping him," he said to Josh.

"You're making a terrible mistake, Bob. Give me that tape and we'll forget all about this," Tyrell commanded. His hand edged toward the phone.

"Shut the fuck up before I shoot you." Bob's hand shook. If the gun went off, the bullet could go anywhere.

Like a gunslinger in a shootout, Tyrell reached for the telephone on his desk. Reacting to the draw, Bob instinctively aimed and fired. The bullet went wild. The vice president grabbed the handset. Bob fired again. Tyrell screamed as the second bullet pierced his hand, splitting the handset in two. The receiver exploded and electrical sparks sizzled amongst the keys as they scattered like broken teeth. Tyrell clutched his bleeding hand to his chest.

"Don't make another fucking move." Bob looked as shaken as Tyrell did.

Tyrell whimpered and clutched his injured hand. He removed a handkerchief from his pocket and bound it around his palm. Bob wasn't taking any chances and kept the gun trained on Tyrell.

"Kate and Abby are alive?" Josh asked.

Bob's eyes flicked from Tyrell to Josh and back to Tyrell. "Yeah. I made the deal with this son of a bitch and he told me Kelso was planning to blow up the house. I got there before Kelso did and I got them out. I know I should have told you when I caught up with you, but I needed you to help make a convincing story. I'm sorry."

Josh didn't care about Bob not telling him. He could be angry with his friend later. He wanted out of this place, as far as possible from Tyrell and his filthy company. He wanted to go home to his family and fix everything, put everything back the way it used to be. But then he remembered that life could never be the same, not now that Bell had told him about her disease.

"You two won't get away with this," Tyrell said. Sweat clinging to his forehead, Dexter Tyrell's face was a mask of pain, but he didn't feel the pain Josh felt.

Josh lunged for Tyrell in his chair. The vice president flinched, anticipating a beating. He turned his head away and raised his hands up to his face. His body collapsed into a fetal position. Josh held a fist above the executive's head, ready to strike, but hesitated when he saw the picture on Tyrell's desk.

Josh snatched up the framed photograph. It wasn't a

picture of his wife or a loved one, but the cover of some business magazine featuring Tyrell. Josh smashed the picture frame down on the corner of the desk. The frame shattered and pieces of glass and broken wood fell from Josh's grasp. Josh dropped what was left of the frame. He picked up the largest of the pieces of broken glass and held it like a knife.

"Give me your arm," Josh snarled.

"What?"

"Give me your fucking arm!" Josh barked.

Tyrell remained curled in a ball. He yelped like a wounded dog when Josh grabbed the man's un-wounded arm. He banged Tyrell's left arm onto the desk blotter.

Bob rushed forward. "What the hell are you doing, Josh? We have him. He's finished."

"Don't come any closer, Bob."

Bob did as he was told and looked on in fear.

Raising the shard of glass, Josh slashed it across Dexter Tyrell's wrist. He yelped again. Blood filled the laceration and crimson poured down the sides of his arm onto the blotter.

"Don't fucking move!" Josh bellowed at Tyrell.

Josh jammed his foot into the pit of the vice president's stomach. He put his right arm on his right knee and drew the makeshift knife across his own wrist.

"Josh," Bob said.

Dropping the glass fragment, Josh took his foot out of Tyrell's gut. He interlaced his fingers with Tyrell's fingers so both cut wrists touched. The two men's blood mixed. Josh pressed down on their wrists with his other hand, ensuring their blood mingled.

Tyrell looked on in disbelief. He fixed his gaze on Josh, then at the bizarre ritual being performed upon him. Slack-jawed, he said nothing.

"Good. We're blood brothers, Tyrell." Josh applied more pressure to their joined wounds. Blood oozed out from between their arms like jam squeezed from an overfilled sandwich. "I'm infected, Mr. Tyrell, and if luck is on my side, so are you."

"Oh, my God." Bob fell into one of Tyrell's club chairs.

"What have you done?" Tyrell demanded.

Josh enjoyed seeing the fear in Tyrell's eyes.

"My blackmailer, my ex-mistress, murdered by your boy, told me one important fact before she died. She was diagnosed HIV positive." Josh relished the moment. The words HIV positive struck terror into all those who had contracted the virus and it was no different for Dexter Tyrell. Josh smiled at the fear in Tyrell's eyes.

Tyrell fought Josh to wrench his arm free. Josh gripped tighter onto the vice president's hand. He pressed down even harder onto Tyrell's arm and head-butted him, ending his struggle.

Tyrell yelped, and the blood drained from his face. His resistance dissipated and Josh relinquished his grip on the vice president's arm.

"Regardless of what happens to you or me, I have the satisfaction of knowing your life is as uncertain as mine," Josh said to Tyrell.

Dexter Tyrell stared at his wounded arm, then at Josh. His panicked expression said it all. He was trying to comprehend what had happened to him and was coming up short. Things like this happened to other people, not him.

Bob stared at the executive then, at his friend. "Oh, Josh."

"Call the police. Let's finish this," Josh said.

Bob started to say something, but let his thoughts die on his lips. He rested the pistol on the desk. He treated the weapon like it was made of glass. He wanted nothing to do with the gun anymore. He got up from the chair and left the office.

Josh righted the chair he'd knocked over and sat down on it. He picked up the pistol and took it out of harm's reach, then sat back and waited for the police.

CHAPTER THIRTY-THREE

The commercials finished and a talk show took over. The first half of the show would retrace Pinnacle Investments's downfall and the second half would be an open forum on the rights and wrongs of the viatical settlement system.

"Leave it alone. Don't you people know when to stop?" Josh said to the TV.

Josh reached across the couch for the remote and switched the channel. He couldn't bear to watch yet another show about the appalling truth he'd uncovered. The subject had been done to death by the television networks, but they insisted on resurrecting the story. He couldn't go anywhere without seeing the word "viatical." It would be on cereal boxes next. He stopped channel-hopping when he came to the cartoons. He couldn't see Tom and Jerry making a viatical settlement on Butch.

Cartoons. Thank God for cartoons. They were a welcome distraction. He'd seen it all unfold on television. The Sacramento Police Department had tracked down John Kelso's address book from the River City Inn. In the book, fifty-seven names and addresses were listed. All but one, Mark Keegan, were clients of Pinnacle Investments. All had been victims of unusual accidents that appeared to be have been choreographed by John Kelso. Josh realized Kelso hadn't gotten the chance to report his final victim's name, Belinda Wong.

If the networks weren't discussing John Kelso, they were discussing Dexter Tyrell. News programs showed stills of the successful executive from financial publications. The images were a stark contrast to the broken man the police paraded before the media. It looked like he had lost twenty pounds since his arrest. Dexter Tyrell never made it to court. On his way to his arraignment, in front of the television cameras, he broke away from the police officer holding him and ran full pelt into the path of an oncoming bus. The executive was killed instantly. Josh watched Tyrell's death on television. He saw a look of total bliss when the vice president saw the bus bearing down on him. Josh had never seen anyone happier.

Josh's eyes registered the cartoon characters on the television, but his mind was elsewhere. The talk show forced him to relive recent events. The last two weeks since his return from Pinnacle Investments had been a blur. Police from two states, along with the FBI, quizzed him about the deaths of Mark Keegan, Margaret Macey, Joseph Henderson—aka Tom Jenks, Belinda Wong and John Kelso. They also questioned him about Dexter Tyrell and Pinnacle Investments's involvement. Josh held nothing back. There was no point in lying any more. Once he started talking, nothing could stop him, and in less than two hours he'd said it all. It didn't seem possible that the deaths and carnage could be explained away in a couple of hours. He thought he'd left something out, but there'd been nothing. Of course, the cops kept him talking until his head swam. They hammered him for days, making him start from the beginning and dissecting the tiniest details.

The police released him after the first long day of interrogation. He and Bob were flown home in the custody of two police officers and were released on their own recognizance. Dexter Tyrell's testimony and Bob's tape recording had seen to that. The executive told the police everything. He explained how he'd hired a contract killer after selecting clients to kill. The name John Kelso was a surprise to Tyrell—Kelso had never told him his real name. Tyrell explained he had only dealt with a voice on a phone and a post office box.

Once the police had Dexter Tyrell, they were no longer interested in Josh and Bob, although charges were still pending. But for revealing the murder-for-profit scandal, it was their lawyer's opinion the charges of intentionally wounding Tyrell would be dropped and the killing of John Kelso would be considered justifiable homicide. For all intents and purposes they were free men; their part was over.

Josh's release resulted in requests for interviews from all quarters. Josh declined them all, much to the media's disappointment. He'd gone from villain to hero. Bell's construction fraud claims were forgotten for the meantime in favor of his vigilante quest for the truth.

But Josh didn't return to a hero's welcome. He'd won his life back at great expense. He had lost Kate and Abby. When he returned from Pinnacle Investments, he told Kate about everything—the affair, the murders, he didn't leave a single detail out. She had remained detached until he told her of the possibility that he was HIV positive. Kate cracked and burst into tears, telling him she never wanted to see him again. He'd discovered Bell had indeed been HIV positive, but he and Kate were clean. Kate didn't care that the AIDS scare was a false alarm. She decided they were finished. He didn't feel much like a hero. Thinking about it now, a tear rolled down his face.

The front door opened and Josh swiftly wiped away the tear with the back of his hand and focused his attention once more on the television.

Bob came into the living room. "Come on, Josh, turn that crap off. You're still in the same clothes you were wearing three days ago."

Josh turned his head toward his frowning friend. He looked at his clothes—a T-shirt and sweatpants. Stains of some sort ran down the front of the shirt. He didn't remember what it was or when it had happened.

"Why are you home so early?"

Ignoring Josh, Bob took the remote from his hand and switched off the television. He sat down on the coffee table between Josh and the TV, the remote held between his clasped hands.

Josh pointed at the television. "I was watching that."

"Yeah and you've been watching that crap for the last week. Daytime will rot your brain. It's about time you did something."

"Like what?" Josh asked.

"Anything. Something. You can do whatever you want now."

"It's easy for you to say. You haven't lost anything. Everything's the same for you."

Bob's grip tightened around the remote and his face flushed. "Fuck you, you ungrateful shit. It's been no picnic for me, you know. I stood by you. You are a guest in my home. It hasn't been easy. Nancy isn't your biggest fan after what you've done."

Nancy's icy reception had been quite clear once she knew of his affair. Josh made it his business to keep out of her way at all times. When she came home, he went to his room and he knew Bob was having his ear bent quite regularly about his stay.

"Do you want me to go?"

"No, Josh." Bob stood and started to walk away in disgust. He threw the remote and it thudded into an armchair. "No, I don't want you to go. I want you to get on with your life instead of pissing it away on watching TV and wallowing in self-pity."

"I don't have much else to look forward to."

A crooked smile spread across Bob's face, and enthusiasm glinted in his eyes. "I think I can change all that. Come on, man. I've got someplace to take you."

"Where are we going?"

"Stop asking questions and get moving. I'll be waiting for you in the car." He clapped his hands together like the king of Siam and disappeared out the front door.

Josh went into the hallway. He caught a glimpse of himself in the hall mirror. He looked at his untidy appearance—hair unkempt, face unshaven and his clothes wrinkled. He hoped Bob wasn't taking him somewhere special. He could do without the hassle. He found his running shoes and slipped them on to his bare feet.

Walking out into the daylight, Josh squinted against the brightness of the morning sunshine and raised a hand to shield his eyes. It had been days since he'd left the house to visit the outside world. It wasn't as he remembered it. The world was a lot more colorful than he recalled, like he had removed tinted goggles after a long day of skiing. He joined Bob in the car.

"Where are we going?" Josh asked again.

"You'll find out soon enough."

Bob didn't divulge their destination until they got there. He indicated a three-bedroom ranch style house on the south side of Land Park with a FOR SALE sign outside. He brought the car to a halt, but Josh wanted to jump out before the Toyota had stopped. Kate stood on the porch to the house, dressed in a loose-fitting summer print dress. Josh fired the car door open, but Bob grabbed his forearm.

"Get over there and win her back. Don't screw this up," he said with a smile pasted across his face. "I went to a lot of trouble to get her here."

Bob released his grip on Josh's arm. Josh leapt out of the car and rushed over to Kate. Fearing her rejection, he slowed as he got closer and stopped about five feet from her.

Bob's Toyota drove away.

"Hello, Josh." Kate's reply didn't exhibit any enthusiasm.

"Hello, Kate."

"I saw you on the TV last week."

"Yeah, I can't seem to get rid of them. They're like flies around a cow's butt."

"Are you working?"

"No. Red Circle offered me my job back, but I said no. It's not what I want anymore."

Kate nodded.

They were silent for a long moment until Josh broke it. "Is this where you're living?"

"No, I'm just looking."

"Oh. How's Abby?"

"She's okay."

"Is she here?"

"No, she's with my mom."

"So you're still at your parents?"

"Yeah."

"You look good."

"I wish I could say the same about you. You look a mess."

It hadn't mattered when Bob mentioned his appearance, but he was embarrassed by it now. Josh straightened the T-shirt and combed his hair with his fingers. He became aware of his smell, the odor of stale sweat. "I suppose I need my two ladies to keep me straight," he said and ventured a weak smile.

"Who, me and Bell?" Kate said coldly.

His smile collapsed under the pressure. Josh winced; the backhand remark hurt. His open-ended comment had left him open to ridicule. "I didn't mean that."

Kate sighed. "Neither did I. I'm not here to fight."

Josh smiled. "Good."

"What did Bob tell you?"

"Nothing. He just brought me here."

"He's been on my case since you came back from Pinnacle Investments, telling me I should talk to you."

"I didn't know."

"That's what he said. He also said you didn't know much about anything these days."

Ashamed, Josh shifted nervously and studied his feet. Had his behavior deteriorated so much that everyone could see him going downhill? Only an idiot wouldn't have seen it. He was an idiot. He wished he'd tidied himself up before seeing Kate. But it was probably part of Bob's plan to make him look a wreck in front of her to stack the odds in his favor.

Tears welled up in her eyes. "You've really let yourself go, Josh."

"I know. I can do something about it. An hour in the bath and a change of clothes, that's all it takes." He paused for a moment. "And for you to take me back."

The welled-up tears, too large and too heavy to remain in place, broke out and rolled down Kate's face. She sniffed and wiped them away with the back of her hand.

"Give me one good reason why," she said. "Just one."

"Because I still love you and Abby."

Kate's brave front couldn't stand up to the bombardment any longer. Her façade cracked and broke into a thousand pieces. Wracking sobs shook her body. She buried her face in her hands.

Scared of rejection, Josh hesitated. But seeing Kate's distress, he went to her, pulled her to him and held her tight.

Kate took her hands away from her face and wrapped her arms around him. She buried her face in his shoulder. He felt the tears soak into his shirt.

He held her tighter. Was this acceptance? He hoped her returned embrace was a sign of forgiveness. He wanted her to lower the drawbridge and allow him entry. He spoke into her ear.

"Kate, I'm so sorry. I can't bear to be without you. If we can't be together, then everything I've done was for nothing." Josh let it all go. He had to let Kate know how he felt; this was his last chance or he might lose her forever.

He felt Kate pull away from him. He let her go. She took a step backward.

She composed herself. "Josh, you betrayed me. You had an affair. You put our family at risk. We could have all been killed because of you. How can I ever forgive you?"

"I was stupid and God knows I wish I could change that. I don't expect you to forgive me. But give me a chance to make up for it." He reached out to touch Kate, but wasn't sure how she would react, so he let his hands drop to his sides.

"Should I give you a second chance?" she asked.

"Abby needs a father."

"*Should I give you a second chance?*" she demanded.

"Yes."

"What makes you think life will be different this time around? You have no job. We have no home. We don't have anything."

"I couldn't ask for more." He smiled. "We have a clean slate. We're free to make life anything we want it to be. We have the chance to start again from the ground up. Nothing to stop us." His enthusiasm spilled over.

"We'll have to take things slow. You have a lot to make up for."

His mouth fell open for a moment. Did this mean what he thought it meant? She was taking him back. It was no time to think, just act. Moving toward her, he said, "I know. I have no expectations other than a second chance."

Kate smiled for the first time. She held out her hand to him and he took it. "Okay."

He smiled back.

"We have a house to look at." Kate opened the door and led him inside.

AUTHOR'S NOTE

As odd as it may seem, viatical settlements do exist and there are strict criteria governing who can and can't enter into them. For the purposes of this book, I've changed those criteria to meet my own ends.

Needless to say, Pinnacle Investments is fictitious, as are all the characters mentioned in this book.

I hope you enjoyed *Accidents Waiting to Happen* and I sincerely hope we meet again on a bookshelf near you.

GOLDILOCKS
ANDREW COBURN

Lawrence, Massachusetts, is a quiet little town. But it's only quiet because the deals have already been made, the police are working hand in hand with the mob, and everyone knows where they stand. That quiet is about to be shattered. Louise Baker has married her way to the top and her mob connections have brought her the power she always wanted. She doesn't worry much about jilting her latest lover, handsome Henry Witlo, known as Goldilocks. But Henry's got a vicious streak and maybe he's a little crazy. Crazy enough to set in motion a chain of events that could blow the town sky high.

THE KOREAN INTERCEPT

STEPHEN MERTZ

Tensions between the United States and North Korea are escalating to the crisis point. And the U.S. space shuttle *Liberty* may prove to be the spark that ignites the tinderbox. Soon after launching, the shuttle lost contact with NASA and was forced to crash-land…in the mountainous frontier between North Korea and China.

Aboard the shuttle is a defense satellite created with the latest American technology. The North Korean government has stated that an American search-and-rescue mission would be considered an act of aggression. But the U.S. president cannot let the precious payload be lost so easily. As he orders American forces to prepare for a military incursion, the race begins….

DEAD
WEIGHT

JOHN FRANCOME

Phil Nicholas was one of the best jump jockeys around, winning championship after championship...until the fall. His body has recovered from the devastating accident, but now his confidence is shattered. This could mean the end for a jockey, but Phil has a more urgent need to get his nerve back—a killer is on the prowl.

A racing fan's love of the sport has turned dark and deadly. He's become convinced that cheating and corruption are responsible for his recent bad losses at the track, and he won't stop until he's punished the cheaters. Phil himself will need nerves of steel if he hopes to save his own life and that of the woman he loves.

FEAR & GREED

LAWRENCE LIGHT

It's the impossible dream of every trader and dealer on Wall Street—an accurate means to predict the ups and downs of the stock market. The Reiner sisters have made that dream a reality in the form of a computer program they call Goldring. The sisters have kept Goldring their little secret, even when a magazine story by financial reporter Karen Glick showcases their sudden wealth. Everything was working so well, but now one of the sisters has been found murdered, Goldring is missing— and Karen Glick has a hit man on her trail.

SMOKE

LISA MISCIONE

A late-night visit from an NYPD detective rarely brings good news. But true-crime writer Lydia Strong is especially surprised to hear that one of her former writing students has been missing for more than two weeks. Before she disappeared, Lily had tried to get in touch with Lydia, seeking her help. Could it have something to do with the death of Lily's brother, the one Lily refused to accept as a suicide? If she wants to find the truth, Lydia will have to follow the trail Lily left behind, a trail that—like Lily herself—seems to disappear like smoke.

SHAME

ALAN RUSSELL

Gray Parker's execution is front-page news and his case inspires a bestselling book. Everyone wants to hear about the man who strangled all those women. Everyone except his young son. As soon as he is old enough, Caleb starts a new life and denies any connection to his infamous father.

But now new bodies have started to turn up, marked just as his father's victims, and all the evidence points to Caleb. His only ally is the sole survivor of one of Parker's attacks, the woman who turned his crimes into a bestseller. Together, these two must desperately try to prove Caleb's innocence—before the law or the killer catches them.

AMERICA'S LAST DAYS

DOUGLAS MACKINNON

Is the United States of America the nation our Founding Fathers intended it to be? Or has the government lost sight of our ideals? To some of the most powerful men and women in the country—including a former Chairman of the Joint Chiefs of Staff and a former Director of the FBI—the answer is growing increasingly obvious, and so is the only possible solution: The time has come to revolt. Their daring plans will not only drive a government to its knees, they will change the course of history.